Haven's War

Safe Haven Book Two

By
Parker Williams

COPYRIGHT

DEDICATION

This story is dedicated to those who assured me Haven and Sammy had another story to tell. And then demanded I let them tell it.

TRADEMARK ACKNOWLEDGEMENTS

The author acknowledges the trademarked status and trademark owners of the following trademarks mentioned in this work of fiction:

Austin Powers: New Line Productions, Inc.
Boss Mustang 429: Ford Motor Company
Chivas: Chivas Holdings (IP) Limited
Darth Vader: Lucasfilm Entertainment Company Ltd.
Desert Eagle 50AE: Saeilo Enterprises, Inc.
Escalade: General Motors LLC
Facebook: Facebook, Inc.
Instagram: Instagram, LLC
Luger: Stoeger, Inc.
Mac: Apple, Inc.
Mario Kart: Nintendo of America, Inc.
McDonald's: McDonald's Corporation
Monopoly: Hasbro, Inc.
Porsche: Dr. Ing. h.c. F. Porsche AG Corporation
Skype: Skype Corporation
Spider-Man: Marvel Characters, Inc.
YouTube: Google, Inc.
Zelda: Nintendo of America, Inc.

HAVEN'S WAR

With Haven on an extended honeymoon with Sammy, bad guys around the world are breathing a lot easier. No one is better at permanently removing these lowlifes who target children—and the brutal murder of two teenage girls makes clear it's past time to return to work. Haven's first assignment back results in a new family member and a renewed sense of urgency to protect and avenge the innocent.

There is nothing 'usual' about the business of hunting predators, but when several of Haven's fellow agents are killed, a pattern emerges. The hunters have become the prey, tools in a bitter vendetta for a perceived wrong.

Despite years of working alone, when the target shifts to someone unexpected, Haven calls in reinforcements—a friend to stand between the family he loves and a ruthless killer. Teamwork may be the only way to win this fight—unless it's already too little, too late.

Haven tries to approach this as he would any other assignment. Find your enemy and make sure they suffer before you eliminate them. But when a member of his team goes off-book and ends up dead, everything changes. It's no longer a battle.

Now it's war.

PROLOGUE

He glanced up at the evening sky. A haze enveloped the quarter moon, giving everything an ethereal glow. Though the night would be considered sultry, it lent itself to romance, walking hand in hand with someone you cared for, sharing whispered words, promises that might last an evening or be the foundation for a lifetime commitment. These people had no idea how quickly something like love could be ripped away, how those things said to one another would be worth less than the air you spent on saying them.

He shook his head. Now he needed to focus, not lose himself in memories of what might have been if things had been different. God, how he wished things could have been different.

The street could only be described as quaint. Small houses, each nearly identical to the next, but with a few tweaks that marked them as individual. The place he focused on had a small flowerbed, bursting with a variety of a flower he recognized, but couldn't recall the name. Tulips, maybe?

The slate gray siding, the maroon shutters on the windows, and the solar-powered pathway to the door that lit up in beautiful colors at night. The overall effect could only be described as charming. A lot of love went into making the house something special. It reminded him of what he'd lost.

He'd taken refuge in a house across from the home for six days, getting the lay of the land, taking note of the occupants' arrival and departure schedule. Then every night, he drifted off, thinking about the place. It had been a dream of theirs, to own a little farm of their own, where no one would send them off to the corners of the world to handle problems. And for one very brief instant, they'd achieved it. But that dream had died in more ways than one. One day it was there, the next it was gone, as if it had never existed.

He tugged the collar of his black jacket and wished for a cool breeze. The earlier rain had sent the humidity soaring, and sweat was building up under his bulletproof vest, matting the sparse hairs. What he wouldn't give for a tall glass of iced tea about now. He tried again, lifting the bottom of the vest up, hoping to let a little air in to cool him down, but nothing helped. He glanced at his watch. He'd need to make his move tonight. No way could he stand to be in this place any longer. The memories and wistful dreams alone threatened to drown him, but this heat had him sweating to the point where even he could smell himself. When he grabbed a coffee at the convenience store down the street while his target was out, the man behind the counter had a hand on the phone. Probably thought he was a vagrant. He sure as hell looked like one. He hadn't showered in days, and his dark blond hair felt greasy to the touch. The beard he'd grown over the last year hadn't seen a razor either. He looked like shit.

When he heard the hum of an engine on the quiet street, he crouched down. Though his patience had long ago come to an end, he needed to see this through. He would wait as he'd been trained, even if every fiber of his being rebelled against the idea. He was an assassin and he had a job to do.

The woman—Sarah, according to facts he'd assembled—slid from the driver's seat, her blonde hair pulled back into a ponytail. She laughed at something the other occupant shouted, then opened the rear door of the van. It took several minutes for her to get set, then she stepped away as a ramp slid down to allow the man in the back to wheel out and be lowered to the ground. She bent over and kissed him, then walked to the passenger side where she took a baby from the car seat. She held the child up, and then blew a raspberry on his belly, which caused the kid to laugh and wiggle. Regret tore through him. He wished there could be another way, but two months ago he'd approached the man—Daniel Tollifson—begging for information. There had been angry words exchanged, as well as the threat of police involvement. He couldn't allow that, because there would be no one else to take down his ultimate target.

He forced himself to focus on the here and now. He needed to remain detached. Better to not let facts like these intrude on his mission. If Tollifson wouldn't help him when he asked, then he'd have to find another way to get his message across. He reached into his pocket and pulled out a photo of a man whose smile had never wavered. Terry had been his whole world, and then had been ripped away from him in a matter of moments. All he wanted had been the name of the person responsible. Why couldn't Daniel see he wasn't asking for much? How would he feel if it had been his wife? Or his child?

Daniel disengaged himself from the ramp, and Sarah started to come around to the other side. It had to be now.

He'd run out of tears a lifetime ago, but again he wished he had another alternative. He didn't. He raised the rifle and peered through the sights. The woman and baby had gotten too near the man, and he refused to hurt the innocent. He understood how devastating that was, because Terry had been innocent, too. He lowered his weapon.

He waited while the two were engaged in conversation. She touched her husband's face, then bent down to blow a raspberry on his cheek, which had them both laughing. She held out the baby to him and gestured to the chair. He frowned, shook his head, and waved her off. Sarah smacked his arm and stuck out her tongue, dodging the swat he attempted to lay on her ass. Then she strode to the house, singing something loud and only slightly off-key. Her husband yelled something about the neighbors, which she apparently found funny and began to sing louder. He could see the obvious love the two of them shared, and that made what he had to do even more difficult.

Regret tore through him. "I'm sorry," he whispered, no longer sure who the sympathy was for.

She opened the front door, and her husband began to roll toward the house. Now would be his chance. Despite his misgivings, he had to take it. He again raised the rifle, closed one eye, and locked in on his target. The wheelchair stopped at the curb, and Daniel tried unsuccessfully to move it. He called out to Sarah, an edge of frustration in his voice. She shook her head and took eight steps toward him when the trigger of the M24 he held in slightly trembling hands depressed, and a loud bang split the quiet suburban street. Less than a second passed before Daniel's head exploded, blood and other materials spattering his wife and child. For a moment, she stood there, eyes wide. She gripped the baby close to her chest, and then screamed.

Before the echo died away, he had already scurried off into the night.

It wasn't a perfect shot. He could hear Terry cursing at him, making him do it again and again until he got it right. But Terry had died, and though two years had passed, he would finally be avenged.

Daniel Tollifson had been the first, but there was no doubt he wouldn't be the last. Though he didn't want to kill anyone, there had to be a penalty for those who refused to help him get justice for Terry. He needed to track down and eliminate the person who'd been responsible.

No matter who had to die in the process.

CHAPTER ONE

The drive from the gun range to the house had a comfortable silence to it. I couldn't be sure what Sammy had going on in his head, but in mine, the thoughts continued to swirl. Rook had called and said it would be bad. Again. The last time, it had been the most complicated case of my career, involving multiple missions, with each target leading me closer to the ultimate big bad. Valerie Mason had been the head of a national cartel with sticky fingers in every imaginable pot—drugs, child slavery, prostitution—and it had been my job to eliminate her. Turned out that Ms. Val had been a cruel, conniving woman who had ruled her vast empire through money, fear, and sex, as well as a good portion of death. A lot of people died—many of them by my hand—before I finally got to face her.

And she kicked my ass.

It hadn't been all my fault, though. Sammy had left me. Walked out when he knew I had to go after the woman. To be fair, she was his mother. The same person who'd given him up to one of her cronies who in turn had forced him to become a prostitute.

So, just as it was fair to say that case had been the worst of my life, it had also been the best, because that was how I'd met him. I'd saved his life from the hellhole he'd been thrown into. In return, he'd saved mine.

I'd lost my stomach for the job. Killing people removed a part of your soul, and I'd helped a lot of people move from this life to another. During that last case, each time I'd completed another of the seemingly endless missions, Sammy reminded me how important people like me were. He also showed me that letting go and allowing him to take control helped to free my mind and allowed me to focus on my job.

Sammy rubbed his hand over my leg, caressing that spot above my knee that gave me weird shivers. He knew exactly where to touch me to get whatever result he desired. "You're thinking too hard."

I sighed, both loving and hating the fact he knew me so well. "Rook said this mission would be bad."

A quick squeeze of my knee drew my focus to him. "So you're thinking about Valerie."

"How could I not? Those were the same words he'd used when we started working against Valerie."

"And you're worried how it's going to affect me." His tone seemed light, but I could sense the bit of tension it held. "It's okay, you know. I've come to terms with what I had to do. If I had to do it all over again, I would still kill her."

He'd shot his own mother in the face. Blown off her jaw. At the time, he tried to tell me that it meant nothing. He said he'd wanted to do it because she'd crushed his soul, but I knew that wasn't the real truth. He'd done it so I wouldn't have to, because he'd thought it would destroy what we'd built. He'd thought it was his responsibility to protect me, because he knew I needed him. The fact remained, I'd told him time and again, my feelings wouldn't have changed because of it, but Sammy knew better. He knew my mind like no one ever had. So even though I'd denied his insistence it would hurt me—us—if he said it, chances were he was right.

"You really need to stop with this guilt trip, Haven. I took someone evil and removed her from the world. Yes, it hurt, just like you told me it would. I still have nightmares, but I can't regret it at all. It's over and done with, and I'm learning to deal with it.

"If I'm honest, it's also helped to free me from some other terrors. When she first turned me over to Arianna, I kept begging for someone to tell me what I'd done. What I could do to fix it. And whether my mother would ever come back for me. As the years went on, I came to realize it hadn't been me at all. Everything revolved around her, and I stopped asking the questions, because I knew the answers. I did nothing wrong when I finally had the chance to face her."

The garage door opened, the lights illuminating the multi-bay port where our collection of cars resided. The Boss Mustang 429 purred into the spot

11

that showed it off best. Sammy loved the car, and I loved the way his eyes had lit up when I'd gifted it to him. On occasion, he'd let me drive it when the mood to watch me struck him. The engine cut off as I turned the key in the ignition, and then I reached for the handle to open the door, but he stopped me.

"Are you sure you're ready to get back to work?"

The question had been on my mind since Rook's call. With Sammy's help, I'd overcome many of my own nightmares. But the thought of seeing the cold, dead eyes of a child again made my stomach roll. Since my handler, Rook, had brought me into his organization, I'd seen too much to ever be *normal* again. The withered shells of kids whose only crime had been being young. Of course, the people who'd mistreated them had taken that life away, and no matter how much therapy they received, there would always be a hovering shadow they couldn't get away from. A taste of fear that they could never be rid of.

Turning back to Sammy, I smiled. "I won't lie, because I know you're going to see through it. I'm really not sure I'm going to be able to do this again. Part of me is already screaming that I should grab my bags, take you, and jump on a jet for parts unknown."

He stroked my arm. "We can do that if you want."

God, I wanted. Seeing what Valerie had done, the children she'd allowed to have their innocence stolen, the bodies that had piled up, had fueled my anger, but also left me raw on the inside. The thought of starting this again scared me to my damned core. Why did it have to be me? Hadn't I given everything already? After everything I'd done, did I have any soul left?

Sammy's voice pitched low, soft when he whispered, "You're a good man, Michael."

He rarely used my real name, but when he did, he laced it with such affection that my heart stuttered. I'd never been in love before I met him. Quick fucks in the backroom I could handle—no emotional entanglements, just a little rough sex, and we parted ways. No numbers exchanged. No plans to meet later. I never had a problem until he came into my life and showed me that I could have more. And when I got it, I needed the whole damn combo platter with a side of chips and guacamole.

He pinned me with an intense stare. "I need you to look at me and tell me you want to do this. If you don't, we say no and plan our next move from there."

The fact he put the ball in my court and told me the decision would have to be mine meant a lot. Usually, Sammy made most decisions for me, and I had no problems with that. I needed his control as a balm for my weariness from too many years as an assassin. But when I gazed into his amazing green eyes, I remembered the first time I'd seen them. He'd been chained to a wall, left to sit in his own excrement. So much fear for someone so young that my blood had boiled. When I'd gotten him out of there, his personality had changed completely. Once free of Arianna's control, he'd finally shored up his defenses and taken charge of not only his life but mine as well. When he'd killed his mother, his carefully constructed wall had crumbled, and he'd fallen apart, needing me to be strong for him. It'd taken more than a lot of therapy to bring him back, stitched together into a whole person. He still bore some of the scars, but they didn't control him.

But those eyes that I'd seen filled with fear reminded me that there were others out there who needed me to be strong for them, no matter what it cost me personally. "I think I have to. If I can stop someone and don't, wouldn't that make me as bad as they are? Isn't it my responsibility to make sure that what happened to you and to my sister never happens to anyone else?"

"You fulfilled your obligations to her a long time ago. Chrissy would want you to live, to find love, to build a life."

He said the pretty words, but deep down my war would only end when I could no longer physically do it. "Thank you. I need to do this, though. If I saw a story in the paper about a child being hurt, I couldn't look myself in the mirror without wondering if the outcome could have been different. I think that would probably kill me."

He laughed, and I realized then he already knew what my answer would be. He'd given me the opportunity to think about it. I grinned at him. "Ass."

"Let's go. We shouldn't keep Rook waiting."

I gaped at him. "Yeah, heaven forbid that should happen."

Rook and Sammy had been at odds several times since he'd come into my life. Rook never took crap from anyone, but Sammy had stood up to him on several occasions, and the two of them butting heads for dominance amused me, because Sammy would always be the one who would win.

The door that led from the garage to the house opened, and my majordomo, Kelly, stood there in a tattered bathrobe. After Sammy started seeing his therapist, Kelly decided to move into one of the spare rooms to take care of us. Once he had, we hadn't wanted him to leave. He had a fatherly air about him that I think both Sammy and I needed—with his dead and me not ever knowing who mine had been—and the three of us worked well together.

He crossed his arms and tapped his foot, looking so fierce. "He's waiting."

Sammy grinned. "And?"

Blowing out a frustrated breath, Kelly walked over to us and grabbed our arms. "I'm too old for this shit. Get in there, talk to him, and then we can play all the games you want."

I laughed. "I call Monopoly!"

Kelly's voice took on a softness I rarely heard from him. "Haven, this isn't a joke. What Rook has is… It's bad. I've got your gear ready to go, and I've packed your bag." He paused and swiped a hand over his eyes. "Please, don't let this one…"

He sniffed and turned away. Something had rattled him, and it scared me. Kelly had been an agent years ago, and he'd seen all kinds of shit of his own. To see him unnerved ratcheted up the tension coursing through me. I straightened and marched to the door with Sammy and Kelly on my heel. I tossed the keys to Sammy, who caught them deftly. "I'll be in the war room."

There were layers upon layers of things you needed to do to enter the war room. Symbols, codes, and about a bajillion numbers were all required information. The room itself held a table, a few chairs, and a desk that had a Mac sitting on it, already open to the necessary information. At my approach, Darth Vader's voice rolled through the room.

"I know it's your anniversary, and I'm sorry to drag you away."

Even though Rook always used a voice modulator, I could detect the sadness in his tone. He sounded so out of sorts that I couldn't even bring myself to tease him about not giving a shit that we were celebrating our anniversary. "No problem. Sammy and I understand."

Sammy had understood since the day I met him. After the mission that freed the world of Valerie, I'd asked him to marry me. Surprisingly he'd said yes and taken my name. The proudest moment of my life had been standing there, his hand in mine, eyes bright with love, staring up at me. His lips had been slightly parted, and he'd licked them right before he'd said his vows. The memory made me smile. At least until Rook spoke and pulled me out of my thoughts.

"I wish…"

Rook's voice broke, and I could hear him trying to gather himself together. I said nothing, because there wasn't much of a chance I could offer emotional support of any kind. Sammy coming into my life had made me face a lot of the problems I had allowed to build up since the death of my sister. Sammy had dug in and rooted them out, allowing the infection that had been slowly killing me to be drained. I'd be the first to admit, to myself if no one else, how much I needed the man. Even though a large part of me worried about jumping back into the cesspool of killers and victims, I had Sammy to remind me that what I did had meaning. Saving kids when I could, and avenging them when I couldn't. If a more noble cause existed, I had no clue what it would be.

I opened the files on the computer and smiled. Two very cute girls, about sixteen, mugged for the camera in one of the endless loops of selfies people seemed to take nowadays. One of them had raven hair with deep green eyes and little dimples that made her seem to not have a care in the world. The other, a stunning redhead with blue eyes, had her arms wrapped protectively around her friend. I knew without a doubt that there had been something between these young ladies.

"Samantha Upton and Tanya Karpinski, sixteen years old. Residents of Portland, Oregon. Samantha was a straight-A student, cheerleader, president of two clubs, including the Gay-Straight Alliance. Tanya struggled with school, but the information we pulled shows that Samantha tutored her and helped her bring her average from a D to a B-. By all accounts, they were lovers, the relationship having developed over the course of the last eighteen months. Samantha was extremely protective of Tanya, who struggled with dyslexia. And we think it's that protectiveness that got them both killed."

I traced my finger over the picture. You could see the love the two of them shared clearly written on their faces.

"Tanya reminds me of my daughter," Rook said softly. "It's been a while since I've heard from her."

He'd told me about his daughter one day when we were talking about why we do this job. It had been the first personal conversation we ever really had. Rook had been brought into the organization and ended up recruiting me after Chrissy had been killed. The two of us shared a bond that few would ever understand. Though his daughter always had someone watching her, it didn't make it easier if he couldn't at least get a hello.

My stomach churned. "I'm sorry." The words were weak, but they were the only thing I could say.

"So am I," Sammy announced as he entered the room and took a seat at the table, looking over the case file.

Of the two of us, Sammy definitely ranked as the more empathetic. Since Sammy had arrived, he'd ridden Rook every chance he got, but he'd be the first one to step up when someone needed comfort. He didn't even know Rook had a daughter, but instead of asking questions, he expressed sympathy for the man.

Rook cleared his throat. "Six months ago, their bodies were discovered in a ravine not far from Tanya's house. The bodies were nude and headless."

Sammy gasped and went pale. As for me, the anger that so often welled up inside me when I got a case rushed to the fore, and I no longer had qualms about going back to work. These two girls, who'd had their whole lives ahead of them, had been ripped from this world by someone who needed to pay. And for the first time in a long while, I actually looked forward to making it happen.

"Please tell me we know who did this," I growled.

Sammy's head snapped up and the look of surprise on his face slowly morphed into a satisfied smile.

"We know everything. The kill order for James Voight has been signed, and if you're ready to work, we can get started."

Kelly entered the room and placed my Desert Eagle 50AE in the black holster on the table. I hadn't held it since I'd put it away after last assignment. If the gun club we had rented on occasion had been geared toward the larger caliber ammunition, I would have taken it with me instead of using the matched set of Ruger .22 target pistols Sammy and I'd bought.

I hadn't touched it since the last mission. In my mind, I thought the gun would give Sammy bad reminders, since it was the one he'd used to shoot Valerie. After we got home, I packed it away. It was easy to see Kelly took care of my gear, and the gleam of the weapon showed he'd definitely given the gun the love it deserved. I picked it up, the weight settling into my hand, as though it was an extension of my body. Which, I guess, it was. I held it up to check the sighting alignment, then went through each of the bits and pieces of the finely crafted killing machine. Beautiful.

I grinned as I put the gun into its holster, then slid it into my bag. "Yeah, I'm ready."

~

The woman looked up at her captor from the inky blackness of the abandoned well. He flicked on the flashlight, which caused her to flinch as the bright beam swept over her. When she finally looked up again, he could see the lines of fear and exhaustion around her eyes. He understood. After all, he'd taken her from her home in broad daylight almost a week ago. Sedated her, then dragged her through the yard and put her in the back of the van. No one saw anything. No one would question. She'd simply vanished.

"What is it about this man that everyone seems so willing to protect him? All I'm asking for is a name. Why is that so hard?"

Despite the terror she had to be experiencing, she glared at him, defiance in her gaze. He sighed.

"I'm not a bad man," he said softly, willing her to realize the truth of his words. "I need to find him, you see. He's got to pay for what he did. For what he…took from me. You understand, right?"

She turned her gaze away and a cold fury swept through him.

"Why won't you help me? Why can't any of you see what he's done?" His voice rose until he shrieked at the woman. "He's a monster and he needs to be killed!"

Still she wouldn't give him the answers he needed.

He snarled. "I will find him, and one way or another, you're going to help me."

He aimed the gun down into the well and put three bullets into her, marveling at the grace with which she spasmed and fell.

"I'm sorry," he whispered into the pit.

He turned to leave, then hesitated. If he walked away, she'd probably never be found here, and that didn't sit right with him. She shouldn't be alone now, left for people who knew her to wonder what had become of Alyssa Benoit. And if he told them where to look, his target would know that his days were numbered. The thought made him smile. One thing he knew from his years on the job, a panicked target made for an easy mark.

He pulled out his burner phone and dialed 9-1-1.

CHAPTER TWO

As we lay in bed, cooling ourselves under the two large ceiling fans Sammy had gotten installed, I figured I finally had to come clean with him. I dreaded this moment, but knew I had to talk to him before I got on the morning plane to Portland.

"You're still thinking too hard," he murmured, sliding his fingers over my skin. "I thought I would have knocked all those thoughts out of your head by now. Maybe I need to try a different approach."

My stomach knotted. It was past time Sammy knew the truth. Since he came into my life, he'd shouldered the responsibility of my wellbeing. That alone entitled him to know. "Can we talk?"

"Always. You know you can always come to me."

I took a deep breath as a frisson of fear coursed through my body. If this went badly... No, I couldn't allow myself to think like that. "You know how you've been going to see your counselor every week?"

When he answered, I could hear the tension in his voice. "Yes."

"I... I've been seeing someone, too."

He sat up, and I could see the hurt in his expression. Like an idiot, I had already fucked this up.

"Not like that! I'm not that stupid. I know what you'd do to me if I ever cheated."

He gave a tight smile. "Castration would be the easiest thing," he answered.

My balls tried to climb back up inside and hide. He might be smaller than I was, but Sammy could be damn fierce if he set his mind to it.

"When I saw how you were getting better, even if you weren't happy with how fast it went, I made the decision that I needed to see someone, too. Her name is Dr. Zee, the psychologist the organization keeps on retainer to help the field agents."

His eyebrows drew together when he pinned me with a scathing glare. "So…what? You're saying now you don't need me?"

Confused, I ran through everything in my head, trying to figure out where I'd said a word about not needing him. Coming up empty, my only option was to ask him directly. "Excuse me? Where the hell did you get that from me seeing someone?"

He sat up and grabbed his clothes from the floor. "Apparently I'm not enough to keep you together after a mission anymore. So why would you need me?"

I rolled onto my side and clutched his wrist, dragging him back down until he lay beside me on the bed. His body was stiff, and his expression could have been chiseled from stone.

"Wow, and you say I'm prickly. Can I talk, or do you want to continue having your meltdown? Because if that's what you want, can you do it quickly? I have a plane to catch in twelve hours."

"Fuck you," he snapped.

"Uh, you did a few minutes ago, but if you need a repeat, I'm good to go."

Despite his words, I could see the tension in his rigid posture. I reached out and rubbed a hand over his chest. Slowly, he relaxed as the anger melted away. I kept up my massage until he sighed and snuggled closer. He gave a soft smile as he leaned in. "So why are you telling me this now?"

Taking a deep breath, I pushed on. "I've never been to see her until recently. I thought that going to talk to a shrink meant I was somehow defective, and not a guy who could handle his issues. Then this man came into my life, and when he finally admitted he needed help, I thought it had to be the bravest thing I'd ever witnessed. I can't tell you how proud of him I was. And I figured if he could be this strong, so could I. So, I talked to Lilah— "

"How's she doing? I haven't seen her for a while."

"Fine. She said to say hey. Anyway, she told me that Dr. Zee would probably be a good fit for me. She's apparently used to working with, in Lilah's words, tough nuts. I made the appointment and went to see her."

"And let me guess. You were your usual 'charming' self."

"You do know that using finger quotes is annoying, right? I mean I can hear the sarcasm, so doing that is like double sarcasm."

He chuckled. "Duly noted. Are you going to finish?"

Giving him a glare, I continued. "Yes, I went in with a chip on my shoulder. I had you, and I shouldn't have needed anyone else. But as we talked, I came to realize that I had so much baggage from before we met that no one would have been able to hold me together indefinitely. You spackled the cracks, but they continued to grow, no matter how much more plaster you put on them. A lot of our conversations centered on you, and do you want to know what she said?"

"That you shouldn't talk about your problems with me, and that you should only do so with her," he answered flatly.

"No, Sammy. Actually, it was quite the opposite. She said that what you told me, about this job being important to so many, was spot on. She said I should make sure you didn't get away, because in this life, you're lucky to find that one person who gets you and who makes you feel complete. She also said you should sign up for some courses, because you're obviously a smart man. If you're interested, she suggested some classes you could take, like maybe to become a therapist. Something where you can help people like you've done for me."

The pink of his cheeks told me how much the words meant to him. And none of it had been embellished. Dr. Zee had berated me for a long time for not seeing a professional. For thinking that I could handle it on my own. She said the fact I had Sammy in my life had been the only thing that saved me, because from what I'd told her, I would likely have self-destructed if I hadn't had him to turn to.

"So why are you telling me this now?"

And now came the moment of truth. "When we were driving home, I felt so conflicted about getting back in the saddle—"

He rubbed a hand over my still nude ass. "My saddle."

"Yeah, your saddle. Anyway, after I read the case file on Samantha and Tanya, I had the urge to track down the bastard who'd done this and do him some serious harm. No hesitation, no regrets. I want him to pay for what he's done, and I need to be the one who ensures it."

A slow smile crept across Sammy's face. "So Haven's back?"

"I think so. But just so we're clear, I'm still going to need you. I will always be better with you by my side. Every day you give me strength to go on. Dr. Zee might help to fill the cracks, but you're the one who provides the love that seals them."

Sammy dipped his finger into my crack, sliding it into my hole. "Speaking of filling the cracks," he joked.

The fact he was back to teasing eased the ache in my chest. It allowed me to let go of the fear of his reaction about my visits to see the doctor and focus on what was important: making Sammy happy.

I rolled onto my back and pulled my legs up, giving him full access to what he wanted. He crawled up and covered my body with his. "I'm sorry that I got pissy. You know how protective I am of you." As his cock sank into me, he whispered the words that let me know how cherished I was. "There are days I still can't believe my luck. But make no mistake about it. You're mine, Haven. Even without the wedding band, without the house, without anything, you are mine."

As he began to thrust in earnest, his amazing green gaze locked on me, and I knew I would never doubt that.

The next morning, Kelly had breakfast waiting when we got out of bed. Several times during the night, Sammy had woken me and taken me again. It seemed he needed the affirmation that I understood I'd been claimed once more. To say that both of us were bone weary would be an understatement. But I found myself oddly energized, too. He'd always had that effect on me, but today, I would find out if I had the stuff to do this job again. To see if everything Sammy and Dr. Zee did for me had bound me together enough to function in the field.

As we dug into the scrambled eggs and bacon, plus the hash browns with the diced onions and cheese, Kelly stood glaring at me.

"Problem?" I asked through a mouthful of food.

"Not sure. You seem…different."

"He's well fucked," Sammy said, not missing a beat.

"Let's add that to the list of things I really don't need to know," Kelly insisted. "But no, it's not that—"

"Hey!" Sammy said petulantly. "Haven, I think he's impugning my ability to fuck."

I loved having these men in my life. The banter between the two of them made me smile when few other things could.

"Don't impugn, Kelly. The man is a sex machine set to high."

"Oh, for the love of— Will you two please stop?"

"Maybe when we get to be your age," Sammy countered.

"Never mind, just eat your food. Haven, your plane leaves in four hours. Do you have everything ready?"

"I do. I put it with the stuff you got together for me. I packed my kit when we took a shower after our…third round of sex?"

"Mmm…I think it was fourth or fifth."

Kelly growled. "You know what? The hell with it."

He stormed out of the kitchen, and as I watched, he grabbed the vacuum from the utility closet.

"You should tell him," Sammy whispered.

Inwardly I cringed at the thought of the conversation, and my breakfast lost its appeal. Of course, if I could get someone else to tell him… "He deserves to know, but I don't really have time. Could you talk to him while I'm gone?"

Sammy cocked his head slightly. "No, I really think this is a conversation the two of you should have."

Of course, he was right. It would feel awkward telling Kelly I'd gone to see Dr. Zee. He'd been after me for many years to do it, and I'd brushed his concerns aside, certain I could handle it. Now, telling him would amount to admitting I'd been wrong—or, worse, he'd been right—but it would also force me to apologize. Still, if anyone deserved it after putting up with my bullshit for a decade, Kelly would be that man.

I rinsed my plate and put it on the sideboard. Kelly would do the dishes later, as he always did. I followed the sound of his grumbles to one of the guest bedrooms that hadn't been used since I'd moved in, where he dusted the window frames. I tapped on the door, and without turning around, he snapped, "What?"

"Got a minute?"

I saw him take a deep breath before he faced me. His pinched expression told me that maybe we'd pushed him too far this time.

"Hey, I'm sorry if we offended you—"

He waved a dismissive hand. "Seriously? After a year, you still think you can embarrass or offend me by talking sex or by Sammy wiggling his naked ass on his way out to sunbathe?"

"Then what's wrong, old man?"

Kelly's pained expression smoothed out. "I'm worried. You haven't done fieldwork in a long time. Are you sure you're ready?"

I admit, his doubt hurt a little. "My skills are as sharp as ever," I insisted.

"I don't worry about your skills, Haven. I've seen the targets from the range, and I know you're as good as always. It's just…it's been a while since you've had to deal with this. Maybe you should let Rook send someone else."

"Have a seat. There's something I need to tell you."

He sat on the edge of the small desk in the room, his expression unreadable. I launched into my conversation, telling him that I'd been seeing Dr. Zee. As I spoke, he relaxed and actually smiled. When I got to the conclusion, he jumped up and gave me a brief hug.

"You don't know how happy this makes me."

"So you're not angry?"

"We all get to things in our own time. I had to go see the psychologist after my first mission. I couldn't get the dead drug dealer's gaze out of my mind. The doctor helped me a lot. It's what made me push you to do it, too."

"Sorry I'm stubborn?"

Kelly's laugh had always been melodic. The sound reminded me of wind chimes tinkling in the breeze. I found it oddly relaxing. "Like I said, everything comes in its own time. I just wanted to be sure you were taken care of. I want to be sure you're in my life for a very long time."

"Even if we joke about sex?"

He leaned in a little closer. "Trust me, with the way you cry out, I always know when you're having sex. Who knew you'd end up being a bottom bitch?"

I sputtered and opened my mouth to say something, when he once again pulled me in for a hug.

"Something I should know, guys?"

"Besides your boy's a bottom?" Kelly asked.

Sammy's jaw dropped, and Kelly laughed as he turned me loose.

"What, you thought I couldn't play, too?" Kelly laughed again, and this time held out his arm to Sammy, who settled in between us. Sammy practically purred as Kelly squeezed him tight. "I love you boys. You know that, right?" he asked, kissing the top of Sammy's head.

Though Sammy would deny it, I could see the sheen of tears. He missed his father, and the life he'd lost out on. His own doctor had helped him a great deal, but the truth of the matter was that he needed this closeness so badly, and no matter what happened to me, Kelly would always take care of him. I pulled back, and Kelly turned us loose.

"You've got this," he mouthed over Sammy's head.

I nodded. When James Voight beheaded those two girls in Portland, he had fucked with the wrong people, and now the time had come for him to pay. "Time to get to work, guys," I said, grinning.

Sammy hefted my bag onto his shoulder, then turned to me. "You're going to be careful," he said, stating a fact rather than asking a question.

"Of course. I'm always careful."

Kelly cleared his throat, and Sammy rolled his eyes.

"Fine. One time I went in angry, and that got the better of me," I admitted, refusing to let thoughts of Valerie intrude. "I'm better now. I promise."

And I told the truth. I'd learned a lot from my confrontation with Valerie. I'd gotten back into meditation to center myself quickly and firmly. Outside distractions were pushed to the back of my mind, because in the field, they would wind up getting me killed. I hated the woman for what she'd done to Sammy, and I could admit, if I could bring her back and kill her myself, I'd sure as hell do it. But looking back served no purpose, so right now, my full concentration had to be on the mission I had coming up.

I went through my mental checklist as Sammy drove me to the airport. I couldn't think of anything I'd forgotten.

"I've got you a rental car waiting in Portland," he told me. "It's booked under Scott Troutman."

"Troutman? What the hell is it with you guys giving me these shitty names?"

"Hey, we have to find fun where we can," he explained. "Now anyway, your hotel rooms are set up. One under Troutman, the other is set up as Willy Loman. Both are suites. You'll find ID in your bag for both names, should you need it."

"So how did you get involved? Usually Rook or Kelly sets up my itinerary."

Sammy beamed. "I need a hobby. I figure if you won't let me train to be an agent, this is the next best thing."

I couldn't tell Sammy that I thought he had the makings of an agent. He'd been working with me over the last year, learning to protect himself, and he had great instincts. But this wasn't the life I wanted for him. After he'd killed Valerie, I knew what his capabilities were, and honestly, I wanted him to retain that little bit of innocence I saw in him.

"Well, I appreciate it. But could we please pick some better names? Even John Smith is more believable than Willy Loman."

"Shut up. I saw Death of a Salesman on cable the other night. I loved it."

"You watch too much television. Maybe Dr. Zee is right, you should take some classes."

Sammy snorted. "In what? Former Child Prostitute 101. Or how about How to Kill Your Mother in Three Easy Lessons?"

The venom that dripped from his lips served to cover how much he'd lost. I reached over and ran a hand across his leg. He covered mine with his own hand.

"Sorry. My doctor said this is the sticking point for me. Letting go of the hurt, forgiving her for what she did to me and my father, and allowing myself to understand I did what I had to. It's a lot to ask."

I knew fully what he meant. Dr. Zee had been helping me try to forgive myself for failing Chrissy all those years ago. Since I'd met Sammy, I'd finally been able to let go of the hurt, but she reminded me that I was transferring my feelings of guilt, not so much dealing with them.

I had to admit, she'd been right. That meant that many of our follow-up sessions helped me to deal with my sister's death, and also worked on not traveling down the same path with Sammy—the man currently doing eighty down the freeway, with the wind tousling his spiky brown hair.

If I had to pick a time when Sammy felt most free, it would be now. He loved his car; he worshiped it, in fact. Because, for a long time, he thought it had the ability to take him from his thoughts and memories, if only he went fast enough. Fortunately, he'd been learning less accident-inducing ways to deal. But he still liked going fast.

"Ease up on the accelerator, Hoss, or I won't be needing a plane at all."

He grinned and stepped on the gas a little harder.

"Sammy, seriously. Please slow down."

He glanced out of the corner of his eye, sighed, and took his foot off the accelerator. "I have to say, for someone who can face down evil masterminds, you're pretty much a chickenshit when it comes to driving."

"Evil masterminds? No more Austin Powers for you."

We both laughed at that.

"So what's the plan?" he asked, getting ready to make the turn into Sedona Airport, where I'd start my three-hour trip.

"Right now, the usual. Going to keep an eye on Jimmy, talk to a few neighbors, learn his patterns. Then, when I've learned everything I need to know, I will have a little one-on-one session with Jim-Jim. Afterward, I'll come home. I figure I shouldn't be gone more than a few days, so don't get too comfortable with having the house to yourself."

His expression turned serious. "I hate being in the house when you're not there."

"You've got Kelly," I reminded him.

"I don't think Kelly wants to bend over for me, though." He said it as a joke, but I could see the tension in his eyes.

"Pull over."

"But we're going to be late."

"Like I care. Pull over."

He sighed and pulled the car to the curb. We could see the terminal from where we were, but none of that mattered right now. I leaned in close to him and asked quietly, "What's wrong?"

27

"Nothing. I'm being stupid. I'm okay."

"And now in the second verse, you open up and tell me the truth."

He sighed and began tapping the steering wheel. "My doctor is concerned that I'm still not willing to go out in public. She thinks I spend too much time online and watching movies."

"And what do you think?"

He sighed again and slumped down in the driver's seat. "She's right. I wanted to ask you earlier if you'd…"

His voice trailed off into a mumble.

"If I'd what?" I pressed.

He turned to me. "When you get home, could we maybe go out? Something small and easy. Like dinner somewhere quiet."

And damn if that didn't have me all perked up and excited. Sammy had avoided any kind of social interactions since we'd gotten together. Even when we went to the gun range, I paid a lot of money to ensure we were the only ones there. And now he wanted me to help him change the situation? To have him take his first steps to reclaiming a part of the life stolen from him? I was so down for that!

"You got it. As soon as I get back, we'll figure out what we can do."

He smiled at me, his full lips drawn back so I could see the pearly white teeth that came from a lot of dental work after he'd come to stay with us.

"Okay, so get me to the terminal. I've got a job to do."

I wanted back to Sammy as soon as possible. To that end, I was already planning how Jimmy would be leaving this world. As I thought about Samantha and Tanya, I knew one thing with absolute certainty: It wouldn't be pretty.

CHAPTER THREE

Though I said it shouldn't take long, I was wrong. After eight arduous days, I discovered James Voight had a reputation in his neighborhood. At thirty-six, he'd been warned many times about approaching young women. His neighbors said he thought himself a player, and they had a lot to say about him—he drove a flashy convertible with the top down, threw lots of money around when he went out to eat or to a bar, and tried to come off as smooth. Most people saw him for what he was, but there were always a few who'd been unlucky enough to fall under his sway.

When Tanya's and Samantha's bodies were found, an eyewitness at the scene linked the crimes to Voight, but Rook said the judge who let him off had done so because the evidence the cop—Alex Michaels—found when he went into his house had been taken without waiting for a warrant. Despite the fact that it linked Voight to the crimes, the judge refused to allow it as he considered it tainted, and therefore inadmissible. So Voight had walked.

One of the mothers, Melissa Karpinski, began a campaign to get Voight driven out of the neighborhood, but it went nowhere, as people simply didn't want to get involved. Then she disappeared, and no trace of her had been recovered.

Rook knew Voight was responsible. After speaking with neighbors, Michaels—the same officer who had been involved in Tanya's and Samantha's disappearances—said a witness had told him she'd seen Voight arguing with Melissa before she disappeared. Michaels thought he had enough reason to check Voight out. The judge disagreed. Of course. Despite the evidence Michaels had collected, the judge again threw it out, stating enough damage had been done to Voight's reputation. When they'd tried to get a warrant, it, too, had been refused for some bullshit reason.

Michaels had ended up on suspension—though Rook said he was being considered for a job in the organization. I hoped it worked out for him, because he seemed to have great instincts. Unfortunately, Voight walked free.

Not tonight, though.

I slipped into his house under the cover of darkness. He had a simple alarm system that I bypassed with no problem. As I entered, a small brown and black puppy yipped at me and made a lunge for my feet. I suppressed a laugh as this little thing danced around, giving short barks, and wagging his whip-thin tail a mile a minute. A quick belly rub sent him dashing off into another room. Voight had never taken the little thing for a walk in all the time I'd been watching him. What a sucky pet owner.

I snuck through the house, mindful of the dog that kept zipping in, checking me out, and then scampering off to another room, barking his fool head off. I hoped that when I'd completed my mission, they'd find him a good home, because he had to be the cutest little son of a bitch.

A flash of light from under one of the doors grabbed my attention. As I got closer, I heard the sound of the television. When the pup scampered back into the room and started barking, Voight shouted for him to be quiet. The dog whimpered, then barked at my feet, before he rushed to another room. This time I followed him and closed the door to keep him inside. No sense in having him get hurt.

I returned to Voight's room and drew my gun. I threw open the door. He lay naked on the bed, watching television. I thanked the gods he wasn't watching porn, because seeing Big Jimmy playing with Little Jimmy—and I do mean *little*—probably would have scarred me for life. But the shock on his face at seeing me with a gun pointed at his head had definitely been worth the price of admission.

"Who the fuck are you?" he shouted, scrambling to cover himself.

"You can call me Haven. I need a few minutes of your time."

His confusion forced me to stifle a laugh. "What?"

"Oh, don't worry. I'm not like a Jehovah's Witness or anything. There won't be any religion discussed tonight. It seems to me that we have a problem here, and I hope we can get it resolved. Tanya Karpinski and Samantha Upton's bodies were discovered in a ravine not too far from here. Someone had assaulted them, then killed them. Now, I can't swear this is what happened, but I want you to hear me out. First, let's get comfortable, okay? Why don't you go ahead and get dressed?"

"You're crazy. Get the fuck out of my house."

I waved the gun around. "See this? Right now, everything in this house is mine, and that includes you. So do what I say, and maybe you won't die tonight. Though I make no promises on that point. Now get some clothes on. I really don't want to see your pasty flesh."

He hesitated, his gaze shifting around the room. Not having the patience, I stalked to where he sat and hit him hard enough across the face to knock him back. He sat up, and found the barrel of my gun pressed to his forehead.

"Get dressed," I ordered.

He pulled on a pair of jeans from the floor, then I dragged him behind me by the scruff of the neck into the living room area, where I dumped him. He sprawled out, still in a daze. For a modest house, it had been done up pretty nicely. Thick wooden support columns were placed strategically to hold up a loft. I thought they'd be perfect for what I had in mind.

"Sit down over there on the floor," I told him, pointing in the direction of one of the columns.

He fidgeted with something in his pocket, and I shook my head. "Now see, I only wanted to talk, and you had to go and change the game."

I held out my hand and made a gimme motion, but when he wouldn't hand over what he had in his pocket, I shot him in the shoulder. The pup I had seen earlier yowled in sync with Voight's scream, and I felt a twinge of regret. But only for scaring the puppy.

"Now, I'd really prefer not to have to shoot you again, so I'm going to reach into your pocket and see what you're hiding."

A cell phone, and it seemed as though he had been trying to dial 911. I shook my head. "Jimmy, so wrong of you." Taking careful aim, I shot him in the other shoulder. He fell to the ground, crying out in agony.

"Baby. It hurts, but they're not going to kill you," I told him. "That's my job."

He went shock white as I grabbed him by the throat and dragged him to where I needed him to be. I propped him against one of the thicker columns, then slipped the gun into its holster. I wrenched his arms behind him, ignoring his cries, and secured them with a zip-tie before I reached into my pocket and extracted something I'd only used a few times. I held it up to Jimbo. "Do you know what this is?"

He babbled incoherently, and it might have irked me a little. I slapped him across the face, ensuring I had his attention. "Now, I'll ask again. Do you know what this is?"

I held up a thin strand of wire, secured at each end by a piece of smooth wood. His eyes went wide. He definitely knew what was about to happen. Before he could move, I wrapped the wire around his neck, and secured it to the pole. I could see his skin turning white where it cut into his throat. Then I stood and started walking around the room.

"That's a garrote. It's a crude, but very effective means of torture. I'm guessing since you know what it is you've had some experience with it. Now that we've covered that and been introduced, I hope you won't mind if I start my story. You see, everyone should know why they're about to die, so I make sure they know before I help them on their way.

"Tanya and Samantha were young lovers. They had that kind of romance that any kid would appreciate. Samantha brought Tanya flowers, gifts, and lavished her with pretty things like butterfly necklaces and shiny baubles. Tanya appreciated the attention, and really liked it when they walked through the mall hand in hand, showing how much they were in love. Then one day, Tanya went to Samantha and told her about a freak in the neighborhood who had been bothering her. Seems he told her he loved her and wanted her to himself. When Samantha heard this, she confronted the man at his house and humiliated him. Personally, I think it would have gone better if she'd dragged the asshole out of his house and shamed him in front of the neighbors, but that wasn't to be. I'm willing to bet Samantha thought she was protecting Tanya, but we'll never know for sure.

"The man—that's you by the way, and I'm using the term man very loosely—was angry—no, more like enraged. A teenage girl had put him in his place, and he hated her for it. He vowed revenge against the girls for rebuffing his advances and then approached them, gun in hand, and forced them into a wooded area where he assaulted them. He started to beat on Tanya, but then something went wrong. One of the girls fought back, and he lashed out and struck her. She went down, probably dazed. Then, in a fit of pique, he hit the other one, too. Then afterward, dragged them somewhere and proceeded to cut off their heads. How am I doing so far?"

He gurgled, the wire slicing the skin, and blood began to ooze from the splayed flesh.

Keeping my voice calm, I leaned closer to him. "I asked a question. How am I doing?"

"Didn't…do…anything," he choked out.

"See, we both know that's a lie."

I stepped behind the beam and gave the wire another twist, forcing it deeper into his larynx. He gasped and his muscles strained, but there would be no way for him to dislodge it. If I didn't remove it, he'd die. Not that I cared.

"I want you to relax a bit. Well, as much as you can." Though he was alone, I still wanted to see if I could find ironclad proof he'd done something to the girls. "I'm going to check out the house, okay? Try not to move too much. I don't want it to tighten and kill you before I get back. Because, you know, it would be a shame if I missed it."

I left him sitting there, choking. As I moved about the house, I opened the door to the room I'd locked my furry friend in. The puppy trailed behind me, strutting proudly. When I turned around, he skittered away. It was pretty comical. I made my way to the basement of the house—surprisingly clean, all things considered. A large chest freezer with a padlock stood in the corner of the room, and I knew what I'd find once I opened it. I picked the lock, then tossed it aside before I lifted the lid.

James Voight had stuffed the body of Jennifer Karpinski's mother, Melissa, in the freezer. There was an indentation in her skull where something had struck her, and I hoped to hell it had killed her right away, because otherwise, Voight had thrown her inside with her daughter's head and left her to suffocate.

According to Rook's notes, when Michaels had called in to let his superiors know what he'd found, they had ordered him from the home. If they had fucking sucked it up and backed his play, Jimmy would never have walked away. This was one of the most frustrating parts of my job. Those who commit violent crimes seem to be given more thought to their rights, their comfort, than the victims. Of course, if it wasn't for that, I'd be out of a job. Wouldn't that be sweet?

I texted Rook to let him know what I'd found and where, then sent a second message to tell him we'd need a cleaning team.

I walked back upstairs, secure in the knowledge that what I was about to do was not only necessary, but justified. James's eyes went wide when I entered the room.

"You know, every time I think I've seen the lowest a person can sink, someone like you comes along and shows me I have yet to scrape the bottom of the barrel. I want you to know that I don't take pleasure in what's about to happen. Well, okay, maybe a little pleasure, but people like me exist to keep people like you from good folks."

I grabbed the ends of the garrote and twisted hard. The crack I heard caused my stomach to knot, but I didn't feel the urge to throw up. I kept tightening the ends until James stopped twitching. The wire had sliced deep into his throat, almost cutting off his head. Seemed somehow karmic to me.

Rook's people would be to the house soon, so I grabbed most of my gear. I left the garrote, because I really didn't feel like cleaning it, and moved toward the door. As I put my hand on the knob, I felt a tug on my leg. I looked down and saw the fierce puppy grabbing the cuff of my pants and pulling on it.

"Yeah, you're real tough, aren't you?" I teased, bending down and rubbing between his ears. It struck me then, when the crew arrived, they'd have to get rid of everything in the house. I had no way to know if that included the dog, and I really didn't want to think about him being hurt, so I made a decision. I scooped the little ball of fur into my arms. He stared at me a moment, then licked my nose. Yeah, okay, he had me wrapped around his paw.

I made sure I had a good grip on him as we stepped into the cool night air. I tapped him on the nose. "Sammy better love you. Think I'm gonna call you Kip." The only answer was a rapidly swishing tail. "Sammy's gonna kill me." I groaned.

I found an all-night grocery store and stopped to pick up supplies I would need if I planned on taking Kip home. Part of me wanted to call to talk to

Sammy, but another part wanted to surprise him. Plus, I really didn't want him to say no. I glanced over on the passenger seat where Kip slept. I reached out and stroked him. He raised his head and yawned, then bounded into my lap. He put his feet on my chest and started licking my face. I laughed as I tried to get him to stop, but my mind went back to when I had wondered if I could love a dog. And looking at Kip, the easy to please smile on his face, I knew I could.

"If Sammy says no, I'm going to have to agree with him," I told the dog. "It's not really fair to him. I don't get called out on assignment often, but when I do, I could be gone for weeks at a time. That means he and Kelly would be responsible for you, and that's a choice they're going to have to make."

With a heavy sigh, I pulled out my phone. I dialed the house, and Kelly answered almost immediately.

"What's wrong?"

"Why do you think something is wrong?"

"Uh, because since I've known you have you, I can count on one hand the number of times you've called home. Hell, we barely get you to send a text when you're on assignment. You're not hurt, are you? Where are you?"

"Still in Portland," I replied. "No, I'm not hurt. I need to talk to you and Sammy. Is he around?"

Kelly called for Sammy, and I heard feet stampeding to the phone.

He sounded slightly winded when he asked, "What's wrong?"

I laughed. "Nothing is wrong. I…um…"

Sammy's whisper cut right through me. "You're scaring me. Please tell me you're okay."

"I'm sorry. I'm fine. I finished the job and will be ready to head home soon, but this assignment seemed to have an unexpected twist to it."

I didn't want to worry them, but I also didn't want to hear either of them say no. I barely knew anything about the dog beyond him being a cute boy, but the idea of what could happen had me nervous.

"Haven? Are you there?" Kelly's voice pulled me back to the here and now.

"Sorry. Okay, here's the thing. Kelly, if I call for a cleaning crew, what happens?"

"They go in and, after they remove the body, they basically torch the house. By the time they're done, nothing is left standing. Why?"

"What if they found something in the house? Would they take it out first?"

Kelly's voice had an edge when he replied. "Something like what? You're being very vague, and I don't know how to answer you."

"Fine!" I huffed a sigh. "Voight had a puppy. What would they do about the dog?"

"He'd be left in the house. Nothing is removed so it can be made to look like Voight did it and then fled."

"That's barbaric," Sammy complained.

"I don't disagree, but we need to make sure that if anyone checks, they don't find any discrepancies. Rook's people plant evidence to build a case against Voight, and make it look like he's fled. There will be a plane ticket showing he's left the country, and they'll make it seem like he torched the place to cover up something."

"You took the dog, didn't you?" Sammy asked.

Not able to contain a sigh, I answered yes.

"Are you bringing him home with you?"

Kelly's question surprised me.

"I might."

"We're getting a puppy!" came Sammy's jubilant shout.

"You don't mind?"

"Mind? I love dogs. What kind is he?"

"Um…a tiny one. He's brown and black. And he's a feisty little thing."

"Can we keep him, Kelly? Can we?"

I knew Sammy was teasing, but Kelly had to be in agreement.

"Let me ask a question before I answer Samuel's. Haven, do you like this dog?"

There wasn't even a hesitation. "Yes, he's so cute."

"Then bring him home. We'll figure something out. Have you given him a name yet?"

"I thought about calling him Kip, but if you want something else—"

"It's safe to say that Samuel and I are both excited to meet this dog that has you all tied up in knots. Do you need us to make any arrangements?"

"I got a dog crate, which he hates, collar, leash, food and water bowls, plus a few other little tidbits. But I need to clear it with the airlines, so I can get him on the plane."

"The plane?" Sammy gasped. "You're going to let them store him in the cargo hold?"

"It's safe, Samuel," Kelly assured him.

"We could drive down there and pick them both up," Sammy protested.

Kelly huffed out a breath. "Okay, two points I need you to think about. One, after what happened the last time I rode with you—and if you need a reminder, it was you going ninety miles per hour while I begged you to slow down—I will never get into a car when you're behind the wheel. Two, it will take almost twenty-four hours to drive there, well, maybe twelve if I was foolish enough to agree to let you drive. I think that might be more stressful on the puppy than a three-hour trip on the plane."

"But—"

"And if he brings him home by plane, you'll get the chance to see him a lot sooner."

"I'll make the arrangements now," Sammy enthused, disconnecting the call.

I looked down at the dog who had curled up and fallen asleep in my lap. "Well, boy, looks like you've got a new home."

He peered up, his eyes bright and shiny, yawned, licked my hand, then went back to sleep.

Yup. Totally in love.

CHAPTER FOUR

Sammy met me at the terminal and the only thing he grabbed turned out to be Kip's carrier. He looked into the door and started cooing. "Who's the cute boy? Aww, yes, who is the cutest little thing?"

Kip barked at him and did his best to run in circles. He reached a paw through the cage door, and Sammy squealed with delight.

"Oh my god, he's adorable. Can you drive home? Because I want to hold him."

"It might be best if he stayed in the carrier while we drive. He tends to get a little hyper."

"Oh, he'll be good." He stuck his fingers through the grate and rubbed Kip's nose. "Won't you? Yes, you will."

I couldn't help the laugh that bubbled out of me.

"Kelly wanted to come, too, but there wasn't enough room for all of us."

The car Sammy had brought was a 2010 Ford Mustang two-tone black and yellow. We'd gotten it six months ago when Sammy had seen it in a car show. He said of all the ones there, it was the one he thought his father would have loved most. His expression when I struck a deal with the owner made it all worth it.

"You could have brought one of the other cars. The SUV would have easily held everyone. As it stands, he's going to have to— You brought the Mustang because you wanted to hold him."

Sammy gave me his patented 'duh' look. "We may have argued over who was coming to pick you up. Kelly thought since I drove you to the airport, he should be able to come get you."

I laughed. "He's never, ever driven me to or from the airport. I always took a taxi. Okay, you can sit and hold Kip while I drive, but you have to keep him in your lap. He seems to sleep pretty easily, but when he's awake, he's got enough energy to power a small star."

Sammy wasn't listening to me, and I really hadn't expected him to. After we got into the car, he opened the carrier, pulled Kip out, and wrangled the cage into the back, behind the passenger's side. Kip snuggled close to Sammy's chest, raised his head, and began to lick his new friend's chin. Sammy buried his face in the dog's fur, then moved him back. "Someone needs a bath."

"I know. Maybe we can take one together."

He frowned at me. "I meant Kip."

Doing my best to look affronted, I pouted at him. "I see how it goes. Cast aside for a dog."

"He can sleep with us, right?" Sammy asked, giving me his own version of puppy-dog eyes.

"Fuck, no. We'll buy him a dog bungalow, but there is no way in hell he's sleeping on the bed."

He lowered his head, and his plump lower lip jutted out slightly. "Oh. Okay."

I glared at Sammy and knew, no matter what I said, tonight Kip would be in bed with us.

The entire trip home, Kip lay in Sammy's lap, occasionally sitting up to look out the window, but otherwise seemingly content with the love he received. Sammy ran his hands over the soft fur, stroking his ears and whispering to the pup, which made his tail wag. The two of them were so serene together, and it struck me that Sammy got as much from the touch as Kip did. They were thick as thieves already, Kip staring intently as Sammy talked.

"He likes you," I said, even though it belabored the obvious.

"I love him," Sammy whispered, then leaned forward and kissed him on the head. "I used to have a dog, you know."

Something else I hadn't known. "No, I didn't."

"She hated him. Said he was messy. Was too loud. I never took care of him, which wasn't true. I walked him several times a day, played in the yard with him, fed and watered him. I came home from school one day, walked in, and called for Buster. He didn't come to me. I wandered through the house, calling his name, and nothing. When I found her in the kitchen, I asked where he was. She told me he got out and got hit by a car. I cried so hard, because there was no way he 'got out.' She did something, but I never found out what."

His words hit me hard, causing my hands to tighten around the steering wheel. "I'm sorry." Lame, but I couldn't think of anything else to say.

Sammy shrugged. "Like everything else, I pushed it down and dealt with it. Six months later, my dad was dead and she gave me to Arianna. Then thoughts of Buster went completely out of my head as I tried to find a way to survive."

I struggled to think of something to say. Feelings weren't easy for me to deal with on the best of days, but after hearing his story, I wanted to find the nearest shelter and adopt another dozen dogs, just to see him delight in their company.

"No, one dog's enough," he said, a slight smile playing on his lips.

"How—" I sputtered.

"It's what you do." Sammy cocked his head and gazed at me, a smile on his lips. "You can't stand to see me sad, so you try to fix things for me. Like you did with the car. So you know, I'm not sad anymore. I have a family, and now we have a new addition," he said as he ran a hand over Kip's head.

The thing about Sammy was that he was the one in charge when it came to our relationship. I knew and accepted it. Hell, I reveled in it. But that didn't mean I wouldn't do my best to make him happy if I could. I let him continue to bond with Kip, saying nothing more.

Our arrival at home showed me that our newest member sure as hell had already wormed his way into the top spot. Kelly rushed out and snatched him from Sammy, cuddling him. Seeing this man who was quickly heading to his sixty-third birthday, holding the puppy like a baby, showed me a side of Kelly I didn't know existed.

"Something you want to tell me, old man?"

He glanced up, and the smile that lit his face could only be called transcendent. He'd barely touched the dog, and he was smitten.

"I've always loved dogs. Well, cats, too."

"So why didn't you ever say anything? We could have had a dog years ago."

He stopped mid-rub and glanced over at me. "Really? Do you think ten years ago you would have been ready to have a companion animal?"

"No," I admitted. I reached out and brushed a hand across Sammy's arm. "But things change. And, sometimes for the better."

"They do," Kelly agreed, pulling Kip to his chest. "Can I ask you something? Why Kip?"

My cheeks warmed as I felt both sets of eyes on me. "When we were kids, Chrissy loved The Jungle Book. When things were going bad in the house, you know, whenever Mom and whoever she had been shacking up with at the time started screaming at one another, we'd hide away as best we could, and I would read to her. She couldn't say Rudyard, but she got Kip down easily. If she needed me to read to her, she'd come over with the book and say, "Kip." As she got older, she learned the author's name, but The Jungle Book was always Kip's work.

"That's a lovely story," Kelly told me. "But, if you don't mind, I'm going to play with my dog."

"What is it with the two of you?" I complained. "It's like I don't even exist anymore."

"I've seen you already. Now I get to meet the dog who enraptured you."

"I wouldn't say enraptured," I lied.

"Mm-hmm," Sammy teased. "Go get in the shower. I'll wash your back."

That sounded good to me. I rushed to the bathroom, turned on the water, and stripped off my clothes before tossing them in the hamper. I stepped into the spray from the multiple showerheads, reveling in their pounding beat on my tired muscles. When a cool breeze washed over me, I knew Sammy had come in.

"How are you doing?" he asked, picking up the soap and a loofah.

"I'm okay."

"Great. So tell me the truth this time. How are you really doing?"

His meaning couldn't be more obvious. I turned to face him, and he ran the sponge over my chest.

"Seriously, I'm okay." I thought a moment, then smiled. "There were so many triggers there for me. The girls' heads, the mother's body, and listening as his neck snapped. Any of those would have messed me up for a long time. But this time, it reminded me how much my job meant. You were right, of

41

course. I can't save everyone, but I can make it right for them. Voight escaped the law, but he couldn't escape justice."

Sammy grinned, then tweaked one of my nipples. The sensation brought a moan to my lips.

"It won't be easy," he reminded me. "We each have a way to go, more therapy, more forgiveness. But at least we're on the right path. I'm very proud of you."

With those words, Sammy dropped to his knees. He washed my legs slowly, sliding the loofah up and down, until it tickled the hairs on my balls. The blood rushed south, and my cock began to rise, standing proudly as Sammy ran a hand over it. I reached out and turned the shower down to a mist.

"No soap for this part," he murmured, leaning in and licking the head. "Hate having my mouth washed out with the stuff."

Then he moved forward and engulfed my dick, laving the underside with his tongue. When his throat opened up, I slid all way the way inside and moaned. *God, what this man did to me.*

"Sammy, please," I pleaded.

He pulled back and looked up, the light spray hitting him in the face. No one would ever describe Sammy as pretty or cute. He would never be a model, but to me he had to be the most gorgeous thing on the face of the earth.

"Please? I like it when you beg," he said smugly. "What do you want, Haven?"

So many images filled my mind, and I couldn't pick out just one. I wanted them all. Sammy down my throat, up my ass, me on my back, my knees, head hanging over the edge of the bed. I wanted multiples of the man so he could do it all at the same time.

My thoughts must have been pretty obvious, because he laughed. "How about if we go to bed, and we'll figure it out from there?"

He held out a hand, and I helped him to his feet. He stood there while I dried him off, patting him gently. When I brushed over his shaft, he trembled.

"No touching," he warned me. "I've been saving up for more than a week, and I don't intend on losing it here on the shower floor. Go in the bedroom and grab the lube. I want you to get yourself ready for me. Don't go too fast, though, because I want to watch."

I grinned and headed into the bedroom. The nightstand drawer stood open, so I pulled out the bottle of our favorite warming gel. I put a small squirt on my finger, then bent over and began to run it around my pucker. God, before I met Sammy, there was no way I would have believed this would feel amazing. Now prepping myself for him was one of my favorite things. Watching his eyes go wide if I moaned or seeing his breathing quicken if I whispered his name, turned me on to no end. I slid my finger in slowly, relishing the slight burn, knowing that Sammy would soon ensure it became more.

"Are you ready yet?" I called out.

"Patience is a virtue," he replied.

"Fuck that!"

He came walking in from the bathroom, the towel draped loosely over his slim hips. Seeing the way the muscles worked, moved provocatively, had me beyond excited. Never before had I desired to have someone for more than a quickie. This man who stood before me? I could have him inside me every day of my life and never get bored.

"You're staring," he said, a grin playing on his lips.

"Thinking," I replied. "Wondering how I can strip that towel off you and get you on the bed with the least amount of steps."

"Oh? And what did you come up with?"

Lunging forward, I grabbed him, tossed the towel aside, and dragged him down onto the bed atop me. He laughed, then stared into my eyes. "I can feel your cock pressing into me. Are you happy to see me?"

He gave a thrust of his hips, our erections brushing against one another. One of us moaned. Probably me. Being away from Sammy for more than a week made me appreciate coming home to him. He leaned forward and licked my neck, which always caused a shudder to run through me. Even though I knew what he'd do next, I still shivered when he latched his lips on my shoulder and began sucking. He loved marking me, and I would never say I didn't enjoy looking at the hickeys every chance I got.

"I wanted to seduce you," he said softly. "To get you all hot and bothered so that you'd beg me to fill you up."

43

I snorted. "I'm a sure thing."

"Maybe," he replied. "But there is never anything wrong with being reminded how much you're loved. Unfortunately, I've been waiting eight days, seven hours, twelve minutes, and a few seconds for this, and I don't know that I can be patient enough to wait to be inside you. Is that okay? Can we make this one quick, so that later we can take our time?"

The expression on his face, the warmth of his eyes... God, I just wanted to lay him on the bed and impale myself. He knew the words to say, the way to make me melt. It all came so easily to him, and I enjoyed being the recipient of his attention. I nodded, and he slid off me.

He grabbed my legs as I raised them and positioned me however he wanted. This one would be rough, because he hadn't given me any more prep than what I'd done myself. Our first time together, Sammy hadn't gotten me ready at all. He knew I needed the pain to take my mind off the assignment I'd come staggering home from. This time he wasn't gentle, and it hurt like hell, but once he was sheathed inside me, he waited until I got used to him.

"Move," I demanded, relishing what he did.

It started out slowly. He pulled out a little, then slid in gently, until our balls touched.

"Love it when you come home," he groaned, shoving in again. "I'll never get tired of this."

He kept his gaze locked on mine as he began to pick up speed, brushing against my prostate and eliciting a grunt from me each time he slammed in. I closed my eyes, reveling in the feelings, when he snapped, "Don't stop looking at me!"

Immediately, I followed his instructions, gazing into the depth of those sinful green eyes. Sweat beaded on his forehead as he drew near his climax, and he grinned at me. "Stroke yourself. I want to feel you clamp down on my cock, milk the come from me. Help me fill you up."

I grabbed my dick and jerked for all I was worth. I wanted to give him this, give him everything. I grunted a few times as my balls drew up, and I shot, splattering my stomach.

"God, yes," Sammy roared. "Love that feeling."

He slammed in a few more times, groaning as he shot inside me. Then he collapsed onto me, kissing me, stroking my chest, my hair.

"Love you so much." He ran a hand gently over my chest. "So much." He rose to his feet, and I struggled to sit up. "Stay right there," he insisted.

He grabbed the towel I'd pulled off him, and with soft strokes, he began cleaning me, wiping my abs, running the towel over my crack—showing me that his deeds matched his words. When he seemed satisfied, he tossed the towel aside, moved me over, and climbed into the bed next to me. He put a hand on my stomach and held me there as we drifted off to sleep.

That night after we'd had dinner, with Kip sitting beside Sammy and barking every time he took a mouthful of food, Sammy put on a movie. We sat on the couch, Kelly in the armchair, and watched Kingsman: The Secret Service. It was a really good movie, if not more than a tad unrealistic. After it was over, Sammy turned to Kelly and asked, "Do you guys have any cool gadgets like that?"

"I wish," came the reply. "Do you know how much easier our job would be if we could make people forget seeing us?"

Sammy frowned as he gave me a curious look. "Would you have used something like that on me?"

The hesitation must have given him the answer he wanted, because his expression turned cold. Kip lay at his feet, and I took in the picture before me.

"Honestly? Yes, I would have. I didn't know you. I had a job to do and would have done anything to keep you safe. But you can't blame me. I had no idea what my life would be like with you in it. Back then, there wouldn't have been a movie night. We wouldn't have been munching popcorn with a dog that snagged any fallen kernels. Kelly would have been gone already, back to the place he lived. What I have now? I wouldn't trade it for the world."

That brought a smile back to Sammy's face.

"Softy," Kelly muttered.

I turned to face him. "Yeah, because you're not loving this life, too."

A bright red suffused his ruddy cheeks. "I won't lie. I am loving this. It feels good to have a family."

And I couldn't deny it. Chrissy had been the only family I would ever admit to having, but these two men and this dog? They'd set up shop in my heart, which I long thought of as having been closed off to emotion, and damned if I didn't enjoy having them there.

Family ruled.

The drawn curtains blocked out most of the full moon, making everything in the bedroom still, but giving a soft glow as well. When a thin shaft of light swept in, I knew the door had opened. I reached into my nightstand for my gun, but the door closed again. It hadn't been open but a moment and never opened far enough to let anyone in. Or so I'd thought.

Small huffs, followed by thumps, then whining caught my attention. I peered down at the end of the bed and saw Kip standing with his feet on the edge, looking expectantly at Sammy. He tried to jump up, but then he'd fall back on his butt. I wanted to laugh, but his determination had me getting up, cupping his rear end, and helping him onto the bed. He stood there a moment, trying to get his bearings, then bounded up toward Sammy. I nearly pulled him back, thinking he would wake the man who'd kept his promise and made love to me nice and slow before drifting off to sleep with me in his arms.

Kip closed in and sniffed Sammy's face, then gave him a lick on the cheek. He moved up onto Sammy's pillow, and did a few steps, turned, and lay down with a sigh behind Sammy's head. I figured Kelly had let him out before he allowed him into the room, but I also knew I'd be getting up in an hour or two to take him back to the great outdoors. I didn't mind, though. The dog made Sammy happy. Sammy made me happy. Therefore, I'd get up at the ass-crack of dawn to make sure the dog got out to pee.

And if that wasn't love, I didn't know what was.

CHAPTER FIVE

He shook his head. What kind of person engendered such devotion from people? Who had so many willing to die for him? He turned to the young blond man—Carter, he reminded himself—whose bright blue eyes shone with tears. He had long since stopped struggling against the bonds that held him, finally accepting the reality of his predicament.

He'd stalked Carter Whitfield for a week before he found him in a place where he could take him. Alone in the park, painting the sunrise over the lake. The kid had the makings of a great artist. The assassin only hoped that he'd have the chance to fulfill the potential he saw.

He'd called Carter's stepfather and told him that, unless he helped, Carter wouldn't survive. Dad had been understandably angry, issuing threats, making demands, then, as time wore on, begging him not to hurt his stepson. And once again, the assassin knew regret. He had no desire to hurt Carter, who was an innocent in something he didn't even understand. The fact remained that the assassin needed information, and his list of contacts was slowly dwindling. It was wrong, but necessary to ensure Terry's death hadn't been in vain.

"Carter doesn't have to die," the assassin said. "Your boy's a good-looking kid. Tell me what I want, and I'll let him go back to college, to work on the 4.275 GPA that I'm sure makes you proud. All you need to do is make a call. Give me what I want."

"I don't know!" the kid's stepfather insisted. "I don't have those connections anymore, I swear. When I left the organization, they cut me loose. That's how it goes. Once you leave, you'll never find them again. Please, don't hurt Carter," he pleaded. "I'll take his place. Just don't hurt my son."

"I really wish that were possible. You need to know that I'm a man of my word, and I swore if you helped me, I wouldn't hurt the boy. But you didn't. If I don't follow through on what I say, then my word means nothing. I'm sorry."

He set the phone down and took a few steps toward the young man. Those eyes went wide and his lip trembled. "John? John, please. I don't wanna die!" Carter cried out.

He could hear John Chambers in the background, begging him not to do this, but his course had been decided two years ago, and nothing now could change it. He whispered in the boy's ear. "Close your eyes. I'll try to make this as painless as possible."

Tears streamed down Carter's cheeks. "Please, don't—"

He pinched Carter's nose and covered his mouth. Asphyxiation wasn't the swiftest method of death, but despite the initial panic, there wouldn't be any suffering. Carter's body spasmed as he strained, every muscle in his body would be screaming now as the adrenaline rushed through him. The fear would make the end swifter as his brain realized there wouldn't be another breath. It would shut down, saving him from the terror. The only problem was that the kid didn't close his eyes. They stared at him, open wide, and he could see the pleading. He wondered if Terry had pled before he'd died.

When Carter's body slumped and the eyes glazed over, he knew that the end had come. He could hear the father sobbing, still begging. He picked up the phone and held it to his ear. "I'm sorry," he whispered. "Your son is at the Williams Arms hotel, room eight. I truly wish there had been another way."

He hung up the phone and staggered into the cool night air. What would Terry say? He'd killed an innocent person, but then Terry had done the same thing on more than one occasion. Still, Terry had argued it had been collateral damage and for the greater good.

So was this. *Wasn't it?*

~

For the next three weeks, Sammy shocked the hell out of me. Where I'd normally find him early mornings was being logged onto Facebook playing the games he enjoyed or watching a movie on television. Now, he was up early, poring over dog training videos on YouTube. I stood and watched as he made every effort to get Kip to learn. And I had to admit, he seemed to be making great headway. When I teased him about it, Sammy glared at me and said the puppy was a lot easier to train than I had been.

I shut up after that.

Kip continued to make his way into the bed at night, curling up on Sammy's pillow. He'd figured out a way to get up on his own, so it no longer made sense to try to keep him out. He had become Sammy's dog—mind, body, and soul. While he still loved being showered with attention by Kelly—who had the treats—or me—who had found relaxation in giving him rubs—if Sammy wanted him, then that was where he went.

The two of them together filled my heart with pride. Sammy had gone to his counseling session and told the doctor about Kip, and she'd been thrilled to hear about him. My own therapist seemed surprised when I talked about the dog, but also said that they were therapeutic and would be great in working out my issues. While it hadn't been the glowing endorsement Sammy had gotten, it still made sense to me.

We were at the koi pond, Kip barking at the fish as they swam lazily in the clear water, when Kelly came out. "Rook is asking to speak to you," he said quietly.

"New job?"

Kelly nodded and began to walk away.

"Hey, Kelly? Why don't you stay out here?" Sammy called.

He glanced in my direction. "I should go with Haven."

Either he or Sammy usually did when Rook called, but I could see him eyeing the chair and Kip.

"It's fine. If I need you, I'll give a yell. Go play with the dog."

Of course, he didn't argue. He sat in the lounge chair and whistled, getting Kip's attention. The fickle beast bounded over and leaped up on the chair, then snuggled onto Kelly's lap. I stifled a laugh and went down to the war room. A chill in the air told me the AC had been left on, and the skin on my arms pebbled. I hated cold with a passion. If the temperature dropped below seventy-five, I wanted to be in the sun or sitting in front of the fireplace.

"How's Kip?" Rook asked.

"Fine. Sammy's got him pretty much house-trained. He's only had one or two accidents, and both times, he did it somewhere easy to clean. But you didn't really want to ask me that, did you?"

He sighed. "You know, I have to admit, one day I'd like to call you just to talk. It would be nice to keep in touch on occasion."

That shocked me. The man known to me only as Rook had always been the consummate professional. Not one to waste time, he came to the point and dispensed the information in clear and concise ways.

"You okay?"

He seemed distracted. "Hm? Oh…yes. I'm fine. So we have something not really in line with our usual cases, but I'd like to talk to you about it and see if you'd be willing to look into it for me."

That grabbed my attention. "Shoot."

The screen on the computer flashed, and a picture of a young man appeared. Long, dark hair. Thick glasses that made his mud-brown eyes seem like an anime character's. "This is Tyler McNab. Twenty-three years old, lives with his mother in Burlington, Vermont. They moved there six months ago after Tyler's release from prison for the sexual assault of an eight-year-old girl.

"Tyler's lawyers said that the offense was the result of Tyler's own molestation when he was a child. His mother vouched for it, stating a neighbor boy had taken Tyler out into the woods and shown him, and I quote, 'games big boys play with each other.' The judge apparently decided Tyler needed treatment more than he needed to be kept away from kids.

"What should have been twelve years got knocked down to five, and thanks to his lawyer's guarantee that Tyler would receive treatment, he got out after serving only a little more than a year."

Rook could have stopped there. He'd told me the story of his daughter and how she'd been abused when she was young. It had been what brought him to the attention of the organization in the first place. The man had gone to court and ended up walking on the charges. When Rook confronted him, the man said his daughter had begged for it. Rook killed him, which led to him being drafted by the organization.

"If the man served his sentence—"

Rook's voice was thick with emotion. "Released on good behavior. Had to register as a sex offender. This happened just after he turned eighteen, and with the claim of his own abuse, the court was more lenient. The girl, Rachel Dunbar, committed suicide on her thirteenth birthday, a few days after Tyler was released. Not only did she have to deal with a trial that dragged on for almost two years, but she also had been shamed for being raped. Kids in her school found out, and harassed her to the point where she obviously thought dying was easier than living."

Rook cleared his throat. I could hear papers being shuffled in the background, and I figured he was taking a minute to compose himself. I couldn't blame him. This one sucked all the way around.

"Tyler's mother moved them from Stanford, Connecticut, because she said she wanted to get him away from the temptation. Problem is that Burlington has kids, too, and I know that Tyler is responsible for at least two assaults since he got there."

"What proof do you have?" I asked, because Rook never gave me an assignment like this.

Rook grew quiet for a few moments. "Call it instinct if you want, or the fact that the girls told the police the man had offered to help them pick some flowers for their mothers. The same thing Tyler had done when he'd been in Connecticut. If you don't want to take the assignment, that's your choice. I know that it's not what you usually get from me. I wish I could offer you more."

His tone belied his words. This case had a personal connotation for Rook.

"I can't kill someone without ironclad proof. You know that."

"Yes, I know. What I want for you to do is watch him. Gather evidence that he's responsible, and I'll turn it over to the police. I just want him taken off the streets so he can't do it again." His voice broke when he said, "Please, Haven."

If someone offered to pay me a million dollars, I doubted I could come up with a time that Rook had said please. I found it disconcerting at the very least.

"When do I leave?"

I heard him sigh. "Thank you. Your flight is booked and leaves tomorrow at ten o'clock. Standard protocol is in place. We've got the rooms booked under John Smith and Tom Adams. Use Smith as your cover while you're there, then check in under Adams, so it would be harder to track you down."

My muscles tensed. "Are you okay?"

"Fine," he said absently as I heard papers being shuffled again.

"Yeah, I'm thinking not so much. While I hate the names you guys pick for me, this seems pretty sedate. What's on your mind?"

He wouldn't tell me, I knew. He never let people in. In his position, he couldn't afford to.

"I've had some reports coming to me that indicate we may have a problem. I'm not ready to talk about it yet, but as soon as I have all the facts, we'll be discussing it."

"I'm going to hold you to that. Something is off here, and I need to know what's going on."

"I promise you, as soon as I get answers, you'll be the first person I contact."

He disconnected, leaving me to wonder what I'd missed.

Sammy stood in the doorway as I pored over the files once again. He didn't say anything, but I could feel him there just the same. He closed the distance between us, and his lips brushed over my neck, causing goose bumps to rise.

"Okay, so I know we didn't get out like we'd planned," I said, closing the files. I stood and turned to face Sammy, reaching out to rub his arm. "And I wish I didn't have to go now, but—"

"It's fine," he interrupted. "Our new addition has kept us all hopping."

He put his arms around my waist and laid his head on my chest.

"You're okay with me bringing him home, right?"

He stepped back and smacked my arm. "Stupid questions deserve stupid answers. No, I wish you had never brought him here. I hate the fact that he makes me happy. And waking up to find him sleeping on my pillow annoys me so much. Of course I like having him here.

"Okay, how about this then; when I come home, we'll take Kip to the vet, have him checked out, microchipped, neutered, and all that other fun stuff that responsible pet slaves do, then you and I will head to the nearest pet store and stock up on things to make him happy."

Sammy flashed me a smile. "I like that idea."

"Then it's a date," I replied, kissing him on the forehead. "I'd love to say I won't be gone long, but you know as well as I do it's always a crap shoot."

"I know. I can be patient."

I snorted a laugh, which earned me another smack on the arm. I was about to protest when Kip zipped into the room and danced around Sammy's feet.

Sammy snickered. "You wanna go outside, boy?"

Kip gave a high-pitched yip in answer.

"Want me to take him out?"

Sammy bent over and patted Kip's rump, causing the dog's tongue to loll out as he whimpered with excitement. I knew that feeling well.

"Nah, I got it. Go ahead and get ready." Sammy stood and Kip followed along as they walked out the door.

As I packed my gear, I heard Sammy and Kelly out in the yard with Kip. Both of them seemed insanely happy, and that gave me a warm glow. Though I swore I never needed anyone, these two men showed me that I did. They both gave me something…important. Love that came in two different forms hadn't made me weak as I always suspected it would. Instead, it gave me purpose, drove me to try to make the world a better place. I put my case in the closet, ready to grab in the morning. I stood at the window for ten minutes or so, watching as Kelly and Sammy chased Kip around. Grudgingly, I tore myself away, grabbed my folder, and sat down to look through the information on Tyler once again.

His first complaint of sexual harassment came when he attended junior high school. A girl had said he'd touched her breasts. Somehow, the school had turned it around, saying the girl had dressed provocatively, that she'd teased Tyler, and that she'd been the one to ask if he'd wanted to touch her. She denied it vehemently, but in the end, it had been for nothing. Her parents took her out of school, and Tyler had been seen as a hero among the boys in his class.

The first time he'd been arrested, he had been taking pictures in the grade school girls' lockers. They'd found him hiding in one of the stalls. That had earned him a six-month stint in the local juvenile facility and a reprimand. Oddly, he hadn't been put on the sex offender listing at the time. The judge said that it would impair his future, and that he'd suffered enough. Damned if that didn't sound too familiar lately.

The one that got him sent to prison was Rachel's. I read about the night when a father heard his eight-year-old daughter talking to someone, then he heard her cry out for Daddy. He rushed to her room, threw open the door, and found a naked Tyler on top of her. Rachel's father grabbed Tyler by the hair and dragged him to the floor, where he proceeded to pummel the deviant mercilessly. When the police came, they arrested Tyler, and when he went to trial, they sentenced him to prison, put him on the sex offender registry, and forbade him from having any contact with a child under eighteen. If Rook's information was correct, and it always had been, Tyler started up in a new place, and that made my blood boil.

"Your new case?" Sammy asked, nodding to the file in my hand as he strode into the room.

Sammy's companion was nowhere to be seen. "Did you guys exhaust Kip?"

"Kelly's in the kitchen with him. He mentioned a treat, and that put an end to play."

Sammy came up behind me and peered over my shoulder.

"Yeah. Tyler is a real piece of work." I went through the pages and told Sammy about what Tyler had done, and how it had been handled.

"You know that I don't believe in a higher power," Sammy said, running his hands over my neck, putting pressure on that point that had me pressing into his touch. "But I can't help but feel that somehow you're here now, at this point in time, for a reason. These kids need someone who is there for them. Someone who can make the tough choices, then make sure they get handled. Tyler is scum. I get that he's not the kind of person you normally go after, but maybe he should be."

He turned my chair and straddled my lap.

"Sometimes you have to prune a sick branch before it infects the whole tree. Tyler definitely qualifies as a sickness. If you waited, how many more people would suffer at his hands? And I don't mean just the kids. What about their families? They'll forever have to deal with the fact that they couldn't stop a predator from destroying their child. How many lives will he have to ruin before he actually becomes your problem?"

What he said made a lot of sense. For years, I mostly went after those who dealt in wholesale destruction of lives. Pimps. Drug dealers. Valerie. When I started with the agency, I got people like James Voight, those who committed horrific crimes and somehow got off. But things changed, and I found myself going after the bigger, badder people, and those smaller cases came less often. Maybe in looking at the overall picture, we tended to miss the smaller details. And, unfortunately, the people. With Sammy's words, I became eager to meet Tyler McNab, and I just knew the man would be dying to meet me.

Early the next morning, I found myself in a taxi headed to the airport. It was funny how both Sammy and Kelly were conveniently busy and each had something to do instead of driving me. I didn't make a big fuss about it, though. Going by cab had been par for the course for years, and I actually kind of missed it. At least until the cab pulled up. The burly driver with the chewed off cigar turned out to be a talker. He had opinions on everything: sports, women, gays, and, mostly, transgender people in the bathrooms and how they destroyed the fabric of society. He wasn't afraid to share his most bigoted thoughts. As we made the turnoff toward the airport, I'd had enough. I leaned closer and smiled.

"Just so you know, I'm a transgender man. Do I really look like I belong in a bathroom with your wife, girlfriend, or daughter? How in the hell does forcing me to use that bathroom make them feel safer?"

He sputtered, spraying the dashboard with spit.

"See, honey, I don't go for bigots. I'm married to a man. We've got a kid named Kip. When I transitioned, my husband stood by me all the way. He loved me, no matter what body I was in. If you think I'm so fucking perverted, then maybe you should examine your own life. It might be you've got something hiding in your closet that you're ashamed to let break free."

He turned his head in my direction, his eyes wide. "I didn't mean any offense."

"No, of course you didn't. But I bet dollars to donuts that the next person who gets into your cab will get the same treatment, have to listen to you ramble on about the people you hate. Most of them won't say anything.

They'll be too afraid that you might hurt them. I mean you are, after all, a real man, right. Me? I'm not afraid of you. If you want to settle this like guys, we can pull over now. If not, keep your fucking mouth shut and do your job."

He chomped harder on his cigar, his teeth grinding. He wanted to say something, and he kept glaring at me in the rearview mirror. Probably trying to figure out how someone as big as me could have been a woman. It didn't matter that I hadn't been. I knew some people who said they were born into the wrong bodies, and were much happier after they transitioned. They certainly didn't deserve to be the new target for so-called 'value voters.'

He pulled up in front of the airport, and I got out, bag in hand. The fare was thirty-six dollars. I thought about refusing to pay, but I didn't have time to get into it with the cops if he decided to push the issue. I threw thirty-six at him, then turned to go into the airport. Before I got to the door, I stopped and walked back to the cab.

"Just so you know, if my husband had been with me and had to listen to you, you'd be picking up your teeth from the floor. You may want to be careful in the future."

I laughed as he sputtered. Tension breakers were always a good thing.

CHAPTER SIX

Tyler McNab lived in a clapboard home with his mother—white shutters, manicured lawn, even a little fountain with cherubs pissing into it. It screamed innocence. His mother saw him off to work each morning with a bagged lunch and a kiss on the cheek. He took the number seven bus to his job as a janitor in a factory. Tyler's employment application history from his probation officer showed he'd tried to get a job at a grade school. It stunned me that this fact had been missed or ignored by all the people who should have been watching Tyler. What made me furious is they should have been safeguarding the children he wasn't even supposed to have contact with, but somehow too many things slipped through the cracks. I texted Rook, and he assured me that he'd have people look into Tyler's case to make sure there wasn't any corruption going on.

As for Tyler ever getting a job with kids? Rook had used his resources to see to it that every school, daycare, children's hospital—shit, any entity involving kids within the state—knew Tyler was on the sex offender registry and nixed any chance of that happening.

Tyler went home at six every night. His mother served them dinner, then he sat down to play video games. Nothing overtly violent. Mostly things like Zelda and Mario Kart. When I spoke to the neighbors, they said he was a good guy. Quiet. Respectful. He often volunteered to babysit for them, if they ever wanted a night out. We had no way to find out if any of them had ever taken him up on the offer. I hoped to hell not.

There could be no doubting the fact that I hated Tyler. To my bones, I loathed him. I read the case histories about his abuse of Lisa McIntyre, Jamie Raspudo, Melanie Tangier, and ultimately, Rachel who had fallen victim to his attentions, and it sickened me. Sammy had been right. We needed to take care of everyone where we could. Waiting for the predators to become big enough to be on our radar meant more bodies piling up in a morgue. Allowing the victims to fall through the cracks now meant they'd have to deal with the problem for the rest of their lives.

Yeah, Tyler had a very bad habit.

Three times, he'd been brought up on charges, and three times, he'd avoided a full prison sentence based on some bullshit his lawyer peddled to the judge or that Tyler's mother had thrown money at. The one time he'd been sent to jail, he'd gotten off easy. He would still be in prison if the prosecutors had done a better job than the defense. The thought pissed me off. It's a shame we couldn't do what Shakespeare suggested and simply kill the lawyers. Like me, though, they were doing their job. They got him back on the streets, and I'd be taking him off.

I watched him for four days, and what I saw had me wondering how the man could still be walking around. His neighbors smiled when they saw him. Every one of them who had children let him play with them. I couldn't believe no one knew about him and his predilections and had gone ahead and offed the sorry fucker yet. Oh well, more fun for me.

On Saturday morning, my fifth day of surveillance, something happened that changed all the plans I'd devised for Ty. He wandered through a park and stopped to watch the children play. I went on high alert. I shot a text to Rook, letting him know that I couldn't wait any longer and to have an extraction ready. Ty glanced around, then began to move toward a young girl, maybe eight, who played in a sandbox by herself. A cute thing with long strawberry blonde hair that flowed in the breeze. I could hear her giggle as grains of sand slipped through her fingers. By any standard, this young girl was sweet and innocent, and my job would be to make sure she stayed that way. I moved in closer, my gaze darting around. I saw the woman, who appeared to be the kid's mother, chatting with another woman. Tyler reached the kid, then knelt down by her. She looked up with big blue eyes and nodded, then took him by the hand. He led her toward the wooded area, and that was enough for me. I moved to intercept them, standing between them and the trees, and smiled at the kid as she gazed up at me.

"Where you going, sweetheart?"

"He said he could help me find some flowers for my mommy," she replied. "She likes flowers. We have lots of them by my house, but he says he knows special ones."

I bit down on my cheek to stop the growl. I didn't want to scare the kid. I reached down and plucked a few dandelions from the grass and handed them to her. "I think she'll love these even better because they came from you."

She gave me the widest gap-toothed grin, said thank you, then turned to go back to play. I pulled the gun out of my jacket and shoved it under Tyler's ribs. "You wanted to go into the woods so bad, then let's go."

"I didn't do anything," he protested, trying to move away until I clutched his wrist.

"It wasn't for lack of trying," I retorted. "You've gotten away with it before, luring young girls in with some kind of promise, then assaulting them. It won't happen again; I can tell you that. Now move."

"I'll scream," he threatened.

"Go ahead. See what happens to you if you raise a fuss." I jabbed him a little harder, and he stumbled toward the darkness and privacy the gnarled trees would provide.

"Who are you?" he asked softly. I could hear the terror in his voice, and it thrilled me to no end that this piece of shit knew enough to be afraid.

"I'm the man whose job it is to stop people like you," I answered simply.

When we were far enough into the trees that no one would be able to see us, I punched him in the back and knocked him to the ground with a thump. He looked up, and I could see him tremble.

"What are you going to do?"

"I haven't decided yet. I had plans for you, but those got tossed by the wayside because you had to go and make me jump the gun. I have to know, why did you go after that poor kid?"

He frowned. "It's her fault," he said, his voice nearly as petulant as a child's. "She had to be so soft. So pretty. If they weren't, I wouldn't even look at them."

Worst excuse ever.

"You know, I have to tell you, normally I believe in an eye for an eye. I had a plan that involved you, me, and an electric cattle prod. I had even slotted four hours in my calendar for you. Now I have to improvise, and after seeing what you were about to do, I simply don't have the patience." I slipped my gun back into the holster beneath my jacket and extracted a knife. This one sliced flesh like no one's business. I knew because I'd watched Kelly sharpen it, then foolishly tried to use it to cut a tomato. Several bandages and a visit to Lilah McQuade, my doctor, showed me there were many other uses for the damned thing.

"Please, don't," he begged, trying to scramble away.

I stomped down on his leg to keep him in place, and he cried out.

"You know, it's funny. I thought I'd lost my taste for the job. I figured I had given enough, lost enough, and paid enough in blood and sweat. But then the most amazing man came into my life and convinced me that I had to give it my all. Because people like you pervert everything you touch. And I swear that you won't be doing it again after today."

I knelt down next to Tyler and grabbed a handful of his long, dark hair. Behind his glasses, his eyes were enormous, and he shed a lot of tears, which barely caused me a moment of regret. "You should know, this is going to hurt. Probably a lot," I told him, then drove the knife into his throat and gave it a twist.

His eyes went wide, and he tried to scream, but all that came out was a gurgle. Blood coated the knife blade and spattered the ground as I yanked it out. I sat next to him as he tried to draw a breath, but only succeeded in pulling blood into his lungs. He tried to get up, but I held him down. No sense in scaring the kids.

"Now that I think of it, this is probably a better idea than the cattle prod. That would have taken hours, and you don't deserve to live that long."

He clutched his throat and gazed at me. I shrugged. "There will be a group coming shortly to dispose of your body," I told him. "They're really good at what they do, so don't worry. People will assume you simply disappeared. Life will eventually go back to normal, but you won't be around to see it. And you needn't be concerned about your mother. She'll get an e-mail from you, saying you couldn't bear the things you'd done. She'll miss you, I'm sure, but she won't have to know that she outlived her son."

His breath came in hoarse wheezes, and he had to be terrified. "A man named Pratchett once said, 'Don't think of it as dying. Just think of it as leaving early to avoid the rush.'" My words didn't soothe him at all.

Ungrateful bastard. His gasped breaths slowed, and his movements became less frenetic as his time drew near. "If it means anything," I whispered, "that little girl will grow up happy."

One final wheezed breath and Tyler McNab's eyes rolled back as he left the mortal coil. I texted Rook my location, and within a few minutes, the area swarmed with his people. I watched them work for a moment before I got up and headed back to the car. Upon leaving the woods, I stopped for a moment to watch the little girl Tyler had fixated on being admonished by her mother for something. I had to wonder if she would ever know just how close she came to her child losing her innocence—or worse—forever. I really wanted to tell her. To make sure she kept an eye on the kid. Instead, I left the park and headed for home.

~

He stood over the woman he'd tied to the chair in a ramshackle house, in a neighborhood where people didn't get involved. There would be no one who questioned when she cried out, no one who would call the police. This gave him time.

She had been a tough nut to crack, but after four days, the assassin had done it. He'd shaved her head, removing the long blonde locks, berated her, hit her until her eyes were black and blue. He refused her requests for water. And when none of those worked, he bled her, slicing off strips of her skin, and entreated her to give him what he wanted. She'd refused, and he thought that this would once again be another person who'd given his target too much trust and would become a martyr for him. After her right arm had been stripped raw, muscle showing through the blood, she cried and begged him to stop. When she'd passed out, he'd waited until she came to, then started again.

"What's his name?"

"I don't know. I swear to God, I don't. Please."

He knelt next to her chair. "I just need a name. That's all I'm asking for. Why is it so hard for you to tell me what I want?"

"I can't tell you what I don't know!"

"Then maybe we should start on your left arm," he said calmly. "I think a little persuasion is really all that you need."

She glared at him, but only for a moment before she ducked her head and sobbed. "Why are you doing this? What did I ever do to you?"

He put his hand on her face. Her skin had gone chalk white, and she felt cold to the touch. He stroked her cheek soothingly, keeping his voice low and even. "Nothing, Shannon. You didn't do anything to me. But I need you to give me the name of the man who did. Someone has to know. Someone has to be able to tell me, because he needs to pay for what he's taken from me. See, I don't want to hurt anyone. I'm not the bad guy here, believe me. I'm more than happy to let you go. To tell someone where you are, so they can come and get you. All you need to do is give me a name. At least a place to start. Something."

She looked down at her arm, blood running off the flayed skin and pooling around the chair she was secured to. A shudder rolled through her. "We're not told much. Only what we need to know. It's safer that way for everyone."

"I know," he soothed, brushing back the few strands of hair that he'd missed. She would give him information. He knew it. So tantalizingly close, he could almost see the moment of his revenge speeding toward him. "What did they call you?"

Her gaze took on a dreamy quality. Loss of blood had made her susceptible to his questions. She'd give him what he wanted. He knew that now.

"They called me Savior," she whispered. "I helped get people out of bad situations and into safe houses. I made sure that no one could get to them."

A bitter irony. She'd devoted her life to helping people, and now she needed someone to protect her. This was his target's legacy. The one thing no one seemed to realize. They were—all of them—disposable. A fact the assassin knew firsthand.

"A pleasure to meet you, Savior. My name is Joel." Her eyes fixed on his face, and he smiled at her. Terry had always said his smile lit him up. "You did a good job," he assured her. "You deserved better than what you got."

She started sobbing, and his heart went out to her.

"I only wanted to help," she cried. "Why should I be punished for that?"

He knelt directly in front of her, wiping tears from her eyes. Her lips twisted into a sneer.

"Such an idiot," she chastised, then lashed out with her leg, catching him in the chest. He tumbled backward, cursing his stupidity. As he got to his feet, Shannon was already standing. Her wrists were still bound to the chair, but she had free use of her legs.

"Nicely played," he admitted, pulling out his gun.

She grinned at him, her teeth coated with blood. "Go ahead and shoot. I'm not afraid to die. I did good work, saved a lot of people. If this is how it ends, so be it."

Her body trembled, and she didn't have the strength to hold back anymore. Her gaze flicked to his hand. She wanted him to shoot her. To end this game now. But he wouldn't. She had information he needed, and one way or the other, he would have it.

He took a step toward her, and she shrank back.

"You used what you had left for that move. You thought you could get me to shoot you, and it would be over. But I can't do that. Not yet anyway."

He leapt at her, sending her and the chair crashing to the ground. She cried out, but he barely heard it. There would be no more fight from her. They both knew it and accepted it as truth. He reached for the knife he'd dropped and brought it to her throat.

"I would have let you go, you know. Now? You're going to tell me what I want. You'll tell me things I don't even care to hear. You think you've screamed before? I'd been gentle with you, because I truly didn't want to cause you any pain."

He slid the blade along her neck, watching as the blood welled beneath her skin, before it turned into a slow trickle down her flesh. He could feel the tears in his eyes as he cut deeper, and her screams ripped through him. Her body shuddered, and then the hoarse voice began to beg. Pleading with him to stop. To end it now. To please just kill her and get it over with.

He gripped her throat, his knuckles turning white as he squeezed. The blood flowed faster. He raised his hand and slashed out, cutting her across her once beautiful face. Over and over, more blood seeping out. The amount that now pooled beneath her fascinated him.

He leaned forward and put his mouth next to her ear, ignoring the blood that soaked his clothes. She was close to death, but he couldn't let her rest just yet.

"I need a name, Shannon. Just give me a name. If you don't know, at least tell me who might."

She coughed as he released his grip on her throat. When she whispered something, it had been so soft he couldn't hear her. He leaned closer.

"Tell me again," he pleaded. So close now. He could feel his righteous anger fueling his rage. What he sought was now within his reach.

She lay quietly, unmoving. Only her ragged breath told him she still lived.

"Shannon, tell me the name!" he screamed at her. "I need that fucking name."

Her eyes could no longer focus. He'd done too much damage, and now he would lose out on the best lead he'd gotten so far. She couldn't die before giving up the name. Goddamn stubborn bitch. Why did they all have to be so stubborn?

"Please, Shannon," he pleaded. "Please help me put an end to this. You dedicated your life to helping people. Help me now. If you do, then others won't die. And isn't that what it means to be a savior?"

Her lips trembled, and he thought he heard a whisper of a voice. He put his ear next to her lips and prayed he'd hear whatever she had to say.

"Tell me again, Shannon. Once more, please."

"Haven," she croaked out.

Haven? Joel's fists clenched. It always fucking came down to Haven. Terry had repeatedly told him that Haven was the best, how great he was at his job. Had Joel realized Haven was involved, he could have started there and saved himself a lot of legwork. But he knew now and could see the end of his hunt. Once he found Haven, one way or another, the end would be in sight. Haven would be the one who ensured Joel finally had the answers he sought. And if he killed Haven along the way? That would be a bonus.

He stood and walked to the door. He turned and gazed at Shannon, whose chest no longer rose and fell. She was gone.

This was another death that needed to be avenged. And when he was done, there would finally be peace for all of them.

CHAPTER SEVEN

I got home about seven that night. As I exited the cab, I could see a silhouette in the kitchen. I slipped off my shoes and entered the property from the backyard. The dew was cool under my bare feet. For what I was about to do, stealth had to be maintained. My enemy couldn't know I was closing in. First, I peeked around the corner, then ducked behind the door. My target stood in the kitchen, music blaring while he burned whatever dinner he was making. I stepped into the warm house and silently glided across the floor, grateful for the fact that I could hear Kip and Kelly in the other room, until I stood directly behind the man. Shock coursed through me when he slammed an elbow back into my stomach, knocking the air from my lungs. He then turned around and tried to kick me in the groin, but I spun out of the way, dropped down, grabbed his ankle, and dragged him to the floor.

"I could have killed you already," I whispered before kissing Sammy's neck.

"And if I had a gun, I could have shot you at the window when you peeped inside, blown you away through the door when you tried to look around it, or simply killed you when you clomped your way through the yard. For an assassin, you need to work on your stealth," Sammy retorted, pulling me toward him.

"Good. You saw me in all those spots. That's great. You're learning."

"Trying," Sammy admitted, grinding against my leg. "I have a good teacher."

"You do. And I'm thinking he deserves a reward," I said, giving Sammy a leer.

"You do, huh?" He reached out and put his hand behind my neck, pulling me closer to him. "What do you think about blowing me here on the kitchen floor?"

What did I think? Fuck. I scooted down and unzipped his fly, reaching in for the prize he offered. He groaned when I wrapped my fingers around his shaft.

"Fuck, I missed you," he whispered.

Talk was overrated, especially when I had my fingers wrapped around almost seven inches of heat. I opened my mouth and laved the head. I wanted it wet enough that I could take him to the back of my throat.

"You are so goddamn good at that," he whispered as he ran his fingers over my cheek.

I had to be. Sammy wasn't one to take it easy on me. When he felt comfortable that I'd be able to handle him, he started tugging my hair. That was when I went down on him. He bit the palm of his hand to keep from crying out. Since Kelly had moved into the house, we'd found our creativity a bit stifled. Plus, if the hound from hell heard, he'd be in, sniffing everything. We learned that lesson very quickly.

After Sammy got used to having his cock in my mouth, he clutched my head. He held it still while he thrust in, not stopping when he reached my throat.

"Take it all." He snapped his hips, driving farther into my mouth. The sweetness of his pre-cum seared a trail across my tongue, enflaming my desire for more of the flavor I'd never have enough of.

"Close," Sammy gurgled.

This had always been my favorite part of sex with Sammy. He held himself in check most times, but in the throes of orgasm, he came apart. The fact I'd been the one to cause it gave me a rush of power. When we had sex, I did everything I could to push him over the edge. While Sammy controlled our relationship and me, there were times when it felt good to remind him that he needed me too.

My tongue circled the head of his cock each time he slid out. I loved it when he lost control like this. It reminded me of his need to claim me each time I came back from a mission. To ensure that he helped wipe away any residual memories of what I'd done. Normally I craved it for that reason. His

66

dominance, originally a source of fear on my part, had become necessary to me.

When he shot, I clamped my lips together, determined not to miss any of his essence. I'd worked hard for it, damn it, and I wanted my due.

"Swallow me, Haven," he moaned.

Even after he'd finished, he still continued with small thrusts into my mouth. I worried for a minute that he'd want another go, and I really wasn't sure I could handle another...enthusiastic session so soon. When his cock finally softened and slipped from between my lips, he stroked my hair.

"So doing that again later," he said, the growl in his voice sending shivers up my spine. "We should probably take care of you."

"God, yes. Please."

His smile bordered on pure evil. "Nah. I think you'll wait until later, too."

"Sammy," I whined. My cock throbbed in my pants. "I already waited almost a week. Just a stroke or two. That's all I'm going to need. Please."

He sat up and tucked himself in.

"Keep it up, and I may make you wait until tomorrow."

"He may have to wait," Kelly said from the door. "Rook is calling."

"Damn it," I grumbled. When I got up, my pants tented obscenely. "What the hell does he want?"

"I'm pretty sure it's not to grade your performance," he said dryly.

"How much did you see?" Sammy asked, a touch of teasing in his voice.

"Believe me, if I had seen too much, I'd have let Kip in here. I'm guessing it would have cooled your ardor very effectively."

"Who the hell uses words like ardor?" I groused.

"People who read and speak at better than a fifth-grade level," Kelly shot back.

I opened my mouth to say something, when Sammy put his hand on my back.

"Go talk to Rook."

I stormed down the stairs to the war room. My erection had flagged, but the ache in my groin had ratcheted up. I needed to come in the worst possible way or else my balls would explode. A moment's thought about ducking into the bathroom to relieve the pressure went away as soon as Sammy yelled out, "And no pit stops along the way."

The fact he knew me so well really pissed me off sometimes. But it also made me feel loved to know how much he'd become invested in our lives together.

"Enough with the sappy shit," I chastised myself as I keyed into the war room.

"Sit down," Rook demanded as I entered.

"No, really. I'm okay. No need to concern yourself for my wellbeing," I snarked as I took a chair.

"Haven, normally I indulge your need to talk, but this time please shut up."

Anger tinged his words. An undercurrent of something else registered. Fear?

The computer flashed, and pictures appeared on the screen. Men and women in before and after images came at a rapid-fire pace.

"Rampart. Carter Whitfield. Savior. Samaritan."

I leaned forward as the images stopped moving. I traced my fingers over them. With the exception of Carter, they'd died in violent, bloody fashions. Still, the fear on Carter's face held my gaze. He couldn't be more than twenty or so. His skin had a gray tinge, instead of the healthy tan it should have. Although he would be older than most of the kids my missions brought me into contact with, I still had that churning in my stomach that I got when a child died.

"Who did this?" I demanded.

"We don't know," came the reply. "Our only clue is Carter Whitfield. His stepfather's name is John Chambers. He used to be an operative, codenamed Keeper."

"Have you talked to him?"

"No. He left the organization. Under normal circumstances, once that happens, all ties are severed. We help them adopt a new identity, and then we leave them to their new life. In fact, with the exception of Carter, these victims were agents at one time or another. They left the organization shortly after the case with Valerie was completed. Keeper and the others left because they were hurt during the assignment. Savior resigned because she said she'd seen too much pain etched on the faces of the women she'd helped."

"So someone is killing former agents, and you have no idea who or why."

"I don't make the rules," Rook snapped. "I also don't agree with all of them. But they were in place long before I started here, and they'll continue well after I'm gone."

"This is bullshit," I shouted, shoving away from the desk. How we could allow people to slip through the cracks pissed me off to no end. It wasn't Rook's fault, though. I shouldn't allow my temper to get the better of me.

"I agree, and I'll be addressing this issue. Again. But for now, someone is out there, and he or she is taking down agents who already gave so much. Rampart lost his legs in the explosion that killed eleven other members of his team. He left the agency, met and married Sarah Brown. They had a newborn baby. The killer ambushed them outside of their home and shot Rampart in the head with a high-powered rifle.

"Samaritan was taken from her home in the middle of the afternoon. She lived on a relatively busy street, but according to the police report, no one saw anything. They later pulled her body out of an abandoned well after a 911 call told them where to find her. The phone used was a burner, so we had no way to trace it back to the owner.

"Carter's body had been dumped in a shitty motel. He'd disappeared from his campus one afternoon, only to be found later. The ME report shows he'd been suffocated. Against the rules, I pulled records to find out what I could. A phone call had been placed to John Chambers shortly after Carter disappeared.

"The final victim, at least the ones we know of, had been called Savior. Her death isn't like the others. She was savaged. Whoever took her sliced the skin from her arm, cut up her face, beat her, and hacked off her hair."

My stomach lurched. None of these people deserved their deaths. The operatives I worked with had protected people, helped to make the world safer by removing from the gene pool bastards who hurt the innocent. And now, after they'd sacrificed their lives doing so and had taken the chance to start building a new one, some fucker had come along and snuffed them out.

"So what are we doing?" I demanded.

"I want you to go talk to John Chambers. Find out what you can. We need information, because I hate being blind. And I refuse to allow someone to get away with killing agents who've already sacrificed so much."

My fingers clenched as I imagined finding the person responsible and wrapping them around their neck, choking the life from them.

"I know you just got home, but—"

"I'll leave right away."

"No, I need you to give me a couple days. I want to have as much information available to you as possible before you go. I also want you to take some time to be with your family."

The regret in Rook's voice couldn't be more obvious. He'd given his family up for the greater good.

"Is this what you were talking about before I left to take care of Ty?"

"Yes. Only Savior hadn't become a victim yet. I'm concerned that someone could take out these former agents. Even if they were no longer part of the organization, they still had their skills. Whoever did it… They're good. Better than they should be."

"Noted," I told him.

"Okay, go be with your people. I have work to do."

"Hey, before you go…"

"Yes?"

"If you ever wanted to come here, we could make up a room for you. You can stay as long as you want."

Rook sighed. "Thank you for that. We both know it won't happen, but I appreciate you making the offer."

"You're always welcome, Rook. Sammy would be thrilled to meet the person he gives so much shit to."

That got a laugh. "He's been behaving himself?"

I had to hold back a snort. "Oh, sure. Definitely. Right. Uh-huh."

"Haven?" Rook's voice broke. "Treasure what you've got. You're the only person I know who's straddled the line and been able to carve out a life of his own while still being part of the organization. There are plenty of people who would give up everything to have what you've got."

Though it was left unsaid, Rook meant himself. He didn't say anything else, and the communications link cut off. I sat for a few minutes, looking at the pictures of the fallen, before I trudged up the stairs to sit down to a meal with my family.

I spent the next three days doing nothing but laying out by the koi pond. Even though Tyler's death didn't bother me, Sammy wanted me to take some time to reflect. I told him he'd been hanging around his therapist too long, but he'd practically ordered me to do as he said. I'd learned long ago that saying no to the man wasn't an option. So I sat, enjoying the fish as they darted around, but having time to play with Kip ranked up there, too. It had taken him a while to warm to me since I got back, even though I'd been the one to bring him home. Sammy claimed I'd been gone for too long and he simply needed a reminder of who I was. I hoped it wouldn't take long, because his constant barking at me and chasing my feet kind of got old, even if I did find it endearing.

Once I'd given him a treat, though, he'd been all over me. I'd become his favorite, a fact that chuffed Sammy and Kelly. I laughed like I hadn't in forever as he climbed my torso to lick my face. When I fell asleep in the lounge chair, he curled up on my stomach, his head on my chest, and drifted off, too.

Sammy woke me, chastising me for not having used sunblock. I protested, but had actually been grateful. I'd sunburned my dick once, back before I met Sammy. I had no desire to repeat that episode, especially with the itch that came as I peeled. The mission Rook sent me on immediately after had been meant to give him and Kelly a good laugh.

"Are you awake?"

I knew Sammy was there, but apparently the dog didn't realize until Sammy spoke. Kip jumped off me, his paws digging into my crotch, and ran for Sammy.

"If I wasn't before, I sure as hell am now." I rubbed where he'd got me, and Sammy chuckled.

"Sorry. I promise to kiss it and make it better tonight. I wanted to let you know we've got an appointment for Kip next Wednesday. I told them he was a stray that we found on the street. The vet said if he had a microchip, they'd be able to track down his owner."

"Don't worry about that," Kelly assured him, stepping out to join us at the pond. "Any information like that would have been purged from records.

Even if Kip is tagged, no one will ever track him back to Voight. Trust me when I say, he is definitely not going anywhere."

Sammy smiled. "Good. He also asked if we wanted to have him…you know…what you said." He made a snipping motion with his fingers, and I cringed. Poor Kip. "The doctor said it would help curb aggression, prevent him from having any baby Kips running around, and overall, his quality of life would improve."

"Yeah, bet you the vet still has his," I groused. While what the vet said made sense, the thought of any guy losing his jewels made me uncomfortable. Well, unless I was being paid to do it. In that case, all bets were off.

Sammy came and threw his arms around me. "You know it needs to be done. He's a good boy, and I'd really rather he stay that way. I've got no interest in him getting out, finding a girl, and ruining our happy home."

Kelly snorted. "At least the pups would be cute."

"Yeah, fine. Get him snipped, but you have to explain it to him when he's old enough to understand." I rubbed my hands over Kip's face, and he smiled up at me, crawling back into my lap. "Just remember, Sammy did it, so don't chew my slippers or nip my bits when they wiggle under the covers."

Sammy smacked me in the back of the head. "You fucking traitor. Just for that, you're sleeping in the doghouse."

"What doghouse? He sleeps on your pillow, then grumbles when I try to get close to you."

"The dog apparently has better taste than I do," Sammy teased.

Kelly grunted and shook his head. "The two of you are sickly sweet together," he complained. "Come on, Kip. I know where the good treats are hidden."

At the word treat, Kip jumped off me and started tagging behind Kelly.

"There's your traitor," I told Sammy. "Tossed over for a bit of kibble."

He laughed and straddled my legs.

"Okay, so now that we're alone…"

I sighed because I knew what was coming.

"We need to talk about this," he insisted.

"No, we really don't. He went after a little girl. I stopped him. Permanently. I didn't even have a moment of hesitation, and I felt no remorse after the fact. You were right. We concentrate on taking down the big guys, but lose sight of the kids that no one else will help. It didn't always used to be that way, but as threats sprung up, they were prioritized."

Sammy stayed quiet for a few moments. I could tell he was working to connect the dots. "I guess I can understand," he finally said. "Better to save ten kids at once, instead of worrying about one."

But Sammy had been that one. Until Valerie hit our radar, we didn't even know about him or the other kids that her group had yanked off the streets. In the long run, were we actually doing our jobs?

"Hey," he said, pulling my attention back to him. "There is no wrong answer here, you know. You can't expect to save everyone. It's impossible. I read the papers and see the number of kids who go missing every day in this country. Multiply it by all the countries in the world, and there would be no task force big enough. You do what you can, Michael. Every day you put yourself out there and you try your damnedest to keep kids safe. No one can ask more of you, and there is no way you can ask more of yourself."

"Doesn't mean I have to like it."

The house door opened and Kelly stuck his head outside. He glanced from me to Sammy and back.

"Haven?" The expression on Kelly's face told me everything I needed to know. "Your bags are ready."

Time to go.

CHAPTER EIGHT

Sammy took me to the airport again. I wanted to tease him about being away from Kip, but my mind went to the mission ahead. It wasn't going to be like any other one I'd ever been on. Usually I'd go in, track my target's movements, and then take them out at a time and place of my choosing. This time, I had to go in and ask someone to relive the shittiest moment of their life.

"You'll call," Sammy told me.

I usually didn't. Even though our phones were encrypted a dozen ways, I feared that somehow someone would break it and track it back to the source. But Sammy wanted this, so I'd do what I needed.

"I'll call," I agreed.

"I don't mind saying, I'm kinda scared."

He hugged me, and I melted into his embrace. There had been a time when I saw such affection as a weakness. I now understood the true meaning, though. It was Sammy offering me his strength in the only way he could.

"Nothing to worry about," I told him. "I'm going to be fine."

He frowned. "This person has taken out three operatives. The only way he could do that is if he took them when their guard was down."

He had a point. While Rook told me often that there were no operatives in the organization who were better than I was, it still required a lot of training to make it. Each of these people had endured the same rigors I had. They'd trained with the best. And in the end, they'd still lost.

"I want to go with you."

Even if it were possible, I didn't want him along. Sammy had already suffered abuse at the hands of his mother and her cronies. He didn't need to be reminded how shitty people could be.

"I want you to go home and take care of Kip. No sense in letting Kelly get an advantage."

His laugh didn't sound genuine.

I ran my hand over his cheek. "Hey, I promise it will be okay."

Sammy grabbed my hand and squeezed it hard. "Don't say something that you can't back up."

"You're right," I replied. "You deserve better than that. I will do what I have to in order to come home. That I promise."

He kissed me lightly. "That's all I can ask for."

I got out of the car and took my bags from the trunk. Sammy waved at me as he put on his directional to merge back into traffic. As I watched him drive away, I wondered if I would have his strength if he had my job. How much must it hurt to wait at home, never knowing if the person you were waiting on was going to come back to you? Before I'd met Sammy, no one other than Kelly had ever worried about me. I used to think it had simply been a part of his job, but I learned he thought of me as his son, and it hit home how my missions affected everyone around me.

Still, I had to do them. Sammy and Kelly understood it and even encouraged me. This mission would show me one thing, though. What happens to the people left behind? And I needed to know if I could truly handle that.

John Chambers had that shattered look of a person who'd had everything taken from them. I could see his core strength, but it lay hidden beneath a veneer of sadness. His blue eyes were bloodshot and had a saline crust from the tears he'd shed. I hated to make him talk about this. When we met, I took him aside and told him who I was. His expression flicked between sadness and rage.

"John, can you tell me what happened?"

"Fuck you. And fuck everyone in that goddamned organization. If they hadn't cut me loose, I would have been able to save my son," he ranted. Then his eyes clouded over. "It's not fair. We worked so hard at building a relationship. Carter had been angry when I married his mother, because he had always thought his father would come back. She and I both knew it wasn't going to happen. She asked me not to give up on him—not that I intended to. I kept at it. At first he refused to have anything to do with me, but finally he seemed to warm toward me.

"I took him to ball games; we went fishing. Eventually he started to talk to me about what was on his mind. We discussed the fact his father had left with his secretary and would probably never come home. It had taken him a while, but he came to accept it. For my part, I did everything I could to be there for him. He wanted to be an artist, you know? I went to all his shows at school. He was good. He had talent. I—"

The tears rolled down his cheeks again.

"I'd been an operative for seventeen years," he told me. "Never cried over my targets. Never felt an iota of remorse. Then I met Molly, and we clicked. The first night I kissed her, I went home and sobbed. It felt like I'd been reborn, you know? Like every stain on my soul had been washed away. Now she won't come out of the bedroom, and I don't have the words to tell her that it's my fault."

Fuck, I hated this. Maybe it would have been better if Sammy had come along. He talked about feelings, knew how to get people to open up to him. This was so far outside my comfort zone that I had no idea what to say. Sammy would hug him, but John would probably slug me. Of course, if he lashed out and we fought, maybe that would help.

Probably not, though.

"I'm sorry, John."

That sounded lame, even to me. I could listen to a man beg for his life and not be at all remorseful for what I would do to him. But seeing this shattered man tore me up.

"Thanks," he replied, his voice cold. "I listened to him kill my kid. Carter begged me to save him. I pleaded with the guy. Wanted him to take me instead. He told me he couldn't. He said that because I couldn't give him the name he wanted, I had to know how serious he was. Then after Carter stopped making noise, he came to the line and told me where we could find his body. I hurried to the motel and broke open the door. He sat there, tied to the chair. His eyes were open and looking at me. You know how it goes. We kill so many people that we think we're immune to the feelings. I threw up. Didn't even make it to the bathroom. Just barfed all over the floor. When the cops came, I told them what I knew, but didn't say anything about the organization. What good would it do? They'd never find it, and I'd sound like a madman."

"What name did he want?"

"That's the part I don't get. He didn't know. He said someone in the organization took something away from him, and the only way to balance the scale would be to get revenge. But he decided to take it out on my kid, because I couldn't tell him."

Bitterness laced his words. The man who'd given his life to service, now hated the work he'd done. It had cost him everything: his son, his happiness, and if he didn't get help, I had no doubt it would cost his life.

He wasn't able to tell me anything more. The only takeaway from this meeting had been the fact the person had been male. Beyond that, nothing useful. I talked to Rook from my hotel room. I rarely took advantage of the reservations, but today I could feel every one of my years. I needed sleep in the worst way. I called Sammy that night, since my flight home wouldn't be until the next day. We talked for a while, until I heard him yawning. I told him to get some sleep, and that I would see him in the morning. When I told him I'd take a cab home from the airport, he said I would wait for him. He needed to see me, to ensure I'd made it home safely, and he wouldn't be satisfied until he could find out for himself.

In the end, it was easier to accept his offer of a ride. And really, after listening to John, hearing the pain of his loss, I wanted to see Sammy, too. I needed him to restore a little faith in me. To prove that not everyone in the world was an asshole.

"You'll be there, right?"

"I will," he promised.

I collapsed in a heap on the bed, trying to catch my breath after being pounded into the mattress. Sammy lay next to me, put his head on my chest, and sighed.

"What?"

"Just listening to your heartbeat," he told me.

No clue why that made me feel so good, but it did. I rolled, pulled him closer, and wrapped him in my arms. Of course, being Sammy, he could read me like a book.

"Wanna talk about it?"

"It sucked," I said honestly.

"I figured. Normally you wait for me to drag you off to the bedroom. When we got in the house and you grabbed my hand, I knew you needed me to take control."

"Always need that," I assured him.

"Glad to hear." He slapped me on the ass, and I relished the burn. He took a few more swats, varying the spot, the strength, and the duration. "Let it out."

"No idea what you're talking about," I insisted.

He smacked my cheeks harder.

"So close to the surface," he said. "I know it's there. Give it to me."

I rolled over and grabbed his wrists, pulling him down on top of me.

"He's going to die," I said, my voice broken.

"John?"

"Yeah. He's shattered. He says he felt nothing on his missions, but we both know it's not true. And now the life he started to build has been ripped away from him. It's not right."

Sammy kissed my neck. "No, it's not. It's like the soldiers coming back from war. They've done their duty, given their all, and they're ignored. I wish it didn't have to be like that."

And it shouldn't have been. The job we did was reminiscent of the military, except when they came home, there was supposed to be a safety net set up for them. With politicians being what they were, that rarely happened. They had advocates, though. People who argued for better care. We had nothing when we left the organization. If I walked away, every person I'd been connected to would be reassigned. Their identities would be changed. I would never find them. Sure, agents made a lot of money, but all the cash in the world didn't help when you couldn't tell people why you were so messed up.

"Sleep, Haven."

Though I usually put up at least a token resistance when Sammy gave an order, this time I did as he said and closed my eyes. Sammy rubbed my chest for a few minutes and drifted off.

The next morning, Kelly woke us. He told us that breakfast would be coming soon, if we were hungry. I opened my eyes and came face-to-face with a tiny pink tongue. Kip crawled off Sammy's pillow and burrowed beneath the blankets between us. He sighed deeply and fell back to sleep.

"He missed you," Sammy told me, then yawned. "Not as much as me, though."

He leaned over and kissed me, but got forced back when Kip came back up from under the covers. He couldn't decide which of us he wanted to attack, so he took turns licking both our faces. It all seemed so normal that I could believe my trip yesterday had been a dream. I knew better, though.

"So how do we find someone if we have no idea who he is, what he's after, or even why? He says we took something from him. What could it be?"

"Could it have been someone working for Valerie?" Sammy asked. "It's not like she wasn't bedding enough people. Maybe someone got promised something, and now they won't get it."

"The thought had occurred to me. It made sense in a weird sort of way."

"I hear a but in there."

"It doesn't feel right. I mean, she kept things close to her vest, so I don't know that anyone even knew about me or the organization. There would be no way they could track down any of us. And as far as I know, Savior had nothing at all to do with Valerie. I worked with her a couple of times a few years back, and she didn't get those types of assignments."

Kip started barking at Sammy, who groaned and got out of bed. He slipped on his underwear and took the dog outside. I lay there, trying to think of a connection. Something that tied all of these people together. When Sammy came back, he finished getting dressed.

"Kelly is putting breakfast out."

"You go ahead," I replied. "I'm not all that hungry."

He snatched the blanket and threw it back, grabbed my ankle, and dragged me to the edge of the bed. "You're going to eat," he insisted. "You didn't have anything when you came home, and I can hear your stomach rumbling."

Despite my grousing, I got dressed and went to the table. Kelly had made blueberry pancakes, bacon, and hash browns. I put a little on my plate, slathered butter on my hotcakes, then poured syrup over everything. After I'd finished eating that plateful, I realized I needed a little more, so went back and repeated the process. After, I leaned back and patted my belly. "Thanks. I really needed that."

"What are your plans for today?" Kelly asked me.

I turned to Sammy. "What are my plans for today?"

He grinned. "We've got yoga to do—and you're going to do it with us, Kelly. You skipped the last two times, so you owe us—and then I thought we might go to the store. I couldn't get an earlier appointment for Kip, but that doesn't change the fact that we need to get him some things."

That caught my attention. "You want to go shopping?"

"Yeah. I do. Want to get ready for my Hawaiian trip." His smile could have knocked me off my feet.

My heart sped up. The thought that he might actually be ready to step out into the world excited me, but also gave me a moment's pause. When the hand smacked the back of my head, I realized he knew exactly where my mind went.

"We talked about this ad nauseam. Get it out of your head. This is my home, and you three are my family. Just because I'll be out doing some shopping doesn't mean I'm going to suddenly find I prefer having my freedom and go running off." His voice lowered. "I walked away once. I won't do it again. I mean, really? Where else am I going to find someone like you? Who else is going to go out and off a bad guy, then come home and get on his knees for me. I'd be an idiot to give that up."

The teasing tone made me smile, especially after Kelly sighed and rolled his eyes.

Sammy put his hand on my arm. "You may not know this, but you do that a lot more now. And it's not nearly as scary as the one you gave me when we first met. I like your smile now. It's genuine."

The whole conversation would have made me uncomfortable two years ago. I prided myself on not letting anyone in, but when I looked in the mirror now, I barely remembered that man. Rook and Kelly both told me that the likelihood of finding someone we could love in our line of work ranked about as high as being able to count all the grains of sand in the world. So what Sammy and I had probably would never happen again.

"Okay, so yoga first, then we go to the store. Sound good?"

Kelly glanced around the room. "I probably shouldn't—"

"You're going to," Sammy insisted. "At your age, you need all the exercise you can get."

Kelly huffed. "I used to think Haven was the biggest asshole. Congratulations on proving me wrong."

Still, he joined us for our morning workout. I submitted to Sammy in nearly every aspect of our lives, but when it came to our regimen, he let me plan it out. I made sure we rebuilt the muscle density he'd lost over the years, as well as working on both speed and balance. I taught him self-defense moves that would get him out of most jams, even though I hoped to hell he'd never have to use them. He made me proud, showing no hesitancy at all when he attacked, and he'd come far on his defensive techniques as well. Though I still held back quite a bit, he had some good moves. He'd successfully tagged me a few times, a fact he used against me when I didn't go quite as easy on him.

By the time we'd finished our workouts, the three of us were sweaty messes. Kelly limped off to his room to take a shower and, if I guessed right, some aspirin. Both of us loved Kelly. He didn't let his age slow him down. He protested loudly, but in our hand-to-hand matches, he gave every bit as good as he got. I could believe that during the time he'd been an agent, he had been a force to reckon with. I once told him I didn't think I could handle the more sedate life he had, and he glared at me, lifted his shirt, and showed me bruises from a recent sparring session. I dropped my pants and showed him the marks he'd inflicted on me as well.

After our shower, and Sammy getting me on my knees for a long blow job, he and I got dressed to go to the store. His hands trembled slightly as he put on his chinos.

"You sure you're ready for this? Being outside and being in public are two different things."

He didn't say anything for a moment. After sucking in a quick breath, he smiled and said, "Got to start somewhere. Let's go."

"Who's driving?"

He put his hands on his hips and dramatically rolled his eyes.

"Right. Sorry."

"We'll need the keys to the Escalade," he told me, the glee in his voice obvious.

"We're taking the big car?"

Kip came bounding into the room. Sammy picked him up, laughing at the pup's enthusiasm.

"Well, duh. Our kid needs a lot of things. Let's go shopping!"

CHAPTER NINE

Three carts full of dog stuff—tons of toys, a new water bottle, tags, a food bowl emblazoned with Kip's name on it, and stuff Sammy had tossed in while I wasn't looking—had been jammed into the SUV. How the hell he managed to fit it all in astounded me.

"Can we go home now?" I asked.

"Are you kidding? This is awesome. I mean at first I was really nervous, you know? But everyone has been a lot nicer than I expected."

"Well, when you hand them your credit card and they ring up nearly a grand in purchases, they're gonna love you."

He stopped and I could see the hurt in his expression. "Am I spending too much?"

Of all the things he could have said, that surprised me. I stepped closer to him and wrapped an arm around his shoulder. "Sweetheart, I wouldn't care if you spent it all. What's mine is yours. You've seen the bank statements. You know how much money we have. Pretty sure a few thousand isn't going to send us to the poorhouse."

He brightened considerably. "Good. I saw this doggy playpen online, and you know he'd love it!"

I couldn't help but smile at his eagerness. He headed to the driver's side, and I went to crawl in on my side, when I heard a deep voice growl out, "Give me the keys."

I rushed to the front of the car, where I saw Sammy standing, his eyes wide as saucers. A kid with shoulder-length auburn hair, dressed in a black shirt and torn jeans, stood behind him, a gun pressed into Sammy's back.

I got closer, my hands raised to show the man I wasn't a threat. "Hey Red, take it easy. Everything is going to be fine." I turned to Sammy, working hard to keep my voice low. "Give him the keys."

"No."

"Sammy, give him the fucking keys," I snapped.

"Not happening," he insisted, never taking his eyes off his target.

The would-be carjacker took a step back and held the gun out. His hand didn't shake at all, which told me he had practice at this. When this ended, Sammy would be getting a piece of my mind for arguing with me and the man with the gun.

"Give me the keys, man. I don't want to hurt you, but I will."

Sammy turned and smiled at him. "You're not getting the keys. There really aren't a lot of different ways this is going to end. See him?" he asked, pointing at me. "He's probably got a dozen ways to kill you right now."

"Fourteen, but I'm still counting," I replied.

"I'm the one with the gun," the jerk said, as if we needed a reminder.

Sammy's hand flew up, fingers wrapping around his assailant's wrist. He twisted, and I heard a bone snap before the gun clattered to the ground. Red howled in pain and tried to pull away from Sammy, who wasn't having it. His foot lashed out, hitting Red in the back of the leg, which drove him to the ground. His head made a sickening sound as it bounced off the pavement. Sammy retrieved the gun and placed it against the asshole's forehead.

"You're welcome," he told the douche. "From me you'll wind up going to the hospital, then probably to jail. If I had let him do it, it's more than likely someone would be claiming your body from the morgue."

"Hey!" I protested. "I can show restraint."

He turned his head and frowned at me.

"Okay, fine. You would have ended up dead," I agreed. "Bad enough you wanted the car, but you had to touch my husband."

"I knew you were fags," the guy groaned out.

Sammy dropped to a knee on Red's stomach, which must have jostled the idiot's wrist, because he yowled again.

"This fag kicked your ass. That fag would have killed you," he snarled. "The next time you think about trying something like this, remember that some people have guardian angels who really aren't the nice beings church teaches you about. They're avenging angels, who take absolutely no shit, and would drop you in an instant. Do you understand me?"

When an answer wasn't forthcoming, Sammy bounced on his knee.

"Yeah, yeah. I understand," he cried out.

A crowd had begun to form. At least one person had a cell phone out, probably taking a video. I heard someone murmur they had called the cops, and someone else said something about this happening before, so it seemed likely our friend had himself a good thing going, at least until he met us.

"We should go," I said, bending over to take the keys. Sammy looked as though he was about to protest, but I cut him off. "Getting involved with the police is probably not in our best interest." While I was glad that our license plate number would lead to a dead end if the cops ran it, the two of us showing up on YouTube wasn't something Rook would be happy about. At least with the way the crybaby was wailing, it seemed people weren't as much focused on us as they were on him.

Sammy made sure the safety was on before he put the gun on the ground, kicked it a distance away, then stood, his expression triumphant. I knew the feeling. My heart burst with pride to see him standing up for himself. That lasted until we got into the car.

"What the fuck do you think you were doing?" I shouted.

"Protecting myself," he yelled back. "He had a gun, Haven."

"Yes, he did. One that would have left a hole in your back if he'd decided to use it. When you're faced with a situation like that, you give them what they want and hope to hell they take it and go. You do not provoke them or taunt someone who is holding a gun. That's not being brave, it's being foolish."

"Then why the hell are you training me?" he roared. "Why not just leave things the way they are? I'll stay at home again and cower. Will that make you happy?"

I slammed on the brakes, and the car skidded to a stop. I turned to him, and he must have seen the anger in my expression, but he didn't back off.

"I did what I had to. What you would have done."

"You're not me. You aren't meant to be me. I'm training you and hoping to hell you never have to use what you're learning."

"You would have stopped him."

I grabbed his chin and made him meet my gaze. "Yes, I would have. But not until he shot you and left you bleeding out in the parking lot. It was not an acceptable risk."

85

He blinked, then slumped back into his seat. "I'm sorry," he growled. "I got caught up in the moment."

"I know. Adrenaline is a powerful thing. Most people in a fight or flight situation choose to run. It takes a special person to be able to stand his ground. I'm very proud of you, but if you scare me like that again…"

"What?"

I could hear the tease in his voice, and I couldn't keep the grin from forming.

"I won't put out for a week."

"That's fine. I ordered a chastity device for you anyway."

I glared at him, and he sat there and smiled.

"You so did not."

"I did. While browsing through the catalog of dog toys online, an ad popped up for sex toys. I didn't really get the correlation until I went exploring. It was like a rabbit hole. Dog collars led to leashes, which took me to clothes for your pup, which had me looking up cute things your pup can wear. Well, that gave me a whole new set of things to look at: people who were dressed as dogs—which was fascinating, by the way—and before I knew it, I'd been looking at stuff for over an hour. And then, at the bottom of one site—kinkypups.com, I think—I discovered the mother lode! Abstinence devices. Who knew there were so many different ways to keep someone from getting hard? One ad talked about keeping your partner honest, which reminded me of that incident with you and the guy in the bathroom—Daddy." He shrugged. "It's taken me a long time to get you trained the way I want. I needed to make sure I protected my investment. I figure if you're going to be gone a while, I should make sure you can't get into any trouble."

"You know nothing happened with that guy! Besides, that was two years ago, and I came home and told you all about it!" I complained.

"Yes, you did. But I figured it wouldn't hurt to give you a solid reminder of who's in charge."

I held up my hand, the wedding band gleaming in the light. "I think this does a pretty good job of it."

"I didn't say I'd use it, but it's nice to have on hand. Or on your dick if I decide to try it later."

I shut up then. Arguing would only entice him to see how it fit or some shit, and I'd wind up with my dick bundled up until he opted to let me out. Yeah, no. Not happening. I decided it was best to focus on what we needed to discuss.

"Fighting isn't supposed to be exciting. It's supposed to be a battle within yourself to stand your ground. Not to run in terror. Every time I go on a mission, I feel the dread in the pit of my stomach. Will this be the day someone is faster than me? Maybe I won't see them coming." I stayed quiet for a moment, then dropped the big one on him. "Is today the day I won't be going home?"

He swallowed, and when he turned to me, I saw the sadness in his expression.

"That's how I felt when you said you were going after Valerie. I couldn't believe you told her you'd give her two weeks before you met. In my mind, it showed total insanity," he said quietly.

"And now?"

He gave a one-shoulder shrug. "You know best. You've been doing this long enough."

"Not good enough. I agreed to Valerie's terms, because I didn't have a choice. We weren't having any luck finding her, and if I'd refused, the whole thing would have continued. I sure as hell wasn't in a position to argue that fact. Did it give her time to plan? Yes, but... Look, Valerie was smart. She knew when we talked that I had been taking down her men. She already had a huge advantage over us, because she knew all the players. She held all the cards.

"If she hadn't shown up, if she had only sent men, then we still would have put a hurt on her. Rook, Kelly, and I all knew it would be our best shot, though."

"And I had to go running off."

"And you had to go running off. I never told you, but your leaving hurt me more than Valerie ever could have. When she had me down, cutting me, my only thought was that she needed to be taken out, too. I didn't care if I died, as long as you were safe."

"I'm sorry," he whispered.

"Nothing to be sorry about," I insisted. I put the car back in gear and merged with traffic. "It taught me a valuable lesson, and I've been working hard to remember it. I got careless because I let my emotions get away from me. What happened comes down to me. I should have known better, should have kept my head, but I didn't. I found myself so wrapped up with you nothing else mattered to me. Not even my own life. While I would still give my life for you, I'd do my damnedest to make sure we both walk away."

He didn't say anything else, though he reached out and put a hand on my knee.

"Did you want to do any more shopping?"

"I'd like to," he replied. "It's been years since I've been out, and I don't want one stupid event to push me back."

He had strength aplenty; I'd give him that. Most people would probably be a quivering mess after an attempted carjacking, but Sammy had lived through worse.

"That's great. How many more stores on your list?"

"Seven," he said, then gave me a cheeky grin. "But we don't have to hit them all at once."

"Well, we'll do what we can."

~

It had taken Joel two weeks to track down any useful information on Haven. He'd heard of the man. Who hadn't? If anyone could legitimately be called a legend, it would be Haven. Terry had sketchy records on him. Not really anything that would help to track him down. Mostly notes he'd made about news stories where the disappearance of known criminals had cropped up. Terry would tell him, "That was Haven's work. I'm sure of it." He never understood Terry's fascination with the man.

He tried once to tell Terry that Haven was just a man, no better or worse than anyone else. Terry had argued with him that night. He had told Joel that Haven was the best, and he'd earned the respect Terry showed him. He tried to explain it, but it made no sense. Haven wasn't better. If he had been, then Terry wouldn't have died. Either way, now that he knew Haven was involved, Joel's plans had a whole new set of avenues open up to him.

A quick shake of his head helped to bring his thoughts back to where they needed to be.

The sun had set, and the weather had become much cooler than he'd expected. Who the hell would think that Arizona could get cold? The house lights were dimmed, but that didn't mean anything. Haven would have been trained to fight in the dark, to use any advantage he had to take down an enemy, so Joel knew extreme caution would be needed to keep him alive long enough to finish his mission.

He approached the house quietly. First, he disarmed the alarm system. From the shoddy work, it had to be there to throw people off. Joel doubted it was even hooked up, but he'd take no chances. He ran his fingers over the lip of the doorframe and found another set of wires. He pulled the hood tighter around his face. No way did he want to show up on camera. At least not yet. He slit the wires, then made a final check. There were no other devices or openings for anything he could find. Terry had said the man was the best, but he'd taken out the system in less than two minutes. He couldn't believe Haven could be this sloppy. How Terry found this man to be someone to idolize sure as hell went beyond him. He pulled out a worn leather satchel from his pocket, opened it, and slid out a thin strip of wire, which he used to jimmy the door quickly and quietly. The door opened silently, and he heard nothing inside. He slipped into the house, closing the door behind him. So far, this had been so much simpler than he thought it could be, given Haven's status.

He'd barely gotten through the door when he heard the growl. He froze for a moment, cocking his head to figure out where the sound had come from. Then something pounced on his feet, nipping at his pant leg. He looked down and saw the dog trying to seem so fierce. The urge to kick it away rode him, but it wouldn't serve a purpose, and besides, Terry had loved dogs.

He bent over and the dog sat, looking up at him and wiggling his little butt. He gave the dog a pat, and stood, ready to continue through the house. When the muzzle of a gun pressed against his temple, he cursed himself. Terry would give him so much shit about this.

"You really picked the wrong house to break into," said a gruff voice to his left. It sounded like an older man, so more than likely not Haven. "Don't you know there's a guard dog on duty?"

With those words, the mutt yipped and dashed into the other room. At least now he could focus on the man.

"You might think that, but no, I'm definitely in the right place. You however, are here at the wrong time."

He lashed out, catching the man across the chest and knocking the wind from his lungs with an audible *oof*. He fell, but rolled back to a standing position in one fluid move, looking supremely confident, even though Joel had managed to knock the gun away. His reaction time was beyond belief for someone his age.

"I thought I should give you a chance to get out, but I can see now you're not a common thief."

"No," he agreed. "Not common at all. I'm going to give you an opportunity here. Tell me what I want, and I'm going to let you live. You've got my word."

The old man crossed his arms over his chest. "Yeah, see, that's where we have a problem. Whatever you're doing in this house, I'm not about to let you finish."

"Pretty sure you can't stop me."

"You'd be surprised what I can do," came the reply.

Sammy pulled the car into the garage, turned off the engine, then stretched and let loose with a loud yawn.

"Tired?" I teased.

"Beyond. Shopping obviously takes a lot out of you."

Laughter had always been rare, but somehow Sammy pulled it from me. We got out and closed the door, before we went to unpack the supplies. It took all of a second for me to realize something wasn't right.

"Stay here," I whispered.

"What's going on?"

"Stay here," I ordered sharply. "Get in the car, and if you don't hear from me in two minutes, you get the fuck out. You go straight to a crowded place and call the police, then you call Rook."

Sammy didn't question. He hopped into the car and leaned low in the seat. I berated myself for my lack of preparedness. I had wanted to leave Haven at home and give Sammy a *normal* day with Michael. Everything told me to take my gun or another weapon I could hide on me, but I didn't. If I had, one carjacker never would have lived to threaten Sammy, and I wouldn't be skulking in my own house to find a weapon.

I went to the garage door that connected to the house and pulled it open slowly. The lights were dim, but Kelly usually turned them off when he wasn't in a room.

I slipped into the kitchen and grabbed a knife from the drawer, then made my way toward the gun safe. As I turned toward the kitchen door, I heard a noise.

"About time," came a hoarse voice. "Could use a little help here. I seem to have found myself in a rather strange situation."

Throwing caution to the wind, I yanked the door open and rushed in. Kelly hung shirtless from a rafter in the kitchen, the strips around his wrist digging into the flesh were caked with dried blood. Blood seeped from his mouth as well as from several deep wounds to his chest and stomach. I did a quick perusal and saw the deep gashes down his left side where someone had flayed him. Skin had been peeled back and covered with a white residue. *Salt.* Someone had split him open, then jammed salt into his wounds.

"Not a side of beef," he croaked. "Are you intending on leaving me hanging here all night?"

I shouted for Sammy, then stood on a chair and put the knife against his bonds. "I'm sorry, but this is going to hurt."

"Because it feels so good now," came the weak reply. "You have to know—"

The lump in my throat was nearly impossible to swallow. "Whatever it is can wait," I insisted. My heart lodged in my throat to see him like this. I had things I needed to say, but couldn't get the words out. "Just hold on and…and… shut the fuck up, old man."

91

Sammy rushed into the house and immediately came to our side. I sliced the ties around Kelly's wrists, and we lowered him to the floor.

"Call Lilah and Rook," I instructed Sammy. "Tell them we need a medevac, and Lilah needs to get her ass to the clinic."

Sammy gave a sharp nod, whipped out his phone, and began punching buttons.

"He came in," Kelly croaked. "Thought I had the drop on him, but apparently I'm a little slower than I thought. He took me down like a kid."

I'd sparred with Kelly, and I knew how the man worked. He was downplaying what had taken place. "You must have put up a hell of a fight," I countered.

"Nah. He thought I was a piñata, but I showed him. He didn't get any candy out of me."

The man was so pale, and shivers racked his body. I put a hand to his forehead and found it cool and clammy. "And I'm almost certain I told you to shut up," I said, anguish at seeing him like this choking me, making my voice crack.

"Okay." Kelly coughed, then slumped back. I heard Sammy on the phone with Lilah. I put a hand on his shoulder and pointed toward Kelly. Sammy nodded that he understood. I grabbed a gun from my cabinet, then started searching room by room. The bastard who hurt Kelly wouldn't live to regret his bad choices. I'd make sure of that.

CHAPTER TEN

Sammy stood clutching my hand as they loaded Kelly onto the helicopter. I'd spoken with Rook who ensured Lilah would be the one attending him. As we watched the chopper disappear over the horizon, the dam broke. Sammy threw himself into my arms and sobbed against my chest. I did my best to assure him that everything would be okay, but even I didn't believe the words.

After I got him into a car, we drove to Lilah's clinic. I had no idea how they'd arranged it, but Lilah had had them take Kelly there. Her place was as well stocked as any hospital I'd been in, though, so I had to trust her call.

I sat in one of the outer rooms, my head in my hands. If I had been there, maybe I could have prevented this. If Kelly died— I didn't want to think about that.

"Lilah says he lost a lot of blood," Sammy told me as he handed me a cup of coffee. "She figures he'd been bleeding for hours. I found a pool in the living room, so someone dragged him into the kitchen then hung him there."

"Did he say anything?"

"He didn't regain consciousness before Lilah got him on the table. She's pumping him full of antibiotics; she's giving him blood and has him on about fifteen different machines. Lilah says he should be okay. I have to ask; how did you know?"

"There were a few things. Kip wasn't barking for one, but Kelly didn't come out to see if we needed help. That had me on alert. But what makes it worse? He was in the house when we arrived."

"Where?"

"I'm not sure where he was hiding, but he slipped out as I searched. I heard a car screech off. We missed him by minutes."

"No, if we hadn't shown up when we did, Kelly would be dead now. That's what you need to remember."

No way would I forget it. Someone owed me blood, and I intended to get it in spades. I got up and stomped across the room, trying to peek in the door. When I couldn't see anything, I growled.

"What were you saying about being angry?" Sammy chastised me. "I can see it written on your face. Go sit down."

I opened my mouth to argue, but then noticed his expression. I went and sat. He pulled a chair from the table in Lilah's waiting room and took a seat next to me. I waited to see what platitudes he'd try to give me to calm me down, and when he spoke, I couldn't contain my shock at what he said.

"You need to stay angry." He put a hand on my shoulder and gave a squeeze. "But you need to focus on it and channel what you're feeling. It's what's going to make you come out on top."

"Oh? How do you know?"

He slid his hand down my arm. "Because I used to do it every night when Arianna had me. I'd go to bed, and I would lay there and think about how pissed off I was. I had that anger and hatred inside me for years. I tried lashing out, but that only earned me a punishment. So I started thinking more about how I'd have to be smarter if I expected to make it out alive. I couldn't keep from getting mad, but I could make sure who I directed it toward. I found if I got pissed off at Amber, Arianna would laugh about it. And I didn't get punished, because Amber wasn't allowed to touch me.

"Not that she didn't get back at me in other ways. She might have forgotten to feed me or made sure that she'd be busy when my bathroom breaks were scheduled, and I had to sleep in my wet—or worse—clothes. But I didn't stop. I had that one little bit of power over someone, and I took advantage of it. As much as I hated Amber, she gave me a focal point for my pain."

Sammy had rarely talked in detail about what had happened to him before we met. It had to be awful, but he came out acting as if it didn't bother him. After he'd killed his mother, he'd admitted that he wasn't over it as much as he'd thought and gone into therapy. Now, he could be more open, telling me things that happened. He seemed more like someone recounting the tale of a friend who'd had it happen to them, instead of the fact it was his life, but at least he had been letting it out.

"I'm angry," I admitted. "I want to know how he got in. What the hell happened in the house? Why didn't Kelly just blow the bastard away as soon as he found him? And what am I going to do when I get him alone?"

"You seem awfully confident."

My grin had to be feral, because Sammy's eyebrows knitted together.

"Oh, I'll find this bastard. Believe that."

The door opened before he could reply. Lilah came out of the room, almost sixteen hours after Kelly had been brought in. The front of her scrubs were covered in blood, and I made a mental reminder that when I got my hands on this guy, I'd make him hurt.

"If he hadn't been in such good shape, we would have lost him," she said in her blunt manner. "Honestly, I can't believe he survived in the first place. It took nearly two hundred stitches to sew him up. We had to do internal and external sutures to repair the damage. Whoever did this, knew what they were doing. The wounds were made over the course of several hours, judging by the fact some were clotted, but others still seeped. There's also the salt. They wanted Kelly in pain. It had to be excruciating for him."

"Can I talk to him?" I asked.

"Not likely. Probably not until tomorrow at the earliest. Right now he needs a lot of rest and getting him riled up isn't going to be helpful at all."

"He can tell us who attacked him," I protested.

"Haven, when something this traumatic occurs, the mind can try to block it out to deal with it. Even if he tells you something, I don't know that I'd put any stock in it."

"You don't know Kelly," Sammy grumbled. "The man is a trained agent. He didn't live this long by being weak or stupid."

"That's not what I'm saying," Lilah tried to interrupt.

"No, not at all! You're just saying that Kelly might not be in his right mind. You don't even know him. We do."

Sammy's chest puffed up, and I could see how flushed his face had gotten. He had come to love Kelly. To hear someone disrespecting him, even if it wasn't how Lilah had meant it, had him coming to his friend's defense.

"He's come a long way since Texas," Lilah grumbled. "I think I might miss the old him."

Keeping that laugh from bubbling out probably kept me from being in Sammy's cock cage. We rarely fought—mostly because I deferred to him in pretty much all things—but when those flashes of anger showed, they were damned impressive. At least if they weren't aimed at me.

I stepped behind him and wrapped my arms around his chest. His breath came in short pants, and I knew he wasn't mad at Lilah, but felt the same helplessness anyone else would. When the man you thought of as a father, strong and able, was lying on the floor bleeding out, it tended to rock you to your core.

"He's going to be okay," I promised.

And he would be. When we got home, I would be making a call to Rook, because the situation had become one that needed to be sorted out right away.

Lilah kicked us out of her clinic shortly before midnight. We'd driven nearly two hours, stayed there almost twenty-four holding a vigil, and she said we all needed rest. Sammy protested, as I expected, claiming we could sleep in the waiting room. Lilah wouldn't have any of it. She told us that her best people were looking after Kelly, and us being there served no purpose beyond distracting them. Sammy huffed and would probably have continued arguing, but I directed him out of the room, booked us into a hotel close to her clinic, then drove us there. Fortunately, they allowed pets, because Sammy held Kip close to him.

"I could have driven," Sammy complained as he sunk down into the seat.

"And you're tired and cranky," I replied, not bothering to mention how he was holding his dog.

"Not cranky," he complained, squeezing Kip a little tighter and burying his face in the dog's neck.

I didn't bother to disagree. We were all on edge, and the last thing we needed was a fight. After we checked into the hotel, we slid into the tub. Sammy actually leaned against me and allowed me to take care of him. I knew how close to the edge he'd gotten since this whole mess started. Despite his protests, Sammy drifted off to sleep in the warm water. I got out, mostly because I needed to make a phone call. I drained the water, then lifted him out of the tub and laid him on the bed. He wrapped himself in the blankets, the same thing he used to do when he first came to live with me. It was a defense mechanism for him, a way to feel safe. I rubbed his back until he stopped fidgeting, then made my way to the other room. After ensuring the door to the bedroom was closed tight, I pulled out my phone and dialed Rook.

"How are you holding up?" Rook asked.

"Better than Kelly," I replied, slumping down onto the chair with a panoramic view of the desert scenery. Despite the bath, the tension still had me aching to my bones.

"How's he doing?"

"Lilah says he's going to be hurting for a long while, and that there will probably be some scarring even though she called in a friend of hers to do the stitching. I want to know how that son of a bitch got into the house."

"Our people went over the place with a fine-tooth comb. He snipped the wires to the decoy security system, then doubled back to locate the real system. The video we have shows he wore a dark hooded sweatshirt, drawn tight so we didn't get a look at his face. The techs are trying to pull some forensic evidence from the house, anything that might lead us to know what's going on."

Rook never didn't know. I could hear the edge of frustration in his voice, and it gnawed at me, but I had more pressing concerns.

"I need a favor," I told him, carding a hand through my hair. "Sammy and Kelly are going to need a place to stay. I won't have them vulnerable like this again."

"I've already got somewhere," he assured me. "We're not sure who he is or why he's after you, but we're going to make sure everyone is safe. The three of you are going—"

"Excuse me?"

"You heard me," he said, his tone showing he would brook no arguments.

"You know what? Fuck you," I snapped. "I held the sliced open body of my friend. The pool of blood beneath him had gone sticky, which told me that this fucker had tortured him for a long time. Kelly's been out of the job for years. This never should have happened."

"You're right," Rook roared. "Kelly knew procedure. He should have called as soon as he noticed someone had entered the house. But he didn't. And he paid the price for his mistake. He's lucky to be alive. I've got several agents who weren't quite as fortunate. Whoever this unsub is, he's either damn good or damn lucky."

I slammed my hand on the arm of the sofa. "You're not listening to me," I growled. "I don't give a shit if he's a shadow, he's not going to get close enough to hurt my family again. And say what you want, but if he's after me, *I* will be the one to stop him.

Rook sighed. "No. You can stop there. We're not doing this. You're going to be with everyone else in this nice little bungalow, with a yard for your dog. You'll be watched around the clock by four other agents. I'm not going to lose you to this sick bastard."

"You're right there. You're not going to lose me, but I'm sure as hell not hiding. You're going to find a place for Sammy and Kelly, and I'm going to track down this son of a bitch and make him wish he'd never touched a member of my family."

Rook sighed. "This is why we don't allow majordomos to stay with their charges for an extended period of time. We knew Kelly had been the best fit for you, but we never expected that you'd actually come to care for him."

"I've always cared for him," I protested.

"Yes, like an employee. Which is what he was. Now? You're treating him like he belongs to you."

"He does," I snapped. "Him, Sammy, and even Kip all belong to me. I take care of my own."

"Funny," came a weary voice from behind me. "I thought you belonged to me."

I stood and spun around. "There's no talking about this. You're not going to change my mind. You and Kelly will be going to a safe house, and Rook is going to ensure that no one gets close to you."

"You're going, too," Rook reminded me.

Without acknowledging him, I disconnected the call. Sammy stood wrapped in the fluffy white robe the hotel provided, his glare cold. He stepped away as I went to reach for him.

"You don't learn," he snapped. "You think you're on your own now, but you aren't. You have us."

"And one of you is in the hospital, lucky to be alive."

His eyes narrowed dangerously. "I'm not going to hide while you're out there risking your life," he assured me. "You can try, but I promise you, I will find a way to get back home. You need me."

I rubbed my fingers over the bridge of my nose. In many ways, Sammy was every bit as headstrong as I was. The biggest difference, I'd promised him my life would be in his hands. He would make the decisions for me, because although the therapy had helped us both, I still needed his control to get me through the day. This wasn't about getting me through the day, though. More like making sure he and Kelly made it out with their lives.

"I will have them chain you to the bed if I have to," I threatened.

"Ooh, we played that game before. You looked good all stretched out like that."

His expression didn't match the playful tone. When Sammy got angry, it could be a glorious thing. But when he grew cold, I knew it was best not to push. Still, this wasn't going to go the way he thought.

"Come here and sit down," I told him. "Please."

He hesitated for a moment, then moved toward me. When he sat, he took a chair opposite my own seat. Wouldn't say it didn't hurt, but he wanted me to come to him.

"Do you remember when you told me once that you weren't Mary Jane?"

"I do," he replied, a hard edge to his voice. "And I'm still not. You've trained me, so you know I'm good. We can work together."

As much as the thought intrigued me, Sammy wasn't fit for this life. I had trained for this in both the military and in the organization. I'd had a few brushes with death, and had seen firsthand how killing Valerie had affected Sammy. He might be the one I looked to for direction, and he may control my body, but I hoped his heart would always be too gentle for this kind of wet work. And the training I'd given him hadn't prepared him for it either.

"Okay, help me out here. If Spider-Man was going after a bad guy, would he drag Mary Jane into danger?"

He opened his mouth for a moment, then closed it.

I pressed on. "And if she got captured, would he kill to protect her?"

"I don't know," he answered, his voice wavering a little.

I stood and moved over to his chair. I tucked a knuckle under his chin and tilted his head back so he looked me in the eye. "I do. I have in the past, and I will in the future. This isn't a comic book, Sammy. People don't come back from the dead. You go. You stay gone. I can't be out there, trying to find this guy, if I've got to worry about whether you're safe. That is why you can't go with me.

"Plus, I need you to watch Kelly. Rook says they're going to send people to keep an eye on him, but I want someone I know and trust to do the job. You're the only person who fits the bill. If this bastard tried once, he's going to try again. He wants me for something, and he's already killed a lot of people to get it. Can you do that for me? Can you protect Kelly?"

Sammy huffed and stood up. "You're an asshole," he snapped. "You know damn well that Rook will send his best people to protect Kelly. You don't need me to babysit, you just want me to think you need my help, so I'll be a good boy and stay where I'm told."

"No, that's not it," I promised him. "I don't know where the danger is going to come from. At this moment, there are only a very small handful of people I can trust with absolute certainty. Rook will send people, but do I know them enough to let them watch the people most precious to me? No, I don't. I know you. I trust you with everything. So who else could I entrust Kelly's life to? And I know you'll be able to protect yourself."

And I did know. No bullshit. He'd shown with the carjacker that he had smarts and skills. I needed to believe in him now, because he would have to keep himself and Kelly alive while I hunted. I reached for my shoulder holster and removed the gun, then handed it over to him.

His eyes went wide, as he finally understood the scope of what I'd asked of him. "You're serious about this, aren't you?"

"I am. But you have to be serious, too. I need to know, Sammy. Would you kill to protect Kelly?"

He answered clearly and without a moment's hesitation. "Yes. I won't let anyone hurt him."

That had been all I needed to know. As soon as Kelly and Sammy were safe, I'd be going after this bastard.

And he'd die.

CHAPTER ELEVEN

When we arrived at Lilah's at the butt-crack of dawn, she met us with cups of coffee. We hadn't gotten any before we left the hotel, so the first sip gave a welcome jolt.

"I'd prefer to keep him here," she began as she led us into her office. "He's torn up inside and will require a lot of care."

"Then tell Rook you want to go with us. I'm sure there's room at the safe house for you, too."

Lilah wrinkled her nose. "I'll have to. Kelly needs constant attention. I hate those places," she grumbled, putting bottles of pills, needles, a stethoscope, and other medical necessities together in a bag she held. "Never as nice as advertised, and the conditions usually make me worry about infection."

Sammy stepped closer to her. "I'm sorry about yesterday."

She stopped packing, put a hand on his shoulder, and squeezed. "Nothing to apologize for, Samuel. I know Kelly is important to the both of you. He is to me, too. I've known him for a lot of years, and the man has a way of getting under your skin. Do you want to see him?"

"Is he awake?" I could hear the touch of hope in Sammy's voice.

"No, it'll be several days yet. Kelly isn't one to rest, so I thought it best if he was kept under for a while. But you can make sure I'm doing my best to take good care of him."

"Please. I'd like to see him."

She led him to the door, where she turned to me. "Are you coming?"

"Not yet. I need to make a call."

Sammy frowned. "Haven?"

"It'll be okay," I promised. "I just need to be sure everything is ready."

He gave a terse nod then disappeared through the door with Lilah. I dialed Rook's number then sat back and waited for the explosion.

"How's he doing?"

"Lilah took Sammy back so he could see him. He's not awake yet, but I guess she figured it would calm Sammy's nerves some. Listen, it's probably a good idea if she goes with Sammy and Kelly. Someone needs to make sure the old man is cared for, and she's the only one with medical training."

Rook let loose a deep, long-suffering sigh. "You're the only one who gives me trouble. Everyone else does as they're told, but you've always got to be the pain in my ass. Why is that?"

"It's what makes me a good agent," I replied.

He barked a laugh. "Is that what you call it? You don't follow orders. You give me nothing but grief. And you brought another thorn in my side into your house, and he gives me nothing but shit."

"You love him, and you know it," I teased.

"I'll never admit to it," he grumbled.

Rook and Sammy had an interesting relationship. Sammy had no problem at all telling Rook off when the mood struck him, and he'd done it quite often when we'd first gotten together. He'd mellowed over the last year, and recently, I'd walked in on the two of them having a conversation about Kip and his training. Once, I thought I'd even heard Rook laugh at something Sammy had said to him. When I'd entered the room, they'd both gone quiet, until one of them ended the call.

It wasn't all roses, though. Rook still claimed Sammy should stay elsewhere. He said it was for safety, but I knew if Rook wanted him gone, Sammy would be. Rook never took shit from anyone but me and Sammy. I asked him once why he allowed it with Sammy, and he told me that he liked the fierceness Sammy possessed. And, he said, swearing me to secrecy, he liked the effect Sammy had on me.

"Is everything in place?" I asked, bringing the conversation back to the topic at hand.

"It is. I had to move a lot of resources around, but Samuel, Kelly, and Lilah are going to be watched around the clock. No one is going to get to them. You've got my word."

"I gave Sammy a gun," I told him, figuring full disclosure was important.

"Good. You trained him to use it, you've taught him to fight, and he's got something he cares for, so I think it's an excellent idea."

"Do we have anything to go on? Give me something."

"The agents who scoured the house found nothing beyond Kelly's blood. We found no evidence of anyone being in the house, beyond what you already know about. They're still going over things, but don't expect it to go quickly."

"No, of course not." I huffed out a breath. I hated this. "So what next?"

Rook barked out a laugh. "You're asking me? I still want you in a safe house. You're usually the one with the plan, so if you've got one, you have to let me know what it is."

I didn't have one. My assignments, both in the military and working for Rook, had always been straightforward—get my mission, find my target, learn what I could, kill them. Simple. This required me to be different. To acquire a different skill set.

"I think, this time, I'm going to have to let him come to me," I said, making a decision. I counted to three, waiting for the inevitable explosion from Rook.

"No! Absolutely not. I've got dead agents here, Haven. People who shouldn't have had to die. You're not going to go out there and make yourself a target. I won't allow it."

Rook could be cute when he thought the decision was his.

"Then you tell me how else we're going to do this. What grand scheme do you have to lure him out into the open?"

He stayed quiet, and I knew the man was seething. He hated the feeling of being powerless. Despite his words, I knew Rook considered Kelly a friend, and it had to be tearing him up inside that the man had been nearly killed.

"We don't have a lot of options. This person, whoever he is, seems to be the one holding the cards. What we're going to do is business as usual. He knows where to find me now, so we wait for him to come back. If he wants me, he'll have to."

"I don't like this," Rook protested.

"Neither do I, but I really don't see many options."

Rook grumbled, then disconnected the call. A few minutes later, Sammy and Lilah stepped out of the back offices. He immediately came to me and put his arms around my waist. I could see the tear tracks down his cheeks and squeezed a little harder.

"He can't die," Sammy whispered.

"He won't. Lilah said he'd mend. She wouldn't lie."

"But he looks so awful. His face is black and blue, his eyes and lips are swollen, and he's got so many stitches."

Lilah came over and rubbed Sammy's back. "It'll look better in a few days," she told him. "He needs some time to convalesce, and if he follows orders and rests, he'll be okay." She stepped away and went toward the back room again. "I'm going back in there. If you want to come keep an eye on him, that would be fine."

Sammy nodded, but didn't say anything.

The day Valerie died, Sammy had retreated into himself. It hit him how much he really wasn't over his treatment at his mother's hands. He'd been shaky and scared, clinging to me for support. But seeing him now? This Sammy worried me more.

Kelly had drawn Sammy out of his shell. As strong as Sammy was, there were certain parts of him that had been broken by the he'd been passed around after his father had died. When Sammy first arrived at our home, a simple thing like a hug between him and Kelly would have been out of the question. But Kelly had been steadfast in his love, eventually earning Sammy's trust—and his hugs. Kelly gave Sammy something he couldn't get from me. A father figure. Kelly gave Sammy something he couldn't get from me. A father figure.

"He's going to be okay," I repeated.

"You don't know that," Sammy insisted, his lips drawn into a thin line.

"No, but I believe it. Kelly is tough. If nothing else, he'll get better just so he can bust my chops some more."

Sammy choked a laugh as he guided us to the couch. "It sounds stupid, but when my dad died, this is how I felt. He'd been the only one who believed in me, told me I could do anything. Kelly is a lot like him. After we met, I didn't think I could ever feel comfortable around him, and now I feel cold because he's not there."

"It doesn't sound stupid at all. Kelly's got that skill of worming his way beneath your skin and making himself at home. There's a quiet strength to him. For the longest time, he had been unobtrusive, standing in the background, watching, but still there. I'm sure you know what I mean. But it dawned on me one day how much I needed him there. It wasn't about cooking my meals or keeping house for me. The fact he'd been taking care of me is what did it."

"And now we could both lose him," Sammy whispered.

I hated the expression on his face. So much pain and hurt, and I would do anything I could to take it away, but the only thing that would do it was time. Even if…when Kelly got better, there could be no guarantee he'd come back to work for me. He'd been tortured, and we had no idea why. More than likely, he'd opt to retire from the agency, which meant Sammy and I would have to move. For everyone's safety, the agency didn't allow any connection between the old life and new. I'd broken those rules more than once, and if it came down to it, I would probably do it again so Sammy could keep Kelly in his life.

"Haven?"

A warm hand on my arm jerked me back to the conversation.

"Sorry. I might have been thinking."

"Somehow I doubt that," he teased, but the tone of his voice was flat.

I could tell from his pinched expression the pain Sammy was feeling. "You don't have to pretend with me, you know."

"Gotta be strong for you," Sammy croaked. "That's my job."

I loved this man. No matter what else, my wellbeing would always be his first concern.

"Yeah, not so much," I replied. "Sometimes we have to be strong for one another." I kissed his head. "This definitely qualifies as one of those times."

He leaned against me, putting his head on my shoulder. I wrapped an arm around his waist and sat there with him. We didn't talk, because what could we really say? Each of us knew how the other felt. We shared those emotions warring within us. I needed Sammy to hold onto that anger, like he'd told me to. He had to push the grief aside if he expected to be effective.

He shifted, and his head drooped. I moved as far as I could toward the end of the couch, then pulled Sammy down so his head rested in my lap. Stroking his hair caused him to nuzzle in deeper. I wondered if the decision to put him in the safe house with Kelly had been the right one. I didn't want

Sammy tangled up in this mess. He'd had enough hurt to last him several lifetimes.

"Stop thinking so hard," he mumbled. "You're keeping me awake."

"Sorry. I'll try to think quieter," I whispered, hoping he'd fall back asleep. Instead, he sat up and leveled his gaze on me.

"Okay, spill."

"What?" I replied, not wanting to discuss my thoughts.

"Don't give me that. Tell me what's on your mind."

Saying no would definitely not help. But I also knew what would happen if I told him the truth. He'd get defensive, demanding to know why I didn't trust him. There would be reminders of the training we'd done together and of the carjacking that proved he could handle himself.

"You can handle yourself," I finally said. "But—"

"But you'd prefer I not have to. I know. Honestly? I would rather not have to either. Being at home, curled up on the couch, watching a movie would be a lot better. Kelly would be grousing in the kitchen, saying they don't make movies like they used to, then he'd sit down and laugh the loudest or cry the hardest."

The memory of our last movie night drew a chuckle from me. It wasn't even a matter of what we watched, as long as we did it together. Saturday had become our unofficial movie day. We'd take turns choosing a movie, then sit back and watch everything from classics to horror. The only time we didn't watch a movie was when I had a mission. They both knew they could go ahead and watch something, but they chose not to. It wasn't the same, they'd insisted.

"What I'm telling you is this guy didn't leave us with a choice. I meant what I said. If he comes near Kelly again, I will kill him."

In truth, I hoped that I could find him first, because there would be no hesitation. He'd die for what he did to Kelly, Savior, and everyone else. He made a mistake in coming after me, and it would be one he wouldn't live to regret.

~

Joel pulled back the bandage to check his face and winced at the ugly lines that streaked his cheek. That bastard old man had nearly ruined everything. Terry would kick his ass up and down the block for underestimating an opponent. In truth, he thought Haven would be there and figured that was all he needed to worry about. Instead, some old dude nearly cleaned his clock. He'd fought like a madman. Joel was astounded at the way he kept twisting out of Joel's reach, always keeping distance and items between them, striking out when he found an opening.

If it weren't for the fact Joel landed two lucky hits and his opponent smacking his head as he fell, he could very well have won the fight.

To make matters worse, he didn't give up anything. Not one word did he utter in answer to the questions asked. And he kept that fucking smile the whole time. Like he knew something, but refused to share. After the first hour, and the slices to his skin, Joel had grabbed some salt and forced it into the wounds. When that hadn't worked, he grabbed a bottle of hand sanitizer from the kitchen. It wasn't what he would use if he had time, but it would work in a pinch. What did he get? Not one goddamned thing. The bastard didn't even cry out when Joel forced the gel into the gashes, pushing it in with the tips of his gloved fingers. Through it all, he just…fucking smiled. If this person worked for Haven, what would the man himself be like? Maybe Terry had been right in his awe.

Then again, maybe not.

Joel knew now he had to meet this man. After fighting with the guy—who was probably his majordomo—the urge to face Haven, to glean every single bit of information the man possessed and then kill him sent ripples of pleasure through Joel. If he killed Haven, then Terry would know that Joel could handle himself. He'd be the one who took down the man Terry spoke of in hushed whispers, as if speaking his name would cause him to appear. Like some villain in one of those cheesy horror movies they used to watch.

Joel smiled to himself. At least his trip had one thing go right. Haven knew what happened. Joel had seen him enter the house, then heard him talking with another man. He'd hidden, thinking he could ambush Haven when he got into the room Joel had hidden in, but there were other people in the house now, and he couldn't afford to be taken unawares. Terry had told him repeatedly to fight on his terms, not to let someone else dictate the rules. Terry had been a brilliant man.

It didn't matter, though. Terry had died. And his death had gone unnoticed. Uncared for. But Haven still lived. He got accolades that Terry never would. Once his body had entered the ground, no one had ever thought of Terry again. Except Joel. He could never forget seeing the empty coffin that should have contained his lover. No one but Joel had been at the funeral. There were no witnesses to the casket being lowered into the ground, or Joel collapsing at the side of the grave. No one to talk to. No hand to comfort him.

He'd walked through their house, the emptiness overwhelming. More than once, he'd broken down, crawled into his bed, and prayed to not wake up in the morning. Yet every day, he did. And the pit where his heart used to be grew larger and larger. He tried to look at photo albums, seeing a younger Terry in his uniform. He'd been so handsome, and he'd only gotten better with age. A little silver in his hair, his dark eyes that softened when he looked at Joel, the body, firm and warm, that held him, loved him, consumed him.

And now? Nothing.

Joel scrubbed a hand across his face, surprised to find himself still capable of tears. He wondered what Terry would think if he found him crying. Would he gather him up in his arms and whisper to him that everything was okay? That he didn't need to be afraid, because Terry would never leave him? They'd grow old together, live happily ever after.

Joel screamed his rage to the heavens. "Fuck you, Terry. You goddamned liar. You knew this would happen. You didn't give a damn that you were leaving me alone. I begged you not to, but you said you needed to do this. All I wanted was you. And you couldn't even give me that. You know what? I'm glad you're dead."

The words hit Joel like a hammer and his stomach clenched.

"I'm sorry, baby," he whispered. "I didn't mean it. I just hurt so much. I don't know what it is, but I can't move on. Not until I get satisfaction."

He reached into his pocket and pulled out the phone he'd taken off the old man. Cracking the security had been child's play. He found messages from Haven. Pictures of him with another man, probably taken when they weren't aware. The two of them looked so in love, just as he'd been with

Terry. Would this man grieve when Haven died? Would he feel like his heart had been torn from his chest?

Or maybe he should take the man instead. Let Haven feel what losing everything was like. How it felt to wake up in the middle of the night and reach for your lover, only to find the empty space he used to occupy. Or to see something that you just had to tell him about, then you remembered you couldn't do that ever again. How would the big, bad Haven handle it? Could he go on with life? Would he put a bullet in his brain?

Joel lifted his gaze and looked into the mirror again. He traced the scratches on his jaw with the pads of his fingers, wincing at the pain. He applied a little salve to the cuts, then put another bandage over them. He went into the living area of the hotel room and sat down. He glanced over to the table where his prize lay. Three names. Haven's and two others. Process of elimination and all, Joel knew one of them had to be the person he wanted. But why stop there?

So many options had opened up to him when he'd found Haven, and now he had to decide which would be the best course of action. Kill the man or destroy his life.

Decisions, decisions.

CHAPTER TWELVE

Three days had gone by. Lilah still had Kelly under, much to Sammy's consternation. She told him that she'd only planned to keep him out for a day or two, but his injuries necessitated a third day. She said if she wasn't satisfied with his progress, it might be longer, but she wouldn't keep any information from him. That mollified him somewhat.

Rook had insisted that they be moved right away. Lilah refused, stating that they would go nowhere until she cleared it. I may have laughed when I heard Rook sputter. Either way, she'd called earlier to inform him that today Kelly could be relocated.

Sammy had been resigned when I told him that I'd be going after the guy who'd invaded our home. He knew he'd have to stay at the safe house, but when he gave me a grin, I feared what he would do.

The cock cage did not feel comfortable. He insisted that if he had to be locked up, so did I. Reluctantly, I let him put it on me. As he knelt before me, I could see his expression. Uncertainty, tinged with a bit of sadness. I realized what he was doing wasn't about sex or trust; it was because it helped him to feel like he still had control of the situation we found ourselves in.

"I studied up on them. They're safe for long-term wear, but you need to make sure it's kept clean," he whispered as he handed me a small box. "There are cotton swabs, gentle soap, and baby oil with a bottle to make application of it easier."

His breathing hitched, and he seemed so close to a breakdown that I stepped back and put my hand on the device. "It'll be fine," I promised. "At least you won't ever be far from my thoughts."

Less than an hour later, Rook had a group of agents swoop in and take Sammy, Kelly, and Lilah somewhere Rook assured me was safe. In the back of my mind I wondered, because this was my family's life I was entrusting

111

him with. In my head, I knew Rook would do everything he could to make sure they were taken care of, but my heart demanded I take them and run far, far away. Fortunately, I was able to compartmentalize those warring emotions.

When it came time to go, Sammy had given the most tempting pout, his plump lip jutting out when they hustled him to the vehicle.

"I wish we were going home," he whispered in my ear as we said good-bye. "All of us."

We wanted the same thing, but while we both wanted Kelly back, the fact that he might be able to tell us what happened or give us any clue to his assailant's identity meant he needed to be kept safe. It didn't mean any of us liked it, though.

I spoke with Rook a few days later, hoping for some news that might finally bring this to an end. Living out of my car sucked. Even though it was roomy by most standards, I couldn't sleep for shit. I longed to share a bed with Sammy again. Unfortunately, Rook didn't have good news. He told me the people who were watching the house said our unsub hadn't come back, and Rook began to wonder if maybe it had been a break-in that had gone bad.

"No way in hell. Kelly could handle any loser off the street."

Rook sighed, and I heard him tapping on his desk. Over the years, I noticed it had become a nervous habit for him. "You're right. I don't like this. We don't usually have to worry that someone is coming after us. Well, after you."

"True enough, but if they're after me, at least the others will be safe."

"Will you be?"

I laughed. "That's a stupid question."

"Don't take this lightly," Rook snapped. "This bastard has killed at least six people that we know of—five of them as highly trained as you. Don't underestimate him."

That wasn't about to happen. I'd done my best to keep a close eye out for our mystery man since Sammy had gone into hiding with the rest of our household. Even though I had no way of knowing who he was, it didn't stop me from thinking every person I saw was a potential threat.

Though we couldn't talk, Sammy did send a message through Rook. He'd been teaching Kip some tricks, and I'd be surprised when I got to see them. I told him honestly that I couldn't wait. Being awake for thirty-six hours in a stretch, snagging food wherever I could—usually a burger and fries at some drive-thru place—and not having a mission to occupy my mind, left me stuck in my own head. Not having Sammy around to pull me out of it sucked. I worked out until my muscles screamed, lungs burned, and tiredness forced me to take a break. I'd sleep in the car for an hour, which I knew was a bad idea, but then I'd go at it again. The only clarity I had came during that bone-deep exhaustion, when I realized how much I missed my home and my people.

When we—my sister and I—used to talk about family, it had all been pretend. Fantasies that we wished would be true. If she had lived, I think she'd be shocked that we really could have had one. Even if it wasn't conventional—three men, two of them married, and a dog—it was mine. And no doubt existed within me that she'd have loved it.

The thing of it was, someone out there wanted to take it from me, to destroy the happiness I'd built. And I didn't even know why. One thing that I knew for certain, though…he was watching me. I could feel the hairs on the back of my neck prickle. I stayed in heavily populated areas, hoping that would deter him, or make him get frustrated and do something stupid so I could take him out. Thus far, though, he hadn't made a move.

When the phone rang, it startled me. Too much time without sleep, without real food, and without Sammy had taken a toll on me.

"Haven?"

"Who else would it be?" I snapped.

Rook coughed. "Yes, well… Lilah called. She's bringing Kelly out from his sedation."

I sighed. It had been two days longer than expected, but at least the old man was now to the point where Lilah thought it was safe. "Where?"

He hesitated for a moment. "I'm not going to tell you."

"Excuse me?" I roared. "Why the fuck not?"

"You know the protocol. No communication. I never should have given you Samuel's message, but your nerves were fraying. I figured it was a better alternative than having you snap."

Truer words were never spoken. In all my years, I never believed I needed anyone. Then this gaunt young man came into my life, turned it upside down and inside out. He made me feel, made me want, and made me long for him. I once likened myself to the koi in the pond. They'd become accustomed to touch, swimming near the surface and wanting to have someone stroke them. I felt that way with Sammy.

"Sorry," I muttered.

"It's fine. The house has a secure line. When Lilah thinks it's okay, I'll have him phone you. I know you have questions and don't want to miss asking something you may think important."

Rook was right. There were things I needed answered. Who the hell could have gotten the drop on Kelly? What did he want? If he had the answers to those questions, I needed them.

"Fine. Have him call me when he's able."

"What are you doing now?"

Everything that came to me would be nowhere near the truth, but I didn't want to lie to Rook…unless it served a purpose.

"In my car, sitting outside the McDonald's."

Silence filled my ears for a moment. "Oh, Haven." His voice dripped with pity and, maybe, a little annoyance. "I can still get you into the safe house. You could be with Samuel and Kelly."

It sounded good. Better than good. But I needed to protect them, and I couldn't do it being stuck in a house. A certain amount of autonomy had become necessary, even if right now we were spinning our wheels.

"No," I replied, sliding a hand through my somewhat greasy hair. God, everything had become such a mess. The feeling of helplessness definitely wasn't one I would ever be comfortable with. "How about if you send me on a mission. At least that will occupy my time."

"Well," Rook answered slowly, dragging the word out. "I do have one, but it's going to take you to Tennessee.

My grip on the phone tightened. As much as I wanted something to do, being away from ground zero didn't sound like a good idea. Or maybe the thought scared me, because I wouldn't be in control of the situation. Not that I was at the moment.

"The man you'd be after is named Elijah Jameson. He's wanted in connection with a string of assaults, all young boys aged eight to twelve. Been arrested once, no conviction, because the parents refused to allow the boy to testify."

One of the reasons I accepted my role as Haven was because of the man who'd repeatedly raped my sister. He ruled the house with an iron fist, terrifying us all, until the day I shot him in the head. That event set me on my path to being recruited by Rook and the organization. Over the years, I'd killed many people, both men and women—because evil didn't know gender—who'd flouted the law, thinking they were above it. And in many cases, they were. Payments to police or judges gave them a degree of immunity from prosecution by the courts, but not by us.

We didn't only go after abusers, of course. People who peddled drugs to children, got them hooked and then turned them out as either mules or prostitutes were also at the top of my list. My job, as explained to me, would be to rescue children where I could and avenge them when I could not.

When Rook set me against Valerie, the scope of her organization and how many lives it destroyed horrified me. The one that hit me the hardest had been finding several little girls in a pit located in one of the wealthiest parts of Arizona. They were left there along with the rotting corpses of children who, according to their tormentor, hadn't followed the rules. I gave him a lesson, though. I beat him with a crowbar, then blew off his face. That event was what brought me to Sammy's arms.

The kids who'd survived couldn't tell us anything about their parents or where they were from. Lilah got them placed with people who would look after and care for them. Their lives were going to be hellish, especially considering what they'd witnessed, but the organization had gotten them psychiatric help. When last I heard, they were adjusting to their new lives and holding fast to the families who had taken them in. I marveled at the resilience of children.

"I want him," I snarled. Sammy would understand, I knew. He'd always been the one who encouraged me to go out and protect people, even knowing what it cost me.

"Good. I'll make the arrangements. Let me know when you're ready to go. I can get the ticket on a moment's notice. Before that, though, please take a shower."

He didn't know how very much behind that idea I was. Days of working out, no chance to clean up? I kept the windows on the car open, because even I didn't want to be in the same room with me. A shower would definitely be what the doctor ordered. Unfortunately, I didn't want to take it at the local gym. Too open, nowhere to stash my gear. Oh, and heaven forbid someone see the cage. That would go over well, I was certain.

Only one place I could think of would give me the privacy I needed to wash myself down and take a nap.

Columns had been the preeminent BDSM club I'd been a member of for years. At least until Sammy came into my life. After a mission, it felt good to let loose with one of the subs. Pound him until he begged for permission to come. Now I had more in common with them than I had with the Doms. Not that there could be any shame in that. I admitted that I needed someone to take care of me, to pull me out of the morass I allowed myself to become mired in because of my arrogance and stupidity. Sammy became that one.

Craig had been the doorman and security forever. He grinned at me when I came up the walk. "Well, I haven't seen you in…shit, what's it been? Two years. Longer? We wondered what happened to you. Some of the subs almost cried their eyes out when you stopped coming in."

"You are so full of shit," I grumbled.

"Seriously. Eddie will be glad you're back on the scene. He asks about you from time to time."

The last time I'd seen Eddie had been right before I went after a drug dealer who peddled poison that killed kids. We'd had some fun a few times, but nothing beyond that. Now the thought of him left me cold. Before Sammy, I thought that the release I'd gotten here had been all I needed. I'd learned differently, though. Physical sensations took on a much deeper level with Sammy than it ever had with anyone else. But he also dragged emotions from me no one else had even scratched. My man was the whole package.

"I'm not really into the scene anymore," I told him. "I just need to rent a room to shower and crash in."

Craig narrowed his gaze. "You're not here to play? You?"

I inhaled sharply. "I met someone," I told him. "He's my whole world."

"Wow. The big, bad Alex found himself a sub."

Alex. Man, I hadn't used that name in a long time. There were times I'd come here most weekends when I wasn't on a mission. A break from the blood and guts of my world, where for an hour or two, I could be someone else. A chance to find a bit of warmth. It never occurred to me until this moment that what I'd been looking for was what I'd found with Sammy.

"Actually, I found me a Dom." I'd never called Sammy that, though the thought had crossed my mind more than once that I was submissive to him in all things. It felt good to finally admit it to someone else.

Craig blinked once or twice, the wry grin on his face melting away. "You? Shit, the subs here used to fight over who got to spend time with you. This is…not what I expected."

Giving a casual shrug, I said, "Well, my job is high stress, lots of pressure. He takes me out of my head and just lets me be for a while. You know?"

The smile I got this time had been the most genuine I'd ever seen on his face. "I do. My own Dom keeps me on a tight leash."

He gave me a weighty look, both of us having shared a little bit of ourselves.

"Look, I know my membership has lapsed, but I need a shower and a nap. I can pay, of course, but…"

Craig waved me off. He picked up his tablet, typed something in, and turned to me. "You're listed as my guest for the day. If you need anything, let me know, okay?" He peered intently at me. "And bring your man around. Me and Sir would love to meet him."

He opened the door, told me to have a good night, then allowed me to enter. I went to the desk and asked for a room. The young submissive behind the counter slid a key to me.

"Do you require anything else, Sir? Shall I send someone to take care of you?"

The weight of the cage around my cock reminded me of exactly what Sammy had said. He took care of my needs, and the fact I couldn't touch myself or have anyone else touch me, let me know he stood by my side, even when he wasn't with me.

"No, I just need the shower and a nap."

He gave me a smile and dipped his chin. "Enjoy your night then, Sir."

The best thing about Columns was that the owners spared no expense on their private rooms. The showers were large enough to fit four people—and had, on occasion—with eight jets on each wall. Standing there with the water beating down on my body, loosening the aches of being cramped in my car, was a godsend. After I'd stripped the layers of grime off skin and hair, I moved over to the bed. Though not like the one I had at home, it would serve a purpose. I crawled onto it, forgoing the sheet, and drifted off into the best night sleep I'd had in days.

The loud, shrill ringing jolted me out of my haze. I sat bolt upright and snatched my phone off the table. The number came up as blocked, which had me smiling.

"Hello?"

"Please come and get Samuel," Kelly croaked. I hadn't heard anything so sweet in a long time.

"Why? What's he doing?"

"When I came to this morning, he stood over me, wanting to know if I felt okay, whether I had to use the bathroom, if I needed help getting there. It's creepy."

"He loves you, old man. He cried for you, and I haven't seen him cry for many people."

"I know," Kelly whispered, his voice thick.

"How are you feeling?"

"About as well as can be expected, considering she had a tube down my throat and one in my dick."

I shuddered. His scratchy tone and his cranky attitude told me that Lilah and Sammy were more than likely getting an earful.

"Better you than me."

He growled. "Wait until the next time you need to come see her. Even if it's for a hangnail, I'm going to tell her to put a catheter in you. I'd like to see you laugh about that."

I heard the sounds of a brief scuffle, a lot of shouting, and then Lilah's voice came on the line.

"He needs rest. If you've got something to say, do it now. I can't keep Samuel out of the room forever. He insists he needs to be here to take care of Kelly, and I had to put two guards on the door to keep him out just so I could complete an examination. And after that, he *pouted* and I actually felt bad about having to do my job." She sucked in a breath. "If you don't finish up soon, they may have to shoot him. And you," she snapped, more than likely at Kelly, "finish up talking with him and rest, or I swear I'll put the tube back in your dick while you're awake. And this time it won't be the small one. And I'll do it without anesthesia."

Kelly muttered something that sounded a lot like 'I'd like to see you try,' then Lilah replied, "Trust me, Samuel will hold you down if I tell him it's for your own good."

As weird as it sounded, this had been the first normal conversation I'd heard in days. A weight lifted from my chest at the thought everything might be okay after all.

"She's a harpy," Kelly croaked.

"It's love. I think she wants you to invite her to dinner."

He didn't reply for a moment. Then he whispered, "You think?"

Anyone who hadn't known Kelly had a thing for Lilah hadn't been paying attention. They talked on occasion, and the look on his face when he'd curled up on the couch and simply listened to her did my heart proud.

"Any woman would be lucky to have you," I replied. "But we'll miss you if you decide to leave and move in with her."

He barked a laugh, then coughed. "You are not a nice man."

As much as it pained me, I had to get my answers. "Okay, so I need to know. What the hell happened?"

Kelly sighed. "I'd been out back cleaning up the little gifts that Kip left, you know, the ones you and Samuel always seem to be conveniently gone for, when I heard him barking. I thought at first it might be the two of you coming back from shopping. I walked in and found him near the front door.

119

I thought he was there to rob the place. I held my gun on him and must have gotten too close, because he hit me. Not many people can move that fast. He knocked me down, but I was able to get up. Lost the gun, though. We fought hand to hand, and he countered everything I threw at him. I needed the room, so I tried to keep things between us while I maneuvered to get to a place more to my liking. He never gave me the chance.

"When he lunged at me, I tripped and fell. My head hit the corner of the table and I went down. He was on me before I could move, slamming his fist in my face. He dazed me, and that was all she wrote."

While he talked, my fist clenched. I could picture the fight as Kelly described it. In my mind, I watched him struggling to hold the intruder off until we got home. Knowing that we were so close pissed me off. If we hadn't stopped at all the stores, if that son of a bitch in the parking lot hadn't slowed us down. If. If. If.

"You're growling," Kelly told me. He sounded amused.

"We should have been there," I said softly.

"No, you shouldn't have. You got Samuel out of the house. He needed that, Haven. You both did."

"Did he tell you what happened at the store?"

"Yes! I can't tell you how proud of him I am."

My phone beeped, signaling an incoming call. When I saw the name on the caller ID, I froze for a moment. "Hold on," I growled. "I've got another call."

"Haven, wait—"

But I'd already switched to the other call.

"Well, I know you're not Kelly," I said by way of greeting.

"No, I'm not. Thank him again for the phone, if you don't mind. Assuming he's still alive. I sort of lost interest in him when I saw you. He was good, but you're supposed to be the best. Funny, though. I never pictured you as a client of Columns. Kind of makes me wonder what you're into. Big guy like you? You're probably into spankings. Making them cry for you?" He sighed. "I guess you don't really know someone until you've been watching them for a week, am I right?"

My spine stiffened. He had been watching me. How the hell could I not have known? And worse, he knew where I was now, which meant that everyone I came into contact with would be in danger.

As if he'd read my mind he said, "Oh, and don't worry about the people who work there, *Alex.* They don't know who you are, so trying to get them to give up information would just lead to more dead bodies."

"What do you want?" I demanded.

"I don't think you're ready to tell me what I want to know just yet, but you will be soon. I wanted to make sure you know I'm watching. Don't bother trying to track me with the GPS chip. I've already removed that and attached it to a car heading south. Good-bye, Haven. I'll be seeing you very, very soon."

And he disconnected. For a moment, I sat on the bed, seething at the thought this asshole seemed to know so much. Then I went back to Kelly's call.

"Lose your phone, old man?"

"He took it from me. After he picked it up, he stood studying the screen, then his eyes went wide and he laughed. He bent over, patted me on the cheek, thanked me, and told me he'd make good use of the information I'd given him. Then he strung me up, whistling the whole time he did it."

"So did he tell you why he wants me?"

Kelly didn't reply for a moment, then he said, "Wants you? He doesn't want you, Haven."

"Then what the hell is he after?"

"He wants Rook."

Chapter Thirteen

"Rook? What the hell does he want Rook for?"

Lilah yelled from the background that he had two minutes, then he needed to be off the phone. He didn't say anything, but I heard her say, "Right back at you." I assumed he gave her the finger.

"He held the phone out and showed me the screen. He pointed to Rook's name and told me you were the missing link. He said unless he was mistaken—which he assured me he never is—Rook is the one who took something from him. He said the only way he can move on is if he gets even. He said he wanted to kill Rook, but I'm starting to wonder if that's enough for him now."

"What do you mean?"

"He knew of you. He talked about how disappointed he was that you weren't home. How much better it would have been if he had found you, instead of me."

"I wish he had, too."

"Don't underestimate him," Kelly warned. "He's good, smart, and he doesn't seem to care if he lives or dies."

Anger surged as my gaze flicked to where the gun lay on the seat beside me. "That's okay, I plan on making sure that he dies. And soon."

Kelly let loose a tired sigh. "Don't go in angry. I don't know how many times I have to tell you that. Think about what it almost cost you."

Sammy.

My stubbornness had very nearly cost me my life. I got up and started to pace the room as I thought back to that day. When I'd fought Valerie, I'd gone in angry at the world. All the training, all the missions, everything had gone out of my head. Emotions controlled me, and I almost didn't walk away. The thing of it was, after my sessions with the therapist, I had a better handle on the rage. At least I thought so.

"I'm going to be careful," I promised. "Rook has a mission for me. I'm going to be out of town for a while."

"So you're going to leave Samuel?" he snarled. "What the hell? You're just going to walk away?"

"Hell no," I groused. "This fucker's watching me, old man. He's been following me. I need to get him away from here. Before I leave, though, I'm going to make sure everything is taken care of. I'll need to make a few phone calls first."

"And who do you plan— Oh, no. Oh, hell no. Please tell me you're not calling him."

I couldn't help but smile. Kelly hated Oscar with a passion. It might have something to do with the fact that Oscar used to belong to the organization. At least until he found out his handler, Knight, had been accepting cash for the jobs Oscar was doing for the agency. We don't fight for money; we do it to keep people safe. When Oscar found out that the man in charge of him was dirty, he did what a true patriot would have done.

He killed him.

He stalked Knight, then when he got him alone, put a bullet into his brain. Afterward, he went through his computer and made copies of all the data he found there. The mission he'd sent Oscar on had netted a side benefit. He had found himself a...whatever the hell Max was.

The friendship we shared was...unique. The two of us couldn't be more different. While we were both killers, Oscar killed because he enjoyed it. His conscience wouldn't allow him to take an innocent life—if he could avoid it—but he would do whatever he needed to get the job done. So there wasn't any love lost between Rook, Kelly, and Oscar.

But right now, he was the only person I could trust to protect Sammy. While Rook may have confidence in his team—and I did, too, to a point—I didn't know them well enough to determine if they would be willing to sacrifice themselves in order to save my people. Oscar would do whatever it took—and more.

"It has to be done, and I think you know that."

"There has to be someone else. Anyone else. I know you need to use people you can trust on this, but why does it have to be Oscar?"

"Because Oscar would be willing to die to make sure his mission succeeds. These other guys probably would, but I can't know. And where the two of you are concerned, I have to be certain."

Kelly sighed, a deep mournful whimper. "Just remember to tell that psycho that not all of us are bad guys, okay?"

I laughed. Kelly may be a great person, but he could hold a grudge. "You need to let this go. You never had an issue with him until he killed Knight. And that bastard was dirty as hell. Rook even told us that if he'd known about it, he would have shot Knight."

"Fine, but I want my gun back."

"No, you're not having a gun here," Lilah shouted in the background. "You're in no condition to fight."

"Shut up, woman! I'm talking to Haven."

I chuckled and stretched out on the bed, propping my head up on the pillow. The two of them so needed to admit their feelings for one another. Maybe getting laid would help make Kelly less irritable. Though more likely he'd be so smug, I'd have to kill him to save my sanity.

"Lilah's coming to take the phone," he said. "I don't think I can stop her. I'm tired, Haven. Just...so tired."

"I know, old man. We all are. When this is over, what do you say to the four of us taking a vacation?"

"Four?"

"You, me, Sammy, and your girlfriend."

"Fuck you! She is not my girlfriend."

"Please. I bet you like her more than chocolate milk."

He grumbled. "I never should have told you that story. Lilah isn't my girlfriend. She's..."

"I'm what?" came a decidedly disgusted voice on the other end of the line.

"Gotta go," Kelly said, hanging up.

I put the phone on top of my pillow, closed my eyes, and attempted to calm my thoughts. Having this bastard know where I was, realizing he'd been following me, and I hadn't known? That scared the crap out of me. I needed to know who the hell he was. More importantly, I needed to find out his connection to Rook and me. He said Rook had taken something from him, so it seemed logical that the two of them had a history of some sort. But there were big gaps that I needed filled.

I jerked upright. I couldn't sleep. Not when I had work that needed to be done. The first thing would be a call to an old friend.

I smiled when Oscar picked up the phone and growled his standard greeting whenever the two of us spoke. "What's up, bitch?"

"I don't have time for pleasantries, O. I need you."

He chuckled. It was dark, but for Oscar that was par for the course. The man was a giant. As badass as I thought I looked, he made me feel petite. He stood six foot six and was built like a small tank. He had no neck to speak of, just a head atop a mass of muscle. In a fight between us, I think I could probably take him, but it would be close.

"Finally gonna give up that fine ass, huh?"

"Sorry, bud. Someone's already tapping it."

His eyes probably bugged out when he said, "You're shitting me."

"Nope. We've been together since that mess with Valerie."

"Yeah, sorry I missed that one. I was out of the country dealing with some not so nice people who were trying to ship cocaine into the country. When I got back, I found out about it. Wish I could have been there."

So did I. If he had, things might not have gone to shit. I might not have… I reined in that line of thinking. Dwelling in the past was useless and would distract me from my main objective: Keeping Sammy, Kelly, and Lilah safe.

I turned my thoughts back to my friend. Oscar amazed me. He was the only former agent I knew of who still had resources that kept him apprised of what was going on. He shouldn't have known about Valerie, but I wasn't stupid enough to think it wouldn't have gotten back to him.

I heard a groan in the background that definitely didn't sound like someone was having fun. "Catch you at a bad time?"

"Just finishing up a job. I was gonna take a little longer, but I'd rather talk to you. Gimme a sec."

A moment later, I heard the sound of a knife slicing through flesh, the gurgle of blood, and what I figured was a body hitting the ground.

"Okay, all done," he said cheerily. "So, what's up? And why the hell didn't I know about this mystery man of yours?"

"Sammy is... Well, it's complicated."

"The best ones always are," he reminded me.

"How is Max?"

"Doing great. He's still painting, and he's incredible. We're trying to get him into a gallery to do a showing, but he's being...resistant."

I snorted. "He's being a pain in the ass?"

"Yeah, that." Oscar was quiet for a minute. "So, tell me about this man you got. I need details."

It seemed weird, me sitting in a BDSM club, talking to a man who'd just finished killing another person. But that was our lives. I went through the story of how Sammy and I had gotten together, how I'd found I needed Sammy to be my rudder. Oscar didn't laugh or make any snide comments. When I finished telling him Sammy and I had been married for a little over a year now, he whistled.

"Man, you don't do things by half. Bad enough you're letting him dick you, but being married on top of it?" He gave a sharp whistle.

Guilt assailed me. I hadn't invited anyone to the wedding, but probably should have tried to find Oscar. Then again, knowing his penchant for inappropriate comments, it was probably best he hadn't come. "You never know, bud. One day, you might look at Max and get down on one knee."

"Nah, that's Max's position, and it's right where I like him."

I laughed, because that was exactly the kind of crude reply I'd come to expect from my friend.

"Okay, so what's going on? I can't believe Haven needs my help."

"You're the only person I trust to take care of this one. Rook's got his men on it, but I don't know them personally. I need the best."

"Yeah, I remember those assignments. Back when I was Citadel, I loved doing the wet work. Sometimes I even kind of miss it."

"You know, you could come back," I reminded him. Oscar had been the one who pulled the deep undercover assassination gigs. Where I went directly after those who hurt the kids, he'd infiltrate the gangs, work his way up the chain of command until he found the leader who had them running drugs, trafficking in human slavery, and the like. Then he'd eliminate them.

126

"No, thanks. Y'all did some good shit, but I like the control. Plus, I like taking them out when and where I want, and if any of their crew get in the way? Such is life, right?"

I didn't tell him that I had that kind of autonomy. Most operatives didn't, and it would have galled him. After he killed Knight, the organization made him an offer: they'd forget all about what he'd done, but he had to turn over everything he'd taken and admit he was wrong. Oscar refused. They weren't happy; he didn't care. He had enough things from Knight's computer to implicate a lot of people. He was the reason for the massive shakeup almost ten years ago, where handlers and their charges were purposely kept separated. Not that the powers that be didn't appreciate him taking Knight out, but they weren't overly thrilled with his activities after.

"Okay, I get it. I need your help, though."

"It'll cost you," he said, his tone flat.

After he'd left, Oscar had become a mercenary, selling his skills to the highest bidders. Involved in a business dispute? Pay the man and he'd make sure your problem didn't see the light of day. Got a gang war on your hands? If you could afford his help, he'd take care of the situation. Just don't expect to give the man orders, because he did things his own way.

"Still not touching my ass. Sammy would have my balls."

He barked out a laugh. "What do you need, man?"

I sat at the edge of the bed. Oscar had no love for the agency, but at one time, we'd been close. I worked one operation with him, and the man was a killing machine. He was one of those 'kill them all and let God sort them out' people, even if he didn't believe in a higher power. Still, he was on the side of the angels. Okay, they were really dark angels, but he was on their side.

"Someone has killed several agents, murdered them. Even a few innocents. Now he's after my family."

"Family? I thought they were dead?"

"Sammy and Kelly."

He laughed. "How the hell is Kelly? Fucker doesn't call, doesn't write."

"He nearly got skinned alive by the son of a bitch I'm after," I informed him.

Oscar growled. "Is he okay?"

Kelly didn't like Oscar. He thought the man was too bloodthirsty, too violent. But Oscar? He cared about Kelly, just like Sammy and I did. You hurt Kelly, and it was more than likely no one could hold Oscar back.

"He's on the mend, but he got hurt pretty badly."

"Please tell me you don't want him caught."

"Caught? No. I want him dead. But I don't want it quick and painless. I want him to suffer for what he did to Kelly."

"Yeah," he replied, his voice dark. "I can work with that."

I gave him what details I had. I told him I would find out where Sammy and Kelly were sequestered and give him a call back. Rook would probably be pissed, but I didn't care. I would do whatever I had to in order to protect my family.

I got dressed slowly, playing the conversation through my head. I figured there would be some resistance. As expected, my boss was less than thrilled.

"No," he growled.

"Yes," I stated as calmly as I could. I could hear the ice in his voice. There was no love lost between him and Oscar . Killing your handler, even if he was dirty, was probably a bad thing. Rook certainly seemed to think so. But I thought it was cute that he figured he would change my mind.

"The man is unhinged, and you know that."

"He's not. He just enjoys his job a little too much."

I was understating the case. In the one mission I ran with Oscar, I saw exactly how vicious he could be. We'd needed information on a target that had gone to ground. We found this one slimeball—a guy named Daryl—who worked for our target. Oscar grabbed the bastard by the hair and yanked him down until he was kneeling on the floor. Oscar took out what he called his pig sticker. He told Daryl he would give him one last chance, but before he could even reply, Oscar's blade hit home, embedded in one of Daryl's blue eyes. Then Oscar twisted it. Daryl screamed long and loud. But Oscar got the information. Afterward, he killed Daryl and left his body out in the open where it would be found. When I questioned it, he shrugged and asked if I had a problem. It cemented our friendship. After we finished our mission, we went out for drinks and talked most of the night. Oscar had more than earned my respect.

"Haven, you can't seriously trust him with Samuel and Kelly's lives."

"And yet, I do. I know Oscar. He may be a tad overzealous, but there is no one I trust more who will give their life to protect their client."

Rook sighed. "That's another thing. The man is a mercenary. He does this for money, not because it's the right thing to do."

"I do it for money," I reminded him. I tapped my fingers on the tabletop. It was only a matter of time before Rook gave in, but right now, I wasn't a patient man.

"Bullshit!" Rook roared. "You offered to take down Valerie for free, if I recall correctly. You do it for the kids first. That has always been your priority."

And it was. I would never turn down a job where a kid's life was in danger. I had enough money to last us the rest of our lives, so Rook was right. I didn't do it for the money. Didn't mean I'd turn it down.

"He's a bodyguard," I reminded Rook as calmly as I could.

"A mercenary!" Rook shouted. "If someone gave him more money to give up Samuel and Kelly, don't think for a minute he wouldn't take it."

Now Rook was being stupid. Oscar was, without a doubt, one of the most honorable men— Okay, honorable might be a strong word. But he had a work ethic like no one else. Besides, it would be bad for business if he turned his back on a client.

"Are you even listening to yourself?" I demanded. My patience had come to an end. While I knew Rook had nothing but respect and concern for Sammy and Kelly, he had to understand that I did, too. Arguing would do us no good. I took a deep breath to calm myself, and then made my point as clear as I could.

"Oscar is going to be coming. There will be no arguments on this. You trust your people. I trust Oscar. You can think what you want, say whatever you have to say, but at the end of the day, he's the one I'm going to entrust my family to. Our friend has been following me, and—"

"Wait. What? How do you know this?"

"Because he called me. He told me exactly where I was. And there's more. Are you sitting down?"

"Yes," he ground out.

I allowed my head to drop back as I scrubbed a hand through my hair. The very fact this man was after Rook set my teeth on edge. Knowing I had to be the one to tell him made it all the worse.

"We know who he's after, and no, it's not me."

"Then who? Samuel? Is this something left over from Valerie?"

Having to admit I didn't have all the facts galled me. I scuffed at the floor with the toe of my shoe.

"He's after you. He told Kelly you took something from him, and he means to get revenge for it."

If I thought Rook was going to be pissed off, I apparently didn't know him as well as I thought.

"Fine. Then let's give him a target. If the only way to keep my team safe is by drawing him out, then that's what we'll do."

My anger at the situation, at the fact that the man knew so much about me that he'd stalked me had finally reached critical mass.

"No, you will do absolutely nothing, do you understand me? I will be the one to draw this man out. If he wants to find you, I'm his best bet. And I don't think it's just you he's after anymore."

Rook sighed. "You know, if you had told me all this beforehand, I would have said to bring Oscar in. I don't like it, and I don't like him, but I'd rather not let my prejudice get in the way of you taking this son of a bitch off the map once and for all."

That surprised me, I had to admit. As far as I was aware, there were few things in life that Rook hated more than Oscar. Well, he did mention Brussels sprouts once.

"I need you to call him for me. Our unsub is watching me, and I won't have him finding out where they're at. Tell him I'll pay whatever fee he needs, but his job—his only job—is to protect Sammy, Kelly, and Lilah. Pull the men you've got watching them, and bring them in to guard you."

"But no one knows—"

"I understand that, but this game has changed. Don't tell them who you are. Don't even let them see you if you can avoid it. But get them there. There won't be any arguing over this, Rook. No one else dies, do you understand me?"

"No. You'll keep the men I have there as backup. Oscar hates to fail, but if he does, I need to ensure everyone is safe. There's no arguing about this. If necessary, I will bring in other agents to guard me."

"It's necessary. Do it."

I didn't even give him a chance to answer before I hung up.

CHAPTER FOURTEEN

"Are you sure this is wise, bro?" the mountain sitting next to me asked.

"Yeah, I'm certain. He's watching me, and I need him to understand that I'm not alone. I'm going to drop you off at a hotel. Rook's already given you the details, am I correct?"

"Yeah, he—"

I held up a hand. "Don't tell me. I can't know for sure what this asshole's got going on, and I would rather not risk any sensitive information getting to him, if you know what I mean."

In truth, one of the scenarios I entertained was setting a trap for our unsub by having Rook put Oscar in a place where I could be waiting so that the two of us could take him out, but common sense prevailed in that idea. The man wasn't stupid—he'd proven the opposite many times—and I wouldn't risk tipping him off. If he wanted me, he'd have to go where I was heading, and that would keep him away from here.

"I'm ready to wire the money into your private account. Rook said you wouldn't tell him how much, so I need to know. I want to take care of it before I leave on my mission."

Oscar shifted in his seat and leveled his gaze on me. "You're still a special kind of stupid, aren't you?"

I blinked. "Still?"

"You've always been too good-hearted for this work. You were a Marine. You know you go in, take out the target, then go have a beer. You're not supposed to let these things get to you."

"PTSD is real, you know," I snarled defensively.

"Hell, I know that. When we were in the Corps, it was part of our daily lives. Even though we were Marines, we were still human beings. That kind of shit can easily fuck you up. Even the strongest of people can't stay strong all the time."

"So what's the difference?"

He grinned at me. "We signed up for this, bud. This is who we are. When we were in the military, we pointed at what they said to shoot, and that was our job. Here in the real world, we had the option to walk away. We didn't."

He wasn't wrong. I could have walked away a long time ago. Probably should have. But the mission was too important to me.

"So you're saying I'm weak?"

"You? Fuck no. You're one of the strongest sunnabitches I know. But you have a heart. That's your downfall. Me? Gave it up years ago. Useless organ."

It dawned on me he was trying to mess with my head.

"So why am I a special kind of stupid? I need everything taken care of in case— Well, just so Sammy won't have to worry about it."

His stare actually unnerved me. I hated things that did that. And the bastard knew it, too, because he kept staring. I tightened my grip around the steering wheel, focusing on the leather digging into my palms.

"If I needed you to come take care of...you know...would you come?"

He meant Max. I've never been clear on their relationship, other than to know Oscar had brought Max home with him after the assignment that ended up with Knight being killed. Years later, Max was still with him. For being a hardass, which Oscar always claimed, he had a definite soft spot where Max was concerned.

"Without hesitation," I told him. Oscar was one of the few people I could actually call a friend instead of an acquaintance. We didn't talk much, but that was more the nature of our jobs than anything else.

"So why the hell do you think I'd charge you to protect what's yours? I'm an arrogant prick, and I cop to it, but I'm not that kind of asshole."

"It's your job, O. I get that, and I'm willing to pay your fees."

He reached out and smacked me in the back of the head hard enough to make it snap forward.

"Don't hit the driver," I grumbled, rubbing at the spot he'd just thumped.

"Then tell the driver to stop being an idiot. I came for you because you're my friend. If I had a family, you'd be in it. If someone came after Max, I'd go in both guns blazing, and I would hope yours would be there, too."

"Anytime," I promised.

"Then shut up and let's work on nailing this fucker." He paused for a moment, then turned to look out the window. "Haven?"

"Yessir?"

"I appreciate you calling me." He faced me again, his eyes hard. "And don't you dare make a big deal about that, or hitting the driver will be the least of your concerns."

I laughed, then flinched away from Oscar's hand as he lashed out and connected with the headrest. We drove for a while in relative silence, which was only broken when Oscar complained about the heat.

"Seriously? In July, we hit near one twenty. This is almost sweater weather now."

Oscar glared at me. "Ugh. Couldn't stand it. Give me somewhere cool, like Oregon."

"Where it rains like eight hundred days a year?" I scrunched my nose.

"I'd rather have rain than have my balls sweating every time I walk out the door."

I shook my head. "They do make this thing called air conditioning, you know."

"Yeah, that'll go over good. I can hear it now. Max, I want to move to somewhere with god-awful heat, so you can hear me whine about needing air conditioning."

"So, you told him yet?"

He narrowed his gaze at me. "Told who what?"

"Max. You told him you love him?"

"I don't love Max," he replied, his voice cold.

"Sure you don't. Because everyone has a person they don't love living with them, sleeping in their bed… Why can't you admit it?"

Yeah, I was pushing my luck. It had taken Kelly to get through to me about Sammy, plus what happened with a target that I beat to death with a crowbar. Sammy stepped up and showed me how much I needed him.

"Max and I, we have some good times. He puts out when I need him to, takes care of the house, feeds me. Not all of us have Kelly."

"If I recall correctly, you lost more than one majordomo with your attitude."

"Oh, fuck you!" he roared. "Kelly would have been damn lucky to have worked for me. I'm fucking pleasant compared to you."

I grinned at him. "Yeah, I can see that."

He slumped into his seat and crossed his beefy arms, looking surprisingly like a giant toddler. "You know, sometimes I wonder why I don't just shoot you and put you out of my misery."

I couldn't help but laugh. "Because you know you'd be dead before you got your weapon drawn."

"Never know. Maybe one day we'll test that theory. I have to admit, I would like to know which one of us is better."

The man had come all the way out here to help me. The least I could do was toss him a bone. "In weapons, I have you beat. In hand to hand combat, I think it would be close, but in the end, you'd likely kick my ass."

He snorted. "I can plug the target from two hundred meters, dead between his eyes."

I felt a flush of pride when I answered him. "Sammy can do the same thing. Well, okay, he can hit the bullseye on paper targets at least ninety-five percent of the time."

"Get out!"

"Seriously. We rent the range and go at least once a week. He's good and getting better."

"You thinking about getting him into the organization?"

I told Oscar about our confrontation with the would-be carjacker, how Sammy handled that, and how he didn't panic at all when we found Kelly. "But that's not the life I want for him. He lost it all, and now he needs to find a path for himself."

"What if he decides his path leads him to Rook?"

My stomach knotted at the thought. "He shot his mother. Blew half her face off."

Oscar grunted. "Doesn't sound like a very good shot to me."

"He did it because he didn't want me to pity him when she died."

Oscar made a noise in the back of his throat. "Did you tell him we don't do pity?"

Not able to look him in the eye, I turned away.

"Fuck. You're shitting me. Have you considered maybe this life isn't for you anymore?"

"More than once," I assured him, turning my gaze back to the road.

Oscar rapped on the window. "And?"

It took a few moments for me to choose my words. What I was about to say would be important. "Sammy and I agree that for us, the mission isn't done until I can't do it. There are too many people counting on me for me to walk away."

Oscar cleared his throat. "Sounds like you got a smart one," he said.

I could hear the admiration in his voice. "You'll like him," I assured Oscar. "But…"

"There's always a but, isn't there?"

"I know that you're here to keep him safe, but you have to realize that includes keeping yourself from throttling him."

"Yeah, leave it to you to get yourself one of those." Oscar snorted. "I guess if you're giving your ass up to him, he's got to be either one hell of a lay, or a lot more intense than you are."

"Well, not to be modest, but yeah, he is. A little of both, actually."

"Shit, man. I wish I had known before. I would have slammed you into the mattress so hard you wouldn't have walked for days. You do have a really nice ass. It would have been one great fuck."

"It never could have worked out between us," I assured him. "When we were on the mission together, I was… I was still in control. I started falling apart after that. Sammy is the one who holds me together."

Oscar nodded. "Yeah, it's probably just as well. If I had done you, I would have ruined you for any other man."

Oscar wasn't kidding—or modest. After our single mission together, we'd changed into different clothes, leaving our gear behind for the crew to clean up. There was only so much blood you could get out of fabric, after all. Oscar looked like a mountain and was hung like a bull. His cock was long, thick, and uncircumcised—not that I'd looked, mind you. But it suited the man to perfection. If Oscar's performance in bed was even a tenth as good as he claimed, he'd left behind a trail not only of broken hearts but probably more than a few broken asses as well.

"Yeah, thank you for your concern for me and the well-being of my ass."

He laughed. I laughed. God, I missed him.

We stopped in a restaurant to grab some food. My appetite wasn't up to par, so I settled for some juice and toast. Oscar had devoured a plate heaped with pancakes, bacon, sausage, an omelet, four slices of toast, juice, and coffee. When he'd caught me staring, he grinned.

"Problem?"

"You eat like that every meal?"

He laughed. "Naw, man. I'm on a diet. This is my midday snack."

"That's disgusting," I griped. I ate big meals, but what Oscar had on his plate would probably feed a family of four. It made sense, though. A man his size probably burned a lot of calories, even sitting still.

I checked my watch, then turned back to Oscar. "We'll be leaving shortly, and it's another hour until we get to where we're headed."

Oscar nodded, stood, and stretched, then went to hit the head. I used my time and called Rook. I let him know that I'd be going straight to the airport after I dropped Oscar off. He complained, but knew he wouldn't change my mind. He patched me through to Sammy using his technobabble to ensure the calls remained encrypted. Suffice it to say, Sammy wasn't thrilled to hear my voice after I said my piece.

"Listen to me," I growled, trying to keep my voice low so others around me wouldn't hear. "Oscar is going to be watching over you. There will be no argument on this."

"And you listen to me," Sammy snapped. "I am perfectly capable of taking care of this. I've got my gun, we have guards, and—"

"Which part of no argument are you not listening to?" I shouted, then flinched as people turned their gazes toward me. I softened my voice. "I know you've practiced, and I am so proud of what you accomplished. But this man is a killer. He took down Kelly, and that alone proves he's dangerous. So, this is what's going to happen. Oscar is going to come to you, he will be inside the house, the others will stand watch outside. You will do exactly as he says."

Sammy huffed. "You know what? Fuck you. Fuck him."

God, I loved this man. He was the only person who could get away with talking to me like that. I was glad I'd warned Oscar, because he might not be as understanding about the mouth on Sammy and it could lead to friction between them.

"Sammy…"

"Yeah, I know. I'll do what he says. Doesn't mean I have to like it, though. And this will be coming out of your ass in the near future. I'm thinking that cock cage might need to become a more permanent addition to your wardrobe."

My skin pebbled with excitement, but my boys tried to crawl back up inside my body in fear at Sammy's tone. The little bastard probably had a mile-wide smug fucking grin on his face.

"I need one more thing from you. Oscar is a good man, but he's kind of scary. Be nice to him, please. He's doing this as a favor to us. Even though Kelly doesn't care for Oscar, the man loves the hell out of the grumpy old man."

"Yeah, don't let Kelly fool you. He told me about Oscar, and he respects his talent. He's leery about him, but he trusts him. He's just got to be contrary."

Kelly actually liked Oscar? Hell, that was news to me.

"I need you to take care of them both for me, as well as taking care of you."

Sammy's voice softened. "Michael, you don't need to placate me."

"Just a sec, okay?" I got up, tossed a hundred on the table, then walked outside. Once there were no other people around, I replied. "I'm not trying to soothe your nerves. To be honest, I'd rather have you pissed at me and alive, then happy with me and dead."

"I hate this."

"I know. I do, too. I found out he's been following me. He knew when I stopped at Columns and—"

"Excuse me?" Sammy's voice was like ice. "You went to a BDSM club?"

I'd never kept my past a secret from him. He knew I had been a member of the club before we met. "With a fucking cock cage around my dick!" I snapped. Then I realized that there was an older couple walking toward the restaurant. Her face flushed, and he looked like he wanted to slap me. "Sorry," I mumbled. She sniffed, and he pulled her away.

Sammy laughed. "Who was that?"

"Some couple. They were like ninety! I hope you're happy."

"Deliriously. Can't wait to tell Kelly." He was quiet for a moment. "I miss you. When are you coming home?"

My heart broke at the sadness in his tone. I'd never worried before when someone had to be put into a safe house, because they hadn't meant anything to me beyond a job I had to get done. But Sammy and Kelly were different. I didn't like being away from my family.

"I'm going to be home as soon as I can," I promised. "I asked Rook to send me on a mission, because I need to draw this bastard away from you. I'm hoping that I'll find him and be able to stop him before anyone else gets hurt. Once I'm done, we'll go to Hawaii and, if you want, we won't come back."

"Seriously?"

It had been a niggling thought in the back of my mind, but now that I'd said it out loud, and the whole thing was laid out in front of me?

"Yeah, I want us to do it. Anywhere in the world you want to live."

He chuckled. Definitely not the reaction I'd expected.

"We both know that you won't walk away. And I'm okay with that. The world owns Haven. I own Michael."

My heart swelled. I was about to reply, to tell him that I loved him, when a heavy hand landed on my back and almost knocked me down.

"Shit, man. You really are out of practice if I can sneak up on you."

I glared at Oscar, who stood there grinning like a loon. I held out the phone. "This is Sammy. Say hello."

Oscar took the phone from my hand, put it to his ear, and said, "Hey, Sammy! The name's Oscar. Piss me off, and I'll shoot you." Then he handed it back to me.

"Really?" I groused.

He shrugged. "Not here to make him happy. Best he knows where we stand right now, so there isn't going to be any confusion in the future."

When I put the phone back to my ear, Sammy was rolling with laughter. I had a very bad feeling about this.

"Sammy?"

He calmed down. "You know that I'm going to needle him every chance I get, right?"

Yep. Bad feeling.

I dropped Oscar off at the hotel. I did a cursory examination outside, while he went in and checked out the hotel and his room. Not that it made much difference. As soon as I was gone, Rook would have someone pick him up to take him to the safe house.

Neither of us found anything, but that didn't make the doubts go away. Sure, I'd done my best to watch the roads, and hadn't seen anyone following, but then again, I hadn't noticed the unsub hanging around Columns, either.

Oscar came back outside, his gaze scanning the nearby people. He strolled over to the car, bent over, and stuck his head in the window. "Room is clean. No one in the lobby seemed overly concerned with my presence."

"I don't see anything out here either."

"So, not to add any more to your plate, but…" He ran a hand over the back of what little neck he had. "Well, if you were followed last week, what makes you think he won't decide I'm a better target? Maybe I could lead him to someone he could use as leverage to get what he wants."

Yeah, the thought had occurred to me. Constantly. There were too many variables here that none of us had any control over.

"I think he's too single-minded to be distracted now. He shouldn't know who you are, so I'll be his main focus."

"And if you're wrong?"

"Then you'd better be as good as you claim." My stomach churned. "I'm trusting them to you, O. You've got my number if—"

He waved a hand. "Yes, Mom. And the number of the fire department, emergency squad, poison control, and another babysitter in case I get sick."

I was out of the car and on him in seconds. I shoved him up against the wall, the impact not even making him grunt. "Listen to me, you son of a bitch, this is their lives I'm putting in your hands. Don't fucking joke or dick around."

He stood there and stared at my hands on his jacket.

"So you know," he rumbled, "I consider us friends. It's the only thing that's keeping me from putting you through this wall. Unless you're going to suck my dick, you don't touch me. Ever. Do I make myself perfectly clear?"

His tone would have made most people wet themselves. I wasn't most people.

I released my hold on him and stepped back. "If you can't take this seriously, then say so. I'll go take care of them myself."

Oscar's expression softened. Which only meant the anger wasn't nearly as pronounced. "Bro, you know I'm going to do my job. I get you're worried about them, but I promise, I will never let you down. Now, get going. You've got some pervert's ass to kick."

Part of me wished I hadn't agreed to go on the assignment, but Sammy would have a fit if I didn't protect these kids from Elijah. I gave a sharp nod, turned, and took two steps before Oscar called out to me. I spun around and noted the expression on his face: equal parts anger and sadness.

"I swear I'll take care of them. I'll die before I let anything happen to them."

"I know," I replied. "But don't let it come to that."

While Oscar strode back into the hotel, I called Rook to let him know I was on my way to catch the flight.

"I'm ready. Time for Elijah and me to meet face-to-face."

With those words, I was off to send a man to his death.

CHAPTER FIFTEEN

Leaving Arizona sucked, but I couldn't think of a better way to draw the guy away from Sammy and Kelly. We still had no idea who he was, beyond the fact he could fight well enough to take down the old man. And having sparred with Kelly, I knew that wasn't as easy as it should have been.

I arrived on Sunday and quickly found a place for my surveillance. For four painstakingly long days, I watched Elijah Jameson. The phrase "watching paint dry would be more fun" sure as hell fit this neighborhood. Or maybe it wasn't that I was bored as much as I wasn't focused. Surveillance was never fun, but it was a necessary evil in my job. This time I found myself distracted more than once, my attention being divided between checking my surroundings to see if I noticed anyone who didn't belong and wanting to call Sammy or check in with Oscar. Each time I forced myself back to the task at hand. I couldn't understand what the issue was. Oscar was with Sammy and Kelly, as were several agents, and I knew they were safe, but... fuck, they were *my* responsibility. And even though I had the best of intentions, it felt wrong to entrust them to someone else.

I needed to get this job done and get home. Where I belonged.

Elijah lived in a nondescript house in a nondescript suburb. His place sat wedged in-between two similar-looking properties. All had white plastic fencing that mimicked woodgrain, but seemed rather flimsy. Each plot had a flowerbed with the same types of flowers—not that I knew what they were—and a cutesy little door knocker in the shape of an angel.

The neighbors on both sides worked during the day. Mr. And Mrs. Morrison worked at the bank. He was a loan officer; she was a personal teller. Mr. Kramer worked as a supervisor at a place that made boxes. His wife had a job teaching high school. One couple left at a little after six and the other not until eight. Neither had children, so the houses sat empty until the owners returned home. Neither of them seemed overly friendly with my target, and them being gone gave me ample opportunity to keep an eye on him. At least when I wasn't distracted by other things.

Good old Elijah? He didn't work. The information we had said he received disability from an injury at his old job, and that medically, he could not do the work required of him. It was unfortunate that they hadn't followed-up, because I saw the man doing a lot of things that would not be sanctioned by his doctor. I decided to add ripping off the taxpayers as another of his sins. I didn't mind paying for people who really needed help, because despite what Congress said, everyone needs a hand now and again. Those who leech off the system though? That pissed me off.

What surprised me the most was something I found out via one of the listening devices I'd planted while Elijah had gone to his therapy. One of the couples in the cul-de-sac had a five-year-old boy, Josh, who they allowed Elijah to babysit on Thursday and Friday when they had to work late. The thought of the cute towheaded boy with a face full of freckles being alone with that animal made my blood boil. Fortunately, I'd watched long enough and learned what I needed to know. It was time to move.

Of course, the best laid plans and all that. Something went wrong. Wednesday morning Josh wasn't feeling well, so he couldn't do his half-day of kindergarten. Naturally, Elijah said he would be delighted to help out, telling them he had no problem skipping his appointment. Patsy and Liam McDonald were beside themselves with gratitude. Me? Absolutely livid. No way could I allow Josh to be in that house with Elijah.

I'd begun to stow my gear, when I heard a voice I was certain I recognized. It was muffled, so I couldn't be certain, but either way, it wasn't Elijah's, and sure wasn't Josh. I hadn't seen anyone else enter the house, but chills ran down my spine. Everything I had worked out became inconsequential. I needed to get there right away.

After sending a text to Rook, letting him know of the change in my plan, I worked my way toward Elijah's house. At least his neighbors had left on time, so that worked in my favor. The easiest access point was the back of the house, which led to a large yard that had a small fenced-in swimming pool. I made my way to the back door, determined to get Josh out of the house. Right now, everything else was inconsequential.

The lock on the sliding door opened without more than a flick of the wrist. As soon as I stepped inside, my senses were on high alert. The house had an almost unnatural silence to it. If Josh had a cold, he could be sleeping, but this whole situation felt off. I knew someone else had somehow gotten inside, so where were they? Had I been so distracted I'd missed him? Fuck me if I put Josh in more danger than Elijah.

When I came around the corner that led to the living room, I was stopped dead by the sight before me.

A man, dressed in a dark blue hoodie with white trim, had Elijah on his knees, a Luger pressed to his temple. He also held Josh in his other arm, and talked to him as though they were playing a game. When he saw me, he sneered.

"So, you're the great Haven. I don't really understand what he saw in you. To hear him tell, you're larger than life and twice as lethal."

I stepped forward, and he pressed the barrel of the gun harder into Elijah's head, causing the skin to pucker and the man to wet himself.

"You really don't want to do that. We wouldn't want this little one to get hurt, would we?" he crooned as he bounced Josh a few times.

"Who are you?" I demanded as I pulled up short. "No, wait. That's not important. Put the boy down, then we can talk about what you want."

He laughed, but it seemed hollow. "I've got what I want. You're here, I'm here, and this sick fucker is with us." He gestured toward Elijah. "I take it he's important to you?"

"Please," Elijah begged. "Help me."

It wasn't difficult to ignore Elijah. He was already going to be dead. "No, he isn't. The boy is, however."

"Ooh, now that presents a problem. You see, I thought this piece of crap was the reason you'd come. While you've been watching him, I've been keeping an eye on you. You need to pay better attention. I've been following you since you got on the plane. Not sure why you don't fly first class. I mean, you make enough money and all."

He'd been on the plane with me, and I hadn't seen him. Fuck, that pissed me off. My fingers clenched, the nails digging into my palms.

"As for your target, you should have seen what he was watching before you got here. It made my skin crawl to see what he did to this kid when he was younger, especially the part where he had videotaped it. When I got in here, the boy was in his lap, watching himself be raped." He sneered at me. "How many times do you think it happened? Really, you wasted a whole lot of time outside watching, when you should have been in here dealing with him. Well, if he's not important, then we can dispense with him."

He pulled the trigger and Elijah's body spasmed as blood and bone were blown into a Rorschach pattern on the wall. Elijah's face was gone. Nothing but a pulpy mess remained. Whatever bullets he was using, they weren't standard issue.

Josh screamed, shut his eyes tight, and covered his ears at the same time I launched myself at the man who'd just killed someone in front of a kid. I grabbed the boy, then shoved the sick son of a bitch back.

My main priority had to be Josh. He needed to be away from the house where he'd be safe. I turned for the door and ran as fast as I could. Unfortunately, I couldn't outrun a bullet. The first one hit me square in the back, almost knocking me to the ground. If it hadn't been for my vest, I'd have joined Elijah in the smear of the month club. The next three bullets came in quick succession, each in close proximity to the others, but not overlapping. They ripped the graphene to shreds and drove me to my knees at the door. I opened it and told Josh to run. It didn't matter where. He just needed to be away from the house. As much as I hated to admit it, I could only hope the cops showed up. Blood ran down my back, the pain unbearable.

"Leave him be," I snapped.

"Oh, he's free to go," my opponent said blithely. "If I'd wanted him dead, he would have been first. And after what your friend did, it might have been a mercy to kill him."

Still kneeling by the door, I tried to draw my gun so that I could protect Josh as he ran, but the man was on top of me before I could. This time, though his face was shadowed, I could see more detail. My age, dark hair— the hood making it impossible to tell for certain if it was brown or black— and lifeless blue eyes. I did my best to lunge for the man, but he shoved me and I stumbled. The ache in my back hadn't cleared yet, and my reflexes were shot to shit. Even breathing sucked.

145

"How do you like those bullets?" he asked, knocking me to the ground and pressing his knee to my chest as he glared down at me. "My own design. Capable of tearing through your protection or," he waved his gun toward Elijah, "ripping through flesh and bone like pudding. Bet I could make a mint selling them online. Cops wouldn't have a chance against these, as you just found out."

He reached out with the barrel of the gun and tapped it to my cheek. No doubt about it, this fucker had gone around the bend and wouldn't be coming back.

"You see, Haven... May I call you Haven? Your boss took something very precious from me. I've been searching nearly two years for a way to get back at him. At first, I thought killing him would make it better, but the bastard is nearly impossible to track down. And don't even get me started on the people he's got around him. Not one of those bastards would give him up."

"I won't either," I wheezed.

"No, I suppose not," he said, sounding bored. "That's okay, though. My plans are flexible. When I found you were connected to him—and don't think your man gave you up, because the stubborn bastard wouldn't tell me anything. It took some guesswork on my part, plus putting one and one together—I realized it worked perfectly for me. I would kill you, which would show that I was better than you. Your eventual death will bring him out into the open. Then I can finish what he started."

"*He?* How do you know it's not *me* you're looking for?" I snapped. I needed to pull him off Rook's trail, and if it meant dying, so be it.

He frowned at me. "Please don't insult my intelligence. I know it isn't you because you're a grunt. I'm not stupid enough to think you'd be out in the field without someone directing you. I know each of the people I tried to...convince were pawns in the game, and I know you are, too. The person I want is the one pulling your strings. And as soon as he finds out what's going on, then we can end this."

"And how will he know?" I demanded.

"Oh, that's easy. I have my ace right here." He stood up and pulled out Kelly's phone. The only numbers on it were mine, Sammy's, and...oh, fuck.

146

He held the phone out for me to see as he dialed Rook's number. "This told me everything I needed to know."

"I was wondering when you'd call," Rook said, his voice showing no emotion at all.

"You don't seem surprised. Though I guess you wouldn't be. You didn't get where you are by being stupid."

"Thank you for the compliment."

The wail of sirens in the background caused my new friend to tense, his hand wrapped tightly around the gun.

"Not much time," I told him. "They'll be here in seconds."

Though I hated the thought of other people being his target, it took his focus off me for a moment. Fire seared my back where he'd shot me as I leapt up and put everything I had into a punch that knocked him down. Unfortunately, it was all I could muster at the moment. He was on his feet again, while I was puffing, trying to draw in oxygen.

He turned and smiled at me. "That was impressive. You shouldn't even be able to move yet." He scrubbed a hand over his jaw. "Believe me. I'm well aware they'll get here momentarily. But you're operating under a misconception," he said, keeping his tone flat and even.

"Oh?"

He gave me a smile that sent chills down my spine. It was one of those you saw on the face of someone who no longer had anything left to lose. "You see, this was, shall we say, a test run. I want you dead, but don't want to kill you just yet. I have the pieces on the board, right where they all need to be. I know where you live and who you love—including the new player you added to the game. I could kill them all, but if I do, it will be at a time and place of my choosing."

He paused for a moment, as if considering his next words.

"I didn't want to kill those others. If they'd given me what I wanted, none of them would have had to die. What is it about Rook that those people willingly accepted death rather than helping me? I really only wanted one person. But the thing is? You're part of the problem here. You were involved from the start, and now I have a chance to break you before I kill you. To show that you're not the man people think you are. In the end, you're going to beg to give me what I want. You're going to betray the ideals you claim to

147

hold. For the moment, I have all the advantages. Keep that in mind for the next time.

"As for you," he said into the phone. "Make your peace, because I'm close to finding you, and when I do, what I did to your agents will have been a mercy compared to what's in store for you."

He slid the phone back into his pocket, then sauntered over to me, drew an arm back and hit me upside the head with the butt of the gun. I could taste the blood in my mouth as the floor rushed up to meet me.

"Special Agent Devlin? Can you hear me?"

The voice seemed so far away, it was nearly impossible to focus on it. My head throbbed, and I could taste the coppery tang of blood in my mouth. I attempted to sit up, but strong hands held me in place.

"Whoa, cowboy. Slow your roll. You're bleeding and we're checking you over to see if any gunshots penetrated your vest."

The officer before me was young, probably fresh out of the academy. He carried himself with authority, though. He also seemed to be sharp, and as shitty as I felt, no way could I risk him latching onto something I said.

"Josh?" I said around a mouthful of goo.

"The kid is safe. We've called his parents, and they're coming to get him."

A sharp nod was a bad idea. My head throbbed, and my stomach roiled.

"Can you tell us what happened?" the cop asked.

He'd called me Devlin, which meant that Rook had already been at work spinning the story.

"Sorry, no can do." I struggled to stand, ignoring the EMT who tried to stop me. The cop, probably pissed that I wasn't being forthcoming, didn't offer any help. As I got to my feet, he grabbed my arm.

"We have a nearly headless body, a kid who is splattered with blood and screaming for his mother. And a government agent who we find facedown on the floor. You're going to give me something," he threatened.

It was cute. Really. Any other time, I might have played with him a little, but right now, I needed aspirin and someone to check out my back. Staying here wasn't an option, because there was too much of a chance someone would ask the wrong questions. I stole a glance at his name tag, then glared at him.

"Listen, Brooks… All you need to know is this man, one Elijah Jameson, was dealing in child pornography. You look at his computer, you're sure to find the images. We're going to have a team coming in very shortly, and at that time, all of you will be asked to leave."

I looked at him and could see the anger simmering. I understood it, and it wasn't his fault. Plus, his arrival may very well have saved my life.

"Brooks, this asshole was scum. His crime—which he's already paid for—was a federal offense. Let it go. Report back to your captain that we superseded your authority." I recalled what the unsub had said to me about seeing Elijah filming. "Trust me, you don't want to be involved in this shit. It's disgusting garbage, and once you get it on you, it won't ever come off. That little boy is going to have a rough time ahead of him. Do you really want people to see what happened to him?"

His nostrils flared, but his eyes bugged out. He shook his head and stepped away, his face pale. At that moment, Rook's team came through the door and began to wave their IDs as they shouted orders to clear the area. One of them pulled me out of the house and stuck me in the back of a waiting car, which whisked me away from the scene while they did their work.

The driver, a young man in his mid-twenties, said nothing as he drove me to a nearby motel. He helped me into the room, took my gun—over my protests—and placed it out of reach, before he stripped off my tattered vest, lay me across the bed, then left. A few moments later, an older woman came in. She grunted at me before she set to work, poking at the wounds on my back.

"You're very lucky," she said in a clipped, efficient tone.

"Really? Doesn't feel lucky."

She jammed a finger into my back, a sharp pain shooting up my spine.

"Be quiet."

"You went to charm school with Lilah, didn't you?"

Another poke into a tender spot convinced me that keeping quiet for a while might be in my best interest.

"You'll live," she finally said. She sprayed something cold as hell across my back, which had me drawing in a sharp breath and biting my lip to keep from cursing.

"Baby," she muttered, smearing the stuff around with her fingertips.

After she finished, she got on the phone. Her gaze flicked between the screen and me.

"How is he?"

Rook's voice.

"Multiple lacerations of the skin, there will be some very deep bruises. If the person who did this had grouped his shots better, we would be needing an undertaker, not a doctor."

"He didn't want me dead," I grunted.

She slapped a hand over my back, a loud crack in the quiet room. "I didn't say you could talk!"

I lurched up, my back screaming in agony. "Fuck, woman! Are you insane?" It was no wonder the driver moved my gun out of reach, otherwise me and this woman would be throwing down.

She grunted again, then focused on her phone. "I would say rest, but I'd be wasting my voice." She turned to me and arched her eyebrows. "As for you, get hit less and you'll probably live longer."

She stepped out of the room as I stood there sputtering. A moment later, my phone rang. I picked it up and hit the connect button. "I think I prefer Lilah," I said by way of greeting.

"Don't look at me. Lilah said she's the one I should send."

"Yeah, I'll be sure to thank her later."

"What can you tell me?" Rook asked, now all business.

"The bastard is definitely not in his right mind. He didn't seem to care if the kid lived or died as long as he got what he wanted. Then there's the fact the son of a bitch blew off Elijah's face while he was holding the boy. My main goal was to get the kid out of the house, so I didn't get a chance to fight the man, but he's a damn good shot. The pattern was laid down perfectly, ensuring my vest was shot to shit, and that I knew he could have killed me at any time."

Rook was quiet for several moments. "If your target is dead, then you should return to Arizona. We'll pay you for your time, of course."

"Seriously? I don't give a good goddamn about the money. That asshole could have killed the kid. He's unhinged."

"Yes, and how do you propose we stop him? Did you get a name? Maybe asked him nicely for some ID? We need something to go on, Haven."

His voice was calm, but I could hear the anger beneath it.

"Sorry," I muttered, even though I wasn't. "I can give you a partial description, but not much beyond that."

"You're not sorry at all," Rook said. "That's fine. I get it. I'm going to pull the airline records, see if we can get anything. I'll also request copies of their security footage. Maybe we'll get lucky."

Yeah, and maybe pigs would fly. The unsub was too put together to slip up on something this basic. "What about moving Sammy and Kelly? If the guy followed Oscar, he might get a bead on them." I wasn't thinking rationally. He'd been on the plane with me, so he couldn't have tracked Oscar. Still, I needed to be sure they were safe. And moving them, even if I was near certain he couldn't know, seemed to be my best bet.

"I've already arranged it. Your friend is…unhappy."

"My friend can kiss my ass. He signed up for this gig, so he'll do it and be happy about it."

God, I hoped to hell Oscar never heard I'd said that.

CHAPTER SIXTEEN

The entire flight back, I watched. I took note of everyone in my section: every man, woman, and snot-nosed brat. One smarmy businessman drooled over the cleavage of a sleeping woman, two twenty-somethings joined the mile-high rub club as they masturbated one another under a jacket spread over their laps, and the not-so-hard to spot Air Marshal sitting three rows back. Of all of them, though, the one who held my attention was the kid of about thirteen who, if he didn't stop kicking my seat, wouldn't live to see fourteen.

A few deep, calming breaths didn't help. I was too keyed up after the mission. I kept seeing Elijah, his face missing, in a bloody heap on the ground. I didn't care about that. What did bother me was Josh seeing those things. It wasn't as if he wouldn't have enough to deal with his considering his abuse—which would require a lot of therapy, something I knew Rook would ensure was handled. Still, Josh had been hurt by more than one person, and I'd failed him. That made my blood boil.

A hard thump on the back of my seat had me on my feet in moments. The obnoxious teen sat there, a fucking smirk on his face as though he was daring me to say something to him. I admit to a modicum of embarrassment that I'd let him get so far under my skin, but right now, my aggression was in need of a target, and I figured the young man wanted to volunteer.

I was okay with that.

A quick check showed his seat mates were sleeping, so I leaned in close and growled in his ear. "You know, you little fuck, I'm in a bad mood. I'm a cop and had a shitty day. I watched a man get his face blown off, and the blood and bone went everywhere. So if you think I'm going to put up with your shitty little attitude, you are so fucking wrong. Do it again, and see what happens to you."

As I stepped back, I was hit in the gut by a wave of regret. The boy's pockmarked cheeks had paled, and he looked as though he would be sick. I scrubbed a hand across my face before I leaned in again.

"Look, I'm sorry," I said quietly. "It's been a bad day, and I shouldn't be taking it out on you."

I sat back down and buckled my belt. A moment later, a face appeared from around the side of my seat.

"Did you really see that?" he asked, his voice filled with awe.

I nodded sharply.

"Cool," he replied.

I could see respect in his expression, and for some reason, that made everything worse.

"No, so not cool. It may look awesome in the horror movies and shit, but in real life, it so isn't. That was a living, breathing person." Of course, I left out the part where the pedophile was going to die anyway. "And now? He just…isn't. He won't see the sun come up tomorrow. If there's someone out there who loved him, they won't be able to hold him. Death isn't cool. It's messy, and painful, and…" My voice trailed off. I'd had these thoughts before, and it never led to anything good. "It's just not."

He nodded, but in truth, I still think he saw the whole thing as awesome. When he sat back, I breathed a sigh of relief. It was easy to think the things you saw on-screen or in games were something amazing. With the abundance of videos online, kids today became almost immune to images of violence and death. I prayed he'd never have to find out the awful truth.

Oddly, the thought of killing someone still didn't cause the guilt it had in the past. Yeah, I took lives, but as Sammy reminded me, I saved so many more. If what our unsub had said was true, Elijah had taken something from Josh that he would never get back. That innocence all children should have had been corrupted. Was I sorry that Elijah was dead? No. Was I upset that It hadn't been me who pulled the trigger? Yeah, kinda. I was supposed to be the kid's protector, and the fact I wasn't there for Josh was what hurt. Not Elijah's death.

I settled deeper into my seat. Now that I understood the core of my angst, it became a little easier to deal with. I mostly felt a little jealous that Oscar could go in, slit someone's throat, and feel not a shred of remorse. But I wasn't sure I could live with being that detached. Whatever. It was his life. Maybe Max gave him something that eased his burden. Or, maybe he really was just a heartless prick.

As the plane landed, a sense of relief rushed through me. I was home. Somewhere things made sense. Even without Sammy next to me, I still felt his presence, and not just because of the cage around my dick. As we disembarked the plane, my phone rang. I picked it up, saw Rook's number, and answered. "Haven's place. I stab 'em, you slab 'em."

Rook said nothing for a few moments, then I heard his breath blow out harshly.

"What's wrong?" I demanded.

"There's no easy way to say this. About two hours ago, your house exploded in a fireball. Everything was consumed. The place is a total loss. I'm sorry."

The words didn't penetrate my brain right away. As they slowly filtered through the noise, I realized what Rook had said. "What happened to the agents you had watching the place?"

"He killed them. Three people. The video shows they were outside, patrolling the area. He took two of them out. Then he called me and made me listen as he tortured Paragon. He kept the phone close, so I could hear the screams. Then he picked it up and said this was just a prelude. He said now he understood what he needed to do, then hung up."

"Did you talk to Sammy?"

"Yes. He's upset. He thinks you're going to be angry about the house."

"Fuck the house," I grumbled. "It was only a home because Sammy and Kelly were there. Beyond that, it was a building that can be replaced. We need to stop this son of a bitch."

"Agreed. He wants me, so maybe—"

I knew what he was going to say. "No."

"If it—"

"I said no, goddamn it," I shouted. All around me, heads turned to see the nut job who was screaming in an airport. Fuck them all. I had just about had it with people anyway. "You listen, and listen good," I told Rook. "This bastard doesn't get you. Even if you did go, there isn't any guarantee he'd stop whatever he's planned. I told you, the fucker has a screw loose. It's not politically correct, but I don't care. He's psychotic and needs to be put down like a rabid dog. If you're not going to be part of the solution, then just stay the fuck out of my way."

Something slammed, then Rook roared, "Who do you think you're talking to? Remember who you work for."

"Yeah, I remember, but you know what? Maybe Oscar had the right idea. He works for himself, and he doesn't have to answer to anyone. He doesn't need to worry about red tape and blurred lines. He goes in, he does his job, and he gets the fuck out. No handcuffs, no answering to anyone other than his client."

"You arrogant son of a bitch. Don't you fucking understand? I listened to Paragon die. And the unsub described it as he cut the man up. I could hear Paragon begging. Pleading for his life. And this sick bastard? He laughed. He asked how it felt to know another of my agents was going to die because of me! Before he hung up, he reminded me in no uncertain terms that the agent's death was on my head."

"You've...never heard a man die before, have you?"

"No. Except for the man who raped my daughter. I heard him plead and didn't give a shit. This? It was different. Not something I... I wasn't... Fuck!"

I heard him groan, and I thought he was going to be sick.

"Turn off the phone. Have them disconnect Kelly's."

"I thought about that, but he said if I did, he'd go after civilians. Then he'd mail body parts to random people. He said he would—would..."

Rook did something then that I'd never heard before. He sobbed. His breath was coming in gasps, and everything he said was garbled. My heart went out to him. When I had been a Marine, I'd heard men die. It wasn't something you got used to. As Rook said, it was easier when the person was your target. You could detach yourself to a degree. When you were a sniper, it was even easier, because you didn't hear them die.

"They knew what they signed up for. We all did. We chose this because we believe the world can be a better place. We all know that it may come down to us dying one day, but even then, we still choose to live this life."

Rook continued to cry, and I stood by, powerless. There was nothing I could say or do. The man would accept it, or he wouldn't. Finally, after several long minutes, he spoke.

"I'm tired, Michael. Tired of this life, of the bullshit. Of sending young men and women to die. I just can't— Well, I can't. Let's leave it at that. The only reason I keep at it is my daughter. If it weren't for her, I probably would have walked away a long time ago."

Never once since I'd joined had Rook called me by my given name. That fact alone had me worried for the man.

"We're going to get him," I promised. "I'll look him in the eye as he dies and make sure he knows that I'm vengeance for all of the people he's killed."

"I'm sure you will," Rook said softly. "I'm going to lie down a while, I think. I've got you a room in your regular safe house. Not that I expect it to be completely safe. You'll have to keep on your guard. I've sent a message to Samuel. He should be calling soon. Take care."

"Always do," I told him.

Without another word, Rook disconnected, and I stood there, phone in hand. I wasn't sure what to do to help the man I considered a friend. There probably wasn't anything I *could* do, but I would worry.

I left the terminal and caught a taxi that would deliver me to my hotel, where I'd stay until Rook called. I had to admit, I was at a loss as to what to do. Our target knew too much about us, and we knew next to nothing about him. That made him even more dangerous.

The phone rang a few moments later. Unknown number flashed on the screen. I grinned when I answered it.

"Tell me what you're wearing," I said, my voice pitched low.

"Please tell me that wasn't your attempt at seduction, because it was pretty weak."

"God, you have no idea how much I miss you," I said. Hearing Sammy's voice, my cock tried to stiffen, which, thanks to Sammy's gift, wasn't about to happen.

"Miss you, too. Did Rook tell you about our house?"

Our. There was a time when Sammy would say our, and I would deny it. Now he was the best part about the place.

"Yeah. Are you okay?"

156

"Me? I was worried about you. It's all gone. The house, the cars, the garden, the koi pond."

A fist tightened around my heart. Everything else was just stuff, but not my beloved fish. The ones I'd bought because I loved watching their elegance as they swam. They taught me a lot about patience.

"I'm fine," I assured him, even as I struggled to keep a lid on my emotions. "We'll get a new place. It'll be something we can build together. Tell the old man to start a list of what he wants to see in it."

Sammy chuckled. "I'm thinking he might want room for Lilah. She's been cooing over him since you left. She fusses at him over every little thing he does. Not like a doctor, but something akin to a lover."

"He deserves it," I said. "He's been alone too long. Let him know there's always room for one more person in our new home, if he wants to ask her."

"Hell no. I went in after she left to make some calls. I fluttered my eyelashes at him and called him sugar booger. He grabbed me by the shirt, pulled me down to him, and said if I ever uttered those two words together again, he'd rip my nipples off."

"Sugar booger. Mental note made." I laughed loud, and the cabbie frowned at me in the mirror. "So seriously, how are you holding up?"

"I'm... I guess I'm sad. I loved our place."

"I know, but before you got there, it was just a house. Wherever we end up, it'll be our home. Maybe this is our cue that Hawaii *is* for us."

"You know good and well that you'll never be able to walk away. It's not in you to leave the kids to someone else. You're a lot like Oscar. He grumbles about it, but he won't leave it either. I think it's the best part of you."

"You think the fact I kill people is the best part of me?" I whispered, not wanting the cab driver to bail out of the moving vehicle.

"No, stupid. I think your caring nature, your need to help, and your compassion are the best parts of what make you who you are. That's what made me fall in love with you. The hot sex? That's just a side benefit. And in answer to your question, I'm in my room, wearing nothing but underwear, and I'm stroking myself thinking about your lips stretched wide around my cock, and you looking up into my eyes while you bob up and down."

"You're a bastard," I snapped as I shifted uncomfortably on the seat.

"One who's very close," he groaned. "Should I tell you what I'm imagining now?"

I should have said no. I had to say no. "Yes," I whimpered.

"Before you left, when I had you bent over the bed, your hands spread wide, your face buried in the comforter. You were crying out as I pushed into you, and we were both riding the crest of an orgasm. I thrust in, slamming you against the bed. You were asking me for more, pleading with me to let you come."

"Please stop," I begged. That earned me another look from the cab driver. I gave him the finger, because right now, my cock and balls ached, and I had no patience for his shit.

"Stop? Oh, but, baby… I'm so close. Why on earth would I stop now? I'm so fucking hard. I've been jacking off daily, just thinking about you. Spurting thick ropes of come onto my chest, then dipping a finger into it and licking it off."

"Fuck," I whispered, imagining him doing that.

"Haven?"

"Yes?" I croaked.

"I'm teasing you."

"I know. I'm not sure if I hate you or love you right now."

"No, I mean I'm kidding. I'm not masturbating. I haven't done anything since you left. I'm saving it up so, when we get together, I can show you how much I missed you."

"You haven't jacked off?"

"Nope. Not once. Believe me, it hasn't been easy."

"No shit, Sherlock!" I sniped. "My coc—the cage—okay, I hate you."

He snickered. "I love you, too, sugar booger."

I pulled a face. "Kelly's right. Never use that phrase again."

I heard a knock, and Sammy told me to hold on. Murmured conversation filtered through the phone, then Oscar's voice came on the line. His breathing sounded labored, not unlike a bull.

"He's a dead man," he bitched, his voice dark.

"Who?"

"This fucker who killed your people and torched your house. He is so fucking dead." I heard a door close.

"You'll have to get to him before I do," I said.

"Fuck that," he whispered harshly. "He made Sammy cry. The poor kid was a wreck when Rook told him about the house. He kept wailing about all those things you two had built. And when he was bawling, it made me think of Max. He's at home, painting away. What would happen if someone found out where he was? No, this shit won't work. He's dead."

"Tell me again how you don't love Max."

"Don't push me, Haven. Not now, and sure as hell not about this."

He was right, of course. "I'm sorry."

"Nah, my temper is frayed. I shouldn't snap at you. But your boy—"

"Grew on you, didn't he? He's got that ability."

"How can you not be more upset about your place? Until he talked to you, Sammy was inconsolable. Even Kelly's upset, but he's not reacting the same way."

So I told Oscar a bit about Sammy. I left out the horrific parts, because those weren't mine to tell. Instead, I focused on how the house was the first and only permanent thing he'd ever had in his life. He'd decorated it and turned it from a collection of glass, wood, and metal into a home for the three of us.

"I understand," he replied. "Probably more than you realize. He's been hanging out with Kelly and that dog of yours."

"Kip," I informed him. "He came from…ah…a mission."

"Friendly little cuss. I might take him home with me. Max would love him."

"Sammy would shoot you before he let you take his dog. Kelly might do worse."

"And what about you?" he asked, a tease in his voice.

"Let's just say you'd never have to worry about getting Max pregnant."

Oscar chuckled. "I'm gonna admit something to you, and if you tell anyone I said it, I'll call you a liar."

"Ooh, this sounds good. Lay it on me."

He took a deep breath. "When you told me this was your family, I thought you were crazy. People like us, we don't have them. But I can see these two men, and listening to them talk—and they do a lot of that, by the way—I can tell how deeply they care for you. And the look on your face

159

when you talked about Sammy? I knew you loved him without any doubt or hesitation."

"Did you know that you're the only person who gets to call him Sammy besides me? Rook, Kelly, and even Lilah, all of them can only call him Samuel."

"You think he didn't tell me to call him Samuel? It's not like I'd listen. But he's a good man, and I'm honored to know him."

"You know," I teased, "I'm starting to think you're getting soft on me."

"Say one more stupid thing, and I will bend you over the bed and fuck you while he watches," Oscar snarled. "I don't know why I even bother with you."

Because, as I was coming to learn over the last year, family came in many different flavors. Sometimes they even came with sprinkles shaped like grumpy ex-Marines.

CHAPTER SEVENTEEN

After another two weeks, I was going out of my mind. The idea of being holed up, waiting for something to happen, pissed me off to no end. And so did the stupid cage around my dick. The only good thing was that I could talk to Sammy on occasion, even though he seemed to take great joy in my discomfort. *Bastard.*

Rook… God, he was a mess. Though he hadn't gotten another call, he was on the edge of his seat, waiting for something to happen. It reminded me of one of the horror movies Sammy enjoyed, where he peered at the TV through splayed fingers, waiting for the immortal villain to make an appearance. Then he'd wrap around me as though I could protect him from the killer's hatchet. Rook was poised to curl up and let the world pass him by.

It had to suck for him. The closet he'd built for himself, the safe space where everything could be viewed with detachment, had been ripped away, and now he could no longer wear his blinders. The truth of what our missions cost had finally hit home for him. No longer were the people under his command merely statistics. In one call, they'd become living, breathing beings.

When we tried to talk to him, he insisted he was fine, but Sammy, Kelly, and I knew better. The man was a shell of himself. Even when Oscar called him, he didn't so much as raise his voice.

"So what do we do?" Sammy asked.

That was a question I'd asked myself many times. We'd told Rook to check with his superiors to see if they could grant him leave or find someone to take his place. He mumbled something about his daughter and deflected any other conversations. It got so bad that he wasn't even assigning missions, even when I asked for one. Which I did, repeatedly. The answer I got was always the same.

"You'll get a mission when I give it to you," he told me.

"Then find me one," I insisted. "I hate sitting here waiting for something to happen."

I could hear tapping on his desk.

"Because maid service, room service, and all the other things the hotel provides are a terrible inconvenience, I'm sure."

I carded my fingers through my hair and blew out a shaky breath. I pulled the pen and pad of paper the hotel provided over and began to write down all the swear words that I had to bite my tongue to keep from saying. And there were quite a few.

"Look, I need something to do. What if I go help out another agent?"

He paused a moment too long. I knew then he was hiding something. At any one time, we had dozens of operatives in the field. While most of them could handle things on their own, I'd never known more than a few to turn down help.

"You're not giving out any missions, are you?"

"That's on a need to know basis," he snapped.

"Which means no. Tell me what's going on."

Rook sighed. It was a long, drawn-out sound made by a man who'd found his world turned on end.

"I recalled the agents that were out on assignment. My superiors are unhappy with my performance, but having them out there puts them at risk. I'm not willing to send them to their deaths for something we have no control over."

And with those words, I'd had enough. If he wanted someone to comfort him, he'd come to the wrong person.

"You're a stupid son of a bitch, you know that? While you're indulging your pity games, there are kids out there being murdered. Women who are being sold into slavery. Men who can't defend themselves that are now adrift in a world that doesn't give a shit about them. This is on you, Rook."

"So you'd have no problems sending them out to die?" he shouted. "To listen to their screams as he stabs them to death? You'll sleep fine hearing the knife being plunged into their bodies and them crying out for mercy?"

I smiled at the anger I could hear in his voice. It sounded better than the helplessness that had been there before.

"Nope. I'll have nightmares about it. I'll mourn their losses. I will wonder what I could have done differently. Then I'll send someone out there to finish their job. You're not honoring their deaths by letting them go unavenged. That's what we do, remember? Protect when we can, avenge when we can't. Or have you forgotten?

"Your people would walk through fire for you. Many of us have. We've seen things that would make what you heard seem like nothing. Shit, if this scares you, then you'd better never hope to be with me when I do my job. It's ugly. It's brutal. And it's necessary."

I put the pen down and leaned back in the chair with my arm thrown over my eyes. Rook had to be made to understand. I couldn't insulate him from the truth.

"You can't keep the agents from doing what they signed on for. If it makes you feel better, remind them of the dangers each time. Ask if they're sure they want to take on the job. I can pretty much guarantee you that, to a person, we will accept the responsibility and stand proud when we head out to protect people." My voice dropped to just above a whisper. "Will we all come back? No. You know how many agents have died in the line of duty. Many more will. But that won't stop us from doing our jobs. Do you think Bulwark, Chaperone, and Stonewall would regret their decisions?" I asked, reminding him of the men who'd died in an attack on Valerie. The men who were now buried in the same graveyard as my sister.

Rook sighed. "You can be a complete asshole, but you're right. I signed up to keep others from being victimized like my daughter. You wanted to keep kids like your sister safe. It's hard, but I have to do the job we were meant to."

Thankfully, he listened to me. I needed him to hear what I was saying, because I believed it and knew he did, too. What we did—and how we did it—was important. Something Rook needed to keep in mind.

"The only way this ends is with us taking him out. To do that, we need to know what he knows. He has Kelly's phone, and somehow broken through the safeguards. I thought that was impossible."

Each phone had layers of encryption. No one should be able to get into it. It was the one thing I'd always been certain of. It was the only way I felt safe sending messages to Sammy when I was out on a mission.

"It should be," Rook replied. "Only those with knowledge of how the phones work would even have a chance to… *Oh, fuck.*"

He must have had the same thought I did, and *oh fuck* summed it up perfectly. "He's not just some random person. He knows who we are, because he either forced someone to talk, or he used to be an agent."

It was so fucking obvious, and we hadn't even considered it? The reason he was so good was because he used to be one of us. And wasn't that just a fine kettle of fish?

"You're shitting me?"

It was the third time Oscar had asked the question. I was with him on the disbelief. It seemed inconceivable that someone who had been an agent could have gone over the edge like this.

"You have no idea how I wish I was. I mean, it makes sense. He knows our gear, he knows how we operate, and now he knows who the people closest to me are."

In the history of the organization, there had been only a small handful of people who had gone rogue. Oscar's handler had been one, and there were a few who collected…favors and money for their services. Beyond that? No one had ever resorted to murder that I was aware of.

"Wow." Oscar whistled, sharp and annoying.

"You got out. Has anyone ever contacted you? What about someone who used to be an agent?"

"Only you," he replied. "I tried to find a few of the guys from before, but as soon as I left the agency, they disappeared like a fart in a windstorm. You were the only one who reached out to me, which is a total breach in protocol, you know."

Yeah, I knew. But Oscar wasn't like other agents. Though Rook frowned on how Oscar did his job, I couldn't fault the man. I'd done a lot worse when I was starting out with the agency. Oscar at least had a code of ethics, no matter how screwed up they might be.

"Oh, trust me, I heard about it when they found out I hadn't cut ties with you. But Sammy said something recently, and it stuck with me. When we're out, we are out all the way. There is no safety net for agents who need help.

If there had been resources, maybe Carter Whitfield wouldn't have died. If John could have contacted someone, maybe—"

"The world is full of maybe and could be, bro. It's only going to drive you crazy if you think about them. We were told what the job entailed when we started. We accepted the risks."

He was right, and I knew it. But I also believed Sammy was correct.

"We can't throw people to the wolves just because they no longer operate for us."

Oscar sighed. "You're right," he said. "Well actually, the kid's right. I think about you and what happened. If you had left the agency, would you have been able to handle it on your own?"

"I had the money to help myself," I reminded him. Not everyone got paid like I did.

"You also had Kelly, Rook, and Sammy pushing you to get the help you needed," he reminded me. "If they had yanked your support network, if there wasn't a Kelly or a Rook? What then?"

I would have swallowed the barrel of my gun. "I don't know," I lied.

"Yeah, ya do. You're like a brother to me, Haven." He cleared his throat. "Well, one I wanna fuck, but you get the point. You wouldn't have come to me for help, and I doubt you would have tried to find it on your own."

"So if *I* couldn't do it, how can we expect people who don't have the money or the resources? Sammy said this was a flaw in the system, and now that I've seen it up close and personal, I have to agree."

"Then what can you do?"

A question in definite need of an answer. Sadly, I didn't have one. "I'll talk to Rook. He's as much as said he doesn't agree with the policy, so maybe he can start the ball rolling."

"Nothing is going to change," Oscar said, his tone telling me he knew more than he was letting on.

"Oh? How do you know?"

A deep sigh. "When I killed Knight I...um...inherited his paperwork. It made for fascinating reading late at night when Max slept. The organization was founded thirty years ago. They—are you sure you want to hear this? It isn't pretty."

I went to the minibar in the room, grabbed a sparkling water, then sat at the table. After popping the top on the bottle and taking a long draw, I simply said, "Hit me."

"Thirty years ago, there was a serial killer in Hawaii. He was dubbed the Honolulu Strangler—pretty original, huh?—and he killed five women that we know of. Each of them had been bound, raped, and, surprise, strangled. Their bodies were found in a variety of places, so there wasn't much for the police to go on.

"Someone got the idea that even if this person was caught, they'd plead insanity and get off like countless people before them. From those humble roots, an idea sprang. Why not simply eliminate those who were getting away with murder. And what better way to do it than to task disenfranchised military men and women, or cops, or anyone with some kind of law enforcement experience, with their deaths."

He paused, and I knew he was letting what he told me sink in. Honestly? I saw no problem with it. We did good work.

"Yeah? And?"

"When the organization was founded, there wasn't an exit strategy for people who were in it. Agents were members in good standing as long as they stayed, but once they decided to leave, they were simply cut loose. None of them were expected to live, Haven. The government didn't give a shit. Once those in charge got what they wanted, nothing else mattered."

I swallowed a lump in my throat.

"It's gotten a little better. Once the people who came up with the agency disbanded, someone else stepped in and took over. They seem to care, at least a little Agents who are in the organization are taken care of a lot more than they used to be. But those who leave? They're still hung out to dry. Knight had notes as well as the organization's own version of morbidity and mortality reports. Most people who left killed themselves within a month. Those who managed to last longer still died within six. Only a few made it past a year, and those were people who had been noted as having an exceptionally strong will.

"That changed as psychiatric care became available for agents while they were on the job, but when they left, those benefits were yanked. Now, agents who leave do live longer. Some are even happy. But there are deep stains on some of them that still lead a lot of them to die." He paused for a moment. "The people that the unsub killed? They'd clawed back from the horrors they'd witnessed. They probably would have lived out a full life, but he snuffed out that hope."

It all sounded so unbelievable. I drained the remainder of my water, went back to the bar, and grabbed the scotch. It wasn't Chivas Regal Royal Salute, but right now, even the swill the bar had would do the job.

"It sounds so implausible," I muttered.

"It's why they take those without families, Haven. The selection process is exhaustive. A lot of criteria must be met. No family. No loved ones. Dedicated to their jobs, so not many will notice when they're gone."

The reasons made sense. I couldn't think of too many folks who would walk away from people they cared about to take a job like this. But the way Oscar explained it made it seem sordid at best.

"And they let you keep this information?" I asked.

Oscar laughed, and it sent chills down my spine. "Not exactly. When I shot Knight, there was a kill order signed with my name on it. The files I have were my only bargaining chip. We came to an understanding that as long as they left me alone, I wouldn't send the files to every newspaper in the country. This is why I'm not welcome back. I know too much. And I've only told you a small portion of what I've learned. There is a lot more, but I don't want to break my bond with the agency."

There was a question I needed answered, but I hesitated to ask. If what Oscar said was true, and I had no reason to doubt it was…

"Is the organization dirty?" I spat out.

"No! They're not dirty. Not by a long shot. They do good work. *You* do good work. They're just… How can I put this? Self-centered. Rook, Knight, and the rest? They preserve the status quo. No one wants to rock the boat too much, because they're all single-minded when it comes to the mission. It's not a bad thing, but it's also not all shiny and noble. It was things like this that gave Knight the opening he needed."

I'd drained the first little bottle of scotch, and the goddamned minibar only had two of them. Fuck it. I grabbed the other, and a few more bottles of whatever shit they had, and started chugging them. They'd make me sick, but I needed to blot this out.

"Stop," Oscar barked.

"What?" I demanded, cracking open the seal on the next bottle.

"You think I don't know what you're doing? How many have you had already?"

The urge to snap at him pushed its way up, but I didn't let it out. He was right. I wasn't playing this smart at all. Getting drunk would leave me wide open to an attack by the fucker. I tossed the bottle into the recycle bin, then went back to get a water.

"I understand, you know. When I first went through the reports, I drained a few bottles myself. Did you know that I passed out in the bathroom? Max found me there, cleaned me up. I tried to shoot him, but still, he took pity on me. My whole world had been built around the agency, and when I found this shit, it took away everything I'd believed. But I... Fuck. I clung to Max, and he let me. When the chips were down, and I had no one else I could turn to... That's when he stepped up."

It sounded a lot like Sammy, but I knew better. Many things Oscar might be, but he wouldn't wallow in self-pity.

"He did his best to comfort me, but you know what? I didn't want comfort. I got angry. All the lies, the deception, and then this shit on top of it? That got me through it. It drove me on to prove that I was more than the agency. I was my own fucking man, and no one controlled me. You're lucky, because you got Rook as your handler. There are files on him, too. He's a damned good man. Probably the best in the entire organization. But he's still only one person. You need to be the one to step up now. Support him, but also work with him to change things."

"Until this bastard is taken off the board, I can only focus on him." Anger bubbled up inside me at the thought of all those deaths. I needed to get the conversation directed toward something else. Thinking about this bastard wasn't going to do me any good. "How's Sammy?"

Oscar huffed. "He's an annoying little shit. To be honest, you'd be better off letting me shoot him. The little prick likes to poke, and even when I threaten him, he just laughs and starts in again. What the hell do you see in him?"

"That's easy. He gets under your skin."

Oscar laughed. "One sec." He came back a moment later. "Okay, he's in with Kelly. Truthfully? I can see why you care for him. He rarely leaves Kelly's side, and you can tell how much the old man means to him. He's a good kid, Haven. You deserve happiness. And in case you're wondering, he misses you a lot. He did ask me for one favor, though…"

I braced myself, because I had no doubt it was going to be something I didn't like.

"Go on."

"He gave me this key. Says it's for something on your person. When I asked what, he snickered. Told me he wanted me to hold it in case, you know, something happens to him. Wanna tell me what the key is for?"

I groaned. "Do me a favor. Go ahead and shoot him. But make it slow and painful."

That earned me a snort. "Nah, I think I'm going to keep him around. He's funny, and he… What was it you said? Oh, yeah. He gets under your skin."

Fine. I'd kill the bastard myself. After he reminded me who I belonged to.

CHAPTER EIGHTEEN

Rook contacted me two days later. Another agent's body had turned up, this one bobbing in the water of a local pool. Fortunately, he was recovered before anyone other than the lifeguard, who was set to open, found him. Agent Cole had burn marks over eighty percent of his body. Lilah's doctor friend did the autopsy. Whatever this fucker did, she said, it was slow and excruciatingly painful. She found residue on his body, some type of fuel that had been applied then set aflame. Different sections showed staggered healing patterns, so it happened over a long time. What killed him was when the gel was put into his mouth and torched.

I shuddered at the viciousness of the crime. The man had said he wanted revenge for a loss he'd suffered, and it was obvious he intended to get it however he could. I tried several times to call Kelly's phone, but he never answered, of course. I even went so far as to leave a message. Something to get him to call and talk with me. There was a certain shame that came with knowing I wasn't being watched because he'd gone off to kill someone else.

Rook sent me pictures of Cole's body. This man had worked him over before he'd burned him alive. Shit, looking at those photos, I wasn't even sure we could call him a man anymore. There was only once that I let go like that—when I'd beat a child murderer to death with a crowbar, turning him into pudding. But my target was a monster who had killed little kids he brought to this country, promising to get them adopted. When he couldn't, it was easier to snuff them out. I'd lost control and gotten retribution for them. Our unsub had killed an agent who dedicated his life to helping others.

"What do we do?" Rook asked, the tension in his voice more than obvious.

Wasn't that just the million-dollar question?

"No."

Oscar's voice betrayed no emotion, but I knew he was pissed. It had been four days since they'd found Cole's body. Rook wasn't answering my messages, and I figured he'd gone into meltdown once again. The last thing anyone had heard from him—that I knew of—was another message stating there would be no assignments forthcoming for the foreseeable future. This had to end.

"Give me a better option," I demanded. "He torched Cole alive, then left the body for us to find."

"You told Rook no. Why the hell do you think we'd put you out there as bait?"

"Because I can handle myself," I reminded him.

Oscar sighed. "No. Not anymore you can't. Look, I've been talking with Sammy—"

"And here we go. What did the little shit say this time?" I ground out through clenched teeth.

"He said you could do the job. He told me he has the utmost confidence in you."

"Oh." Well, that wasn't what I'd been expecting.

"I don't. There was a time that you were the best agent in the field. That time has come and gone. This job isn't for you anymore. I think you know it, too, but you're not willing to admit it."

"What the fuck?"

He laughed. "Oh, you're still good, don't get me wrong. But your reaction times are slower. You're not as aware of your surroundings as you used to be. If we were asked to go on a mission together, I wouldn't go with you as my partner."

It felt like he'd stuck a knife in my gut and was giving it a good twist. He wasn't wrong, though. I'd been thinking about it since well before Valerie. I didn't want to stop being an agent, but I wasn't the same man anymore. I was slower, less focused. Valerie had proved that when she'd taken me down. I thought some time away might help, that I could come back from it and be as good as I once was—but that hadn't happened. I'd lost my edge, and the fact I'd allowed this bastard to get so close to me and mine proved it.

171

Fortunately, things were different with Sammy in my life.

Being with him, having Kelly living with us, all of it changed me. Now I looked forward to nights on the couch, the two of us cuddling as we ate popcorn, all while we watched some insipid program. Kelly, who, a year ago, would have returned to his own place in the evenings, now sat across from us, snorting at the funny parts. Sammy made me…no, he made us want more, for ourselves and him.

"I have to see this through," I insisted. "He's killed too many people. Some of them I worked with. I owe it to them to get justice."

"Yeah, you do. But to do that, you need to be alive. This plan of yours is suicide. And, from what I hear tell, you need to ask permission beforehand anyway." Oscar snickered.

"Fuck you," I grumbled.

He wasn't wrong, though. I would need to talk to Sammy before I did this. He would raise concerns, but he'd understand.

"Hey, it's cool," he said.

There wasn't a censure there. I honestly believed he had no issues with it.

"I just wish I had known all this before. I could have given you exactly what you needed. Shit, I would have beat your ass daily."

He chuckled when I groaned. "What the hell has Sammy been telling you?"

"Enough where I'll have blackmail material for years to come. Who knew you liked to be tickled there?"

"Oh, fucking A," I growled. "Where the fuck is he?"

This time Oscar laughed, and I knew I'd been had.

"He doesn't talk much about the slap and tickle you guys do, but thank you for confirming my suspicions."

I dropped back onto the chair, my head banging against it. "I hate you. I hope you know that."

"I do," he admitted. Then his voice softened. "It's Sammy that's made you weak, you know. This job isn't for someone in love. It gives people too much of a hold on us."

"Bullshit," I barked. "Sammy is the best thing that's ever happened to me."

"I don't doubt that for a moment. But tell me something, if I said I'd kill him, what would you do?"

Ice flooded my veins. "What are you saying?"

"Nothing," he promised me. "But from the sound of your voice, the thought of losing him terrifies you. That's what I'm talking about. He told me about Valerie. We were having dinner one night, and he told me about killing her. Kelly was in the other room with Lilah, and Sammy was sitting on the couch, feeding bits of his burger to Kip. He wasn't looking at me, but he said 'you know I killed my mother.'

"I admitted I knew. He told me he had no choice; she had to die. He said he couldn't let you do it, because it would have caused a rift between the two of you that couldn't be healed."

"That's bullshit. I told him—"

"It would have killed you," Oscar informed me. "It would have eaten at your insides, festering like an open wound. There was a time when you could have popped the bitch and walked away like it never happened. Not anymore."

"I've killed since then," I said, though even to my own ears my voice hollow.

"Yes, you have. And you will again. But…and this is where it gets dicey, it wasn't directly related to Sammy. He's the chink in your armor, your one true weakness. He gives you strength, too, but…"

Oscar's voice trailed off.

"But what?" I demanded. "Tell me you wouldn't risk everything for Max. Go on, say it. I fucking know you love him, even if you won't admit it. If he were in trouble, you'd move heaven and earth to protect him."

He was quiet for a moment. "You're right, I would. But, and this is the difference between us, I wouldn't go in angry. If it were Max's mother, I'd put a bullet in her head without a second thought. My feelings for Max are secondary to my job. He knows it, too. I have never made a declaration to him, because I won't be put in the same situation you are."

I shoved my fingers through my too-long hair and scratched my scalp. Was Oscar right? No, I refused to believe that. Sammy stood beside me, giving me the strength to do my job. When I thought I couldn't go on, he pushed me to where he needed me to be. He believed in me.

"You're wrong," I croaked. "Yes, I love Sammy. I would walk away from this life if he wanted it, but he doesn't. He knows what this job means to me."

"Okay, let me ask you something. Are you still doing it because of what happened to your sister?"

Goddamn, at times I hated Oscar. He was like a bug, burrowing into my flesh until he hit the fucking nerve.

"No," I admitted. "Not entirely. Sammy is my reason now. Why? Because he survived. He showed strength of character and will. My sister wasn't weak by any means, but I look to Sammy for inspiration. He gives me the drive to keep moving forward."

"All I'm saying is that you need to find a reason to fight for yourself. It's always been about what you want to do for other people, you know. What does Haven want for himself?"

That was a damned good question. I'd never known what I wanted for myself. Brief glimpses of a life outside of the organization had been tantalizingly close, but I couldn't walk away. Not when there were children out there who needed protection. After my sister had been beaten to death, I'd killed the man who'd done it. There hadn't been a shred of remorse. That came later. Dreams of disembodied voices pleading with me not to end their lives were almost a nightly occurrence. Since therapy, though, I'd gotten a handle on them.

"I want what I've always wanted. To protect the children when I can and avenge them when I can't. That's who Haven is, and who he will always be."

"You know how I feel about you, so you can take this as gospel. That's who Haven is. What about Michael? Who is he?"

Fingernails on a chalkboard couldn't have caused me to wince harder.

"How did you know?"

"I listen. It's one of my skill sets. The old man was talking with Sammy one night. I stood at the door when Kelly took him by the hand and made him promise that if anything ever happened to him, the kid would look out for Michael. I figured it had to be you. And for the record, Sammy promised. Well, after he lit into Kelly for saying such stupid things."

Warmth rushed through me.

"These men do for both Haven and Michael, but what about you? You're constantly willing to put yourself on the line for others, but what about the people you leave at home? The ones who are wondering if you'll come back. You say you love Sammy—and I know you do, so don't start—but think about him, too. Shit, man, think about yourself. You have a life now. Don't throw it away."

There was an urge to continue to argue. To tell him that I was happy with what we had, but what good would it do? I *was* building a life, and I had no desire to give any of it up. Hell, even Kip curled up in Sammy's lap brought a smile to my face and warmth to my chest.

I tried to imagine things if I continued going the way I had been. This fucker who had been stalking me knew too much about me and where I went. Worse, he knew about Sammy and Kelly. It dawned on me that Oscar had been right. Sammy would always be the chink in my armor, because I would kill anyone who dared to get close to him. The unsub had already proven to be dangerous, and the thought he might target Sammy? Fuck no, not happening.

"We're going to do this," I insisted. "Call me weak if you want, but he's already hurt Kelly and he knows about Sammy. I'm not going to let the bastard touch him."

"That's my job. He won't lay a finger on your boy's pretty little head, I swear it." Oscar paused for a moment. "By the way, speaking of head, how does he feel about a threesome? I think having you squeezed in between us would be fucking hot. Shit, I can't even think about which end I want to start with."

"Touch him and you'll never have to worry about having sex again," came a very pissed off voice that I barely recognized.

I heard a deep chuckle. "Oh, come on. Just once. I've always wanted a shot at that ass. I can just imagine banging away at it and smacking his cheeks with each thrust. Yeah, that would be awesome."

I heard a squawk, a loud thump, then a scuffle. I waited patiently until Oscar picked up the phone again.

"Shit, man. The kid's got a good left."

"You knew he was there, so you changed the subject."

"I told you, he's my responsibility. I won't let him get hurt, even if it's his precious feelings. Right now, he's in the other room, telling Kelly what a bastard I am. Kid's got a set on him. He didn't even hesitate to jump me. You trained him good, Mike."

Pride flowed through me, and I sat up just a bit straighter. If Sammy impressed Oscar, it was saying a lot. "Yeah, he's one of a kind all right. Sorry if he hurt you."

"Meh. I've been hit harder. Can I say I love how protective he is of you? The two of you are a good fit. And this is why you need to start thinking about him, too. You say he wants you to continue being Haven because he understands the need for you in the world. Will that keep him comfortable on those nights when you're gone for a month? When the bed is cold and lonely? When there isn't anyone he can talk to?"

"Sammy would never cheat on me!" I insisted.

"Not saying he would. I'm asking you if it's fair to him that he has to be alone so often? Is it fair to you when you're away from him? You might be together, married and all, but you're still going to have to leave him alone to take care of someone else's life. It was one thing when it was just you, but are you willing to make Sammy wait? Who will he cling to? The old man? If he and Lilah hook up, where does that leave your boy who, by the way, just told Kelly I'm an obnoxious fucker. Kelly's laughing."

When I opened the door to the mini-bar, I found the booze had been restocked. I really wasn't in the mood for anything hard, so I grabbed a cola. I popped the top and took a sip while I contemplated what Oscar had said.

"Well, he's not wrong." I sighed. "Maybe you aren't, either. I have to think about this. I guess I took him at his word that it was something I needed to do. Maybe I never thought about life beyond the next six months because, like you know, our longevity isn't usually measured in years."

"Amen, brother. It's why I'm never going to discuss feelings with Max. I can't guarantee I'll be there for him tomorrow. If I die, all that matters is he's taken care of. You, though? You had to buy the milk and the cow. Although, I guess you're the one being milked."

I was in the middle of a sip when he said it, and I snorted soda out of my nose.

"Seriously, Mike— Can I call you Mikey? I like that."

I sighed. No matter what, he'd take whatever would irritate me the most. "No. Get on with it."

"Bitch." Oscar cleared his throat. "Anyway, Mikey, you've devoted your life to the organization—to the kids—forever. You need to take a breath, step back, and see what you need from life. Neither of you wants to face the big picture, and that's part of the problem as I see it. Sammy says he's willing to wait for you to come home. He'll step back and let you go save the world. But what's in it for him? There's a difference between Sammy and Kip, other than Sammy hasn't yet chewed up a pair of my alligator shoes."

He paused, probably waiting for the obligatory comment, but at the moment, my mind was focused on what he was saying about Sammy.

"Okay, well, the difference? It's that when you come walking through the door, Kip will always be wagging his tail, grateful to see you. Sammy will wag his for a while, but each time you go away, it becomes more difficult to remember why you're doing it. I fully expect that, one day, Max won't be there when I get home. He'll finally realize that what he's waiting on is a dream, one I can never give him. Don't do that to Sammy or to yourself."

"He wouldn't..." I said, though now the thought was in my head.

"You're right. He probably won't. Many people make it work, but not everyone has a life filled with danger like you do. Will he be able to deal with sitting at home, night after night, not being sure if you're alive or dead? It's going to be hard on him; you've got to see that. You know the life he's had, the things he's lost. What happens if he loses you, too?"

Shit. Oscar was never serious about things, and now he was turning my world on its ear. Sammy was giving me everything I wanted out of life and pretty much handing it to me on a silver platter. He'd been there for me since the day I'd rescued him and had never once asked me for anything for himself. I'd taken it at face value, not really giving thought to his needs.

"You know I hate you, right?" I grumbled as I drained the remainder of my soda then belched. A flick of the wrist and the soda can arced in the air before it clattered to the floor.

"What can I say? I like the kid. And I like you. I don't have a lot of friends in my life, and I want you to be happy."

"Dude, are you getting emotional on me?"

"Bend over and I'll show you," he replied.

I was about to ask to speak to Sammy when my phone chimed.

"Hang on a sec," I said to Oscar, putting the call on hold.

I pulled the phone back and worry gripped me. It was Kelly's number, and the words had ice freezing in my veins.

"One more down. It was so much fun, I figure why stop there?"

CHAPTER NINETEEN

A few moments later, the phone chimed again and another text popped up. This one was gut-wrenchingly brutal. It showed pictures of a man who lay in a pool of blood that flowed outward from a multitude of wounds. He'd been savaged. I could see stumps of fingers, a missing eye, on his mouth lay an ear, skin ripped off as though whoever did it was in a rage as they were doing it. A large hole in his chest showed where his heart used to be—now just a gaping hole.

Through the blood and gore, one thing popped into my head. I knew this person. Well, I'd seen him before. It took several moments for me to figure out where. When Sammy and I had gotten married, this man had stood in the back of the room, watching us. When I asked Kelly who it was, he said he hadn't seen anyone. I thought it was... Oh my fucking God...

"Rook," I whispered as I traced my finger over the screen.

"What do you think of my handiwork?" came the next text a few moments later.

This time I dialed Kelly's phone, stabbing the speaker button. My anger ratcheted up as did the questions in my mind.

"Hello?" came the singsong voice, so different from the Darth Vader filter Rook used.

"What the fuck did you do?" I demanded.

"Pretty sure you can see what I did, but if not, I'd be happy to give you a play by play," he replied, and I could hear the grin in his voice. "Or, if you prefer, I can send you the video. HD and everything."

Admittedly, I was having problems processing what I'd seen. I had no idea what to say to this...man. Sadly, that didn't stop him from talking.

"With the person who was in charge of this branch of the organization, I expected it to be an epic knockdown, drag-out fight. I went in, ready to take everyone out who was protecting him, but there wasn't anyone. I have to admit, it went a lot smoother than I'd thought it would. I didn't even have to track him down. He called me. Think of how many lives would have been saved if we could have done this earlier?"

My thoughts went to my fellow agents and their families, all innocent, but taken out by this psychopathic son of a bitch.

"When I saw his number, I was so intrigued I couldn't help but answer. Can you believe how courteous the man was? I told him I would make an exchange. His life for yours and everyone else in your precious agency. He agreed, just like that. Not even an attempt at negotiations."

I couldn't force myself to look away from the pictures. I could see the blood hadn't set, so it must have been taken while he was alive or just after he died. I'd been cut before, but this? Vicious didn't even begin to describe it. Even at my worst, I'd never done anything like this. As the man talked, I couldn't stop looking at the pictures.

"Of course I didn't trust him to keep his word. He never does—well, did. So I told him to give me an address and I would come to him. After I arrived at the designated location, I watched everyone. There were only a few possibilities among all the people. I dialed the phone, and the one I most suspected answered. I gave him another address, and he got up and walked out. I couldn't believe it when he really did come alone. But, being as he's a smart man, there was no way I could take chances with him. He walked out of the shop and slowly moved along the sidewalk. I knew he was watching, waiting to see what I'd do. When I blocked his path, he stopped and said how nice it was to meet me.

"He assured me he had no tracking device on him, and that he was going with me willingly. I directed him to a car I had waiting and took him somewhere else. We had a very nice conversation. I have to tell you, Rook impressed me. I'm not sure what I expected, but it wasn't this. He told me he knew who I was, which surprised me, because I was certain I'd covered my tracks well enough. Everything about the man was…just wow. The way he kept his cool, stayed calm, even though he knew what was coming? It's hard to believe he wasn't an agent at some point."

I didn't want to hear anymore. I wanted him to shut up, because the images rolled through my head like a movie. My hand curled into a fist, my nails digging into my palm. It was the bite of pain that kept me from lashing out.

"When we got to our destination, he got out of the car and went where I directed him. Believe it or not, I almost reconsidered my plan. I found that I actually could like the man, but I'd waited too long for this. When we got where we were going, I told him to sit in the chair. For some reason, I expected him to lash out, to try to fight back, but he didn't. He merely went and took a seat. As I bound him to the chair, I could see the sadness in his eyes. There was no way I could miss it. It's the same thing I see every time I look into the mirror. It pulled me up short, at least until he said he was sorry for my loss. Then I remembered why I was so angry. What he'd taken from me. Suddenly, I no longer felt bad.

"Still, he surprised the hell out of me. As I cut off his fingers, I told him why I was doing it. Every cut, there was an explanation. He screamed…a lot, but he didn't beg. He didn't try to bargain. I hope when it's my time, I can be half as strong."

"You're insane," I muttered, staring at Rook's empty eye socket.

"You might think that," he replied. "It's not true, though. I'm frighteningly sane. Because I thought through exactly what I was going to do to him. He took my world from me, so I took something from him for each thing he cost me."

"What the hell could he have taken away from you that would lead you to do this?" I demanded.

"My world," he repeated. "The only thing in my life that made sense. And Rook sent him to his death. He underestimated Valerie, and it cost me Terry. He was everything to me, and now he's nothing. Eye for an eye, isn't that what they teach us?"

Us?

"Holy shit. You were an agent," We'd already figured that out. Still, we were no closer to having anything we could use against this sick fucker. I needed to get him to tell me something—anything—that would clue us in to who he was. "I can't believe they'd take a sick fucker like you as one of us."

His voice hardened. "Terry and I both were. We fell in love over the course of a month-long mission, but kept it secret, since the agency frowns on it. But at night, when we lay holding one another, he and I would make plans about our life after we were done. And your precious Rook took them away from us."

"Who was Terry?"

"You called him Bulwark. He said he fought you once. Told me you were the best. So you understand why I had to do this."

"No, I really don't," I answered. "Why did you have to…cut him?"

He laughed. Loud, maniacal. Then it turned into a sob, as woeful as any sound I'd ever heard. "He had to pay, so we did it in kind. I would never see Terry again. That cost him an eye. I will never hold him again. That cost him his fingers. I could never hear him say I love you, so he lost an ear. His lips would never move again, so I cut open his mouth. And I'd never feel his heart beating against my chest again. I'm sure you'll find that around here somewhere, too."

My stomach heaved at the thought of Rook being tortured and dismembered. After what had been done to the others, I knew it wasn't fast or painless.

"But Bulwark… Terry? He knew the risks of the job. He still took it. It wasn't Rook's fault that—"

"It was!" he shouted. "Rook knew he didn't have the intel to go after her. He threw Terry and the others at her like cannon fodder, all so you could operate safe and sound. They died so you could live."

None of it was true. Bulwark and the others died trying to save people by taking down a monster. Just like our job description had always been, Bulkwark had gone where angels feared to tread. Since this bastard had been an agent, he would have known that, too.

"So, what now? You've killed Rook, avenged Terry. Now what do you do?"

"Oh, that's easy," he said cheerily. "I realized the only way Terry's death would make sense is if the agency doesn't exist. Plus, killing these people hasn't been nearly as hard as I thought it would be. I'm saving them, really. From being used like pawns, then having them tossed out when they're no longer needed."

"Like you were?" I hazarded a guess.

"I left the agency before Terry. He said we were going to go together, but then Valerie came along, and Rook asked him for help. He swore to me one last mission, and we'd go to live the life we wanted. We'd get our happily ever after. When he didn't come home, I had no idea what to do. I had no numbers to call, no one who could tell me what happened. I found a book Terry kept, and there were a few names of friends he'd had in there. One of them remembered me and told me Terry had died on his mission. My whole world gone… Poof. Just like that. And I didn't even know.

"Do you know what it's like? Having to hold a funeral when you don't even have a body? How many nights I lay awake, certain it was a mistake and that he'd walk through the door at any moment?"

If this man hadn't just killed someone I considered a friend and mentor, I might have had sympathy. Even with the other deaths he'd caused, maybe I could possibly work up regret for him. Now? He'd be dead before he knew he was.

It was a struggle to keep my voice even. I wanted to threaten him, let him know his days were numbered. But I still didn't have the information I needed. I had to continue pressing him. "So, you've gotten what you wanted. That should be enough to satisfy you. I'm sure it would make Bulwark very proud to see what you've become."

He sucked in a breath. "You know," he drawled, "I thought it would be. I figured once Rook was dead, and Terry was avenged, it would be over. But it's not. There are others out there who will never know if their loved ones are ever coming home. So, I'm going to do this for them. You'll understand eventually."

Like fuck. "How?"

"Terry always said, *Joel, you don't leave a job half-done. If you're going to do it, you have to go in with the intent to finish it.*' So, that's what I'm going to do. When I kill you, who will tell your precious lover? Or maybe I'm going about this the wrong way. If I kill him, who would you go to? Because why should you have happiness, when it's been denied me? Or maybe I should just kill you both. Hm. I've got some thinking to do. You'll know my answer soon enough. For now, though, you can find your friend in the storage room at the ice rink down the street from McDonald's." He rattled off an address. "It was closed for the week after 'unforeseen' mechanical problems caused the ice to become thin. It made a perfect place for Rook and I to…chat. If you hurry, maybe they'll be able to open by the end of the week."

And then he disconnected.

I sat there, thumbing through the pictures, each one a reminder of why this fucker had to be taken down. Memories of Rook flashed through my head. From my first meeting with him, the introduction of Sammy and him, and my beating death of a child killer, Rook had never once questioned me. He'd always had my back. The man had been my handler for over a decade. He'd seen me at my best and my worst. He was the one who got Kelly to take care of the house while I was away on assignment. He was…fuck, he was my family, and this son of a bitch had just…

The bathroom was too far away. I grabbed the wastebasket and emptied the contents of my stomach into it. There wasn't much more than some soda, but it definitely tasted better going down.

Though I knew very little about Rook, still I wondered what would happen with his daughter—she'd been assaulted as a child, and Rook had killed the man who'd done it. It had brought him into the organization, but cost him his marriage. He still had someone keeping an eye on her, though. Shit, I didn't even know if she ever heard from him.

I'd taken Rook for granted. Never really told him how I felt about the things that he'd done for me. Getting my sister buried where I could visit, finding me the house where I'd brought Sammy back to heal. Hell, allowing Sammy to remain, even though we'd gone back and forth about it.

"How many times in our lives have we let things like this slip by? A moment where we could have made someone's life better, simply by saying thank you? When the moment is gone, you think it's no big deal, but the time comes when you'd give anything to go back so you could say the words. Let a person know how much they meant to you?" I muttered to the empty room.

It wasn't unlike what Oscar was saying about Sammy. Yes, unless I was on a mission, I told him how much I loved him every day without fail. But what about Sammy caring for me? Did I ever really thank him for that? For giving up a life he could have had, instead of getting hooked up with an assassin. Just the way Sammy had dealt with the carjacker showed that he had potential beyond what I had given him credit for.

But this wasn't about Sammy or me. It was about Rook. And how without our handler, the whole team had no rudder. There should be someone I could call, let them know what had happened, but there wasn't. It struck me then how fucking stupid the organization was. Yeah, they did it for the safety of everyone involved, but how were we safe now?

The why and wherefore didn't matter. First thing I had to do was find Rook. I called down to the concierge to have my car brought around to the front of the hotel. As soon as I was in it, I programmed the GPS with the address I'd been given. For all I knew, the lunatic was there waiting for me to arrive, but right then, I didn't care. For some reason, it didn't surprise me that the address was close. A few times Rook had mentioned something about Arizona, but it never dawned on me that he lived here. Another failure on my part.

My phone rang again, and I realized I had left Oscar on hold.

"Man, that must have been some good shit if you forgot about me," he groused.

"Now's not the time, O," I said.

He must have heard something in my tone, because his voice went frosty. "What's going on?"

"Rook is…" I swallowed hard. "He killed Rook." Fuck, even saying the words out loud didn't make it seem any more real.

"Tell me everything," Oscar insisted.

So I did. In graphic detail, I told him what Joel had told me. I also stopped so I could forward him the pictures. His breath hitched. Oscar, like me, was a man who was used to violence. It was part of our lives, and we lived with the repercussions daily. In fact, we were responsible for a lot of the violence in our lives. But what Joel had done went far beyond getting revenge for the death of a loved one.

"He's psychotic," Oscar growled.

"And that makes him even more dangerous," I added. "I want you to bring Sammy and Kelly here. They're safer with us together."

"Agreed. What are we going to do?"

"I'm almost to where he said I could find Rook's body. I'll figure it out after that." I told him where I was headed. If Joel was waiting—and if something happened to me—I wanted to be sure they knew where to find us.

"Are you stupid?" he snapped. "What happens if he's still there?"

"Then I take him out and we end this."

"Don't be an idiot!"

"What the fuck do you want me to do?" I shouted. "Leave his body to be found by someone else? To have the bits and pieces of him swept up and taken by the police? Bullshit. I need to be the one to get him. Rook is...he's my responsibility."

Oscar was breathing on the other end of the line, so I knew we were still connected. Finally, he sighed. "Be careful. I'm going to get everyone packed up. What do you want me to tell our guards?"

"To await further instructions, I guess. Don't tell them about Rook yet."

"Understood."

I hung up, got out of the car, and drew my gun before I moved toward the building. The images were seared into my brain, and I knew that they would never go away. Right now, though, I didn't want them to. They gave me something to focus on, a direction for my anger.

I pushed open the back door to the place, and the scent of blood struck me immediately. It wasn't difficult to track it to its source. As bad as the pictures were, the scene I found was infinitely worse. I stared at the amount of blood that pooled on the floor; I couldn't believe the body held so much. Joel was tidy, though. All the pieces were easily found, with the exception of Rook's heart, which I found under the chair he'd been tied to.

My hands were shaking as I dialed Oscar. "I found him," I said, the quaver in my voice obvious. "I have to admit, I don't know what to do. Rook would send a cleaning crew, but I have no idea what—"

"I got it covered," Oscar said. "I called in a favor from a friend. She's sending her people now. They'll take care of Rook, I promise."

"But there's so much blood. No way they won't know something happened here."

"Trust me, by the time they're done, the blood won't matter. There won't be a building left standing for them to go through. It's taken care of, Mike. We need to plan our next move, though."

I'd had that thought in the back of my mind. I knew exactly what needed to be done.

"I'm going to see if I can find someone else in the organization. They need to know what happened. Then, once we do that, we're going to war."

CHAPTER TWENTY

Oscar's friends arrived about an hour after we hung up. Six people got out of an SUV that they'd parked near the rink, then headed directly into the building. The person in charge, who introduced herself as Gina, was a slender woman, with short, dark hair and a devious twinkle in her eye. She didn't talk as she and one of her men went to work setting up barricades to cordon off the area. After they removed Rook's body, Gina came over to me.

"Torch job?" she asked as she made a series of hand gestures to one of the men, who nodded.

"Yes."

She grinned. "I like someone who lets me do my job without second-guessing. Oscar said this man was a friend of yours. I promise by the time we're done, there won't be any way for them to know what happened here."

I swallowed hard and nodded. "How much do I owe you?"

"Already taken care of," she informed me. "Oscar has us on retainer."

"How the hell did you…"

Gina shook her head. "Best not to ask. I owe Oscar more than I can ever repay. If he needs me, I don't bother to wonder why. I get my ass in gear. You're just lucky I was nearby."

If there was one thing I didn't believe in, it was luck.

"There's no way you could have been nearby."

She sighed. "Fine. Oscar called me, told me to have my men here on standby. We usually are when he goes on a job."

Anger churned my stomach. "He knew something like this was going to happen?"

She frowned at me. "Nah. He had no way of knowing, but he likes having me and the guys close at hand if he needs us. Like I said, it's why he keeps us on retainer. We're not usually needed, but we're a good asset to have when the situation calls for it. So, what… What do you want us to do with his body?"

I hadn't thought that far in advance. Shit, I hated not having Rook to turn to.

"We've got him packed in a container," Gina said, betraying no emotion. "Oscar usually has us take them back home, where he's got someone who disposes of them. I know it's not the same, because those aren't the bodies of friends. It's up to you what you'd like us to do."

"I… I really don't know," I admitted.

She put a hand on my arm. "Hey, it's fine. We'll take care of him. When you figure it out, let Oscar know and he'll contact us. I promise, nothing will happen to your friend."

She said it so calmly that it made me pause. "How did you two get mixed up?"

She shrugged. "Like I said, he got me out of a situation. If you need to know more than that, you can talk to him."

She turned and walked away from me. Gina moved with a fluid grace, but also a determined set to her shoulders that could only belong to someone who'd been through a traumatic experience. I saw the same thing when I looked at Sammy. Like him, Gina was a survivor. Whatever she'd been into that Oscar had gotten her away from must have been bad, but she hadn't let it ruin her life. A few minutes later, the SUV was moved and she came back to me.

"You'll want to clear the area," she said. "Good thing this is the only building in the vicinity, because this one is going to burn hot."

"What about the McDonald's?" I asked, worried the blast might cause innocent people to be hurt.

Gina frowned at me. "It's McDonald's. The people there are going to die one way or another." She laughed when she noticed my expression. "Relax. They won't even feel the heat from the fire."

We vacated the area, and I watched as the fireball engulfed the place where my friend had been murdered. It brought me a sense of calm, but I wouldn't know peace until Joel paid for what he'd done.

By the time the first sirens could be heard in the distance, Gina and her crew were gone. I headed back for the hotel. It had been several hours, and by now Sammy, Kelly, and Lilah would be there. I knew Oscar wouldn't tell them what had happened, so I would have to explain that myself.

As soon as I put the keycard into the door, it was yanked open, and I found myself with an armful of Sammy, as well as an excited puppy dancing around our feet. I pulled Sammy close, allowing his scent to fill me. God, I'd missed him so much. Lilah was perched on the arm of the chair where Kelly sat, looking pale and thin. His expression told me he knew something was wrong.

"Okay, so what happened?" Sammy asked as he extricated himself from my grip.

I took a chair near the window. Kip rushed over and jumped in my lap, peppering me with kisses. It was a strange juxtaposition for what I had to say. I glanced at Oscar who gave me a nod. There wasn't any sense in beating around the bush. I turned to Sammy. "Rook is dead."

Kelly gasped and clutched Lilah's hand. She leaned over and wrapped him in her arms. Sammy's gaze narrowed as he regarded me.

"Are you okay?" he asked.

Our friend was dead, but his first concern was for me. "I love you," I said softly.

He stepped closer, knelt, and pulled me down into a kiss.

"What happened?" Kelly asked as he scrubbed at shiny eyes.

I told them what I knew, but left out the more graphic details. Those would come later when they had time to understand the ramifications of Rook's death.

Kelly turned to Oscar. "Can your friend have Rook's..." He choked back a sob. "Rook's body delivered to one of our people? I'll give you a number. They'll make sure he's taken care of."

Oscar nodded, his expression grim. I was relieved Kelly knew how to contact others in the agency.

I turned my full attention on Kelly. "I need to find someone higher up in the organization. They need to know what happened and tell us how to proceed."

Kelly inhaled sharply. "We could go to his house," he said, his voice barely a whisper.

"Do you know where he lives?" I asked.

He folded his arms over his chest and nodded. "I'm one of the few. I went there one weekend. It's about an eight-hour trip. I just… Rook planned for every eventuality. He had a circle of friends who knew where he lived, so if something happened, we could make sure—" Kelly's voice hitched. "Make sure everything was covered."

It killed me to see Kelly's expression. I hadn't been aware he and Rook were as close as it seemed, and I hated that I needed him to tell me the information I had to have.

"I need to know where he lives," I said. "Maybe there are notes or something that we can use. Right now, we're all flying blind, and that includes any operative in the field, not just the ones who worked for him."

Kelly nodded and stood. He was still shaky on his feet. I could see Lilah was about to protest, but he held up his hand, and she stopped. She did wrap an arm around him to keep him steady though. I could see him lean on her and give a weak smile. It warmed my heart. He could protest all he wanted, but Kelly obviously had feelings for her that went beyond friendship.

I turned to Oscar and Sammy. "I'm going to need the two of you to come with us. I have no idea what we're looking for, but it'll be easier if we have extra sets of eyes. No one goes anywhere alone. I don't care if we're all in the same house, you don't leave your partner. Sammy will go with Oscar; I'll go with Kelly and Lilah."

Sammy frowned, but said nothing. I knew he wasn't happy about my assignments, but I needed a clear head and being close to him would have me wanting him to touch me. Rook's death had rattled me, and right now, only force of will allowed me to hold myself together.

We piled in the car. With five of us, plus Kip sleeping on Sammy's lap, it wasn't a comfortable fit, but we made it work. Kelly directed me out of the city proper and through winding, dusty back roads into the middle of nowhere. After a few bathroom breaks for Kip, we finally came to a compound of buildings with a two-story home smack dab in the middle of nowhere. From a distance, it looked like any other house. A little more opulent, but nothing special.

"Don't let the looks fool you," Kelly said, his voice soft. "This structure has been built to protect the occupant against forced entry, climate change, chemical/biological/explosive attacks. There are vaults for firearms and ammunition, remote control offensive and defensive systems, hidden compartments and sliding bookcases, emergency escape routes, alternative energy systems, the windows and walls are fortified to withstand up to .50 caliber gunfire. There are underground bomb shelters and storage areas with supplies of food. This place is a fortress, even if it appears to be more like a resort."

And that was exactly what I thought of when looking at it. It reminded me of a spa in middle of the desert. There were dozens of smaller buildings, each connected to the other by wrought iron footbridges. The main house was a split-level tan brick building with wraparound porches on both top and bottom. High, arching windows with tinted glass were set into copper-tinted frames. The area in the courtyard appeared to be bluestone planking that surrounded an infinity-shaped pool with crystal-clear water. Kelly led us up onto the porch where he used his fingerprint to allow access, then entered a security code. He pushed open the door, allowing a blast of cold air to escape as we stepped inside.

"Holy shit," Sammy whispered.

The front room was massive, with a network of computers set against one wall. The other wall, with a faux brick laminate, had shelves of books surrounding a marble fireplace. The flooring seemed to be hardwood, but had a bit of give when stepped on.

"There are pressure sensitive steel panels beneath the floor," Kelly said as I knelt down to examine it. "Rook told me there were also several trapdoors that will allow you into the lower area in case of attack. There is also an elevator system that runs from the bottom levels to the upper floors."

"It's like the ultimate doomsday prep," Oscar noted.

Kelly nodded. "I always thought it was overkill, but Rook said in the event of a catastrophe, he could bring agents together so that they could mobilize and help where needed. It's why there are so many buildings. He had them built as housing should they ever be needed. They're not much more than dorm rooms, but they're functional."

It made perfect sense to me. Rook put the wellbeing of people above all else. It was the code he lived by, and the one that killed him.

"Do you think he's got any of the security armed?" Sammy asked.

Kelly went to one of the computers on the nearby desk. He tapped a couple of buttons and scanned the monitor. "No, he's got everything but the front door disabled, which makes no sense."

"It does if he wasn't expecting to come back," Oscar mused. "One thing I remember about Rook is that the man is—was always three steps ahead of everyone else. He knew what was going to happen, and he made sure that we could get in here."

The truth of Oscar's words were a lance through my heart.

"The stupid son of a bitch," I growled. "He should have trusted me to handle it."

"Like you did with the kid?" Oscar whispered. "You were told to wait, not to go in angry, but you did. How is Rook any different than you?"

Oscar didn't wither before my glare.

"Fuck you," I snapped. "That's different."

"Not to Rook. He was doing what he thought he needed to in order for his people to be safe. What he did wasn't any different than something you or I would do. He willingly gave his life so others wouldn't be killed."

His words made sense, but the outcome didn't. It didn't matter what Rook thought. It ended up killing him and leaving the rest of us with targets on our backs. "And a fuck of a lot of good that did him."

"Haven?" Lilah called, her voice filled with panic.

Oscar and I rushed to where she stood with Kelly, her arms wrapped around him as he sobbed. I had never seen the man cry before. Sammy entered the room and immediately went to Kelly, pulling him in for a hug, while Lilah moved around to rub his back.

"What's wrong?" I demanded.

Lilah pointed to the desk where several envelopes were laid out. Each had a name on it. Kelly's lay open on the table. Sammy looked at me, his lip trembling as I picked up the one addressed to me and tore it open. A single sheet of creamy white paper slid out into my shaky hand. The words were penned with a deliberate care. Every letter was neat and easily read.

Michael,

So apparently I'm dead, otherwise you wouldn't have gotten this. Man, that sucks. I was hoping I could talk some sense into him, or at the very least take everyone else out of harm's way. I know you're probably complaining that I didn't listen to you. Maybe next time I'll know better.

What can I say that would make sense in a letter? It has been the greatest privilege of my life to work with you. You are a strong, capable man, who is destined for something more than being an assassin. You have Kelly and Samuel at your side, and I think that will help lift you to a much higher place.

Don't be angry with me, okay? I went through the list of agents he's killed and realized I couldn't stand it if the next name on the list was someone I considered family to me. I guess it's a moot point now, though. You're reading this, so I blew it. I had to try to stop him. Guess that went over well. Or not. Do me a favor, would you? Don't show this to anyone else. What I'm going to say here is really for you alone. Each letter is only for the person to whom it's addressed, so don't complain when Samuel and Kelly don't show you theirs. Though knowing Samuel, he'll still tell you what I said. The kid will always find a way to bust my chops, I'm telling you. Love him, Haven. Hold him close. Now, more than ever.

With me being gone, the organization is going to need someone to fill my shoes. Someone who has the respect and admiration of many people. That's going to be you.

I blinked back the tears. I wasn't Rook. Didn't want to be him. I wanted the man here where he belonged.

I know you're going to argue and fuss. It's what you do. But if you think about it, you'll know I'm right. You have a family to take care of now, and you can't be traipsing around the world, trying to put out small fires when there is a chance to coordinate efforts against them.

I've already spoken with my superiors. They know I want you to take my job when I retire. Of course, they don't know that I've apparently already done so. (It's a joke, so you can laugh.)

As for our killer, his name is Joel Timmons. He was in a relationship with a former agent, who died on a mission. There is a document about him on the desktop of my computer. It wasn't easy to obtain. I ran into a lot of roadblocks trying to dig up anything on him. Read it and know your enemy. And for God's sake, don't go in angry. That never works out for you, and I don't need to see you any time soon.

A few other things. This house? Yours. Even if you decide you don't want the job with the agency. Keep your family safe. Make this a haven for all of you. I'm entrusting Kelly to you. This will be hard on him. We've known one another for years, and he's got a good heart. Don't let him be alone.

I do have one request of you. There's an envelope taped inside the drawer. It's for my daughter, Mary Jessup. I need her to have it. I want her to know that her father never forgot about her, and that he loved her so very much. Watch out for her. She's all that was good in my world.

Okay, well… I have a meeting to get to. I'm sure it probably won't end well, but if the man has any honor, this will be the last we hear from him.

Michael, you don't know what having you as a friend has meant to me.

My best to you, Sammy, and Kelly. Oh, and tell Oscar he still owes me.

Nathan Jessup aka Rook

My tears stained the sheet of paper. I couldn't deny how it tore me up inside. Glancing over, I saw Sammy reading his own. Big, wet streaks left a shiny trail down his cheeks. He looked up and our gazes met. He crumpled the paper in his hand and rushed over to where I stood, took me in his arms, and buried his face in my chest.

"Rook wanted us to have the house," I whispered to him. "He wants us to make it our very own haven."

Sammy barked out a laugh. "That fucker. If he were here, I'd kill him right now." He sobbed. "He's really gone, isn't he?"

"Yeah, I'm afraid so."

"What are we going to do?"

"Rook left us some information on Joel. He said it was important to know the enemy."

"Please, tell me he's a dead man," Sammy said, a fierce expression on his face.

"Can't get much deader," I assured him.

As I looked up, I saw Oscar. He stood in the doorway, seeming very uncomfortable.

"What's up, O?"

He shook his head.

"Rook says you still owe him. Care to tell me what that's about?"

He gave me a watery smile and stood straight. "It was supposed to be our secret, but I guess now it doesn't matter anymore. When I killed Knight,

Rook may have been the one to tell me what files to take. He said it would be my insurance policy. To say he wasn't happy about the situation would be an understatement, but he also understood why I had to do it. He believes—believed—in the job, but knew there had to be a better way. Without him, I'd probably be dead and buried by now. At the very least, they'd have locked me away and I wouldn't have seen the light of day ever again."

I chuckled. Rook was a man of many surprises.

"Okay, we have work to do. Rook said he's got a file on Joel, so first we need to go through the information. In the meantime, I want Lilah to put Kelly to bed, assuming you can find a bedroom."

Kelly opened his mouth, likely to protest, but stopped and nodded. He seemed to have aged ten years. "I am tired," he admitted.

He let Lilah lead him from the room, and for a moment, I worried how much this would affect him. But I had to focus on the task at hand. I took a seat at the heavy, dark wood desk. I tapped on the space bar and the computer came to life. I glanced over the files on the desktop. Each folder had a lock on it, except for one marked as Joel. I clicked it.

Contrary to what Rook told me, apparently there was information on people who used to be agents. Joel's file wasn't large, but it told a story similar to mine. Brother killed overseas, parents couldn't handle it and took to drinking, which led to harder drugs. The mother would take out her anger on Joel and his younger sister.

He wasn't a great agent. There were several infractions noted in his file, mostly small things like being rough with an informant. There wasn't anything that stood out in his career. He received a few slaps on the wrist; though, there were notes that even though he wasn't part of Rook's squad, Rook wanted him watched more closely.

Joel may have thought the agency didn't know about him and Bulwark—Terry—but he'd been wrong. I smiled to myself, because there wasn't much Rook didn't know. The two of them had bought a property together in North Carolina. A few dozen acres with a small house on it. Rook hoped that it might be a stabilizing influence on Joel, but then he'd quit the agency.

Bulwark, on the other hand, contrary to what Joel had said, had continued to take missions. I noticed a progression in the ones he took that had me quirking an eyebrow and formulating my plan of attack.

"Oscar?"

"What's up?" he asked, a frown on his face.

"I've got something special for you to do." I waggled my brows at him. That made him smile.

CHAPTER TWENTY-ONE

To say we moved like a well-oiled machine would not be wrong. Joel had given us the impetus to put an end to his rampage, and we were all committed to seeing it through.

Oscar was given his marching orders, and he left to take care of our first offensive strike. Sammy was familiarizing himself with the computer system, and Kelly reached out to Rook's superiors to let them know what had happened. Suffice it to say, they gave us carte blanche to deal with the situation as we saw fit, since we were at the epicenter of the events. Then they balked when we told them what we needed from them.

Talking with the men who gave Rook orders was weird. I'd never really given them much thought beyond what Rook had said. They were a shadowy organization, who had their fingers in a lot of pies. They weren't perfect, but we lived in an imperfect world. Now, I understood what he meant.

"I'm sorry. I can't give you that information."

There was no way I could stop the growl from escaping. "This is bullshit! Rook is dead. Does that mean nothing to you?"

"Of course it does," the man on the other end said haughtily. "Rook was a valued asset to—"

"Stop. Just fucking shut up and listen to me. I need access to everything you have on Joel Timmons. I don't care if you have to dig up Bulwark so I can question him myself."

"There is no cause for you to—"

"Are you listening to me? Because obviously you're not hearing what I'm telling you. My friend is dead. The man who was my handler. You know, the one who kept me on a short leash? He's not here anymore, which means I'm not bound by your rules. Tell me no again, and see what I won't do to find you."

The man gulped audibly. "I'll have to talk with a few other people."

"You do that. Talk to whoever the hell you need to, but I want that information by tomorrow."

"But that's not possible!" he complained. "Even if we agree, it will take time to get it all together."

"And you have time. Until tomorrow. This man is singlehandedly responsible for killing several agents that we know of, in addition to Rook. He knows about us, and he could very well blow the lid off the entire agency."

The man on the other end sniffed. "He'll never find us."

"And yet, he tracked down the other agents from a few notes that Bulwark had made. He found me, destroyed my home, nearly beat my majordomo to death, and made threats against my husband. Do you think he's not motivated to find you? For that matter, do you think I wouldn't be?"

Even though I expected him to hang up on me, he drew in a sharp breath. "I'll call you back within the hour."

Then he hung up.

After my call, I went in to see what Sammy had found. He shot me an annoyed look when I asked.

"Computers aren't my thing," he complained. "Unless it's Facebook or Instagram, I don't know much about them. Even with the passwords, I'm being blocked at every turn. I'm not going to be much use to you."

His shoulders muscles were knotted as I began to knead them. He groaned and tipped his head back.

"I'm sorry. I wish I knew more about this"—he fluttered his hand at the computer—"beast."

"It's fine," I assured him. "We have the information most important. I was hoping there might be something we missed. Rook left us what he found on Joel, but I was more interested in Bulwark. Anything we find may be the piece we need to find Joel and take him down."

"I'm not giving up," he said. "I've been looking online to see how to crack files. It's gotten me a little further than I had been. Pretty sure these hackers never found a system like this before."

He was right. The organization hired some of the world's best hackers to make the system safe. Passwords were changed and encrypted every day.

Important files were safeguarded with sophisticated traps and loops that, unless you knew what you were looking for, made it nearly impossible to find.

"Don't knock yourself out," I told him. "There is still the chance that we'll get the information from the higher-ups. Oscar is also checking with his contacts. One way or another, we'll get what we need."

"Why are they being so fucking anal about this?" he groused.

I shrugged, digging deeper into his muscles, which elicited groans of pleasure.

"In this world, knowledge is power. It's why they were so angry when Oscar left with stuff from Knight's office. It put them in an awkward position, and they're not likely to want to put themselves out like that again. Bad enough Knight made it easy for Oscar to get the info, but knowing that he's holding onto it pisses them off."

He said nothing else while I continued to massage him. I'd missed being able to touch him, to fall asleep at night with him spooned around me, to have him take me out of my head. The problem was even if sex were an option right now, I felt certain that neither of us was in the mood.

"Hey," he said, putting a hand atop mine, "come here."

I took a deep breath and stepped away. My mood was all over the place, but even this loss of contact had caused my anxiousness to ramp up.

"You're not centered, are you?"

There wasn't any way I could lie to him, so I shook my head. He grinned at me as he turned the chair around so we were face-to-face.

"Kneel down here and put your head on my knees."

Getting down there wasn't easy. A man my size simply isn't made to drop down quickly. Once I assumed the position he wanted, I lay my head on his lap. He dug his nails into my scalp and began scratching. The sharp bite of pain ensured that he had my complete attention.

"You're handling this well," he whispered. "I admit, I've been off-kilter since I read his letter. This whole thing seems too surreal. But you're holding yourself together, and I'm very proud of you."

If anyone saw us, they'd wonder at the whole dynamic between us. I was much bigger than Sammy, but he was the one who held the power. I needed him like a life preserver thrown to a drowning man.

"What did Rook's letter to you say?"

He chuckled. "Nice try. Rook said not to share, and I have no intention of doing so. The one thing I will tell you, however, is that he held you in the highest regard. Oh, and he said he'd never seen you look more handsome than you were at our wedding."

The words brought a stab of pain to my heart. To know that he'd been so close, that Sammy and I could have hugged him?

"Why didn't he come in and say something?" I asked.

"Maybe it's just who he was. But don't think of it in those terms. He came to see you, his friend, get married. I have to wonder how often he got out of this house. Being Rook was a full-time job and probably didn't allow for much time off. And to have a house this big for just him? Crazy."

The house was immense. As large as ours had been, Rook's was easily four times the size. Multiple buildings spread out over several acres of land. On closer inspection, we'd found the compound had four main buildings. As we'd explored them, we'd discovered one was an enormous library, another held even more computer equipment, and the third had been setup as a training room. What we had initially taken to be an infinity pool was actually two smaller teardrop-shaped ones. On the first side, it was like a Jacuzzi, all bubbles and heat. The other, a regular pool, but the water was much cooler. We'd found at least six hidden passages that led out from the main area to the sixteen smaller buildings that dotted the landscape. There were probably that many hidey-holes in the flooring. Rook's house was a veritable fortress.

When the phone rang, I was off the floor and answering it by the second ring.

"Hello?"

"Haven? This is King. I have to say, I am not used to being threatened in the manner you relayed to my assistant."

King? I admit, I knew the whole organization's power structure was based on chess, but never did I think I would be talking to the top dog.

"Yeah, well, extenuating circumstances and all. By the way, I won't be calling you King. Unless that's really your name."

He gave a dry chuckle. "You're a real charmer, aren't you? I knew you would be when Rook told us about how you handled your interview."

Being held in a room, tied to a bed, and having the shit scared out of me had been their idea of an interview? Nice.

"He did say you would be... What were his words? Oh. A breath of fresh air. For the record, my name is King. You can call me Alexander if you prefer."

Alexander King? Shit, even I had heard his name whispered as being a major player in the halls of power. The man was supposedly a myth, whose boldness in both business and in his life made him fodder for many urban legends. It was rumored that he had more money than Bill Gates and Warren Buffett combined, but lived so far off the grid, most didn't believe he existed at all. There were no pictures of him, and quotes attributed to the man were more often than not made up by someone else. He held no meetings, spoke to no one. The business that bore his name was run by a group of men who signed affidavits they'd never had contact with him. Of course, it gave him a perfect spot from which to run the organization.

And now, he was on the phone with me.

"I won't deny it was self-serving to base the organization on my name. I quite liked the whole intrigue angle. So you're looking for information on Joel Timmons—codename Seeker—and Terry Michaels—codename Bulwark. You do know we don't hand this information out for a reason, correct? The security of our organization and the safety of our active field agents is one of our highest priorities."

"I do. And you know that Joel already had enough to piece together where some former agents lived, as well as killing innocent people in his misguided desire to get to Rook. Our friend sacrificed himself for the ideals of the organization, not to mention to keep people safe. You owe him."

King's voice was dark when he answered. "I don't owe anyone, Mr. Phelps. Everyone in this organization is well compensated for being part of it. Each of them—Rook included—accepted the risks the job came with. While I understand how upset you must be after having found your friend in that—"

"Say another word, and I will track you down. I'll make sure they never find a piece of you. You don't disrespect Rook; do you understand me?"

King chuckled. "I can see that Edgar wasn't embellishing. You certainly do have a temper."

"Yes, well, finding a friend chopped into bits does tend to put one on edge," I snapped.

"You're right, of course. I do apologize for my lack of compassion." He cleared his throat. "It's not how we normally do things, but these aren't normal circumstances. I'll have Edgar forward to you everything we have on the two men. As you've already been told, you can deal with the situation however you see fit. Should you need anything, don't hesitate to let us know."

"Thank you."

"One last thing, for the record. You and Samuel wouldn't be the first people who have disappeared after getting on my bad side. I suggest you not do it again."

With the final warning, he hung up, and a cold shiver ran down my spine.

"What did he say?" Sammy prompted.

"He's sending the information to us." No way would I tell him about the mega-rich man who'd said he could make us vanish.

"These files fill in quite a bit of missing information," Sammy said as he thumbed through reams of papers. "Bulwark was an amazing agent, if these sheets are anything to go by. He was involved in some big-time disappearances. One of these men was dubbed by the papers as the Long Island Serial Killer. It says that Bulwark tracked him down and dispatched him on the very first mission he took. To this day, the papers say the case is unsolved, but it isn't."

Bulwark was impressive. I'd fought him during my training and gotten a nice scar across my chest as a reminder. He was a broad man, with a face not unlike a roadmap of scars of his own. He wasn't a handsome man by any stretch, but he did have a presence.

"Look for anything we can use against Joel," I instructed Sammy. "It's time we end this once and for all."

Oscar stepped into the room as Sammy and I were poring through the paperwork. He gave me a cheeky grin. "It's all set. Let me tell you, it's going to be spectacular."

Sammy glanced between us. "What did the two of you do?"

"A surprise for Joel," I said, not going into detail.

A quick shake of his head was Sammy's only reply. He did, however, pin Oscar with a stare. He swept a hand toward the table to indicate the stacks of folders. "Grab a pile and get to work."

Oscar turned toward me. "Is he always this bossy?"

I grinned. "Pretty much."

He frowned at Sammy. "And you're still alive? I don't get it."

Oscar picked up several folders, then flopped down on one of the leather sectionals spread about the room. I'd wondered if Rook had used this room for meetings, considering the amount of seating available.

"Where do you want me?" came a soft voice from the door.

"Back in bed," Sammy insisted. "You're not looking well."

Kelly shrugged. "Well enough. I... I need to help."

It didn't sound like Kelly at all. The man who stood before me wasn't the one who'd sparred with me or fought Joel. He wasn't even a shadow of his former self. Hell, the man looked broken. Deep, dark rings under his eyes let me know Kelly hadn't been sleeping well. His mouth was pinched, not showing the easy smile he always wore. He trembled as he shifted from foot to foot.

"Lilah?" I asked, addressing the woman behind him, who stood close to prop him up.

"I think he should be in bed, but he said he would feel better if he had something to do. It'll be okay, as long as he doesn't get too worked up. He's got company with him, though."

"Oh?"

Kip sat next to Kelly, leaning against his leg.

"He jumped on the bed, and curled up next to Kelly. I tried to coax him out of the room, but he wouldn't move."

Kip was a smart dog and seemed especially sensitive to moods. Maybe he could sense Kelly's and wanted to make the man feel better.

"Please," Kelly said, his voice breaking. "Let me help."

I pointed to a place for him to sit. "There," I said as I pushed a coffee table in front of him. He sat down and sighed.

"What are we looking for?" he asked as he began going through the first folder.

I blew out a breath. How Rook had made this seem easy was beyond me. "Anything that stands out about Joel or Bulwark. If you find something about the two of them together, all the better. Rook left us a basic outline, but I need more meat."

Oscar grinned and was about to say something.

"Shut up, Oscar," Sammy said with a sigh.

"Fuck. He left himself wide open for it, and you had to ruin it."

"If Haven needs meat, I'll be the one giving it to him."

Oscar cackled. "I may have to visit more often. I haven't laughed this much in a long time."

"Sounds good. Next time you can bring Max. I'd love to meet him," Sammy said, his gaze narrowed.

I couldn't help but laugh when Oscar's eyes went wide. "Fuck no. I'm not getting the two of you together. That's a recipe for disaster right there."

Everyone but Kelly laughed. Seeing him like this was killing me. The man was nearing his sixty-third birthday, yet right now, he seemed decades older. I put down the file I held, and Sammy glanced up. I nodded toward Kelly and he dipped his chin once.

"Kelly, come with me."

"But I just started—"

"Leave it," I insisted. "Let's go."

Lilah started to stand, but I stopped her. "Just Kelly."

She sat back down and didn't look happy.

I directed Kelly to the training room. Blue mats covered a section of the floor, with free weights and a few exercise machines scattered about the large, open space. I led Kelly toward the mats. He'd just stepped on, when I whirled and aimed a blow at his face. He stepped back, barely evading my fist.

"What the fuck are you doing?" he snapped.

"Looking for Kelly, because what I see? That's not him. I don't know who the hell you are, but you aren't the man I know."

I swung again, and he tripped, trying to move back. He fell to the ground with a thump and a grunt.

"Stop this!" he pleaded, raising his hands to shield himself.

"No." I stomped a foot near him, and he shoved my ankle, pushing it away. "Get up," I told him.

He lay back on the mat. "Fine. Kick me if you want. Pound my face into a bloody pulp. I don't care."

The front of his shirt gaped open as I pulled him off the floor and to his feet. It was then I noticed how much weight he'd lost. The man was a shadow of himself, and that was something I could not—would not—accept.

"Pathetic," I snarled. "You're ready to lie down and die? Is that it?"

He stood there, and I saw his fingers curl into fists as color rose in his cheeks. It was the first real reaction I'd seen since Joel beat him.

"He's dead. Do you not get that?" he asked, his eyes wild. "He slaughtered Rook. Wild animals are less vicious."

I closed the gap between us until our chests bumped. "Is this about Rook, or what Joel did to you?" I demanded. "Tell me!"

Kelly's face contorted in anger. "Fuck you! You don't know a goddamn thing!"

"No, of course not. We came home one night and found someone we care about beaten to a pulp hanging from the ceiling. It made us feel helpless, because we weren't there for him. Joel shot me in the back while I was protecting a kid. Could have killed me right there on the floor, but he didn't. He left me lying there, bleeding, while he mocked me and threatened to hurt you all. Then he killed someone I considered a friend. And let's not forget, he also killed people who were my comrades. So yeah, I don't know anything about feeling like I've lost control of my life and I'm watching it spiral down the fucking toilet. How stupid of me to think I might know a little of how you're feeling."

I turned and stormed toward the door.

"Haven… Michael, wait."

My breath was coming in sharp pants. I'd bared my soul to Kelly, telling him things I would only ever let Sammy know. When I turned to face him, he stood, head bowed.

"Do you know how I met Rook?"

"No," I replied tersely.

He looked up and gave me a smile, one so sad it served to make me angry at Joel all over again. I moved toward him, then directed him to yet another in the myriad of chairs Rook kept. He sat and patted the seat beside him. He waited until I sat before he leaned forward and put his head in his hands.

"I'd been working for another agent. At the time, Bishop was his handler. Out of the blue, I get a call from someone named Rook. I'd heard of him, but my charges weren't part of his network. Anyway, he called me one day and asked if I was willing to work with a real hard case. He said this agent had chased away four other people who couldn't stand working with him anymore. I said sure, I'd do it."

He grinned slightly, and it loosened the knot in my stomach.

"This guy? He had a chip on his shoulder the size of Phoenix. He thought he was hot shit, and don't get me wrong, he was. But the arrogance everyone saw hid a vulnerability that no one bothered to look for. I came to realize he pushed everyone away, because he felt it was better to be alone than it was to be hurt again."

The chair was suddenly hard and uncomfortable. I got up and started pacing, remembering how Kelly had refused to allow me to force him away. How he showed me his playful side and brought mine out. The bastard was infuriating, and I loved him for it.

"Almost a year passed, and I grew closer to this prickly son of a bitch. Rook commented on the change in you and said he was sure it was down to me. But he also told me the assignment was over, and it was time to find me a new person to work with. I told him no. Now, in my job, you don't argue with your employer. Rook was surprised by my vehemence. While you were out on assignment one day, he came to the house and introduced himself. Definitely not what I thought he'd be, but he did have an air of authority about him. Anyway, he repeated that it was time for me to move on to my next assignment and that you would be getting a new majordomo. I refused.

"He raised his eyebrows and said, 'Excuse me?' I said that you needed stability in your life. You needed me. I told him the stories about the squirt guns, the koi pond, and other things that focused and centered you. And I told him that it was that which made you the agent you were. We argued about it some more, but in the end, he moved heaven and earth to make sure they kept me here. For some reason, Rook had a soft spot where you're concerned."

I remembered the conversation we'd had last year, where he'd told me about his daughter. It seemed out of character for him, but after that moment, he'd opened up a little more.

Now, he was never going to open up again.

We were nearly ready to make sure Joel paid for his crimes. And this time, I was looking forward to it.

CHAPTER TWENTY-TWO

Our eyes were burning by the time we made it through half the paperwork. Six days, countless hours, and lots of coffee. But we were no closer to finding the information I'd hoped would be there. Kelly had grown stronger since our conversation. He seemed to face the piles of folders with a new determination. It was on the sixth day that he cleared his throat and waggled his eyebrows at me.

"I think I might have found the connection you're looking for."

He held out the tattered folder. I went through it, scanning the dates, and a smile bloomed on my face.

"Oh my god, this is totally what we need! This gives me something to use against him, to knock Joel off balance." I handed the file back to Kelly. "Keep looking. I want any and everything that we can find on this man. He's had the ball in his court long enough. Time for us to make a play of our own."

"You know I get all quivery when you start talking in sports metaphors," Oscar said as he continued looking at the file he held.

He yelped and jumped. I frowned when I saw the smile on Sammy's face.

"Did you just kick him?" I asked.

He shrugged. "Maybe."

"He did!" Oscar protested. "The little shit got me right in the shin."

"Only because I couldn't get my foot high enough to nail you in the balls," Sammy retorted.

"Haven, handle your man, before I take him into the gym and show him what a real fight is like."

Sammy jumped up, knocking his chair back. "Bring it!"

Oscar shook his head. "Not worth it," he grumbled.

"Chickenshit."

"Whatever you say," he drawled.

Sammy picked his chair up and shoved it under the table. He stormed from the room.

"Let's go," I said.

"Where?" Oscar asked.

"You're going to make this right. I know we're all tired and on edge, but you guys need to get this settled."

Oscar shrugged. "Fine. His funeral."

He got up and we followed Sammy into the gym. I found him standing at a punching bag, hitting it hard enough to cause me to wince.

"Okay, I'm here. You wanna spar? Let's do it."

Sammy turned and glared at Oscar. Without saying anything, he opened a cabinet on the far wall and pulled out a pair of gloves. He slid them on, then came to me to help lace them. Oscar did the same. The two of them walked out onto the same mats Kelly and I had been on recently. Sammy powered in and swung first, but Oscar blocked it. Sammy danced around, the way he'd been taught, and jabbed, but to no avail. His attacks were clumsy and uncoordinated. Oscar continued to put his gloves up and deflect the blows. This went on for several minutes, until Sammy was huffing for breath.

Oscar frowned. "Is that the best you got, kid? I've seen at least five openings where I could have had you on the mat already."

Sammy snarled. "So do it! Prove to me you're as tough as you claim."

Oscar grinned. Two hits later, Sammy was laid out on the floor, looking up at the ceiling.

Oscar stepped back and crossed his arms over his chest. "Had enough?"

"N-no." Sammy struggled to get up. He was shaky when he swung again, and this time Oscar let the strike through. It was barely a tap.

"Fight me!" Sammy demanded.

"No, you're doing a good enough job of fighting yourself," Oscar replied. "What are you trying to prove here? That you're as badass as me? Newsflash, you're not. You've got heart, I'll give you that. Keep in mind, heart alone isn't going to stop someone who is determined to hurt you. Rook found that out already."

"Don't you talk about Rook!" Sammy shouted. "He was a better man than you will ever hope to be."

"And his death is eating you up inside. I get it, kid. But so you know, it's killing me, too. I have to compartmentalize it, though. I need to keep it buried deep; otherwise, I wouldn't be able to do my job. You, on the other hand, are being ripped apart because Rook gave you something you never had."

"Oh? What's that?" Sammy challenged.

"A family. A sense that you belonged."

Sammy's eyes went wide. I wanted to push Oscar away, to stop him from hurting Sammy, but Sammy needed to hear what Oscar was telling him. He had to let go of the pain.

"Don't think I don't pay attention. I saw how you fussed over Kelly. How your first instincts were to take care of Haven. And how devastated you were when you heard about Rook. You're looking to let all that anger out on someone, and I get to be the target. If that's what you need, I'm okay with that. Shit, I'll stand here and let you hit me as much as you want, if you think it'll help."

Sammy stopped and dropped his arms to his sides. "It's not fair," he whispered.

"No, it isn't. But it's the life we lead, and sometimes it sucks. The question I have for you is this. Are you going to let it eat you up, or are you going to do something about it?"

Sammy's chin dropped to his chest. "What can I do?"

"Exactly what you've been doing. Help Haven. Keep him on the straight and narrow. Help him however you can. Honor Rook by holding your family together." Oscar stepped closer to Sammy. "Don't let his death stop you from standing up for others."

When he took Sammy in his arms, I tensed. Oscar looked at me over Sammy's head and gave me a sad smile. He backed Sammy up until they were next to me, then turned him and pushed my husband into my arms.

"I think this is yours," he said before walking out of the room.

"I'm sorry," Sammy whispered.

I leaned in and began to unlace the gloves, then slipped them off. I took his hands in mine, noting their dampness. "For what? Being human?"

He shook his head. "I'm the one who is supposed to have a handle on things. The one you can lean on. Right now? I'm falling apart. Rook's letter got to me, and I don't know how to deal with it."

"You can start by telling me what he said."

Sammy sighed. "How much he wished he could be here to see me emerge from my shell. How he would one day like to meet us in person, and how he knew that even with him being…gone, we would still fight the good fight. He said he was entrusting you to me, and that I'd need to keep you safe."

My throat closed up. I wasn't sure if I would hug the man or kill him if I had him here. He did what he thought was best, but in the process, he tore us all apart. How were we supposed to move on without him?

I took Sammy back to the room we'd been sleeping in and pushed him down onto the bed. I crawled in next to him and he molded himself around me, wrapping me in his arms. We didn't speak, simply lay there and soaked up each other's strength. The coming days were going to be hard, but we needed to be able to depend on each other. Not just me and Sammy, but all of us.

After he fell asleep, I got up and watched him for a few minutes. He hadn't been sleeping well, either. None of us had, really. The time for this to end had arrived, because I would be damned if any of my family would continue to suffer while Joel was out there. I slipped out of the bedroom, went into yet another one of the rooms the house had. This one seemed to be a library of sorts. Books lined the dark cherrywood shelves, their light covers a striking contrast. I took out my phone and dialed a number.

"Mr. King has been expecting your call," came the terse voice on the other end of the line.

I was transferred without further delay.

"Were the files helpful?" he asked.

"More than," I assured him. "I know now what to do."

"And you're calling me because…?"

"Your assistant said you were expecting me to call."

"Oh, I was. Just wondering if it's for what I think it is."

I took a deep breath and laid out my plan. From beginning to end, I told King every step that we were going to be taking. He said nothing until I finished, then he whistled.

"Okay, it takes a lot to surprise me, but you've done it. I must admit, I did not see that one coming. Are you sure this is how you want to proceed?"

"Not really, but to me it's how it has to be."

King hummed. "Okay then. Let me make some phone calls, and I'll make sure it's taken care of. You are good to go. And, Haven?"

"Yes?"

"I'm glad I didn't make you disappear." He laughed. "After this is over and done with, I'd like for us to have a conversation."

"About?"

"That'll wait until you've cleared this whole thing up. I want Joel taken off the board and am entrusting that to you."

"Thank you. I'll be sure to give him your regards."

After we hung up, I took a deep breath. *Showtime.*

"Is everything ready?" I asked.

"It is," Oscar replied, showing off his gleaming smile.

"Sammy?"

He thumbed through a new folder. "I have everything here I found on Terry and Joel. Now are you going to tell us what's going on?"

"He told *me*," Oscar teased.

Sammy frowned. "Just because I can't beat you now, doesn't mean I won't be able to do it later, you know."

Oscar made a motion like he was jacking off. "Baby, you can beat me whenever you feel like it."

This time, instead of an impotent display of anger, Sammy laughed. "Asshole."

"Oh, I can work with that, too!" He leered at Sammy. "And I'm really, really good."

A quick shake of the head, and Sammy turned his attention back to me.

"Okay, so give with the details."

"No, sorry. Not this time."

He glared at me. "And why the hell not?"

"Because he's protecting us," Kelly answered from his perch on the couch. "This is something he and Oscar are going to keep close to the vest. In other words, this is going to be ugly."

"Oh, so ugly." I laughed. "Personally, I can't wait."

"Is everything set on your end?" Oscar asked.

"King said we were a go. So I think it's time we get started."

I slipped my phone from my pocket and dialed Kelly's. Not surprisingly, Joel didn't answer. When the call got kicked to voice mail, I grinned.

"Hey, it's Haven. Though I'm sure you know that by now. Listen, I think we need to talk. There are some things—important things—that I think you need to know about. I'm not sure whether you'll accept my word as good enough, but I swear I'll come alone. If you're at all interested, give me a call."

After I hung up, Oscar said, "And now the wait begins."

After two days, Joel still hadn't called. I was itching to try again to leave a message, but patience was necessary for this game. All of the pieces were in play, I just needed him to step up.

We were sitting in the living room. The television was on, but it didn't seem that anyone was paying attention to it. My gaze swept around the room, trying to figure out what was going on in everyone's head. My knee was bouncing a mile-a-minute, and I found myself wishing something would happen.

"Stop fidgeting," Sammy groused.

"Can't help it," I replied. "Nervous energy."

"I think I know a better way to work that off." He waggled his brows. "Come with me."

It had been several weeks since we'd had sex. With Joel and everything he'd done, and now with Rook, there hadn't been any desire. Now? I could see Sammy's eyes blazing. He needed the release as much as I did.

I followed him to the room we'd taken as ours. It wasn't as comfortable as what we had in our old house, but it wasn't bad. Rook apparently had a thing for dark wood, as the bookcases, bed frame, and desk were all made from the same cherrywood that permeated the house. It was masculine, but welcoming. I hated to admit it, but I could see us living here once this mess was over with.

"Take off your clothes," Sammy insisted, his voice husky. He turned and closed the door. The flipping of the lock loud in the quiet room. He then turned a heated gaze in my direction.

I began to strip down, but then he held up a hand.

He slinked across the room and perched himself on the bed, legs spread wide. "I want you to do it slowly. I think after all this time, I deserve a good show."

He grinned as I lifted the hem of my shirt, displaying my stomach.

"Man, that's enough to make me wish I had dollar bills," he said. "Don't stop."

Though I wanted to get to the main act, I also needed to get Sammy back on track. I peeled the shirt off, incrementally showing skin as I turned slowly so he could see front and back.

"Fuck, I missed seeing this," he whispered.

"Wait until you get to touch it," I teased, tossing in a hip bump like I knew what I was doing.

"No talking. Just do what I said."

He wanted uninterrupted pleasure? Sure, I could do that. My shirt came off, and I spun it on my finger before tossing it onto the floor. After I toed off my shoes, I began to fumble with the button on my pants. My cock was like an iron bar, so damned hard I hurt. The zipper came down, and I shimmied out of the jeans, allowing them to drop to the floor. All I wore now was my socks and underwear. I hitched my thumbs into the waistband and began to peel them off, but Sammy stopped me again.

"Come here."

I closed the distance between us and knelt next to the bed. He reached out and began to trace a finger over my scars. When he touched the one I'd told him Bulwark had inflicted, his breath hitched and he began to draw back. I grabbed his wrist and held it to my chest.

"Don't back away," I told him, worried that this would shut him down again. "You need to take what's yours, and that includes me. If you want me, that is."

His gaze snapped to mine. "Don't you ever think I don't want you," he snarled as he pulled me to my feet and yanked my underwear down. He wrapped his fingers around my shaft and buried his face in the crook of my neck. "God, you smell so good."

We'd decided to take a shower together that morning when we'd woken up. When he'd told me he'd gotten the key back from Oscar, my heart had sped up. He'd made a show of it, unlocking the damn thing slowly and sensually. When it'd clattered to the floor, I'd wanted to cry out in relief. He'd finally taken off that blasted cock cage, and I'd breathed a sigh.

"Don't get excited," he'd insisted. "I may put it back on when we're done."

Then the bastard had chuckled as he'd turned on the water. The bathroom had a strange soap—black peppercorn was something I'd never heard of, but it had an amazing scent that didn't linger. You'd catch a whiff of it now and again, but it wasn't strong or cloying.

He knelt down and nuzzled my crotch, rubbing my dick along his cheek. The slight stubble there caused my cock to ache even more.

"Please," I ground out.

"Please what?" he said, a smile lighting his face.

"Need you naked, too," I insisted. "I need to see you."

"You saw me in the shower."

"Fuck. Sammy, please. Get undressed."

"No," he said. He stood up in front of me. "You want me naked, you do it."

My hands trembled as I reached out to take off his shirt. He stood still, and I had to force myself not to rip the clothes off and throw him on the bed. I knelt to take off his pants and underwear, the awe I felt at being able to touch him again near overwhelming. After he stepped out of them, I started to stand. He put his hands on my shoulders.

"Stay down there," he said. "Open wide."

I did as he commanded. He grabbed my head with one hand and gripped his shaft with the other as he guided it toward me. As it slipped inside, he pushed all the way in, past the back of my throat where he held it for several seconds.

"I was worried you'd be out of practice," he teased as he began to withdraw.

I whimpered and gripped his legs.

"No." He pulled out completely. "Hands at your sides. You're only going to kneel there and let me do what I want."

He wrapped his hands around my head and jammed his thick meat back between my lips.

"God, I've missed fucking your mouth," he panted. "So goddamn hot, it's like you were made for me. I've needed this, and now I'm getting what I deserve."

He pumped faster, pushing beyond my throat muscles. When his legs began to tremble, I knew he was close.

"Swallow me, Michael," he grunted as he began to unload.

The taste was like ambrosia. I would never get enough of this man. I could tell from the copious amount that it had been quite some time for him, too. After he stopped shooting, he held my head until his cock softened slightly. He reached out, took my hand, and pulled me up beside him.

Sammy sagged back onto the bed. "I so needed that," he said. "Gimme a minute to catch my breath, because I'm going to want round two right away. Hell, I may go for round three, too." He sat up and stroked my face. "We've been running since we got here. I know we've spent several days together, but it's like we were still separated." He kissed me. "I've missed you so much, you don't know. Your touch, your scent, hell, simply being able to hold you while we sleep."

My stomach fluttered at his words, because he felt the same as I did. I hated being gone from him for weeks on end. Everything Oscar had said was true. In fairness to Sammy, I was leaving him behind. Yeah, he had Kelly and Kip, but he needed me, too. And heaven knew, I needed him.

After a few moments, he sat up. He rubbed his hand over my hair as he grinned at me. He nodded down toward his once again erect dick.

"I want you to stand up and bend over with your hands on the mattress."

When I assumed the position he asked for, he ran his hands over my body.

"Love the way you feel," he murmured.

217

As he got to my ass cheeks, he ran a finger along the crack, drawing a shudder from me.

"Okay, here's what's going to happen," he started. "You're going to stay just like that. I don't care if you have to bite your tongue or chew your cheek, but you're not allowed to move, speak, or make any noises."

What the fuck?

CHAPTER TWENTY-THREE

"Do you have a problem with that?" Sammy demanded.

"Uh, yeah. How the hell can I help it if I make a noise? You know what you do to me."

He swatted me hard on the ass, and I relished the burn. "You're going to do it because I told you to. Now, no more talking. I don't want to have to gag you. And, if you want to keep the cage off…"

The rest of his threat went unvoiced, but I got the message loud and clear. No talking or sounds of any sort. I leaned over the bed, my arms spread to keep me upright.

"Very nice," he murmured.

He dropped to his knees behind me and spread my cheeks. When the initial waft of his breath blew over my pucker, I knew I was in trouble. At first, it was nothing more than a slight poke of his tongue, but even that was enough to make me sweat. Sammy knew how to play my body. He could tell you what kind of noise I'd make depending on where and how he touched me. My ass was especially sensitive to his ministrations.

When he jammed his tongue against my hole, my first instinct was to cry out, and that bastard knew it.

"Problems?" he asked, his voice light and lilting.

I shook my head. I refused to give him the satisfaction of breaking me. He added a finger in next to his tongue, prepping me for his cock. It had been weeks since I'd been under him, and he was taking his time, teasing, taunting, making me want to plead with him to get on with it. It felt too good, and I had sweat on my brow because I wasn't allowed to beg him for more.

"You're doing well," he muttered, letting his finger slide in deep as he probed for my sweet spot. When his digit brushed over my prostate, I nearly flew over the edge of the bed. I heard the drawer open and the pop of a cap. A cool fluid drizzled down my crack, Sammy's fingers massaging it into my hole.

"Bet you're wondering where this came from," he said.

Fuck no, I didn't give a shit where it came from. I wanted him to get on to the main event, because even though he'd come, I hadn't. My cock wept pre-cum, a long strand that pooled beneath me.

"I ordered some things and took them with me when we went to the safe house. I packed them away in my suitcase, because I knew I'd have you like this. In fact, one of the things I have is something I bought to use on you before this whole mess started. He held it up so I could see it. At about seven inches, it appeared to be made of plastic. The tip was curved and…oh, fuck no.

"I see you know what this is for," he said with an evil laugh. "I've been wanting to try some toys with you. It seems like a good time to try out a prostate massager, don't you think?"

When I shook my head, he patted my ass.

"That's okay. I think it is, and that's what matters, right? So this toy? It has several speed variants. I thought we'd start you out with the lowest one, then see where it leads us."

He added a little lube to the device, then slid it inside me.

"Very nice," he said, pushing it in deeper. He twisted it, and it brushed against my hot spot. A flick of a switch and it began to vibrate in my ass. I clenched hard, because there was no way I could keep from screaming if I didn't.

"The nice thing about this toy? It comes with a strap to hold it on."

A moment later, a band encircled my waist, then clipped. I couldn't figure out why he wanted that, until he crawled underneath me and slid up onto the bed. He waggled his cock at me.

"Suck me," he said, his voice husky.

I opened my mouth and took him in deep, delighting in his groan. He dropped a heavy hand on my head and began thrusting.

"Take it, Michael."

And I did. I held perfectly still and let him use me how he saw fit. At least until my ass started vibrating harder.

Sammy chuckled. "Oh, did I forget to mention it came with a remote?"

Never in my life had I been so turned on. I swallowed around Sammy's cock, taking it into my throat. When he pulled me off, I glared at him.

"I think that's enough for now," he said as he turned the device off. "I really want in that ass. It's been too long."

It took him only moments to unhook the belt and slide the wand out of my ass. He said nothing as he stepped in behind me, pushed me down a little more on the bed, then thrust in deep. My head arched up at the sudden intrusion, but Sammy didn't even give me time to adjust before he was pounding deep inside me.

"I'm sorry," he grunted, slamming harder. "I need you so much."

His fingers dug into my hips as he ground himself against me. The friction caused a delicious ache in my balls. It had been so long since I'd had release that it wouldn't take much to push me over the edge. Sammy howled as he came. The sound was feral.

"Come for me!"

I cried out as jets of come shot from my aching balls, spilling all over the bed. It had been so goddamned long, and the release, while always intense, had never felt like I'd stuck my dick into an electrical outlet. I collapsed onto the bed, Sammy atop me.

"Wow," he groaned. "That was…wow. I think we should do that more often."

It took a few minutes for my sex-addled brain to understand what he meant.

"Fuck no!" I roared as I rolled over and dislodged him. "You're not caging me for weeks on end, just because the orgasm is so intense."

He quirked an eyebrow. "I'm sorry? When did this become a democracy?"

Aw, shit. I wasn't in the mood to argue with him. All I wanted was…

He rolled over and wrapped an arm around me. "I love you," he whispered. "Missed you so much while you were gone. I know how important you are to the world, but when you aren't here, it's like my world isn't complete. Does that make sense?"

It did. "Mine, too. Um…not to be a buzzkill or anything, but could you let me go?"

"Why?"

"Because I'm lying on the wet spot, and it's cold."

He laughed and rolled off me. We took another shower, then changed the sheets. We lay back on the bed and lingered as we reconnected. Every touch from Sammy was a gift. He held my heart and my body in his hands, and it was where I felt the most grounded.

By the time we got out of the shower and changed the linens on the bed, the sun had begun to set. Seeing the sun go down in Arizona had always been a thrill for me. The sky bursting with an amazing rainbow of color that muted as it sunk beneath the horizon, until it finally faded to black. Nowhere I'd been in the world had made me feel like I could call it home, until I'd brought Sammy to live with me. Now I couldn't imagine my life any other way.

"What do you want to do tonight?" Sammy asked.

I thought about it for a moment. Since this mess started, we'd all been run ragged. On edge because we never knew when the next attack would take place, whether one of us would be the target, or if any of us would be the next one for Joel to turn his rage on.

"I think tonight we need a break. Maybe a family movie?"

When his lips curled up and his eyes shone, I knew it was an idea he liked. Of course, he was the only one. When we returned to the living area, our announcement wasn't met with enthusiasm.

"A movie?" Oscar grouched.

"Yep. Sammy's going into the kitchen to make snacks with whatever he can find. Might not be more than PB & J, but something to nibble on while we sit back and watch something together."

Oscar rolled his eyes dramatically and stomped off toward the kitchen, Sammy following close behind. Out of the corner of my eye, I saw Kelly and Lilah curled up on the sofa. Her head rested on his shoulder, while Kelly's head lay against hers. Kip nestled in at Kelly's side. They sat there, eyes closed, fingers laced together, and seemingly very content.

"I can feel you staring," he said. His right eye opened a crack. "You have something to say, I'm sure."

The moment was perfect to tease him about Lilah. He'd denied his attraction to her for a long time, despite Sammy trying to push them together. But seeing them there, curled up on the couch? After everything with Rook, it made me realize how short life could be, and how we had to take our happiness where and when we could.

"No, nothing," I said. "If you're happy, then I'm happy for you."

This got me some raised brows from both of them.

"I admit, I thought about ribbing you, but you deserve happiness. And it's good to see you smile."

He nodded. "You were right, as much as I hate to admit it."

"So you like her more than chocolate milk?" I said, remembering the story about Kelly falling in love with a girl whose eyes were like chocolate milk. It turned out they were both in grade school at the time. He used it as an object lesson of why Sammy and I should be together. For that, I owed him so much.

He opened his eyes. "Fuck you," he said, but there wasn't any heat to his words. "Lilah and I are going to head to—"

"The hell you are, old man. Family night. All of us, together, watching a movie. It's a tradition we've missed out on for far too long. You're going to sit your ass down there and deal with it."

Lilah grinned as she turned pale blue eyes to Kelly. "I'd like to watch a movie," she said.

"Then we're watching a movie," he replied.

She sat back, and her gaze told me the depth of her feelings for Kelly. She'd waited for him to wise up and realize how much she cared for him, and now that he had, she was waltzing on the clouds.

Tearing my gaze away from them, I thumbed through Netflix to see if I could find something we'd all enjoy. On the enormous curved screen, we'd have a good angle no matter where we sat. When it landed on an animated film I'd never seen before, Lilah perked up.

"Oh, I love this movie," she said, her voice filled with a glee I'd never heard from the normally staid doctor.

I turned toward her and Kelly and could see a beseeching look on his face. He desperately wanted to make Lilah happy, and I wanted him to get what he'd been waiting for.

"Then it's what we'll watch," I answered.

When Oscar and Sammy came back with two plates loaded with snacks, we all settled in. As soon as the credits started, Oscar groaned.

"This is the shit Max loves. I've already had to sit through it once. Do we have to do it again?"

Lilah's expression fell. "No, we don't—"

"Yes, we do," I answered. "There are other TVs in the house if you want to watch something else."

Oscar glared at me. "This is fine."

Throughout the movie, Sammy sat next to me, holding my hand. He seemed to relish the contact as much as I did. One thing though, I kept glancing toward Oscar. He complained about watching the film Lilah had chosen, but it dawned on me as it played that his complaint was more about being away from Max than the movie.

Though I had to drag it from him bit by bit, I did learn some things about the young man who was with our friend. Being with Oscar, Max had grown. He still questioned his worth to Oscar, but he'd come into his own. He discovered his love of painting and would sit on their deck overlooking a lake, and lose himself in the joy of his pastime. And now, Oscar was here, away from Max, for weeks on end. At least I knew now how the man understood so well the separation issue.

I tugged my hand from Sammy, who cocked his head. He'd figure it out soon enough. I got up and went over to Oscar, bent down and whispered in his ear, "If you want to go call him, do it. There's no reason to sit here thinking about him when we have phones or computers you can get in touch with him on."

Oscar shook his head. "It's not like it is with you and Sammy," he whispered. "Max understands that."

"Maybe, but I don't think you do. There isn't anything wrong with how you feel, you know. Call him. Let him know you're thinking about him. I bet dollars to donuts he'll be glad to hear from you."

He sat there in silence for a few moments, then his arms flexed as he pushed up out of the chair. "I'm going to bed," he announced. "See you all tomorrow."

Kelly and Lilah waved, but didn't stop watching the movie. Sammy seemed concerned, but I shook my head, and he sat back and pretended to be interested in what was happening onscreen. After Oscar left the room, I went back and took a seat beside my husband, who immediately took my hand in his.

"What's going on?" he asked, his voice soft.

"Oscar needs to call home."

"Oh, Max? Yeah, he misses him."

I was surprised Sammy knew. Max wasn't a topic of conversation very often. "Oh?"

Sammy glanced around, then leaned in close. "It's written all over his face. He's got it bad for the man, even if he won't admit it."

It was good that I wasn't the only one to see it. It made me wonder if Oscar was hiding it or was simply in denial. Either way, it was his life, and aside from a little goading, there wasn't much we could do. What we needed to do, however, was take care of Joel. He still hadn't called me back, so it was time to up the game. I took Sammy's hand and pulled him from the room, leaving Lilah and Kelly to watch the movie.

"Breakfast meeting in the morning," I told Sammy once we were in the bedroom. "Tomorrow we're going to move forward with the plan."

"But Joel hasn't called yet."

"I'm aware, but I won't wait for him to decide. It gives him more time to lash out, and that's something I can't have. Right now, King's pulled all the agents back in. This means no assignments are getting done and innocent people are suffering. That's got to stop."

"Are you ready to let me in on this big plan of yours?" He smiled and batted his eyelashes.

"No."

That earned me a scowl. "I can make you tell me, you know."

He could. He had probably a dozen ways. "You can, but for right now, just trust me, okay?"

Sammy locked a hand around the back of my neck and pulled me in for a kiss. "You know I do."

For a few moments, we enjoyed the closeness, the touching. All too soon, it ended.

"I'm going to Rook's war room," I said. "If you see Oscar, send him in, please."

"Will do, chief!" he replied, adding a snappy salute.

I left Sammy and went down the hall, out into the evening air. This compound was remarkable. Rook's war room was a separate building, which, like the others, was heavily fortified. More computers were located here, high tech stuff that I barely understood. Whatever King had Rook doing went way beyond being my handler. I sat in one of the high-back leather chairs on wheels. Incredibly comfortable, especially for someone who spent a lot of time in here.

I pulled up the files again, reading through Joel's and Terry's history. For a brief moment, I might have felt a twinge of regret for what we were about to do, but I snuffed it out quickly. This man… No, he wasn't a man. He was a fucking animal. He needed to be taken off the board completely.

The door opened, and Oscar strode in. He seemed more relaxed than he had previously.

"Lemme guess. Skype sex with Max?"

"Fuck you," he snarled. "What makes you think I even talked to him?"

"You have the look of a man who had one hell of an orgasm."

Oscar grinned. "I always have one more in me. Why not strip down and let me show you?"

I ignored the teasing. "Have a seat, O. We're going ahead with Plan B tomorrow morning."

He slid into another chair, identical to the one I occupied. "Are you sure?"

"It's the only way I can think of. Unless you've got something else in mind."

He shook his head. "Nope. I liked Plan B anyway. Waiting really isn't my style."

"Then we're agreed? Tomorrow, we'll sit down with everyone and let them know what's about to happen."

"Are you going to give them the details?"

I thought about it for a moment. I trusted every person here, but with what we had planned, I was afraid that someone would object, and that would make us have to debate it.

"No. Executive decision."

"You can make decisions without Sammy? You think I believe that?"

I sneered. "Sammy has a good heart. He'd be the one to try to convince me there was a better way. I can't afford to have that happen."

"Yeah, that makes sense." He paused. "So, I looked like I had one hell of an orgasm?"

There was an innocence to his question that caught me off guard. "Is there something you want to talk about?"

"No. Nothing at all. I did what I needed to do. And I'm ready to end this little game."

That made two of us.

CHAPTER TWENTY-FOUR

Oscar and I stayed up the rest of the night, confirming that everything we had planned was in place. Once we were satisfied we'd covered all our bases, we went in and started breakfast for the troops.

"Hand me berries from the freezer," I said.

Oscar pulled out the bag of blueberries and tossed them to me. I tore it open and poured them into the pancake batter. Meanwhile, Oscar broke open a dozen and a half eggs and whipped them, then poured them into a hot, greased skillet. He tossed in a few pinches of herbs and a handful of shredded cheese, which made the kitchen smell amazing.

He slid a pan of bacon into the oven, then went back to scrambling the eggs.

By the time we were done, we had a mountain of food. Easily enough for five, unless Oscar was hungry. I got on the intercom and called everyone down.

Sammy marched into the kitchen. His hair was mussed and he swiped a hand over his eyes. He stalked toward me and jabbed a finger in my chest. "If you ever use that device again, I'm going to put you back in chastity for the rest of the year."

Oscar grinned and opened his mouth to say something. "Shut the fuck up," I snapped. "Sit down and eat."

We sat around the table, no one talking about anything other than breakfast. Lilah put some butter on Kelly's pancakes, then poured on a bit of syrup.

"That's it?" he grumbled.

"That's a serving," she replied. "You don't need that much sugar."

He frowned at her. "I like syrup," he complained

"And I like having you around. So shut up and eat."

His cheeks pinked, but he dug in. "This is great," he said around a mouthful of pancake. "Would be better with more syrup, but it's really good."

"Better than some of the stuff you've made me eat," I teased.

"Don't start on my soup," he groused.

The conversation stayed light. Mostly about the weather, the house, the food. When everyone had their fill, Sammy cleared the table, then we all adjourned to the living room and took seats around the perimeter of the table.

"Okay," I started. "Oscar and I were at it all night and—"

"And I'm surprised he can sit this morning," Oscar said, looking at Sammy and waggling his brows.

Sammy refused to take the bait and kept his attention on me.

"We've given him more than enough time, and he's obviously decided not to get in touch with us, so we're going to switch to Plan B." I glanced at Oscar. "Is everything ready?"

He pulled out his phone and tapped a few buttons. "Are we set?" he asked the person on the other end. Then his gaze swept in my direction and he nodded.

"Give me five minutes, then do it."

Kelly narrowed his gaze. "What are you doing?"

"Taking the game to Joel," Oscar replied.

I dialed Kelly's number and waited for the voice mail to kick in. "Okay, since you've decided to ignore me, I'm going to do something that should have been done from the start. You'll be getting another message from me in about three minutes. I strongly suggest you pay attention to it, because it's going to affect your life."

I hung up the phone. Oscar did a group call between my phone, Kelly's, and the person on the other end of Oscar's. It would be scrambled and untraceable. A few moments later, the video kicked in. It showed a small house, blue trim and white shutters. The lawn had been ignored and now grew so long it bent back toward the ground. A cute place.

Or at least it was. A moment later, it erupted into a fireball, with flaming chunks of the place landing in the grass and setting it ablaze. You could hear Gina barking orders in the background, and see masked men as they rushed around, not trying to put the fire out, but stoking it to ensure the blaze consumed everything on this tract of property.

"Holy shit," Sammy said. "What the hell did you do?"

Oscar grinned. "Just destroyed Joel's memories."

"That was his house?" Kelly wanted to know.

"It was. Nice thing about public records, you can find out who bought properties. This one had been purchased under Joel's and Terry's names not long before Terry died."

"And you just destroyed it?" Sammy asked, obviously aghast.

"Yup," Oscar said, his tone clipped. "That's phase one."

"And now we wait," I said. "But I'm sure it won't be for long. Oscar sent the video directly to Kelly's phone."

My phone rang two minutes later, and I grinned when I saw the name on the screen. "And now starts phase two." I slid my thumb over the screen. "Hello?"

"What the fuck did you do?" Joel demanded.

"Destroyed your house and property. The place you lived with Terry, the one where you made love. Where he told you how much he cared for you. Where you were supposed to build your life together after the mission where he died. Now, just like your dreams, it's nothing but a pile of ash."

I could hear him weeping in the background and felt not one shred of remorse.

"I just destroyed your life, like you destroyed others. Tell me, Joel, how does it feel? To know everything you had is now gone. And that's not the end of it. I know other things, too. And I'm going to make sure that everything precious to you is stripped away. Your memories, your fantasies. All of it is going to be dust, Joel."

"I'll kill you!" he screamed. "You and your lover are so fucking dead. Do you hear me? I'm going to take him and skin him—"

At this point, I hung up the phone.

"Mission accomplished. Tell Gina to bring her team home."

There were several calls from Joel, each demanding I answer. I ignored them all. I wanted him angry enough to get sloppy. I needed him to realize he was no longer the one in charge. Considering the tone of the messages he'd left, the man was on the brink. I needed to keep his attention focused on me, though. Oscar had mentioned the fact he could go after innocent people, thereby trying to force me out into the open. And damned if I wouldn't go.

"You're playing a dangerous game," Kelly said.

"Tell me about it."

He poured a cup of tea and joined me at the table.

"I thought you hated tea," I said, thumbing through another of the endless sheaves of papers.

He rolled his eyes and huffed. "I do." He added a ton of sugar and lemon to the cup and stirred it vigorously. "Lilah says it's full of antioxidants and healthy stuff. I asked what good does it do to have stuff that's good for you if it tastes like crap. She...didn't approve."

I couldn't help but laugh. I put down what I was reading and stared at my oldest friend.

"What?" he asked, his spoon clinking against the mug as he stirred his sweet hot water.

"You like her. I'm happy."

He frowned at me. "What? No jokes? No *told you so?*"

I reached out and put my hand atop his. "No. I really am happy for you. I've always liked Lilah, even if her bedside manner leaves something to be desired. And the way she looks at you? She's totally in love."

Kelly took a sip, then put his mug down. "I love her, too. If we survive this, I'm going to ask her to marry me."

The news wasn't as much of a shock as it could have been—if I'd been blind. "So you'll be leaving?"

"Says who? Like I can trust you to take care of yourself. You and Samuel are stuck with me, but I'm hoping you'll be able to accept Lilah, too."

"This is a big place," I told him. "I counted six buildings that could be made into housing. If we stay, I'm sure one of them could be converted into a nice place for you and her. So you know, Sammy's already making wedding plans."

Kelly laughed. "When I was in the safe house with him, every day he kept asking why I didn't ask her out. Eventually I had to tell him that the two of us had been seeing each other for a while. It was just dinner and a movie as friends, but I found myself wishing it could be more. I was surprised when she kissed me one night after I dropped her off. A few weeks later, she asked me to stay the night. If I'm honest, I thought it was a 'friends with benefits' arrangement. Only it became more than that for me. Honest to God, Haven, I didn't know she felt that way, too."

"All you had to do was look at her. You could see the adoration in her eyes. And who the hell else would let you drag them across the country to take care of a scared young man? She didn't do it for us, you know. She did it because you asked."

He put his cup down and turned his full attention to me. "Was I really that clueless?"

"*Was* infers past tense. Still are? Yes. You told me that when I found Sammy I needed to grab him with both hands and not let go, because love didn't come around for people like us. Seems to me it did for you, so what are you going to do about it?"

He blinked a couple times. "What? I already said I was going to ask her to marry me if we survived."

"Stop thinking like an agent. Think like a man who is in love. Ask her now. Even if something happens, she'll always know how you felt about her. Every time she looks at the ring on her finger, she'll know she was cared for."

He drained the remainder of his tea, winced, and went to rinse out the cup. "How did you get so good at this love stuff?"

"I had someone who taught me that it was okay to let people in. And I owe him more than I can ever hope to repay."

In a surprise move, Kelly came closer, bent down, and kissed my cheek. He'd never been one for open affection before, but when he stood back up, I could see his eyes glisten.

"You can never repay what you don't owe," he said. "I had expected my life to be one of servitude to you and Samuel. When the two of you married, you showed me that I wanted more for myself. It's what pushed me to seek out Lilah's company."

"Then what are you waiting for? Go. Carpe diem."

He smiled and strode over to the door, then turned around. "You know, I think Samuel's had a good effect on both of us," he said, then left the room.

Maybe he had.

Two days and about fifty calls from Joel later, I decided it was time to move on to the next part of my plan. I listened to the messages he'd left, each one more unhinged than the last. Because of what I'd taken from him, he threatened me. Sammy. Kelly. Even Kip. It was a shame that he didn't realize he had so much more left to lose.

I sat at the kitchen table and called King's assistant and told him what I needed. Apparently, his boss must have put the fear of God into him, because he snapped to right away.

"Of course, I'll get you that information within the hour," he promised. "I know a man that we use for sensitive work like this, and I guarantee you, it's untraceable."

"Great. Could you ask him to do it as soon as possible? I need to keep the momentum going."

"Yes, sir. Of course."

We disconnected, and when I felt someone staring daggers at me, I turned around. Sammy stood there, hands on his hips, and a frown marring his face.

"Is this really necessary?" he asked.

"I'm not even going to dignify that with an answer. You know what he's done, and what he's capable of doing. He killed Rook and would have killed Kelly if we hadn't gotten home in time."

Sammy's chin dipped to his chest. "I know. After Rook…died, I thought I wanted Joel killed, but now I just feel…" His words trailed off.

"You feel bad for him?"

He nodded. "I know it doesn't make sense, but I do. He worked for the organization, gave them everything, and when he wanted to leave, he was out in the cold. Maybe if there had been someone there to help him through his grief, none of this would have happened."

If we were going to have this talk, I needed coffee. I got up, went to the pot, held it up to see if Sammy wanted some. He nodded, so I poured a cup for each of us. I put a splash of milk in his, then took them to the table. He sat with me, each of us sipping our life-saving caffeine.

"He's angry and hurt. I get that, Sammy. But he's killed people. And not just agents, but innocents. A college kid who will never see a sunrise again.

233

He smothered him without remorse. He flayed Savior, whose only crime was that she was an agent. Never mind she dedicated her life to getting women out of bad situations. How many people are going to suffer because of her death? How many of them will die?

"I wish there was a better way. If I could drag him in and strap him to a psychiatrist's chair, I would do it in a heartbeat. But that ship sailed already. He's got to be taken down, not just for our sake, but for those people we protect."

Sammy sighed, sipped his coffee, then put the cup down. "In my head I see the logic. In my heart, I wish there were another way. I know how I'd feel if you got killed. I can empathize with him."

"No!" I slammed my cup down hard enough that it cracked along the side. "You can't empathize, because it's not in you to kill an innocent person. If I died, you'd grieve. You'd go through all the stages of loss, but you'd move on. You wouldn't fall into the same mire as Joel because that's not in you."

"We never know what we're capable of until the time comes," he countered. "I killed my mother because of what she did to me, and what she might have done to you. Is it so hard to believe I could kill someone else?"

When he put it that way, no, it wasn't. "You're right. It's in all of us to snap. Every day, people walk outside and they could very easily go off the rails and kill someone. But it's different here, because he's planned these killings, and don't for a moment think what he's done is anything but murder. That's the difference between what you did and what he's done. You killed your mother to save me. Who is Joel saving? What he's doing isn't justice. It's revenge."

Sammy shrugged. "I guess."

I reached across and took his hand. "No, don't guess. I need you to understand this. I'm not saying there isn't enough blame to go around, but most of it rests squarely on his shoulders. What he's done is worse than the people we go after, because he knows better. He's seen what people do to each other. Witnessed the atrocities that can be inflicted on those weaker than he is. That can't be allowed to continue."

Sammy sighed, drained the rest of his coffee, and folded his arms behind his head. "You're right. Everyone involved in this knows it. But isn't what you're doing right now akin to torture? You burned his house down. How is that not going to make him die on the inside?"

"I'm doing what I have to," I explained. "I don't know where he is, so I need to draw him out. He's got to be angry enough to stop thinking rationally and just react. Only then can we put an end to this whole mess."

"Fine, I'll shut up."

I was out of the chair and pulling him up before he finished saying the words. "No. I don't ever want you to stop talking to me. What's happening now is something we've never encountered before. This man has the same training I do. That makes him at least as dangerous. More now because he thinks he's got nothing left to lose. That's how I need him to be because, as you learned, going in angry is a bad thing."

He pushed away from me and sat down again, his arms crossed over his chest. He looked away as I took the chair next to him. "How much more can you take away from him?"

"The thing about hitting the bottom? You start to think there's nowhere else to go but up. He's about to learn that there are levels he never imagined he could sink to."

Sammy's brow furrowed. "Please tell me you're not enjoying this."

"Haven doesn't enjoy his job the way I do," came Oscar's voice. He stepped into the kitchen, went and poured himself a cup of coffee, then sat at the table with us. "Your man has a soft spot. Yes, he's one of the best assassins I know, but it costs him every time he kills someone. Me? I enjoy my job. I like to kill the bad guys. They get what's coming to them because of the lives they lead. This douche, Joel, needs to be ended so he can never hurt anyone again.

"I get that you want to help everyone, and I think it's noble. But even if we get him into counseling, there isn't any guarantee it will help him. What we do now is going to have to protect everyone from him. That's our job. We can't afford to let emotion come into the equation. We've got to be decisive in our actions, because too much depends on us. What we do has to cut the problem off at its source, and if that means we take him out, then it's what we do."

Sammy listened, nodded at all the right points in Oscar's speech, then turned to me.

235

"I don't like it," he admitted. "I understand it's your job, and I know what you do is important, but there's more to this than some asshole selling drugs to kids. Joel was one of you, and he should have been taken care of. He wasn't, and that isn't his fault. I know it's not going to stop you from doing whatever you need to, but I don't think it's right that people are...disposable."

With those words, Sammy got up and walked out of the kitchen.

CHAPTER TWENTY-FIVE

"You should tell him," Oscar said. "The kid has a right to know what you're about to do."

"No. I tell him, and that's something else he's going to worry about. For right now, it's best if he doesn't know."

Oscar grunted and shook his head. "You're a real piece of work, you know that? You tell me how important this kid is to you, then you leave him out of conversations that directly affect him."

I sighed. Oscar didn't understand. Not that I thought I did, either. Sammy was a capable man, a fact he'd proven many times over. My problem? If he disagreed with me, I would probably do things his way. I'd ceded control of a large part of my life to him because he kept me grounded in the present. This time, I had to remain resolute, and couldn't second-guess myself.

"So when you go on a mission, you're all about sharing with Max what you're about to do? Did you let him know when I called you and asked for help that you sliced someone's throat? That you watched as he bled out on the floor while you were on the phone with me? How much do you share with him?"

He rubbed his eye with the heel of his hand. "You don't get it. Max and I aren't like you and Sammy. We're not married. He can walk away any time he wants, and if he's smart, he will. This isn't the life for anyone. How you and the kid make it work, I will never understand."

"You're right. I probably won't ever be able to explain it. I look at Sammy and realize he's the reason I do what I do. To keep people like him from having to live in a world like we do. You know that if it weren't for us, what we do, there would be a lot more awful stuff that would happen to them."

Oscar hummed. "How about if we agree to disagree? There will always be bad stuff happening, and we can't protect them from it. The only thing we can do is make sure they're not victims of it."

"Fair enough," I replied, getting up and tossing my cup into the trash, where it fractured along the crack. I turned back and leaned against the counter. "Tell me something, though. Isn't keeping them safe enough of a reason?"

Before Oscar could answer, my phone rang. I pulled it from my pocket and saw 'Unknown Caller.' I slid my finger across the bar, said hello, and waited.

"Mr. Haven? This is King's assistant, Edgar. I'm calling to let you know that your request has been approved and taken care of. Is there anything else I might do for you today?"

I did a fist pump. "Edgar, my man, you've just made my day. How can I thank you?"

"I could give him a good fucking," Oscar called. "I bet he likes it nice and hard."

I scowled at Oscar. Even though I couldn't see him, I knew Edgar had to be blushing like mad when he stammered, "N-no, that's really not necessary."

"Don't worry. I'll make sure to keep him on a short leash."

"Ooh! Yeah, a leash would be nice, and I bet Edgar would look amazing in a collar!" Oscar shouted. "Being led around through the club, a dog tail butt plug sticking from his ass."

I glared at Oscar, who simply chuckled.

Edgar couldn't keep his stutter under control. "Mr. K-King would be very upset if...uh...never mind. Please forget I said anything," he whispered, then quickly hung up.

I put my phone back into my pocket and turned my attention to Oscar once more.

"I think King might be a tad put out if you touch his young man. Sounds to me like they've got something going."

Oscar shrugged. "His loss. So what did he have to say?"

I rubbed my hands together before I realized I probably looked like a cartoon villain and stuffed them in my pockets. "Step two is underway."

"I'm not sure what you've got planned, but can I be the one to call him this time?" Sammy said from the doorway.

"No. This is all on me. He's already got you and Kelly on his radar, so no way are you interacting with him."

Sammy's eyes got big. "Please. Maybe I can talk him into… I don't know, turning himself in?"

Oscar's expression softened as he regarded Sammy with a sympathetic look.

"Aw, kid. Your heart's in the right place, but I agree with Haven. You need to stay as far away from this nut job as possible. I read his file. He's a good shot and an expert at hand-to-hand combat. Think me or Haven, only more crazy. He's pissed as hell at Haven, so he might well decide to take you out at a distance just to get back at your us for torching his place."

Sammy's shoulders slumped. "Okay."

I walked toward him. "Okay? That's not like you. Usually you'd be insisting you were going to help. What's going on?"

His gaze fell to the floor. "This seems wrong to me and I don't know why. He's hurt a lot of people, and I get that. But he's doing what he was trained to do. He's doing what you do."

"No," I insisted, lifting his chin. "I would never kill an innocent person to find a way to get to another innocent. Rook did nothing wrong. It's his job to send in the troops, and we all understood that. Bulwark died believing he was trying to do the right thing. It's the price we're all willing to pay. You've got to let it go, Sammy. Joel's made money from when he was with the agency. He could have sought help, just like I did. Instead, he went out and started hunting people."

"Maybe Bulwark was his anchor," he said emphatically. "Once he lost him, Joel was a man without a rudder."

"You saw his files. Joel skirted the edges in his assignments. People died there, too. It's not that he was an agent; it's that he was a bad one. For that sake alone, he's got to answer for what he's done." I sucked in a deep breath. "Look, maybe it would be better if you, Kelly, and Lilah took Kip and went somewhere."

Sammy jerked away from me and pinned me with an angry glare. "What? No way am I leaving you here alone."

"What am I? Chopped liver?" Oscar grunted.

"You know what I mean!" Sammy grabbed my shoulders and pulled me closer. "Get that thought out of your head right now."

"Are you two gonna fuck? If so, can I at least watch?"

"Sure, maybe we can teach you something," Sammy retorted, though he didn't stop gazing into my eyes.

I stepped back, a tad uncomfortable, because Sammy didn't know exactly what I was going to do with Joel. Oscar had said I should tell him, but the fewer people who knew, the better. If Joel even had an inkling Sammy had information like that, he'd probably do whatever he could to learn it.

"Will you trust me to handle this my way?" I asked him.

He sighed. "Yeah, you know best. I just worry about what it might cost you."

"I can honestly say, this won't be a problem for me," I assured him. "And now, it's time to move forward with our plans."

I pulled my phone out of the pocket of the jeans I was wearing and dialed Kelly's number.

"You fucking bastard!"

"You should work on your greetings," I said. "Otherwise I might not call you back again. I mean, I have information for you, but if you don't want it…"

I let my voice trail off.

"What?" he demanded.

I grinned at the anger in his voice. "So you remember how you got on that flight with me where you killed Elijah? Well, we did some checking and found out you paid for the ticket with your credit card. So, I dug a little deeper, and found a fascinating paper trail showing purchases of guns, ammunition, incendiary devices, hotel rooms. The list goes on and on. I had a friend do me a favor and, guess what? Your money supply? Cut off. No bank account, no credit cards, no cash advances. You're also listed as a bad risk for a loan, so there won't be any money there. Essentially, unless you've got a large supply of cash on hand, you're tapped out."

I expected a blowup, but the rage I'd figured was coming never appeared. Instead, his voice was cold, calculating. "You think you're smart. You're certain you have all your bases covered. Guess what? You don't. Take the money. I don't care. It's not going to stop me from coming after you. By the way, nice place you got yourself in. I'm guessing they were Rook's old digs. I especially like that you brought the old man to stay with you. You think maybe he'll be able to hold me off this time? Or what about that pretty kid you've got? I'll bet you anything he'll scream real nice."

A hard shiver went through me. He knew where we were.

"Nothing to say?" he taunted. "That's fine. I've got plenty we'll need to talk about when I see you. Actually, I plan to start with your sweet young thing. I'm going to do to him what you did to our property. I'm going to douse him with lighter fluid, then burn him alive. Imagine the smell of the charring flesh, the sound as it sizzles. And, of course, the cries for mercy. How long do you think it'll take him to die? Minutes? No. I plan to ensure he lives for hours, maybe days. Once I've burned him to the bone, he'll beg for death. Then, after I do kill him, I'm going to make sure there's nothing left for you to bury. The only thing you'll have to keep you warm at night will be the memories."

He hung up and I turned to Oscar. "Get them out of here. I don't give a fuck where you take them, just go."

"What's wrong?"

"He knows where we are. He must have eyes on the ground. Probably hired someone to tail me and report back to him. Fuck me for my stupidity!"

"Honestly, do you think there's anywhere safer than where we are?" Sammy wanted to know. "This place is our best defensible position."

Oscar grinned. "Listen to the little man spouting war tactics."

Sammy frowned. "Which is safer? You trying to escort three people to safety, knowing that there is someone out there who could probably pick us off one at a time, or to hunker down here, where we have a fireproof building, bulletproof windows, hiding spots, weapons, and more?"

"Kid's got a point. Out there, we're targets. In here, we're more likely to hold our own."

I thought about it for a moment. "Fine. Do we have all the security rearmed?

Kelly strode into the room. "No, we can't release it without a password."

That made things a lot more difficult. "Should have been the first thing we did," I snapped. This situation had me off-kilter from the moment I'd found Kelly. We'd be lucky if I didn't get us all killed.

Kelly glared at me. "It's not like Rook left us a manual for this stuff. Sammy's been trying to get things running again. He's got a few of the outside sensors active, but without knowing what everything does, we're flying blind."

And that was my fault. I was so focused on Joel I failed to plan for contingencies. I should have had all of this thought through in advance, just like Rook would have done. "Fine. I want everyone in one wing, with one of us standing guard at the console all night."

"Sounds like a plan. I'll take first watch," Oscar stated.

"No heroics, O. If you see anything, even something as innocuous as a fucking mosquito, you raise the alarm." I turned to Sammy. "And you, the minute you hear it, you're going to do whatever you have to so you keep safe. Hit the access panel in the library. That'll take you outside the range of the main house. From there, you get the hell away. Give me your phone, and I'll program King's number into it. You call him. Tell him what happened, and ask him to hide you all. Keep Kip with you at all times, too. I don't want any of you being left behind. If it comes down to a fight, you get the hell out of this house."

"But I—" Sammy started to protest.

"But nothing," I shouted. "You do what I say this time. Keep our family safe." I turned to Oscar. "If it comes down to it, you throw each of them over your shoulder and get them the hell out of here."

"I'm not leaving you," he said, his voice flat. "We never leave our team behind. You better than anyone should know that."

"You'll do your job, which," I reminded him, "is to protect Sammy, Lilah, and Kelly."

Sammy huffed and strode over to the intercom where he jammed his finger on the button. "Lilah? Family meeting in the library, now." He turned to me and Oscar. "Library, both of you."

Oscar laughed. "Gotta tell you, the kid's got a brass pair," he said with a grin.

The conversation had been tense from the moment everyone gathered in the library. They'd each spread out, but their attention stayed focused on me. I knew Sammy had chosen this room because of the size. Big enough to give everyone room to sit, but intimate enough that no one needed to shout to be heard.

I was pissed at myself for letting this farce go on. Joel was a murderer, which he'd proven more than once. How could I look myself in the mirror if I let any one of these people get hurt?

"The smart play is for you to get the hell out of here and not stop until you get to another safe house," I said, my voice strained.

Sammy's nostrils flared. "That's stupid! The only ones who should go then would be Lilah and Kelly." He turned to them both. "No offense."

"None taken," Lilah replied. "But I'm not leaving either."

"Yes, you are. You're going to get the hell out of here so you won't be hurt," Kelly whispered, and even I could hear the pleading in his voice.

Lilah, to her credit, gave him a steely glare. "You don't own me. This is my decision to make, not yours."

He sighed. "Please. Do this for me. I want you safe."

"Both of you need to go," I insisted.

"No," Kelly growled, wagging a finger in my direction. "This is non-negotiable."

"I'm not going anywhere," Lilah said, casting a glare in Kelly's direction. "None of you have medical training, so you may need me."

"Definitely not," Kelly snapped. "You're going with Samuel."

She glared at him, and he actually withered under her scrutiny. "Like hell I am."

"And who the heck said I was going anywhere?" Sammy ground out as he added more fuel to an already tense situation.

I scrubbed a hand over my cheek. This conversation had been going back and forth for over an hour. "Enough!" I roared. "This isn't up for debate. Each of you will do as you're told."

Four pairs of eyes regarded me from couches around the room. Some with anger, some with amusement.

"Really? Keep in mind, you're not the boss of me," Sammy said, crossing his arms over his chest.

Lilah raised her hand. "Me neither." She turned her attention to Kelly. "Neither of you are. I'm a medic, served two tours in the Middle East, have been under fire countless times. I've pulled men from firefights. Do you truly believe either of you scare me?"

Kelly, the traitor, actually snickered at what she said, before he shook his head. "I love you," he said softly. "When this is over, the two of us should look into getting married."

Her gaze softened, but her voice stayed rock steady. "Fine. When this is all said and done, and you ask me properly, we'll see about it. But that's only if you stop treating me like I'm an appendage. I'm a smart, capable woman, and I will never let anyone think of me as being weak. Do I make myself clear?"

In that moment, even I was afraid of Lilah McQuade. Kelly grinned and his eyes sparkled. He lifted her knuckles to his lips, placed a gentle kiss on them, then pulled her close. "Yes, dear." He turned to me. "Sorry, none of us are going anywhere."

"You all know what could happen here, right?" I demanded. "He could kill you. Kelly? Do you want to see Lilah lying dead on the floor? Lilah? What about you? He almost killed Kelly once. Do you seriously want to give him the opportunity to finish the job?"

They looked at one another, then joined hands. "We've lived good lives, surrounded by those we consider more than friends. If we have to go, it's an honor to do it in service to them," Lilah told me. "We're always going to be stronger together, Haven. If we let Joel separate us, then he can pare our numbers down until he gets each of us alone. Without having each other to depend on, none of us will stand a chance."

Her speech was pretty, and she said all the right things. The problem was that being under fire wasn't the same as having a bullet tear through your body. What bothered me most was the thought of her bleeding out in front of Kelly, him watching the light go out of her eyes. He'd already lost too much, and the thought of him losing Lilah made my next decision an easy one.

"Fine. You won't go? Then I will." I walked to the door and turned around. "If I have to face him, I'm going to do it alone. No one here needs to die."

Sammy pushed up off his seat and stalked toward me. "You're one stupid son of a bitch, do you know that? We are not doing this again. I'm not running away, and you're not alone in this fight."

"But—"

"Listen to the kid, Mike." Oscar stood and put a hand on Sammy's shoulder. "This isn't just your fight. Rook was our friend, and we aren't about to let you be the only one to face this fucker. Besides, five of us against one of him?"

An explosion shook the ground and had us rushing for the windows in time to see a fireball launch itself toward the sky, brilliant reds and yellow trails reminiscent of the morning sun. It seemed that the choice had just been taken out of our hands.

CHAPTER TWENTY-SIX

In short order, there were several other explosions. Kelly assured me that the buildings could withstand them, but his expression when he glanced in Lilah's direction told me he wasn't willing to trust it to keep Joel out.

"How the hell did he find us?" Oscar barked.

"No clue. Not important right now. Keeping him away from the others is."

I could see fire in several areas around the property, and I knew what he was doing. Joel wanted to draw us out, make us vulnerable. The thing of it was, I didn't give a damn about the buildings, only the people in my care.

Sammy came up from the armory, handed small caliber firearms to Kelly and Lilah, passed me my Desert Eagle 50AE, then peered out the window. "How did he get so close?" he asked.

"We never turned the security system back on," Oscar replied as he slipped on a graphene vest. "None of us knew enough about how it worked and didn't want to chance setting it off."

"That worked real well," Lilah said. "Men. No wonder the world has gone to hell."

"Hey!" Kelly protested.

"Except you, sweetheart," she soothed, patting his cheek.

It was incredible. Even under siege, the two of them were calm and collected. Kelly didn't leave her side, and Lilah soothed him with a touch now and then.

"So what do we do, boss?" Oscar asked.

It was a good question. We had no idea where Joel was. He could be somewhere on the property, setting off the explosives. Or he might be a mile away, detonating them by remote control. I didn't buy that, though. He'd

246

want us afraid and making mistakes. He had to be close enough to take advantage of them.

"We could try and draw him out of hiding," Sammy said.

"How?" I asked, putting on a vest.

"Well, we know trying a bulletproof vest is of limited use, since he has shells that almost pierced what you were wearing." He nodded in the direction of my chest. "Wear that anyway, because anything will help. As for the other stuff, what if we turn the alarms back on? Maybe they'll pick him up and drive him from wherever he's holed up. Or, at the very least, they'll show us on camera where he is."

"Good call. Kelly? Do you know the system well enough to rearm it?"

"Hell no," came the reply. "Rook never really talked much about it."

"Well then, I suggest you figure it out. Sammy, you go with him. Lilah, gather as much as you can to do a triage. Cut sheets, towels, whatever. Oscar, you and me will be the ones in the field. I want him taken down hard, but don't risk yourself to do it. Get a bead on him, let me know where he is, and the two of us will converge on him."

"Right." He rushed from the room and returned with communication equipment and night gear. He tested the batteries on each as another explosion rocked the main house. This was too close for comfort. "Equipment checks out," he said, handing me an earpiece and a walkie-talkie. "Sammy, can you monitor the discussion while you're helping Kelly?"

Sammy gave a terse nod.

"It's important that you listen in," he said. "You have to be able to do both. If you can't—"

"I have it covered," he snapped. "Get out there and do your fucking jobs."

Oscar laughed. "Kid, you're a pain in the ass, but I respect you." He grabbed Sammy and pulled him into a quick hug. "Keep everyone here safe, okay?"

"Will do," he promised.

With the push of a button, a panel opened in the wall. A soft green glow lit the tunnel, allowing us to move swiftly while preserving our night vision. A small door opened in a rocky crag not far from the compound. Sammy checked in with each of us to ensure we were all connected. When the test went well, Oscar and I began to scan the area.

"Too much light and smoke from the fires to see anything well," he said softly.

"He was counting on that," I said. "You guys got eyes yet, Sammy?"

I made a gesture and the two of us began moving in different directions. Oscar would approach the house from one side, while I went in from the opposite.

"Coming up now," came the reply. "It doesn't look like he's done too much damage yet. The fires aren't doing more than burning desert shrubs and some decorative fencing. I see a few trees that are smoldering."

"Copy. We're going to move in and try to find him. If he's on property, I'm willing to bet he's making his way toward the main house."

"Do you want me to call the police?" Sammy asked.

"Definitely not. That would bring the organization under scrutiny, and Joel could hurt more people. Call King, tell him that we believe Joel is probably here. Let him know we're trying to find him." I paused for a moment. "Sammy, if he gets into the house, I don't care what you have to do, but you grab the dog and get out of there with him, Lilah, and Kelly. Turn the fucking gun on them if you have to."

"We already discussed—"

"No!" I growled. "I can't... No matter what, you three have to live. Do you understand me? Oscar and I are doing our job. We're expendable."

"Speak for yourself," Oscar mumbled. "I intend on getting home."

"So do I, but things happen." I wish I had the words for how I felt. How being with Sammy made me feel whole. But everything I would say simply paled to the truth. Without him, there wasn't a me anymore. "Sammy, please. For once, do what I say."

"No."

"If you can have your feelings seminar later, that would be great. Kid, if he wants you to go, you go. He's in charge of this operation."

Another explosion, this one near the house, had me nearly pissing my pants.

"Ask Kelly how sure he is about the security of the house."

Sammy murmured something, then came back. "Well, the house was never attacked while he was here, and Rook never said anything about it happening. He only knows what he was told, and he says we should be perfectly safe as long as the security system has been engaged. Which, of course, it hasn't."

I slid down a sandy hill as I moved closer to the house. "Did you call King?"

"Edgar is overriding the command codes. He should have it up and running in a few minutes."

"Lock down everything. Doors, windows. Anything you think might be big enough for a man to get through, you close and seal. If you won't leave, at least move to the safe room."

"I love that you worry about us. You don't know what it means to me. But we already told you, none of us are running. We're going to fight to defend Rook's legacy. So shut up and get this son of a bitch."

"Yes, dear."

Sammy's chuckle warmed my heart. Not something you'd say on a battlefield.

As more explosions tore up the compound, I entered the area from the far side of the house. The damage was scattered, making it seem as though destruction wasn't the main goal. I saw Oscar twice as we patrolled the area, and each time, he shook his head at me.

We'd been checking the buildings, ensuring Joel wasn't hiding inside any of them. Without words, each of us knew what had to be done. As I approached one of the outbuildings, another blast knocked me off my feet. The heat swept over me and the concussion had my ears ringing.

"Haven? Haven! Are you all right?" Sammy called.

"Fine. Just rung my clock. You guys got anything at all yet?" I figured it wasn't likely, since he hadn't said so, but I needed information.

"Just got off the phone with Edgar. The system has been rebooted. We entered new pass codes, so everything has been armed. Once we told the computer that there was an event going on, panels covered the windows, all the doors were sealed, and the room we are in was locked down. No one is getting in here unless they've got the code."

I breathed a sigh of relief. At least now I could concentrate on what I was doing, rather than worrying about my family.

"Haven, Oscar check in. What's your location?" came Sammy's harried voice.

"I'm by the building near the eastern edge of the property," Oscar replied.

"I'm in the main compound, near the pool. Or what's left of it."

Large divots had been blown out of the concrete, pieces scattered across the entire area. Water sluiced over the side, to be absorbed by the thirsty ground.

"I have movement," Sammy said with barely contained enthusiasm. "West side, near the building with all the books."

"Copy." I took off running in that direction and knew Oscar was doing the same. As I approached the area Sammy was talking about, I spotted a figure in the darkness. I crept closer, wanting to wait until Oscar was in position.

"No, Haven! Not there! He's behind—" Sammy cried.

Too late. A shot rang out, and I was thrown to the ground as the bullet hit me in the back. Shit, that hurt worse than I remembered. Before I could get back to my feet, the gun was pressed against my temple and I was relieved of my weapon.

"Terry must be pissing himself laughing right about now. He said you were the best, but guess he was wrong."

"You caught me off guard, I admit it." I needed to stall for time to get Oscar here. "How did you find us?"

"It was a lot easier than I thought it would be. My codename was Seeker. I was the one who tracked down and eliminated people who went underground. I'm the person who connects the dots. Everyone leaves a trail, and I know how to follow it. Whether it's on the computer or simply by doing the same things every day, people can be found if you know where to look."

"My hat is off to you," I said, genuinely impressed.

"I know you're waiting on your friend, but what say we dispense with him trying any last minute heroics?"

He reached out and yanked the headset from me. "You can come out now Oscar Goodwin."

It shocked me to hear him call Oscar by name.

"Don't look so surprised," he said to me. "I told you, there isn't much I don't know, and if it's important, I will find it." He stood, straightened his spine, then called out, "Step out where I can see you, Oscar. Otherwise Maximillian Kearney might not look too pretty come morning."

"What's to keep him from dropping you where you stand?" I demanded.

He shrugged and gave a twisted grin. "The bomb I planted. I'm the only one who knows where it is. Don't worry. It's a simple device. I tell Oscar where I've hidden it; he calls Max and instructs him on how to turn it off. Easy enough. But if he kills me, then boom, no more Max."

I heard Oscar cry out then rush from behind the house where he'd been. He launched himself at Joel, who sidestepped the punch aimed at his head. Joel then took aim and shot Oscar in the back. He fell to the ground, trying to suck in air. Joel strode over, bent down, and took Oscar's gun.

"Hurts, doesn't it?" Joel snarled. "One of the things I learned from Terry was how to bypass most of the equipment currently in use by the organization. He said it was important, should something ever happen where someone else got hold of it. Guess what? Lesson learned."

He waved his gun in the air and shouted, "The rest of you have a choice. Come out here or watch them die from where you are. Either option is fine with me."

"Don't you dare," I growled. "You stay the fuck inside."

Of course, no one ever listened to me. A few scant minutes later that the door opened, and Kelly came out, followed by Sammy and Lilah. Sammy rushed over to where I lay and dropped next to me.

"Are you okay?" he asked.

"Why don't you ever do what you're told?" I whispered to him.

"Because I won't let you go, stupid."

With that, he pressed something against my hand. I glanced down and saw him sliding a knife into my sleeve. That was my man. Always thinking on his feet.

"Enough," Joel snapped. "Get up and stand together where I can keep an eye on you."

Sammy pulled me up before he went to get Oscar. He held out a hand, and Oscar reached up and grabbed it. The pass of an item didn't escape my notice, but apparently Joel missed it.

The five of us huddled together, the men forming a wall around Lilah almost instinctively. I heard her huff, but she said nothing.

"You know," Joel said, "Terry used to tell me stories about the organization late at night when no one else was around. He was always so proud of being part of it, of helping others. The man was a fifth-generation Marine, you know. He had duty to God and country drilled into him his whole life. When Rook came to him and made him an offer, Terry couldn't say no."

Joel paced nearby, just out of reach. I waited to see where this was going to go before I decided what to do.

"He was their best agent." Joel turned to me. "Until you came along. He told me what happened in your training. How you bested him and others. He said he'd never seen anyone like you. I admit, I was jealous, hearing the tales of how amazing you are. You're the reason Terry started to keep a journal. He clipped articles about pedophiles who disappeared, certain that it was your work. It became like a bible to him. As time went on, the number of people he tracked grew. I listened to all the tales. Each one a feat of skill and pride. But you, Haven? You were the one no one else could top."

Next to me, Oscar's muscles coiled. I figured he was wound tight and ready to spring. If he did, I needed to be ready to move, but I hoped he'd wait until it was time.

"It took months before Terry finally saw me. I was so used to being in the background I couldn't believe it when he finally noticed me. In the organization, there wasn't a lot of time for dating, so we grabbed our moments where we could. When we were filing reports and stuff, there would be a quick round of sex in the bathroom, surreptitious touches as we passed one another. Eventually it got to be more than I could stand. I didn't want to waste our lives being out there, when we could be together. Finally, one night I told him how much I wanted to leave. For it to be just the two of us. He surprised me when he said he agreed. He wanted that, too."

Joel inched closer. The weight of the knife in my sleeve a comforting reminder.

"One day he went to Rook and told him he was through. Then I went in and said the same thing to my handler. It wouldn't be long before we were free. I imagined our lives together. It was quite a shock, knowing that you no longer were beholden to anyone else. It took us both time to adjust to sleeping in, to making love when we felt like it. Then almost a year later came the call that neither of us thought would ever happen. Rook asked Terry for help with one more mission. He wanted to take down a woman named Valerie. He said she was bad news. Terry couldn't say no."

This was my moment. The one I'd been waiting for. And I wasn't about to let it pass.

"Apparently Terry couldn't say no quite often."

Joel glared at me. "What the fuck does that mean?"

I grinned at him. "Did you know that Terry kept working for the organization after you left?"

"You're lying!"

"Hardly. I can show you the proof. You're the one who follows paper trails, so you'll be able to see it. For over a year, he took quick missions. In— boom goes the bad guy—out and back home to you. Usually the same day. He never told you, did he?"

"No, because there's nothing to tell," Joel snapped.

"So no unexplained trips he had to take suddenly? No hedging when you asked where he'd been? How long do you think he lied to you, Joel?"

I could see uncertainty in Joel's expression. "Fuck you! You don't know what you're talking about. You're trying to poison my memories, but it's not going to work. Terry loved me, wanted to be with me. No, you're not going to throw me off my plan. Killing you will prove that I'm the best. The one who deserved the happy ending. Before I do that, I'm going to tear your soul out the way mine was."

He waved his gun in our direction. Pointing it at each person in turn.

"You have four friends here, willing to stand by your side to die. You're going to choose one to kill, then I'm going to kill you."

I laughed. "I'm not killing anyone."

"You're going to kill one, or I'll shoot all of them and you'll watch them die. You've got a chance I never had. You can save your lover, and all you need to do is kill a friend. Of course, it's your choice, but I'd make it soon, because this offer won't be repeated."

Oscar stepped forward and held out his arms. "Kill me." He glanced in our direction. "No one else needs to be hurt."

"You've got your volunteer," Joel said, a certain glee in his voice as he held up my gun, emptied of all but one bullet before he tossed it onto the hard-packed earth in front of me. "And don't worry, I promise to call Max to tell him where the bomb is. He doesn't need to suffer like I did."

Everything from that point was a blur of motion. Sammy pulled Lilah and Kelly to the ground as Oscar spun and threw the knife Sammy had handed him at Joel. It struck and embedded in his shoulder. Though he didn't drop his gun, it threw him off enough that I was able to dive to the ground, recover my weapon, and hold it on him. His eyes went wide as he realized I now held his life in my hands.

"Bang," I said. "You're dead."

CHAPTER TWENTY-SEVEN

Joel stood there, eyes wide. "No, it won't end like this!" His hand shook as he tried to raise the gun. Oscar tackled him before he could fire a shot. He had him on the ground, pummeling him.

"You don't threaten Max. You don't even fucking think about him. You're going to tell me where the bomb is, or I'll kill you with my bare hands."

Joel smiled, and the blood in his mouth made his teeth gleam in the lights of the compound. "He's gonna die," Joel spat. "And it's going to be your fault."

"Fuck that!" Oscar said. He punched Joel once more, then grabbed his phone. He called Max, and I could hear him pleading with him to get the hell out of the house. The expression on the man's face told me more than his words ever could. He was afraid. Oscar could look down the barrel of a gun and not know fear. But with Max's life on the line, he was terrified.

"There's no bomb," Sammy said as he stood.

Oscar turned and glared at him. "What do you mean?"

"Where do you live?"

"A town outside of Seattle. What are you saying?"

"That there isn't a bomb," he repeated.

"How can you be so certain?" I asked.

"Because Joel didn't have time. Edgar and I worked it out. For a man so obsessed with the comings and goings of others, Joel left a wide paper trail of his own. Purchases he made here in Arizona, each with timestamps. He paid for them by credit card and bought several things each day for the last two weeks. There's no way he could have gotten to Seattle, planted a bomb, then come back here to do his shopping."

Kelly got up and pulled Lilah along with him. She dusted herself off and brushed back her hair.

"Samuel showed me the sheets," Kelly said. "I agree with him. There isn't a bomb. Joel's playing you."

"Couldn't he have hired someone?" Oscar asked, his fingers clenched tightly.

"No. Joel doesn't play well with others. The logs Edgar supplied show his travel. We know exactly where he's been. This was his game from the start, and he wouldn't allow anyone else to be a part of it. I promise you, he's lying."

Oscar snarled as he slammed Joel into the hard-packed ground. "What the fuck are you playing at?" Oscar demanded, driving a meaty fist into Joel's face, snapping his head to the side. When Joel didn't react, Oscar gripped the knife, and with a feral grin and a violent twist, he tore it out of Joel's shoulder. He howled, which seemed to satisfy Oscar.

"I believe I know," Lilah answered. "He wanted you to kill him. He wants to be dead so his pain will be gone and he can be with his lover. But it didn't go away, did it?" she asked.

Joel's eyes watered. "You were supposed to shoot me," he said, his voice cracking. "You want me dead, so do it. I killed Rook, and the pain didn't go away. Why didn't it go away?" he wailed.

I strode over to where Oscar sat on Joel's chest and nudged him. He got off, and I straddled Joel, pushing the gun against his head.

"Haven?" Sammy's voice trembled.

I ignored him and stared into the eyes of the man who took Rook from us. They would be black and blue soon. Oscar had not held back on his punches. I pressed the gun into Joel's mouth.

"When Rook got involved in the organization, it was because a man raped his daughter. She was ten years old when it happened, and she never fully recovered. Now I have to be the one to tell her that her father is dead. To look her in the eye and tell her that you ended the life of a good man, because you couldn't fucking handle the death of another man whose only goal in life was to keep people safe."

Joel's eyes watered.

"When Rook killed the man who hurt his daughter, he put the gun into the asshole's mouth and blew his head off. It seems to me that's karmic justice for you."

Joel closed his eyes, obviously ready for the pain to stop. I took out my phone and dialed a number.

"It's time," I said.

"Understood," King replied. "I'll have a team there within the hour."

Sammy was obviously confused. "I don't understand."

I grabbed Joel's bloodstained shirt and yanked him to his feet. "That was a good throw, O."

"I wanted to put it in his face," Oscar growled, his expression dark. "Are you sure about this?"

"Oh, yeah," I replied, then turned my attention to the man whose life I held in my hands. "You deserve to die, Joel. In fact, of all the people I've ever killed, no one has deserved it more than you." I pulled the gun back. "That's why I'm not going to do it."

"What? Why?" he said, his brow furrowed. "You have to kill me. Rook deserves to be avenged."

"No," I corrected. "Rook deserves to be remembered. And I want you to do that every day of your life. You see, you may be a genius when it comes to following people's movements, but apparently when it came to your lover, you were blind. Rook never asked Terry to go after Valerie. It's all in the files we got. Terry fucking begged to go. The life you wanted so desperately, with the white picket fence, and the happily ever after? That may have been what Terry thought he wanted, too, but in the end, the job meant more to him than you. That's what killed him, Joel. Not Rook."

Joel collapsed onto the ground. "It's not true. It can't be. He loved me. He told me he loved me."

I ignored his whining. "Now we're going to toss you into the deepest, darkest hole we can find. You're going to live out your life there, buried beneath the ground just like Rook is. Only he'll rest in peace, while you're going to wish you could."

Whether he heard my words or not, I didn't really know. Joel was sobbing so hard I wasn't sure any of my words penetrated his anguish. Our group

257

moved away far enough to keep an eye on him, but not nearly far enough for him to make an escape.

"Was that true?" Sammy asked me. "Is that really how it happened?"

I shrugged. "Who knows? In the end, it doesn't matter. Joel believes it is, and that's going to haunt him for the rest of his life. I can't think of a worse punishment for him."

"What made you change your mind?"

Now came time to fess up. "I didn't. This was the plan all along. I didn't want to share it, because I needed everyone to play their parts, just in case he was watching."

Sammy nodded. "Okay, I guess that makes sense. But you're going to owe me big-time for this."

I had no doubt he'd collect, and quite often. Hopefully it wouldn't involve that fucking cage.

Joel sat on the ground, his hand over his bleeding shoulder. He had nowhere he could go, and all the fight had seemingly gone out of him. With the revelation that the perfect life he'd envisioned may not have been at all as he expected, I think he simply gave up.

No one else spoke as we waited for King to send the team that would take Joel somewhere no one would ever find him, nor that he would ever find himself. King wasn't sure my idea was a good one, but he'd given me the leeway I needed to ensure it came off as planned. Now came time for the aftermath. The mission was over, Joel had been taken down, and still there were no winners. I guess we simply had to accept we did what we could to ensure Joel would never hurt anyone again.

Life sucked.

We'd tracked Rook's daughter to an assisted living center in New Mexico. Sammy had insisted on coming with me when I was making the arrangements. I didn't argue, because I didn't want to go alone. We'd submitted our request to see her, grateful when it had been approved.

The building was bland. The paints were muted, and there were no splashes of color on the outside. It was an innocuous place that held one man's most precious treasure.

"Are you sure about this?" Sammy whispered.

"No, but he asked, and I have to see this through for him."

I rapped on the door to apartment seven. A soft voice called out, "Who is it?"

"My name is Ha—Michael Phelps. I'm looking for Mary Jessup."

The door opened a crack. I could see the security chain on it.

"Yes? What do you want?"

"I work...worked with your father. He asked me to come here and give you something." I held up the envelope, then slid it through the gap in the door. "I don't mean to bother you, but I promised him I'd deliver it."

I could see her hands tremble as she took it from me. The door closed, and I thought we were done, but a moment later, it opened. She was a pretty young woman, with long, dark hair that stopped at her shoulders. She was slender, and you could tell by looking at her how hard it was for her to talk with us. Her eyes had seen some horrible things, and they were reflected in the cool, green gaze.

"Please, come in," she said, taking a step back.

Sammy moved a little closer. "We don't need to come in," he said softly. "If you're more comfortable talking to us out here, we can do that."

She shook her head. "No, it's fine. Really."

We entered the apartment, and I was amazed at the difference. While the building itself was boring as hell, Mary's apartment was whimsical and fun. She collected music boxes that she'd displayed around the room. She must have seen me looking at them, because she put the envelope in her pocket, then went over and picked one up.

"They're gifts from my father," she explained. "They were my favorite things when I was a little girl. I loved listening to them and watching them move and dance. I never really felt the same after... Anyway, Dad kept sending them. He'd order unique ones and have them shipped to me. They weren't what I wanted, but I accepted them." She put the one she held back on the shelf. "If he had come to see me, that would have been so much better. But he had his work, and that always came first."

"He wrote you the letter, maybe if you read it, you might understand better?" Sammy prompted.

She pulled out the now crumpled envelope. She tore it open gently, as if afraid of what would come out. I could see her eyes scanning the page, and as she read, they began to tear up. When she got to the end, she sobbed, "Oh, Dad."

She sat on the couch, with the afghan spread across the back, the letter crushed in her hands.

"What happened to him?" she asked.

There wasn't any way I could tell her the truth. The letter alone had devastated her, and knowing the details would probably be more than she could handle.

"He did important work," I started. "He helped people who had been hurt, like you. Someone was upset about something that happened, and they decided they needed to hurt him, too."

She pulled the corner of the afghan, slipping it over her shoulders.

"He was always a good man. He cared so much about people. I'm sorry that they couldn't go to him for help."

"So are we," Sammy said. "We miss him."

Her eyes gleamed as she looked up at him. "You worked with my father? Can you… tell me about him?"

She patted the couch, and Sammy took a seat beside her. He started with how he'd come to meet Rook, and how they'd argued, but also how much he respected the man. By the time he finished his story, he had her laughing.

"So he was still a good man? Why didn't he come to see me? I missed him so much."

Sammy turned to me. "His work was dangerous," I explained. "He was afraid that someone might find out about you and he didn't want that. But you have to know, what he did? It saved countless people. So many owe him their lives, including both of us."

She smiled. "Yeah, that's him." She held up the letter. "Thank you for bringing this. Can I ask you where he's buried?"

We hadn't invited Mary to the funeral. The decision, made by all of us, was that none of us knew how fragile she was, and we worried she might ask to see Rook's body. I opted to go ahead and take care of things, then invite her to visit the grave.

When we'd had the service, it had been a small affair—just me, Oscar, Sammy, Kelly, and Lilah. I'd stood staring at the closed coffin, before I reached into my pocket and withdrew my dog tags. I hadn't thought of them for years, but I'd retrieved them before we'd left for the ceremony, because I'd wanted to give my friend something that had at one time meant everything to me. I put them atop the casket before it slid into the crematory oven. Rook's urn was buried in the same cemetery that Bulwark rested in.

I held out a plane ticket to her. "We can do you one better. If you'd like to come with us, we'll show you."

We sat for a while longer. The silence was uncomfortable for me, because I had no idea what to say. Sammy talked with Mary, his voice low and even. I was grateful he'd come along.

"I'd like to go," she finally said. "I'll have to make arrangements, though."

"It's fine," Sammy told her. "We've got a room at the Holiday Inn, so whenever you're ready, we can leave."

Her caretaker at the house was leery when Mary said she wanted to go with us, but after I showed her our government IDs, which were completely falsified, she allowed us to take Mary with us.

Mary took time off work, explaining that her father had passed away, and she needed to go to his funeral. They hugged her and wished her the best. She smiled, said thank you, and told them she would be back in a few days. After that, we boarded the plane and headed back home.

When we got to the cemetery, I put a hand on Mary's lower back and escorted her through the gates. As we passed by the graves, I pointed out a few of them to her. "This is my sister," I said. "She was the light of my life, and I miss her every day. Over there are some people who worked with your father. They put their lives in his hands, because they trusted him. When they died, it was because they believed in what he was trying to accomplish. Your father is buried here, in the row reserved for my family. I know it might not make much sense, but I considered him a part of mine, too."

She took my hand. "No one could ever earn greater praise than to be remembered," she whispered, her voice breaking. "Thank you."

"We'll give you some time," I told her. "When you're ready, we'll be at the gate."

She nodded then sank to her knees. She wrapped her arms around Rook's tombstone, and we could see her talking to him. It broke our hearts that we couldn't save him, and that Joel had left one more person who'd already lost more than anyone should.

"So what happened with Joel?" Sammy asked as we approached the car we'd bought. We'd fallen in love with the 2017 Porsche Cayenne as soon as we'd seen it online. We discussed it and decided it would be the first car in our new collection. Sammy, of course, already had a list of vehicles he'd like to see.

King had arranged to have repairs done on the damage Joel caused to the compound. At Sammy's request, the pool had been removed and a new koi pond put in its place.

It would be some time, but eventually the property, now called 'Haven', would become our home.

"I talked with King. About twenty years ago, there was a bunker built in the Mount Denali area. Very remote, almost impossible to get to. Someone convinced him he needed it in case war ever broke out and he had to go somewhere safe. Eventually he realized that hiding wasn't his style, so it sat empty. Joel's been confined there. He's under constant guard, never allowed to leave his cell. He has no phone, television, computer, or any way to get information about the outside world. No one is allowed to talk with him. His only recreation is a stack of fiction books. He hates it, because he's a man whose entire life was about gathering data. Now, he'll never be able to do that again."

Sammy sighed and stared at the ground. "If you had told me a week ago, I'd have protested that it seemed to be cruel, but looking at that woman, whose entire life has been shredded again? Now I think it's a kindness to him."

I wrapped an arm around Sammy and pulled him close. The week since Joel had been hauled off had been chaotic at best. So many things going on, including calls from Edgar who was insisting that I needed to appear before King. He made an appointment for a few days after we got Mary back home, so I got to wonder why the man wanted to see me. I told him it would have to be rescheduled, because we had a wedding to attend. He sputtered and said that Mr. King wouldn't be happy. In the end, King's unhappiness changed nothing, because my family came first.

Mary's head was bowed when she approached us. She had a tissue in her hand that she used to wipe the tears from her cheeks. Seeing the pain etched on her face had me reaching for her. She clung to me. I wrapped an arm around her and let her cry. Eventually she stepped back and gave a watery smile.

"I'm ready to go," she told us. "Thank you for this. For…well, for everything."

She gave each of us a tentative hug.

"Would it be okay if I wanted to come back and see him again?" she asked. "We had a nice talk, and I think I'd feel better if I could do it again some time."

I handed her a card with both mine and Sammy's names printed on it. "You call us whenever you want. We'll make sure you're always able to come here."

She gave a watery smile, then slid back into the car. We had reservations for her at a local hotel, but she said she would feel better if she could go back home. Of course, we accommodated her request and took her back to the place she'd be among friends. I hoped one day we would be counted in that number.

"I now pronounce you man and wife. You may kiss the bride."

Kelly glowed as he lifted Lilah's veil and kissed her. Around us, people I'd never met were clapping. When Kelly turned toward the assembled crowd, he held up his hand, showing off the ring.

"She's stuck with me now!" he crowed.

Lilah wrapped her arm around his waist. "Don't worry," she said. "I'm going to make him regret this day."

He turned to her, his eyes shining. "That's never going to happen," he swore. "I've waited my whole life for you, and now that I have you, my life starts anew."

It was a beautiful moment from a man I never knew had a poet's soul. I glanced over at Sammy, who dabbed his nose. He saw me and quirked an eyebrow.

"Something to say?" he asked. "Before you answer, keep in mind what's in my toy box at home."

I smiled at him. "No, nothing is wrong." I leaned over and kissed his nose. "Just like seeing your softer side sometimes."

"Yeah, well… When we get home, I'll show you my soft side. I have new toys to try out."

His grin was positively evil, and I couldn't wait. The repairs to the compound were fairly extensive. The damage added up, but we were happy to let King pay to get the property back to what it was. We even added a few things to make the place our own, including a special playroom that Sammy wanted. We hadn't used it yet. In fact, he hadn't even let me see it. Couldn't wait, though.

CHAPTER TWENTY-EIGHT

After the ceremony, a young man tapped me on the shoulder then bent down next to me. "Excuse me, Mr. Haven? King would like to see you. Now, please."

Without waiting to see if I followed him, he turned and marched toward the door.

"Well, that's intriguing," I said to Sammy. "I'll be back."

Sammy's brow furrowed and he started to get up. I put a hand on his shoulder and pushed him back down.

"Stay here. I won't be gone long."

I followed the guy—who I assumed was Edgar—out of the church, and to a long, black limousine. He opened the door, and I slid in. There was a man sitting there, drink in hand, looking as though he owned the world.

"Haven, nice to meet you. I'm King."

Okay then, maybe he did.

The man I'd followed out got into the driver's seat. "Edgar, take us away from all these lights, please. They give me a headache."

"Right away, sir."

Edgar put the car in gear and off we sped. King sighed and leaned back against the seat. "I'm not used to being told no when I want to speak to someone," he said.

"And I'm not usually summoned, so we each got to try something new."

He grinned. "You're a real piece of work."

"I try my best to piss off authority figures at least once a day. It keeps me on my toes."

"I'd try it, but there isn't anyone I consider an authority figure. Pity. Edgar, make a note for me to see who I can piss off, would you?"

"Yes, sir. I've got it noted."

King smiled fondly at Edgar. I could see the affection in his gaze.

"So, I don't mean to rush you or anything, but I've got a reception to attend. Lilah's family is in town, and I'm looking forward to meeting them and doing what a best man does. What can I do for you?"

King grinned. "I like direct and to the point." He paused a moment. "As you're aware, with Rook's passing, there is an opening in the organization. Rook left me a message and said he wanted you to take the job."

I shrugged. "Not really the type of man Rook was," I said. "No way could I do what he did."

"Ah, but you have people to help you," King countered. "Your Samuel is willing to stand by your side. I admire that kind of loyalty. If he's interested, we will give him all the training he'll need to handle the computer side of the job. He can track the agents, find out who is available to send on missions, as well as their expertise in the field."

"Sammy may be more interested in becoming a therapist. My doctor said he would be good at it, and it seems something he'd be perfectly suited for."

King gave a sharp nod. "Done. Any classes he wants to attend, we will provide. He's a strong man and your perfect counterpoint. Perhaps it's time Kelly took a more active role with the field agents. He's a very detail-oriented man, and I think it would do him some good to get back to the fold, as it were."

"What about Lilah? Kelly won't do anything without her."

King shrugged. "The compound is expansive, as you know. We could easily convert one of the outer buildings to Dr. McQuade's clinic, allowing her to be nearby should you require her services. It's a win-win for everyone, in my opinion."

"And what am I supposed to do?"

"You're going to make the tough decisions. Who's worth going after, how best to take them out, and finding evidence of how they were able to slip through the very flawed justice system we have. It's not an easy job, I'll admit. It's going to take a toll on you, but it also allows you to spend time with your young man and the family you've built."

It struck me then how much I wanted this job. The chance to make things better for everyone? Hell, yes.

"Okay, but if I say yes, there are going to be some changes."

He quirked an eyebrow at me.

"First off, if and when an agent leaves the organization, they're going to have a contact number if they need help. I don't care if it's the assistance of a doctor, a psychiatrist, or a fucking babysitter. They sacrifice so much, and if they need a hand, we're going to give it. No one should be dropped on the corner and left to fend for themselves after giving years of their lives to protect us."

King hummed and put a finger to his chin. He caught Edgar's attention in the mirror. "Edgar? Your thoughts?"

It surprised me that a man in King's position asked Edgar's opinion, but if they were partners, it made sense.

"It's a good idea, sir. As I've said in the past."

"Yes, you have. I should have listened to you. Please, forgive me."

"Forgiven, sir."

"We're not done yet," I said.

"I never thought we would be," came King's droll answer.

"As you've seen, it can work with partners. Having to hide the fact they're in a relationship, or lying about it, doesn't help anyone." I swallowed hard, hoping that what I was about to say wasn't wrong. "The two of you being together should prove that."

King opened his mouth, then closed it.

"What makes you think Mr. King and I are together?" Edgar said, his voice quavering just a little.

"I got the feeling from the phone calls with you. You care deeply about him, and I assume that they're reciprocated. If not, please forgive my presumption."

"It's not really—"

"It's fine, Edgar. Yes, the two of us are partners. We have been for six years. I trust Edgar in everything and welcome his counsel. You make sense. If agents had someone to talk to, whether it be a professional or even someone they could depend on, it would make them a stronger unit. Is there anything else?"

I grinned. "Not at the moment, but I'd like to keep this line of communication open. Sammy, Kelly, or Lilah might have something to add at a later date."

"Very well, I'll agree to your proposal, but I need your answer now. Will you take the job?"

I should ask Sammy, but he'd once said my life was divided into two parts. One he held, and the other that belonged to the world. I had to believe he'd agree to this. "Yes, I'll do it."

King extended his hand. "Welcome, Rook."

The name came as a shock, but it was also something that made me want to be good enough in the job to be worthy of the man who'd held the title before me. If I could be half the leader Rook had been, then I would know he'd be smiling down on me, wherever he was.

"I can't believe you said yes," Oscar said as we waited for his plane.

"I can," Sammy replied, taking my hand. "It's perfect. Haven— I'm sorry, Rook cares what happens. He's going to make it a better job for everyone involved."

"But aren't you going to miss the excitement?"

I looked at my friend and realized he was baiting me. "No. You were right, O. This is where I belong. Are you sure you won't stay? There's a position for you."

Oscar chuckled. "The only position I'm interested in requires you to be on your hands and knees, with me at the back, and Sammy at the front. You haven't lived until you've been spit roasted by me and another dude."

Sammy let go of my hand, put it on Oscar's chest and pushed. "Back off," he said, though there wasn't any anger in his words. "This is my private playground."

"Yeah, I know, kid. The two of you are amazing together, I have to say. Thank you for the offer, Mikey, but this job isn't for me anymore. Not that I'm sure it ever was. But if you ever need me, you call and I'll be there. Got it?"

"Same goes. We're a phone call away."

Oscar hugged Sammy, who surprised me by allowing it. Then he put his arms around me and gripped my ass cheeks. "God, what I wouldn't give to have one shot at this," he whispered in my ear right before he kissed me hard on the mouth. When he broke the kiss, I turned to see Sammy trying to contain his laughter.

"Hope you enjoyed that, because it won't happen again," Sammy assured him.

Oscar gave a cocky grin. "Never say never, boyo. That might be what the man needed to see he has other options."

But Sammy and Oscar both knew I didn't. Sammy was my choice. My only one. Just as Max was Oscar's, even if he hadn't admitted it yet. They called Oscar's flight over the loudspeaker and my chest tightened as he strode away with a wave and a smile. I missed the annoying fucker already.

Sammy took my hand and gave it a squeeze. "Ready to go?"

I felt a pang of regret at seeing our friend leave. I would have loved to work with him again, but he had his own path to travel, as did we. "Let's go home and address the troops," I said.

We said nothing as we drove home. Sammy hummed quietly as he watched the miles disappear out the window. When we got home, Kelly and Lilah met us at the door, with Kip bouncing around wanting affection. Sammy bent over and picked him up, snuggling him to his chest.

"This is really happening, isn't it?" Kelly asked.

"As long as you're all with me, yes."

"I have nowhere else to be," Lilah said. "After all, my husband is here."

She smiled up at him, then lay her head on his arm.

"I need to set up a call to all of the agents," I told them. "I'd like you there with me."

We went to Rook's—our—war room. Sammy pulled up the names of the forty-six agents under my command as Kelly, Lilah, and I took seats around the large table in the center of the room. The monitors lit up, showing all the names in a grid. Sammy pressed a series of buttons on the keyboard. One by one, the screens flashed with faces. Some of whom I knew, and others I'd yet to meet.

"Good evening, my name is…" I said, then stopped. The Darth Vader voice filter was on, and that just wouldn't work for me. Sammy turned it off,

269

and I gave him a sharp nod. "Sorry, let's try that again. Many of you knew me as Haven, but I've been given the title of Rook. As you know, the man who held that title fell in the battle to keep people safe. Nathan was our leader. He was the one who told us who needed to be taken out of the system in order to save those who couldn't save themselves. He was the most steadfast person, always there for us, and we honor his memory by continuing to do his work."

I shifted uncomfortably. Saying good-bye to someone who'd held such a place of esteem in our lives was probably one of the worst things I'd ever had to do.

"The man who killed him has been removed from the playing field," I continued. "He was a former agent, who turned his back on us, and killed our friends and colleagues. The fault wasn't all his, though. We are an organization who prizes secrecy above all, but we can't be that group anymore." I paused, lending further weight to my words. "You, the people who fight for others, are our most valued asset. Starting today, we're going to be changing how things are done. Should you decide that this job is no longer for you, you will not be abandoned. We will continue to be there for you, to help you in whatever way we can. Though we'll still protect the privacy of our other agents, you will not be forgotten or pushed away."

I typed a number on the keyboard in front of me. Sammy turned and nodded, letting me know it had gone out.

"The number I just sent you is a helpline. It's going to be manned twenty-four hours a day, so if you ever need it, you call and someone will answer. Don't try to handle hard things by yourselves. If you're having a crisis, you need to talk to us. We want everyone here to live a long, happy life."

I swallowed the lump in my throat, remembering Carter Whitfield and his stepfather, John. King had sent someone to check on him, only to find out from his wife that he'd committed suicide a week after I'd met with him. That couldn't be allowed to happen again.

"Moving forward," I continued, "I'll be taking over. Please be patient with me as I learn the system. Computers aren't really my best friend. That's why I've assembled my own team." I gestured to Sammy. "This is Samuel, my partner. He's going to be available to talk whenever you need it. He's not a trained therapist. Yet." Sammy beamed. "But he will be taking classes and working toward a degree. Either way, he's got a willing ear to go along with a good heart.

"Some of you have already had the pleasure—and I use that term loosely—of the kind ministrations of Dr. Lilah McQuade-Michelson. She's going to be monitoring agents' wellbeing. If she feels there's a problem that needs to be addressed, she will do whatever she thinks is necessary. And, finally, her husband, Kelly Michelson. He was my majordomo, but… Well, if I'm honest, he's no longer suited for that role."

Kelly's eyebrows went up and I heard a small gasp from Sammy.

"He's meant for so much more," I continued. "Going forward, Kelly will be a trainer, ready to work with whomever needs to brush up on their skills. He's going to be testing you, seeing to your limits, and then helping you push past them. Don't let his age fool you, because he's a son of a bitch."

A few people chuckled, and Kelly smiled at me.

"I know I'm not Rook," I said. "No one can ever fill his shoes. I am, however, a pretty good tactician. I won't leave you in the lurch. Together we will carry on Nathan's legacy, and make sure our friends, family, and neighbors are safer. If you would rather have a different handler, or if you'd like to reconsider your job, please feel free to call on me and we'll discuss options. I won't hold it against anyone who prefers a more seasoned person at the helm."

None of the people spoke for a few moments, then one person, a young man with the codename Passant raised his hand.

"I don't know that I can speak for all of us, but I'm with you. I can't tell you the number of times Rook… I'm sorry, Nathan, was there for me. To know that he trusted you with this job is good enough to earn you a shot in my book."

All the others on the screen nodded. I was humbled by their trust.

"Thank you, Passant. I hope I'll never let any of you down. Now, one more thing before we go. I've got a list of assignments a mile long, and starting tomorrow, I'm going to be handing them out. For tonight, however, this line will remain open. Call if you want to ask questions or talk. One of us will be here for you."

I was about to tell Sammy I was finished, when one more thought came to mind.

"Oh, by the way. One thing I've learned recently is that we can't solve all the problems. Not alone, at any rate. Together, though? We can do anything. And with that in mind, I'm going to say to you, it's time we got on with our mission. We have people to save when we can and avenge when we can't."

Sammy disconnected the calls, but left the line open. He got up, walked over to where I sat, and plopped onto my lap. He snuggled in against me, rubbing his hands on my side.

"I'm proud of you," he said.

"Why?"

"Because you're going to be an incredible leader. You're already an amazing man. You care enough about these people to ensure none of them are ever left behind, and for that, I'm grateful. Though I hate what Joel did, I can't hold him completely responsible. If this had been in place before, maybe—"

I put my hand over his mouth. "And if wishes were horses, beggars would ride," I said. "We can never know what might have happened. We can't second-guess anything. Maybe Joel could have been helped, but there's a possibility he still would have ended up doing the same thing. We can only do our best to ensure this never happens again."

"We're going to do it together," Lilah said. "I'm already making up new standards for healthcare."

"And I'll ensure that King puts them into place for everyone," I promised.

"Now what do we do?" Kelly wondered, bending down to pick up a squirming Kip.

I couldn't help but smile as I transferred the calls to my phone. I'd promised to work to keep my people safe, and I would. "The same thing we do every night, Pinky. Try to save the world."

They all laughed as we left the room, the future ahead of us one of uncertainty and excitement. But it was one we'd all—agents and us—travel together, as a unit.

I had to believe that somewhere Rook would be as proud of us as we were of him.

PARKER WILLIAMS

~~The End~~

ABOUT THE AUTHOR

Parker Williams believes that true love exists, but it always comes with a price. No happily ever after can ever be had without work, sweat, and tears that come with melding lives together.

Connect with Parker on:
Twitter: @ParkerWAuthor
Facebook: https://www.facebook.com/parker.williams.75641
Or you can visit his website: http://www.ParkerWilliamsAuthor.com

www.ingramcontent.com/pod-product-compliance
Lightning Source LLC
Chambersburg PA
CBHW050720180626
46814CB00002B/520